The Return

Roland Merullo

The Return

PFP INC
publisher@pfppublishing.com
144 Tenney Street
Georgetown, MA 01833

October 2014
Printed in the United States of America

First PFP edition © 2014

ISBN-10:0991427599
ISBN-13:978-0-9914275-9-8

Front Cover & Author Photo © Amanda S. Merullo

(also available in eBook format)

Also by Roland Merullo

Fiction

Leaving Losapas
A Russian Requiem
Revere Beach Boulevard
In Revere, In Those Days
A Little Love Story
Golfing with God
Breakfast with Buddha
American Savior
Fidel's Last Days
The Talk-Funny Girl
Lunch with Buddha
Vatican Waltz
Dinner with Buddha

Non Fiction

Passion for Golf
Revere Beach Elegy
The Italian Summer: Golf, Food and Family at Lake Como
Demons of the Blank Page
Taking the Kids to Italy

For Pa
With Thanks

Praise for Roland Merullo's Work

Leaving Losapas

"Dazzling . . . thoughtful and elegant . . . lyrical yet tough-minded . . . beautifully written, quietly brilliant."
— Kirkus Reviews [starred review]

A Russian Requiem

"Smoothly written and multifaceted, solidly depicting the isolation and poverty of a city far removed from Moscow and insightfully exploring the psyches of individuals caught in the conflicts between their ideals and their careers."
— Publishers Weekly

Revere Beach Boulevard

"Merullo invents a world that mirrors our world in all of its mystery... in language so happily inventive and precise and musical, and plots it so masterfully, that you are reluctant to emerge from his literary dream."
— Washington Post Book World

Passion for Golf: In Pursuit of the Innermost Game

"This accessible guide offers insight into the emotional stumbling blocks that get in the way of improvement and, most importantly, enjoyment of the game."
— Publishers Weekly

Revere Beach Elegy: A Memoir of Home and Beyond

"Merullo has a knack for rendering emotional complexities, paradoxes, or impasses in a mere turn of the phrase."
— Chicago Tribune

In Revere, In Those Days

"A portrait of a time and a place and a state of mind that has few equals."
— The Boston Globe

A Little Love Story

"There is nothing little about this love story. It is big and heroic and beautiful and tragic . . . Writing with serene passion and gentle humor, Merullo powerfully reveals both the resiliency and fragility of life and love . . . It is, quite utterly, grand."
— Booklist

Golfing with God

"Merullo writes such a graceful, compassionate and fluid prose that you cannot resist the characters' very real struggles and concerns . . . Do I think Merullo is a fine, perceptive writer who can make you believe just about anything? Absolutely."
— Providence Journal

Breakfast with Buddha

"Merullo writes with grace and intelligence and knows that even in a novel of ideas it's not the religion that matters, it's the relationship . . . It's a quiet, meditative, and ultimately joyous trip we're on."
— Boston Globe

Fidel's Last Days

"A fast-paced and highly satisfying spy thriller . . . Merullo takes readers on a fictional thrill ride filled with so much danger and drama that they won't want it to end."
— Boston Globe

American Savior

"Merullo gently satirizes the media and politics in this thoughtful commentary on the role religion plays in America. This book showcases Merullo's conviction that Jesus' real message about treating others with kindness is being warped by those who believe they alone understand the Messiah."
— USA Today

The Italian Summer: Golf, Food & Family at Lake Como

"This travel memoir delivers unadulterated joy . . . [Merullo's] account of those idyllic weeks recalls Calvin Trillin in its casual tone, good humor, affable interactions with family, and everyman's love of regional food and wine . . . A special travel book for a special audience."
— Booklist

The Talk-Funny Girl

"Merullo not only displays an inventive use of language in creating the Richards' strange dialect but also delivers a triumphant story of one lonely girl's resilience in the face of horrific treatment."
— Booklist

Lunch with Buddha

"A beautifully written and compelling story about a man's search for meaning that earnestly and accessibly tackles some well-trodden but universal questions. A quiet meditation on life, death, darkness and spirituality, sprinkled with humor, tenderness and stunning landscapes."
— Kirkus [starred review]

Vatican Waltz

"Merullo's latest is a page-turning novel of religious ideas written with love and imagination. . . With fillips of The Da Vinci Code conspiracy and Eat Pray Love gourmandism, this book will speak loudly to Catholic readers . . . It also sings with finely observed details of family relationships, ethnic neighborhood life, and the life of prayer. The shoulda-seen-it-coming ending is a miracle . . ."
— Publishers Weekly [starred review]

One

Holding a vintage Sauer P226 with a silencer screwed onto the barrel, Chelsea Eddie Crevine stood at the sliding glass doors of his Florida home and stared out at the pool. From the minute he'd been chased away from Boston, he'd thought of this pistol, gift from his late father, as his stay-out-of-jail ticket, his emergency exit, and it was beginning to seem to him that the time had come to use it. Johnny Cut hadn't called in two days. As of last night's news there were pictures of Alicia on the TV. Outdated, maybe, but recognizable. Find the woman and you find the man; that was the FBI for you. It made his mood sour.

As he stood there considering his options, the sour mood was confirmed by pulses of pain echoing up through the middle of him. Sharp, merciless, timed to his heartbeat, they made him think of a laborer with a sledge hammer driving in spikes on the MBTA tracks. He knew exactly what it meant. There would be no more surgeries now. No more checkups or treatments or new drugs he could pay for in cash from his own pocket. He'd been running down a dark alley his whole life, shitheads chasing him, and now he'd come to a wall and there would be no climbing over, no side alleys, no door. . . . But this was the weird part: it didn't matter very much. For the past seven months his life had been reduced to nothing: going out into this fenced-in yard and sweating in the fucking Florida sun, or walking on the beach at night if Alicia wanted to, or, once, on his birthday, with a cane he didn't need and dark glasses, going out to eat. It was no life anymore, and he told himself he wouldn't be sorry to let it go. He thought of his old man and the lousy way he'd checked out. He felt the weight of the pistol in his fingers. For a guy like Chelsea Eddie, he told himself, dying would be nothing. Like a haircut, a dentist visit. Nothing.

Still, he kept the Sauer where it was.

Three things bothered him. One, he wanted to see his sons and say good-bye. Two, he was tormented by the idea that the prick who sent him here was still alive and nobody could find him. And three, stupid as it might be, he didn't want Alicia to go on being alive while he wasn't. Eating, getting her nails done, fucking somebody else—who knew. The idea of that was like a nest of hornets in both ears.

So when she came in through the door—garage to hallway to kitchen, and called out "Hi, Eddie!" like he could have been anybody, as long as the guy had just paid for her manicure; when she came in like that, pretending they had a normal life, and stood at the counter with her back turned, taking cans of soup out of a grocery bag, when he heard her voice and looked at her, he decided it wasn't his time after all. His mind had just been playing tricks again. The pain had already gone away. There were still things he had to do. He padded over in his bare feet and before Alicia could say anything or turn around he put one bullet through the back of her head. Splash of warm red flesh on white cabinets. Her hips had gone big and there was a funny noise—like a big fish on a dock—when her weight hit the floor. One eye was still there. It looked up and past him, brown glass in a broken doll's face.

He was surprised at himself for two seconds, then he laughed. "What a vicious bastard you are," he said, and he walked upstairs to get ready to leave.

Two

Standing behind the counter of his video rental shop in Maddles, Montana, Peter found himself, as he often did, thinking about Chelsea Eddie Crevine. He didn't know why. The mind just worked that way sometimes. You knew there was another human being out there in the world who wished you were dead, and so, from time to time, your thoughts just naturally went in that direction. You knew Chelsea Eddie's guys were looking for you, you knew pretty much exactly what would happen if they found you—it was perfectly natural for a little spider of worry to crawl across your brain now and then.

The TV was on above and behind him, and a regular customer—Carol or Cheryl—was standing at the counter. She'd been telling him about the make-up business, Hollywood-style, and inside him the conversation had sparked a crazy idea.

"La-look at this huge na-nose," he said. "You're telling me you could d-do something to disguise a beak like this here?"

"Of course I could, Peter."

"You're bragging now. You could nev-never in a million years make it so people didn't take one look and say, "There goes Peter the Nose"."

"You'd be amazed," Carol said. She was holding two DVDs against the front of her white wool sweater and glancing up every few seconds at the TV.

Peter had left the volume on low—morning in Montana—but he caught the words "Linda Tripp" and "grand jury".

3

"Ba-but you'd need all your equipment and everything, wouldn't you?" he said. "I mean, the stuff you had in Hollywood. All kinds of giz-giz-gizmos and that?"

"One carrying case," she said. "Ninety minutes. With the kinds of treatments they have now, your own father wouldn't recognize you."

At the mention of his father, at the hint that his new idea might turn out to be something other than a ridiculous fantasy, Peter suddenly found it difficult to be still. He stopped listening to the TV. There was a *Directory of World Cinema* in front of him on the counter, a well-thumbed paperback, tall as a water glass. He pushed it from one hand to the other, sliding it across the countertop, back and forth, back and forth. "So who-who-who-who-who'd you do the makeup for when you were wa-working the studios?'

"Pick any star off these shelves and I likely patted his or her face at some point . . . Eastwood. Streep."

"The gr-greatest . . . DeNiro?"

"Did you see Godfather, Part Two?'

"F-f-f-fourteen ta-times!"

The woman laughed and slipped the DVDs—shoot-em-up thrillers with a bit of family drama—into a cloth shopping bag. "That was one of ours."

"What brought you back here, then? I mean, Mon-Mon-Montana. After the high life."

"Once I was retired for a while I could never picture myself growing old and dying anyplace but Maddles. A lot of people go home to die, don't you think?"

"Sha-sure, but ya-you—" The front door squeaked and a man in a gray topcoat and sunglasses stepped into the store. He was dressed, Peter thought, like a city guy, a sign from God, maybe. Peter watched him turn his head this way and that, as if the man were confused, as if he'd expected, upon entering a video shop, to buy shaving cream or a hunting rifle or milk.

"Help you f-find something?"

The man looked across the small distance, dark glasses still in place, hands in his pockets, and said nothing for the count of three. "Nah, wrong store," he said. And then, as he turned to walk out again he tossed a half-hearted "Sorry" over one shoulder.

Nothing to worry about, Peter told himself. Just a stranger passing through on his way to the ski resorts. If it had been one of Eddie's guys he wouldn't have just stood there and looked around. He wouldn't have said sorry. Carol slipped the twin cloth loops over her arm, glanced one last time at the TV, and sadly shook her head. "Any time you want to turn into somebody else for a day, just let me know," she said, and she smiled and followed the stranger out into the cold.

Three

Because she'd been Boston's most popular news anchor for six years in a row, and because people still tuned to Channel 8 at noon and six just to see Joanna Imbesalacqua, Mike McGowan the producer went to the trouble of asking if she wanted to read the story of John Denok's arrest, or if she'd prefer to have her new co-anchor read it. "Of course I want to read it," Joanna said. "Why wouldn't I want to read it?"

Because, McGowan almost said, *the man would kill you and your brother and your father in a nanosecond if he thought he could get away with it.* But he just nodded and marked the script accordingly.

When she read the report—top story that day—Joanna had to draw on decades of practice in order to keep a note of triumph from her voice. John Denok, known also as "Johnny Cut" because of a looping scar that ran across his left cheek, had been arrested at dawn in his Winthrop home, without a struggle. According to FBI sources, he'd been under surveillance for the past twenty months. The charges included murder, conspiracy to commit murder, obstruction of justice, extortion, and narcotics distribution. He was being held without bail at an undisclosed location. She read it in her just-the-facts voice, and then, as if there might still be anyone in Eastern Mass who didn't know, she went on to say that, for years, Denok had been the first lieutenant to Edward "Chelsea Eddie" Crevine. Crevine had been at large for the past seven months and was still the subject of a massive FBI manhunt. She looked straight at the camera, mouth muscles under control, tone of voice neutral, and said, "There remains a half million dollar reward for information leading to his arrest."

It turned out to be a big news day in Boston, the kind of news that paid the bills. In addition to the Denok story there was a report of a police officer shot in Mattapan, and a home invasion in the ordinarily safe neighborhood of Beacon Hill. Even the weather forecast promised trouble—a late-season snowstorm moving up the coast. Hoping to end on an upbeat note, Mike McGowan tacked on to the tail end of the half hour a ninety-second piece on something called The Family Repair Project. The project was the brainchild of a Methodist minister in the city's Brighton section. The piece opened with video of a little boy leaning against his daddy's knee, paging through a picture book, and then segued to the minister saying that the father had recently served time. Offense unspecified. After initially filing for divorce while her husband was incarcerated, his wife had reconsidered. The church was offering a neutral space where the couple could be together for a few hours every week, receive counseling and encouragement, and engage their child in what the minister called "healing play activity" in the hopes of "making a broken family whole again."

The interview ended, Joanna paused for two beats with a thoughtful pinch of her lips, then floated a soft pitch in the direction of her rookie co-anchor, Marty Lincoln: "Nice idea, isn't it."

Marty nodded, blinked twice, said: "Wonderful thing . . . to keep an emphasis on the family in our busy lives. Let's hope it catches all on over all the city . . . on the, all—sorry—catches on the city . . . Let's hope it catches on all over the city."

They turned to the camera. She said, "I'm Joanna

7

Imbesalacqua. For Marty Lincoln and everyone here at Channel Eight, have a peaceful and joyful afternoon."

The WSBT theme song played, credits rolled. There was another stretch of banter, inaudible to the viewers at home, then the red Talley light over the Number One camera blinked out and the pleasantries ceased. Joanna leaned back and let a technician release the clip from the microphone on the collar of her dress and loop the wire over her head and away. The cameras were wheeled toward the walls. The assistant producer walked past with her headphones on, stepping over a tangle of cables, showing thumbs-up.

Marty brought one fist down gently on the desk, and drummed out a frustrated staccato. "*On all*, Marty," he said. "*On all*, for God's sake. Twenty-nine minutes and forty-five seconds perfect, and then you destroy the whole thing. That's three broadcasts in a row now, isn't it?" He looked around as if for confirmation, or encouragement, and, receiving none, he pushed his shoulders back and smiled his leading-man smile at Joanna. "Would the glamorous Ms. Imbesalacqua care to have lunch with her bumbling new co-anchor?"

"Have an errand to do. Sorry. I'll be back by quarter to four to go over the six o'clock script."

"They're making jokes about me all over New England, aren't they. I'm an object of ridicule."

"You'll be fine. Stop obsessing."

"Easy for you to say. The glamorous, the perfect, the ultra-professional Joanna Imbesalacqua who never messed up anything in her life."

She returned to her office for coat and gloves and the gun permit, rode the elevator down to the basement garage, worked her car free of its reserved space, and drove out into a March

8

afternoon that was as damp and heavy as wetted wool. "Never messed up anything in her life," she said in a Marty Lincoln voice, as she maneuvered through the streets of Chinatown and toward the expressway north. "Never messed up her life in anything . . . Never anything in her life . . . Messed up . . . sorry. Never . . . " But she was smiling as she said it. After thirty years of being untouchable, the filthy muscle behind the Crevine operation, Johnny Denok, was going away. If he didn't know about it already, Chelsea Eddie would soon find out. Little by little, associate by associate, board by board, the house of terror he'd built in Greater Boston was being torn down.

Four

Five miles north of the Channel 8 studios, in a ranch house with a car port to one side and tall shrubs beneath the front windows, the telephone rang on a hand-made wooden end table. As he pushed himself out of the armchair and walked toward it, Vito Imbesalacqua wondered if the person on the other end of the line had been watching Joanie, too, and had waited for the end of the broadcast to call. An old friend just wanting to say how good she looked. Or Joanie herself, asking if she could come by and have lunch. He walked over and lifted the receiver to his ear, but there was no one there. A buzz like bees, a nobody. Two times now today. Ten times this week. They were trying to make him afraid, he knew that, but all Eddie and his friends were doing was making him mad. Let them come to this house, he thought. Let them come here and see what they get. He set the receiver on the table beside the phone and went to the kitchen window to see if the snow had started yet.

It seemed to him, staring out at the bare tree branches and heavy gray sky, that a death-feeling hung in the cold air around his house. Lucy had died in the bed in the next room—he thought about her and prayed for her every hour—but this feeling wasn't about Lucy. This was something else. Dying didn't make him afraid now. Even with all the heavy weights God put on his shoulders these last few years, he still held onto the belief that there was another life after this one, something better. Even so, there was a sadness tied onto it. You got used

10

to people being in this world with you, and then they were gone. You got used to summer, and then the snow came, and the cold, and the gray. Maybe God set it up that way so you were ready when your time came. You had enough of the cold. You had enough sadness. You were ready for the next place.

Five

Upstairs in the bedroom, Eddie took his time. Nobody would come to the house today, he knew that, and it was important now to think a little bit before making his move. He took two suits out of the closet and tossed them onto the bed. But his mind wasn't working straight. Alicia had a crucifix on top of her bureau, something he'd told her a thousand times he didn't want to look at. "God is God," she used to say back to him. She liked rubies and two-hundred-dollar haircuts. She fucked like a dog in heat. But "God is God," right?

He went over and grabbed the crucifix and dropped it into the pile of used tissues in her little wastebasket. That made him feel calm for a few seconds, then not so good again. So he reached down and grabbed the piece of metal—that's all it was—and stuffed it in her underwear drawer, but a little crumpled-up sheet of tissue came with it, and some perfume was on the tissue, then on his hands. He washed it off in the bathroom like it was a sickness then came back and looked outside. The fucking Mexicans were cleaning the pool! With both hands Eddie threw open the window and pushed his face against the screen.

"You!" he yelled.

The Mexicans looked up.

"Get the fuck outa my yard. Now! It ain't today . . . Go!"

After hesitating a few seconds, the two men set the long-handled cleaning nets on their hooks and walked fast through the gate. Fast . . . for them anyway, Eddie thought. He listened for their van to start up before he closed the window. Perfect. All they had to do was come over to the sliding doors and look in and see a little blood or something and he would have been fucked.

He tried to remember where Alicia kept the suitcases.

Six

Joanna took the expressway to the bridge over the Mystic River, where three lanes climbed in a shallow asphalt arc, offering a view of cranes and freighters to the left, and to the right a cold-looking Boston Harbor. The view changed as she descended: brick tenements, metal fire escapes, graffiti in three languages, but the littered streets and puddled rooftops called out to her in a language she knew. There was an exit for Chelsea, then one for Revere, and just that flash of white letters on a green highway sign—REVERE—lifted a chorus of voices to her inner ear. She knew her father had been watching the noon broadcast just on the other side of this hill, in the house where she and Peter had been raised. And she knew how happy it would make him, in the middle of his empty day, to see her car pull into the driveway. She eased her foot off the accelerator for just a moment, then changed her mind and drove on.

Nineteen miles farther north she left the highway and traveled east on a two-lane road. Pure suburbia now, the towns here had been farmland when she was a girl. Driving through them she was surrounded by a memory of a particular Sunday outing: her mother turning to look at them over the top of the seat, the fierce love, the buried anger tightly packed inside the skin of a dutiful Catholic wife; her father gripping the wheel as if it were an umbrella in a gale, as if the sinews in his hands and arms were composed of wariness and worry and outdated ideas about what a man was supposed to be; her brother hiding a

14

book of matches in his palm until their mother turned forward again, then flipping the cover back and forth in a hypnosis of disobedience.

A line from the last part of the broadcast—"making a broken family whole again"—echoed in her thoughts. Over the past thirty-odd years the farmland she drove through had been bought up by developers, divided and sold, and the landscape of intertwined fates that went by the name "Imbesalacqua" had been divided up, too. Her mother had been dead seven months. Her father had kept the house, and now passed his lonely days sawing and sanding in his basement workshop, betting pennies on hands of whist at the Soccorso Club, making his weekly trip—septuagenarian pilgrimage—to church and cemetery. Her brother had evolved from mischievous child to irresponsible adult, from casual card-player to casino addict. One morning not far from his fortieth birthday, with his mother on her deathbed, he'd awakened to find himself buried to the eyes in debt to Eddie Crevine. And then, in an incredible reversal of fortune, he'd captured Crevine's threats on tape and sent him fleeing into exile. Peter was living in an exile of his own now, with a wife and adopted eighteen-year-old son, somewhere in North America. New identity, new profession, ward of the United States Marshals; stool pigeon or hero, depending on who you asked. In the physical sense he was gone from her life, and her mother was gone, but there remained something nagging and unsolved in the memory of them, something hidden in shadow. Tattered family dramas invaded her dreams and ran like smoke-colored threads through the white linen of her waking thoughts. Nice as it was, Johnny Denok's arrest wouldn't ease that pain. Even if Eddie Crevine himself were arrested—the thing she hoped for most in life—it wouldn't erase the huge question at the center of herself: what was the point of it all?

Since her mother's death, since Peter's sudden departure, it seemed she was being asked by every event of every day to dig down and down, to unearth every layer of buried emotion and trouble, to find some secret key that would unlock the door into the territory of peace of mind. It was a Revere dig, a daily tour of the shadowy catacombs of the past, and so far it had gotten her exactly nowhere. Well off, locally famous, supposedly beautiful—she would trade all of it for one measure of lasting peace.

According to the letters that reached her—relayed through censors at the Office of Witness Protection—her brother had stopped gambling, stopped smoking, embraced the domestic routine, and found, in his secret exile, the contentment that had eluded him for forty years.

Nothing was harder to imagine.

She followed the road into a small village; two church steeples and a triangular park coated in old snow, a few fresh flakes falling now. Beyond the park she found Firehouse Road. Gas station, a row of clapboard houses, the firehouse itself, then, right where it was supposed to be, a one-story, white-shingle bungalow with a circular dirt driveway out front and a wooden sign cut in the shape of a pistol. She put on her blinker and turned in.

Seven

In recent months, Eddie had come to believe that the best piece of advice he'd ever gotten had come from a man named China Louis. Many years ago he and China had worked together in a complicated business—the moving of eight kilos of heroin from a warehouse in the Bronx to various distribution points around New England. It was the start of an intermittent and uneasy association. He did business with the Chink because it never seemed possible—at least for certain things—*not* to do business with him. Louis had his fingers in all the darker Boston neighborhoods, and employed guys—kids, really—who weren't afraid to kill and steal and go away for it. Eddie often wondered how much Louis paid them.

Still, in some weird way, Eddie had to admit that he half-liked China Louis. And the Chink—no matter what Johnny Cut said—seemed to like him in return. One time, over a lousy meal in Little Hell, at a rib place called Jo-Jo's that made him half-sick to walk into, China Louis had told him this: "Eddie, listen to me. You're gonna be top of the heap one day on your side of the city. The people above you are gonna die, or be sent away, and you're gonna be sticking up there like a weed in a nice suburban lawn. You don't want to wait until they take you out of your house in handcuffs. You want to have a plan. You want to have everything all set up for that day so you can just disappear if you need to."

"I have a lawyer," Eddie said. "I have cash put away."

"I'm not talking about that. They put you inside with no bail and none of that's gonna do you any good, see? Listen to me now, I have a guy in Philly who set everything up for me in case I have to leave in a hurry—new Social, new I.D.s, a house all paid for in somebody else's name, a registered car, a bank account in this other name, safe deposit box, a secure way of staying in touch with one or two people I know I can trust."

"I'm glad you care about me so much."

"I don't care about you. I don't give a shit about you, tell the truth. But they catch you and squeeze you, or somebody who works for you, I don't want any leakage in my direction. Purely self-interest on my part, see?" Louis slid a business card across the table. "Here, you just helped me make six hundred thousand dollars. Take this as a sign of my gratitude."

The card advertised a Boston masseuse. Eddie looked at it for a minute then flipped it over and saw a phone number on the back, written in pencil.

"The plan-man," China Louis said. "Combination financial advisor, insurance agent, and angel. Name's Leon. See what he can set up for you."

Eddie had kept the card for two and a half years before he came to trust China Louis enough to finally make the call.

Eight

Lunch in the rectory that day was ham steak with a pineapple slice, green beans on the side. Together with Father Alberto Bellini and Matilda the housekeeper, Vito and Father Dom took their food at the communal table and talked about the weather. Outside, Rosalie said, she'd already seen a few snowflakes. The weathermen was predicting six to eight inches by morning.

Afterwards, Vito and Dommy retired to the parlor, where the cook sent out a dessert course more to their taste: two thick slices of gorgonzola cheese, wedges of pear, two cups of espresso on tiny saucers. The parlor curtains were drawn. Held in a tent of yellow lamplight, the two old men sat leaning toward each other on worn leather chairs, sipping coffee and pressing cloth napkins to their mouths, and seeming to consider, in silence, a great puzzle. Upstairs, Father Alberto was playing a tape of Shostakovich—the gloomy fifth symphony, much too loud. After a few seconds a door closed on the sound and an awkward silence came over them.

"What do you hear from Peter?"

Vito broke off a corner of the gorgonzola with his fingers, put it on his tongue and let it dissolve there. "They don't let him call me."

"Joanie?"

"She calls on the weekends and tells me sell the house, Papa, move out, make you life easy."

"She wants you to move in with her?"

Vito shook his head. "A condalinium. She says then you won't have no work around the house, Pa. I try tellin her the work around the house is the same to me now as stayin alive. She don't listen."

They ate and drank. A police car went past on Revere Street, siren wailing. When the sound faded and died, other than an occasional frenzy of clicking and knocking in the old radiators, the room was quiet—books on the shelves that no one had looked at in a decade, a statue of the Virgin in one corner, dusted tables and vacuumed carpet and drapes drawn against the day. In a little while, Father Dom said, "What's wrong, Vit?"

Vito had knocked a crumb of gorgonzola onto the carpet. He bent over, making a small grunt, retrieved it between his thumb and second finger and pressed it to the edge of the plate.

"Vito."

Vito turned his brown eyes squarely upon his friend.

"Since Christmas you haven't been to confession. Some weeks I don't even see you at Mass. I had to call and invite you four times to get you to have a meal with me. Nothing's wrong?"

"The dinners here ain't that good, Dommy. Since the new cook."

"I'm serious, Vit."

Vito looked down at the front of his sweater. He brushed the fabric there with his fingers, chest to belt, twice, and looked up. "I lost my wife, Dommy," he said, as if the priest might somehow have forgotten.

"I know that. I know how terrible that must be."

"How can you know?'

"A priest can imagine."

They heard the old furnace go on beneath them, whir and

rumble, more knocking in the pipes. Vito touched a finger to the slices of pear on his plate, adjusting them so they sat parallel.

"I'd take away the sadness if I could."

"I know."

"You have Joanie, at least."

Vito nodded, started to say something, and then closed his mouth and looked away.

"It used to be when things were like this you'd come into the confessional and we'd talk."

For half a minute Vito said nothing. When he at last spoke, it was in a slightly forced tone, as if he'd stepped back from the raw intimacy of their friendship and then forward into it again with a certain resolve. "Last time in confession you lied to me."

"Lied how?"

"Are you a man who goes with men? Are you that way? I'd still be your friend, but tell me."

"When I was young I went with women, like everybody in our gang, you know that. Now I don't go with anybody in that way, I don't look at people that way even, anymore. I'm a priest, an old man now. Put those two together."

"But you told me in the confession you were a man who goes with men."

The priest glanced at the cup in his hand, shook it in a gentle circle so the brown outline reformed itself. "I was trying to make you understand that it doesn't matter that Joanie likes women. I was trying to say something like that shouldn't matter between a father and his daughter."

"And you couldn't say it straight?"

"You were upset. I thought it would be a more powerful way. I was going to tell you afterwards, but then Lucy died, and Peter had to go away, and it didn't seem like the type of subject I could just bring up out of air. I came to see you six, seven times after the funeral, thinking we could have a talk, but it felt like all you wanted was for people to leave you alone. You wanted to be angry at God."

"Wouldn't you wanted to be? Wouldn't you wanted not to have your best friend lying to you about somethin like that?"

Dommy rubbed the side of his thumb across an old stain on the leather arm of the chair. "You're upset about something else, Vit, I can feel it."

Vito shifted his weight. The leather squeaked. "Last night Joanie called on the phone and said she was getting a gun for me."

"A gun?'

"In case Eddie comes breaking in the house in the night. I have my crowbar next to the door, I told her. You keep the gun for yourself." Vito's eyes came to rest on the statue of Mary. "She talked to me like I was the little boy, and she was my mother. How I should be worryin about Eddie, how he must be thinking this, thinking that, how I gotta take care of myself now, not work too hard, not shovel the snow but pay somebody else to . . . a kid—"

"She cares for you, Vito, that's all."

"I was thinking now, driving, that all my life people been talking to me that way. Why, because I don't speak that good English? Because I worked all my life with my hands?"

"You invite people to do that, Vito."

"How invite? Tell me."

"You act a little bit like a child sometimes, in confession especially but other times too. Even with Lucy I used to see it sometimes. Even with Joanie and Peter. It's like you think if you're nice enough in the world nothing bad will ever happen, nobody will have a reason to dislike you, or hurt you, not even God . . . We've been best friends since I was thirteen, fifty-seven years, and I think this is the first time I've ever seen you get angry at me."

"And what? Gettin mad makes you a smart person?"

"It makes you human."

"*Better* than human was what I thought you were supposed to try to be."

"You want me to tell you the truth, I'm telling you. There's something in you trying so hard to be perfect, never to hurt, never to say a word that anybody doesn't want to hear, that people end up not giving you all your full credit as a man. I made a mistake in the confession, I apologize. I'm not making excuses. I'm just saying there's a way, by trying to be too good, you invite people to look down on you. People want to attack if you're too good. If you have no defense set up, then they get out the weapon and attack."

"But why should that be?"

"It is. I don't know why. You must have noticed this."

"I don't understand, Dommy. It wasn't that way in the old country."

"You were a kid in the old country, Vito. You left when you were ten."

"Eleven, I was. It wasn't that way."

"Your family was the exception, maybe. They were good people, your mother may very well have been a saint. But look at the world now the way it is. If you want to succeed now, you succeed at the expense of someone else, somewhere else."

But Vito was shaking his head, pushing the idea of such a world away from the air around him. "It wasn't that way," he insisted.

"God isn't that interested in *nice*. The world isn't built with simple rules like that—nice and bad. If you're nice you get a good life, if you're bad you get a bad life. That's what would make sense to people, but God has another sense, not like ours."

"You're so sure how God thinks, Dommy?"

The priest sipped the last of his coffee and wiped one finger across his lips.

"To me it looks like now that if you live the way you supposed to live all your life you end up in your own house by yourself, and God takin all the things that matter and one by one ripping them out of your hands to see how long you can go not gettin mad on Him . . . Lucy, Peter, Joanie."

"Alfonse you ripped out of your own hands, though, Vit."

Vito looked down into his hands for a moment, as if Father Dom had meant this literally, and he might see the scars there where the son he had fathered and not raised had once been attached. At that moment it was all too much for him—Peter, Joanie, Alfonse, Lucy, Chelsea Eddie . . . just too much. A giant wave of feeling washed over him, regret and self-pity, an old man's cocktail. He pushed himself to the edge of the chair, stood, and went out of the room, around the base of the staircase, gathered his topcoat and hat from the standing rack and went out the front door into the first snowy gusts of the afternoon storm. He stood in the empty lot for a few seconds with his felt hat on against the swirling snow, the topcoat still folded over one arm. The door opened behind him and he turned and saw Dommy caught there in a box of light. "We have three empty bedrooms going to waste and there's a big storm predicted. Why don't you stay? Matilda will make us supper. Eggs and peppers in the morning."

Vito couldn't seem to speak.

"You know the way I meant it about Alfonse, don't you? You wanted me to tell you the truth, I was just telling you. He calls you "Uncle" to this day, for God's sake, Vito. It isn't right."

Vito lifted one arm, a farewell, an apology, and left a line of footprints in the new snow as he went.

Nine

The door was metal and windowless, with a hand-lettered sign on it that said, "WE'RE HERE CMON IN!" Joanna turned the handle and pushed. A buzzer sounded above her. She stepped into a room with small barred windows high up on the walls, a linoleum floor, and display racks and glass counters instead of furniture. A woman in her twenties was standing behind the middle counter, fingers spread on the glass as if drying her nails, a small silver ring through the left side of her lower lip.

"You expected a guy, I know," she said. "Everybody expects a guy. Close that door or the alarm will go off in about another two seconds."

Joanna pushed the door tight. She took off her gloves and held them tightly together in her left hand. "Raw today, isn't it."

The woman turned down her lights so that the ring sparkled once in the fluorescent lights. "Snow, they're saying on the TV, has it started yet?"

"Just now."

"Speaking of the TV, what are you doing here at this time of day? Aren't you supposed to be at the station?"

"You recognized me."

"You're not exactly just another anonymous face, you know. My dad recognized your voice on the phone in about one second."

"It would be better for me if this were confidential."

"Sure. Confidential's our middle name. But I bet you'd be surprised who comes in here. Half the people in your business, for example."

"Susan Ellerson referred me."

"My dad handled Susie."

Joanna stepped closer and looked down through the glass at the neat displays.

"You look more stressed in person than on TV, if you don't mind me saying so. Kind of rough being a star, huh? Weirdoes calling you all the time, I bet. Stalkers and everything."

"Some of that, yes."

"No trouble getting a date, though, I bet, with your looks."

Joanna shook her head, pinched up the corners of her lips in a small signal which the young clerk didn't catch.

"They just killed a TV lady down in Rhode Island, didn't they? Last summer?"

"Shot, not killed. She lived."

"Lived to read the news another day, right?"

"I think she went on to another career, actually. I need something that will fit easily into this handbag, and something you don't have to be an expert to use."

Taking the hint this time, the young woman asked to see Joanna's permit, then unlocked the case in front of her knee, and with a practiced deference brought out a pistol and placed it on a piece of felt on the glass countertop. There was a small blue butterfly tattooed on the skin between her left thumb and index finger.

"Is that powerful enough . . . it looks so . . ."

"A .22 wouldn't be, but this one here's a .38. Powerful enough to knock the guy stalking you on his butt and make it so he never gets up again."

"No one's stalking me."

"Knock your boyfriend on his butt then, if he—"

"Is there a place I can try it?"

"Town wouldn't give us permits for a range. I'll just show you. Squeeze here, pull this part out. Here's the clip, you push it in like this. Hold your arm straight out and put the other hand here, like this." She turned and pointed at the wall. "Always aim a little low, because if it was loaded the kick would lift the barrel up, okay?"

"Is this the one you recommend?"

"Swiss, brass-plated. Top of the line." She removed the clip, passed the pistol across the counter, handle first, and stood in an envelope of professional stillness while Joanna turned the weapon this way and that, hefted the weight of it against her palm, aimed at the freshly-painted wall. "There aren't any bullets in it, are there?"

The woman held up the clip and smiled.

"It's alright to pull the trigger then?"

"All you want."

Joanna flexed her index finger three times, making three small snapping noises, louder than she'd expected. Move one finger, she thought, and you end a life. It was a bit like playing God. Leslie would think she'd gone completely mad.

"It reminds me of one of my father's tools," she said. She set her handbag on the glass countertop and reached for her wallet. "Credit card okay?"

"Credit card, cash. Just don't give me a check because my dad's such a fan he'll have it framed instead of cashing it, and he'll hang it in the living room."

Joanna watched the woman swipe the card and work the machine. She looked down through the glass to her left at antique Lugers and derringers and revolvers laid out like holy objects on the red felt. The details of a hundred city shootings came back to her. Always the top of the news: friends killing friends, brothers killing brothers, lovers killing lovers for sleeping with neighbors. Guns, Leslie said, existed only to show a rich nation how angry it was.

"You helped catch that Mafia guy, didn't you," the clerk said, half turning over her shoulder.

"My brother did that."

"But you were there, too. I remember they made a big deal of it on the news."

"I just sat there. I did next to nothing, really. And the man who we really needed to catch got away."

"That's not what it said in the *Herald*. They said a hired killer had a hand on your throat and was about to strangle you, and you just sat still. To save your brother."

"You know how they exaggerate."

The woman finished with the machine and brought the credit card and sales slips back to the counter. On her face was an expression Joanna had seen a thousand times. The intense curiosity. The sense, almost, of worship. The desperate hope spawned by encountering a life that seemed larger than ordinary, as if that imagined largeness would make the world something other than what it was: a dark chamber speckled with passions. Prelude to an eternity of nothing whatsoever.

She stood there, captured in the bubble of her fame, waiting for the clerk to set the slip of paper down so she could sign it and escape. A country music song played on the radio. The lyrics had to do with a father gradually coming to approve of his daughter's boyfriend.

"There's a rumor you like girls, you know," the clerk said suddenly.

Joanna did not flinch. "All kinds of absurd things get said about women in this business."

"I told my dad that. I told him: I'd know one if I saw one, Daddy. And the Channel Eight lady, she just doesn't fit the mold."

The clerk, at last, presented her with the slip, and Joanna had the pen poised, and was holding the top of the paper to keep it still, when she stopped and looked up.

"Void this please."

"What? It's a good pistol. Was it what I asked? I was just curious. People say I'm pushy, but it was just that my dad has always been such a fan of yours, and when he heard—"

"No, it wasn't anything. I want two of them, actually. Same model if you have it."

The young woman hesitated one second and then smiled, showing a set of teeth as white and even as snow on a porch railing. "Make my day," she said.

Ten

It was a beautiful day for skiing—sunny and crisp, with last night's snow lying like a family of sleeping white creatures on the tree limbs. Elsie wished Austin would have come with them, but Austin was eighteen, and eighteen, she had to keep reminding herself, was the age when you didn't really need parents anymore, probably didn't even want them, certainly didn't feel required to spend a sunny weekend day with them instead of with your friends. For a moment she tried to picture herself as she'd been at eighteen. No father, a mother adrift on the winds of addiction . . . She steered her thoughts back to the present. Why spoil the last run?

The chairlift caught her behind the knees and hoisted her into air. She kicked her skis gently back and forth, tilted the tips back toward her. The shadows were long on the hillside now, a cold edge to the wind. No one sat beside her.

The chair crested a rise and bumped past a pole. Above and to the left she could see the trail. As she was drawn closer, she began to look for Peter, playing a little game with herself, predicting she'd be able to identify him by his skiing style first, before she could see his clothes or face.

She was right. High up on the slope one dark figure cut back and forth like a playboy in a gathering of priests. It was one of the easier intermediate runs—they'd learned to ski only three months ago—and most of the skiers and snowboarders using it were stiff with fear and inexperience, making slow, clumsy turns, wobbling, toppling over and slowly getting up. And then there was a solitary man in a red wool cap, moving three times as fast as anyone else, traversing the slope at steep angles, cutting back, going up precariously onto one ski, poles waving, nearly toppling over sideways, catching himself, letting out a joyful whoop that echoed in the basin like a madman's signal for sunset prayers. Her husband.

She leaned over to watch as he came almost directly toward the lift line in a spray of powder, cutting someone off, yelling back, "Sa-sorry!"

"Peter!" she shouted, when he was as close as he would get.

"Ell-say-ay-ay-ay!" he shouted back, without looking up. And now that he knew she was watching he bent into an amateurish approximation of a racer's crouch and sped diagonally across the slope. The chair swung upwards, pulling her away. She had to turn and look over her shoulder to keep him in view. He planted his pole and tried a fancy turn, one of those effortless little hops the better skiers made. But he managed to get his skis only halfway around, and flew up and over them sideways, sailing through the air and splashing down in a berm of new powder, three feet shy of the trees.

A second passed, two seconds. She had to twist all the way around. She saw him sit up. She heard his stammering echo knock against the smaller trees near the summit. "I'm oh-oh-oh kay-ay-ay, Else Else Else". The chair bumped over the end of its climb and leveled out, and she could see the lift shack up ahead, a man—he bore an eerie resemblance to Peter's half-brother, Alfonse—waiting there to catch her so she wouldn't fall.

Eleven

He grabbed the cell phone and carried the suitcase and suiter down the stairs, along the short hallway, and out to the car without looking at Alicia's body. His mind was whistling and gusting like wind in a blizzard, a million and a half thoughts flying around. His sons. The fucking Imbesalacquas. Why Johnny Cut hadn't called or written his regular letter, disguised as a bill and sent in a roundabout route and usually including some cash. Why the fuck he'd done Alicia like that. The Mexicans and what they might have seen. How he was going to cover it. Where he was going to go. What he was going to do.

He looked at himself in the mirror to see if the hair color was still good, the little bit of nose work. Nice.

He sat back in the seat a minute and tried to settle down. First thing he had to do was give himself a little time. Part of Leon's plan had been to hire illegals to tend the grounds and pool and clean the house—no chance of people like that causing any trouble, or going to the authorities about anything. But still, Eddie thought, bad as they wanted to stay clear of the law, even the pool guys, even Lorena the maid would have a hard time ignoring a dead body. What was he going to do about Lorena? Where did she live? He didn't even have a number. He went back in the house and, carefully stepping around the blood pooling on the tile floor, and avoiding looking at his wife's broken-up doll-face, he found a number on the list next to the phone and dialed. No answer. He left a message. "Lore-

32

na, listen. This here's Mister Echeverria, Alicia's husband, you know. Eddie. The house is 565 Tangerine, Citrus Estates, right? You know it, right? Well, listen, me and Alicia we're goin' away for a while, a week, two weeks probly, so we don't need you to come and clean and everything. We'll pay you just the same, don't worry, just don't show up for the next two weeks, all right? Just leave the house the way it is, we'll be fine, okay? All right? Bye."

Two weeks that would give him, if the pool guys didn't come back and look in the windows. Two weeks was enough. Eddie went back out to the car, and sat there thinking things through.

Another part of Leon's plan—along with the house, the help, the car, and the money—was to set up a secure phone line that Johnny Cut could use to call him, and he could use, only once in a while, to talk to his son. With a little money this wasn't hard to do. Leon had a connection at the phone company, a guy there who could set up a line under a fake name, and check to see if it was being tapped. But something told him not to use it now. Johnny Cut hadn't called, something was off. He took the cell phone out of his pocket and turned it on. This was the backup. If the Feds expected him to call anybody it would be his son John, so this phone was for calling James. One time. Emergency type situation. Make the call, Leon said, then ditch the phone someplace by the side of the road. Eddie poked his finger into the numbers and pushed the phone up against his ear. Two rings, and then a girl's voice came on the line. Jimmy's secretary, it probly had to be. He hadn't expected that. Shit.

"Crellin Accounting," she said, in a happy voice.

"Yeah," he said. "Listen." Then he gave the secret code and yelled at her to tell Jimmy. He realized he didn't know how to hang up, so he just threw the fucking phone into the bushes. His mind was on fire. Alicia's face. The fucking crucifix. He

33

could barely get the keys out of his pants pocket. Day after to-morrow he'd told the secretary. What if she didn't pass it on? He should write that down. This was Monday, Alicia's day to get the manicure and shop. Day after tomorrow was Wednesday and he had no idea how long it would take him to drive to Washington, D.C. He had the address in his pocket, he'd thought of that, at least. Washington, Wednesday. He'd have to remember.

He got into the car and backed down the driveway and into the cul de sac. Think straight, he kept telling himself. Think straight. But his fucking mind was spinning. Fucking Alicia did it. Think! There was twenty-two thousand dollars cash in his pocket, and twice that much in a paper bag in the corner of the trunk. He had his father's gun, the map, a week's worth of clothes in the suitcase, two good suits on hangers in back, a piece of paper with the hotel address. Something wasn't right. At the end of it all, a few days in the future, something waited for him, a dark something he didn't want to look at. He turned on the radio to block it out of his mind. The news was on. Two guys shot in Liberty City because of a five-dollar bet. Eddie laughed. It was what now, end of March? April? It was maybe going to be cold up north. Where did you buy fucking leather gloves in Florida?

Twelve

Sleet whistled past the corner of the building, and gusts of wind pressed against the glass like the shoulders of insistent ghosts. Joanna opened one of the windows that looked down on Boston Harbor and was able to get a sense of the force of the storm. Not as bad as predicted, she could tell that already. Even from this height—fourteen floors—she could hear the No Parking signs buckling against their metal bolts, and something—a plastic bottle—rolling around in the parking lot. But the precipitation was mixed snow and sleet and not particularly heavy. She stood looking out for a while, watching the last gray daylight fade to black behind the swirling clouds, then she turned back toward the kitchen.

The meal wouldn't be anything special—vegetables over pasta in a light tomato sauce, a ready-mixed salad of field greens. But she'd gone out and bought a seventy-dollar bottle of Montepulciano di Nobile, Leslie's favorite, and she'd set the table with her best cloth and napkins, her silver cutlery, the gold-banded glasses Leslie had given her for their anniversary the previous year. On one of their antique-hunting trips to the Berkshires, she'd picked up a pair of British candlesticks, Scofield 1795. She set them on the table now, fitted into them a pair of green tapers, checked the clock, the stove, opened the wine.

Their dinner was set for seven-thirty. Candlelight, music, a bit of privacy for once—it was not an ordinary evening for them and she didn't want to mark it in an ordinary way. Five years now. There was a sense—she had the sense at least—that she and Leslie were approaching some kind of decisive moment: more of a commitment, it felt like, though precisely what shape that commitment might take was difficult to tell. Maybe Leslie would move in instead of just sleeping over on occasion, and they'd live openly as lovers, and to hell with public opinion. Other people in the business did it.

The night seemed filled with possibilities. There was a beautiful onyx necklace in a gift box in the night-table drawer, and, in the air of the apartment, a sense of her life opening out into some luxurious stretch of commitment and warmth. It occurred to her that she might finally be finished mourning her mother's passing; at least that one part of the family puzzle had been set in place.

At twenty past seven she took the salad out of the refrigerator and brought it to the table. The vegetables were sizzling gently in the pan, the pasta ready to go into its pot. Earlier, she'd tuned into an NPR talk show about addiction—the guest was encouraging a much wider definition of the word—but she was no longer really listening and switched it off. The telephone rang. Out of habit she waited until the machine picked up, but the person on the other end closed the connection without speaking, something Leslie never did.

At seven forty-five she went to the window and peered down at the street, looking for a gray Volvo, an open parking space, a blond beauty hurrying along in the wind and snow. She put in a Bonnie Raitt CD, poured herself half a glass of the wine and wandered into the dining room in a slow choreography of forced optimism. It was a bad driving night. Just as she herself had done, Leslie had probably spent a few hours in the office and was home now, fixing her hair, wrapping a small gift, or driving all over the city looking for some special dessert.

Nothing to be concerned about.

At eight-fifteen she lit one candle and turned off the lights. The burner beneath the vegetables had long ago gone cold. The pasta water waited on the stove, cool as metal. She was on her second glass of wine now and had cut up some Syrian bread into triangles and taken a small container of hummus from the refrigerator.

At eight-thirty she dialed Leslie's apartment and got the answering machine, into which, in an absolutely calm voice, she said she hoped everything was all right, that she was making a meal at her place as they'd agreed. Seven-thirty, remember? She should be careful driving on her way over.

Joanna waited until ten minutes after nine before blowing out the candle. For a long while, with snow and sleet knocking against the windows, and the little yellow light on the security panel flashing its comforting pulse, and the bump of the elevator doors sounding from time to time beyond the walls in muted notes of false promise, she sat at the table, spinning the exquisite wine in her glass, drinking, struggling to get some clear view of herself, to step back and get some clear view. She was a fool, that part was clear enough. As foolishly sentimental, in her own way, as her father and brother. In spite of the thousands of news reports she'd read on air, in spite of everything she knew about life, she still had a made-up future going on in her imagination, and that was going to kill her long before Chelsea Eddie Crevine ever did.

When the digital clock moved from 10:59 to 11:00, she stood, one hand on the back of the chair, waited until her head stopped spinning, then walked to the sliding door, opened it, stepped out onto the balcony, and let the hard pellets of sleet blow against her, stinging her cheeks. She put one hand on the rail and leaned over, looking straight down two hundred feet to the white sidewalk. A few icy flakes settled on the backs of her fingers. The white world swung and shifted, cars gliding past like eels sending beams of light along the bottom of a silver sea, and it seemed then as if her mother's voice were calling out to her from the other side of a curtain as thin as the sleeve of a silk shirt. One step now and no pain.

Thirteen

Outside the house where she and Peter lay in bed, the night was soundless and still, a Montana night, all ice and stone. Elsie heard the soft thump of Austin's music in the walls, all the comfort a teenager's mother was allowed at this hour: he was home, he was safe. With every passing night the worry about him being abducted or hurt by Eddie or one of Eddie's men lessened one hundredth of one degree, and sometimes she let herself imagine the day when that vile excuse for a human being would no longer cast his shadow over them. It seemed to her—and she felt like she could claim some personal experience with the subject—that killers and mobsters poured their dark slime over the whole society. Even if they didn't touch your family as directly as they'd touched Peter's and hers, they reminded you of a certain kind of horrible possibility. They showed you one end of the human spectrum. They kept fear alive in people's hearts, feeding it the way zookeepers fed vipers in a cage.

There were no sounds from outside the house, no traffic in the street, no sirens, no noises from the neighbors. Beyond the bass beat in Austin's room, there was a particular flavor of quiet that she'd almost gotten used to. Nice, in its own way, but there was a loneliness associated with it, too. The cold, the dark, the quiet—she wondered how long it would take for a city girl to really, truly come to love it.

She and Peter had stopped for dinner on the way home

from skiing, and it seemed to her that the cleanness of the mountains had stayed with them all during the meal and the ride back to Maddles, but also that this country loneliness had been draped around them like black cloth. They'd come home late and made love after their own fashion—a playful, unexpectant, easily satisfied fashion—and were lying under the sheet and quilt now with moonlight cutting through the curtains and the pleasure of the fine, clean day still in the room.

They were touching at ankle and hip, lying on their backs. Peter took her hand and ran his thumb gently across the top of it, something she liked. After a time he said, "I'm hav-hav-having urges to go back to Revere."

She turned her head slightly, changed the pressure against his ankle in a familiar way. He was joking again. Seventy per cent of everything he said was meant as a joke. "The marshals would be a little bit upset to hear that, don't you think?"

"I'm not going to ask them. I'm j-just going to g-go."

She rolled onto her side and ran her eyes over his face in the half-dark. The thumping in the walls stopped suddenly, as if Austin, two rooms away, were listening as well. "You're not serious?"

Peter didn't reply.

"What do you mean, go? Go how?"

"I'm ga-going to sn-sneak back. I'll be ga-ga-ga-gone exactly ta-two and a half days. I have it all planned out."

"All planned out! A second ago you were just having urg-es!"

"The urges were c-connected to the plan. Some-somebody came into my shop last week, and I started talking to her and I got-got-got an idea."

She laughed quietly, tried to let herself relax again, settle toward sleep.

"I'm serious. I've ba-ba-been trying to wa-work up the

40

courage to tell you."

"You can't be, Peter."

"Turn on the la-light and la-look."

When the lamp went on he covered his eyes with a bent arm. She propped herself up on one elbow, pulled his arm away, studied his mouth and eyes for a few seconds, then fell back.

Peter reached across her body and turned off the lamp, and then held her. He wiped his fingers along the wet track over the bone on the side of her eye. He said, "La-la-listen, Else. Please. I na-know it's la-lousy for you."

She sobbed for another little while, intermittent burps of misery, then lay still, breathing, hammering the bottom of her fist into the sheet.

"Else, sa-say something."

But she wouldn't, or couldn't. An owl called not far from the house, three short sharp syllables, a long fourth.

"El-Else."

"You see already how much more you're stuttering?"

"Th-that's the fa-first time you ev-ever said anything about m-my stuttering. Ev-ever. In fa-four years."

"You were getting so calm inside you almost stopped stuttering. You didn't notice it?"

"What does calm have to do with st-stuttering."

"We were all so calm. Look how much Austin has changed over the last few months."

"Austin w-w-was always a g-good kid. He was j-just ticked off at first that we ya-yanked him aw-away from D-Darcy. Th-that's all."

"He's different than he used to be and you know it, Peter. We're all three different. This is the most beautiful place I've ever seen. The kids are good to him, the people have been wonderful to us."

"Won-wonderful? You're wa-with them an hour and they sa-say twelve words. Na-nine of them are about the wa-weather, the other three about ca-cows."

"They are very kind, good people, Peter, and you know it."

"They're not Italian."

"Neither am I."

"You ha-have-have all the qua-qua-qualities, though."

"Now you're making a joke to just try to get me to forget what you said. But you mean it, I know you do."

"Of cour-course I mean it. You can ca-cook as ga-good as my f-father. You ha-hair color is a little off, ba-but up in the na-north they—"

She let go of his hand and pushed a few inches away from him. "You're Peter Drinkwater now anyway," she said. "You have to remember not to mention the Italian stuff."

"I sa-say I'm half. On my m-m-m-mother's side."

"No one here cares about those things anyway."

"You think so? The guy at the post office yesterday asked if we were Ja-Jewish. I said no, ba-but that there was a little Na-negro blood there. Wa-way back."

"You didn't."

"Sure I did. What-what of it, if we're Jewish? Wh-what, they ga-give you diff-different stamps? Ka-ka-ka-ka-kosher glue on the back in case you la-lick?"

"Stop, Peter."

"There was a bi-bi-big scandal downtown yesterday. I didn't tell you. I guess one guy actually hugged another guy. It-it ta-turned out to be his cousin, but people were all upset about it anyway. Hug-hug-hugged him and actually—"

"Stop."

"Alright, I'm stopped . . . Look, Else, it's na-nice here, I admit it. Skiing is fun, it is. And you na-know I ah-pre-pre-preciate you and Austin ripping your lives up and ca-coming

42

here with me. But look at it from m-my side. I stopped smok-ing. I gave up ga-gambling. Completely. Nobody ever thought it was possible. I da-da-do my best to fit in here, eve-even though for me it's like Mars. I r-rent out my movies and I t-take back my movies, and I pretend I like ten feet of snow all winter and mac-mac-macaroni and cheese for the la-lunch special at the cafe, on those days when they run out of meatloaf. But my-my-my f-father is ga-getting on. I c-couldn't live with myself if I didn't go back to see him."

"The new agent says when they catch Eddie we might be able to go back for good."

"Sure. Wa-when are they ga-gonna catch Eddie? The ya-year two-thousand, eighty-eight? Eddie's out in the Bahamas someplace on a yacht. You think he lays awake at night worry-ing about me? He's at the crap tables with a new face and a vodka t-tonic and twenty thousand dollars worth of chips in front of him, and we're thinking about him day and na-night."

At this, she began to cry again. Peter squeezed her hand. "They'll kill you," she said through the tears. "They're watching your father's house, and Joanie's apartment, you know they are. Just waiting for you to do something like this. We finally get—" the tears choked her for a few seconds, she let go of his hand and swiped at her eyes. "I finally get a little calm and logic in my life—after thirty-six years of nothing but craziness—crazy parents, a crazy drug addict for a first husband . . . Finally . . . and . . . you, you can't stand it when things are too quiet. You always need to make the boat rock until it's just about tipping over, or else the ride is no fun for you."

Peter tapped a finger on his belly. "G-give me a little cr-credit, at least. Gam-gam-gambling is no pic-picnic of an addic-tion to give up."

"I give you huge credit. So does Austin. We talk about it all the time. But isn't this just another kind of gambling, only with your life? With our lives?"

"It wa-would be, Else. If I didn't have a per-perfect plan worked out, and if-if I was j-just doing it for the r-rush."

"Aren't you though? Couldn't your father come here?"

"They arrested Johnny Denok today, it was on the news in a story about Eddie."

"Who?"

"John Denok . . . Johnny Cut. Eddie's right-hand guy for as la-long as anybody can remember."

"Eddie's still out there, Peter."

"Za-Xavier's at Walpole. Da-Denok's going away. Ed-Ed-Ed-Eddie would never come back now. There's nobody left now except his ka-kids. John and Jimmy. And Jimmy could-couldn't sha-shoot somebody if—"

"Tell Willard, then. Maybe they can arrange a trip, or a meeting at least."

"You na-know Willard and the other marshal guys, Else. They won't even let me make a ca-call, ra-write a letter. They-they-they'd nev-never let me ga-go."

Elsie turned her head away from him, and stared at the moonlit window. "You're going back to gamble, aren't you. You have some idea that you'll make a fortune there, at your lucky track, and buy us out of this ordinary life into something fancy."

"Ab-ab-absolutely not. If I wa-wanted to gamble I c-could g-gamble on Austin's computer. I'm g-g-going back to sa-see my father. I have a d-debt to him. Forty ya-years of na-nothing but trouble. Some nights I lay here, I cho-cho-choke on the ga-guilt. You-you don't have that with your folks. Ya-you don't know what it's la-like."

"My parents are dead, Peter."

"Eve-even moreso then."

"And guilt never once, never once in the history of the

world was a good reason for doing something. It only ends up crushing you around the edges. You keep running, keep going, but there's this crushed look to everything you do if you're guilty. Look at your poor father, and what he's carried all these years."

"Fa-first time you ever sa-said anything about my fa-father like that."

"I love the man," she said. "I miss him as much as you do. But he made one mistake in his life and now he believes God's going to punish him for it for all time unless every other thought is "I'm sorry". . . . You can't walk around always thinking about every wrong thing you did in the past, and how God is disappointed in you, and people are disappointed in you, and what a bad person you are, and how you need to spend the rest of your life making up for it. All that ends up doing is making you do something like that again in the future, creating more things to be guilty about. More dents in good things, more crushed edges of things that are clean and right."

Peter was silent for a long time.

"I'm saying this out of love," Elsie said.

"La-la-love. La-love means seeing some-somebody once in a while. La-love ma-means t-t-t-taking a risk na-now and then."

Elsie turned onto her left side, away from him, and let those words settle onto the quilt and carpet like a thin cloud of dust. She could feel Peter lying perfectly still on his back beside her, and she knew it would hurt him for her to keep silent now, to turn away from him like this, but she felt like she needed to go to a private place, inside herself, for a little while. She thought—briefly and not seriously—about what it would be like to leave him, just take Austin and go someplace and start all over again. Most likely she'd fall in love again after a short while, and most likely the new man in her life would be addicted to something. For a long time now she'd had a theory about people that they repeated their mistakes over and over and over again, like a phone answering machine programmed to say exactly the same thing every time a little zip of electricity came through the line. She took care of troubled people, that's what she was programmed to do in this life. Her mother had trained her, at first, and then there had been Doug and then, after a lot of suffering and another few years, Peter. Her heart reached out and wrapped itself around them, she couldn't help it. Other than that she had such a straight, logical life. If she had to make money, she worked. If she had a toothache, she went to the dentist. If Austin called and needed a ride, she got in the car. Life seemed so simple that way; not easy, but simple, straightforward, understandable. And for her mother and Douglas and now Peter it was a case of turning a simple, straight bus ride to the grocery store into a massively confused conversation. Which bus to take? Maybe a taxi instead? What about a side route to make it more interesting? Have an argument with the driver. Forget your money at home. Drop the gallon of milk as you were putting it in your shopping cart. Make sure the checkout girl didn't cheat you. Argue with her. Flirt with her. Keep the taxi waiting so long you had to walk. Then it started to rain. You'd forgotten your umbrella. Your wallet got soaked. There was a lottery ticket in the wallet, a winner probably, but now it was unreadable . . . and on and on, over and over and over again.

Still, of all of them, Peter had by far the kindest heart. He'd never been mean to her, never been anything but a loving father-figure to Austin. He bought her flowers, candy, earrings he couldn't afford for Valentine's Day, insisted Austin go out with them to celebrate, ordered the most expensive steak, held her arm as they went out the door, kissed her like they were sixteen-year-olds, joked with them when they were down. This was the deal, she told herself, and he had never really tried to

46

hide it from her and she had understood it from the first night she'd let him take her home: she got all that, the generosity, the laughter, the thrill, the caring . . . and in return she knew that one day he'd do something like this. Not leave her. Not cheat on her. Just step out to the railing on the roof of the building and see how far over he could lean before gravity brought him down.

He put his hand on her hip and she touched his fingers, just for a second, then turned back away from him and tried to stop thinking and go to sleep.

Fourteen

In the time Vito had been at the rectory the snow had accumulated to a depth of two inches, but now, this close to the water, it was starting to mix with sleet. Revere Street was a parade of blurred white and red lights, a city plow blinking at the head of it, throwing sand. Without noticing, he drove through a yellow light turning red at the highway, a tractor-trailer already revving up to cross his path. He turned left onto Broadway, climbed the small rise there, but then, at the top of the rise, instead of continuing east, downhill, toward the corner of Proctor Avenue and home, he made a sudden left in front of a slow, oncoming line of traffic, past Rigione's Market, past the Do Not Enter sign, and onto Tapley Avenue. A horn sounded angrily behind him; he didn't hear it.

Narrow to begin with, Tapley Avenue was made narrower by the line of parked cars, and Vito needed all his concentration to guide the Pontiac down the slick slope and bring it to a stop by the curb. For a short while he sat there opposite the house where his parents had lived when they came over from Italy, where he and Lucy had lived when they were first married, until they'd been able to save up and buy the newer house on Proctor Avenue. He sat there a moment, wipers knocking, snow and sleet tapping on the windshield like fingernails, then he looped around the bottom of the block and up Ambrose Street. The house he stopped in front of—8/8 pitch to the roof, a small porch that needed new supports—shared a back fence with the one on Tapley Avenue. There were shrubs—lilac bushes, he knew—to either side of the front porch steps, and the limbs sagged under the weight of the new snow so that he could see the windows of the front rooms. The trim needed painting. Alfonse's car wasn't in the driveway, not parked in front of the house, so probably he was at work. Vito turned off the engine and sat in the stormy afternoon light, looking through the passenger window, a spy from another world.

The aspect of life that seemed so strange and inexplicable to him at that moment was the fact that there existed an invisible wall between people, and that wall kept you from really feeling what pain there might be on the other side. It seemed to him that in this one respect God had designed the world very badly. Because of it, you could be the source of tremendous suffering in someone else's life—hurt a person, humiliate a person, kill a person—and not truly feel what you'd done to them. Forty years ago he'd walked through the gate in this backyard on a December afternoon with snow and sleet coming down in just the same way it was falling now, wearing his carpenter's clothes and a worn denim cap and carrying a toolbox in one hand, and in half an hour he had done enough damage to his wife and children to last an entire lifetime.

Lucy had been pregnant with Peter then, and had taken their Joanie—a young girl—into Boston for Christmas shopping. He'd spent the morning making a cradle for the new baby. When he finished gluing the pieces of the cradle together, he tapped the dowels snug with his rubber mallet, folded up the newspapers and lay them in a box beside the stove. He set the cradle on top of the kitchen table, so Lucy and Joanie would see it the minute they stepped through the door.

It was still three hours before he was supposed to drive to the subway station to meet them.

The snow had turned to sleet while he was working on the

cradle. He went out the back door in just his overalls, flannel shirt, and hat, and carried his toolbox across the back yard and through the gate, leaving a trail of boot prints on the thin wintry sheet. He was a strong man then, young, handsome, people said, even with the oversize nose.

Nasone, they called it in Italian. Extra big, it meant. Black hair, strong shoulders, strong hands. Though so much of that had changed, some essence, some core of him, had stayed exactly the same. He was still the type of man who'd walk across a snowy yard to help somebody, a woman especially; but there seemed to him now a stain on that generosity, as if all his life he'd been locked in a nightmare with people going about their business on all sides of him, while he scurried this way and that, offering his help, his sympathy, his money, the work of his hands, in exchange for their approval. What Dommy had said about him must be true, then: there would always be a stain on what he thought of as his goodness. It wasn't a pure thing, wasn't true.

When Carmellina answered his knock at the back door there was so much pleasure in her face. It seemed to him now that he'd been perfectly ready to sell his soul, ruin his marriage, hurt his wife and his children just for those few drops of sweetness and gratitude. He'd felt like such a good man then, in spite of what he was thinking underneath.

Carmellina offered him something to eat, and although he was hungry, he refused. She led him upstairs to show him the place where the cold air was coming through two bedroom windows, and water leaking in when it rained or the snow melted. The carpet was stained, the little trunk she kept there was stained. She told him he'd saved the house from being completely ruined with the other work he'd done. She used the Italian word. *Rotta*. Broken.

Carmellina's old mother had just died. Her husband, a no-good, had gone away. There were no children, but on that afternoon, there seemed to be a third person with them in the bedroom. It was as if her thinking about him over the past weeks, and him thinking about her had combined to form another spirit, and all that had to happen to give that spirit physical form was for one of them to say or do something that acknowledged it. One moment. Forty-two years ago now and as clear to him as the upholstery of the seat of his car underneath his spotted, wrinkled hand. Carmellina was standing close to him near the window, wearing a lilac dress. A little perfume, he could smell. The iron radiator was clanking. All he would have had to do was set down his tools and start to work, and his life, Carmellina's life, Lucy's life, Peter and Joanie's life would have been different lives, easier, better. Carmellina was looking at him. He set his toolbox down, reached out and put the tips of two fingers on the bone of her hip under the dress, and that was enough. All of a sudden she was kissing him, the way a woman who hasn't eaten in a week puts food in her mouth. And, instead of stopping her, he was kissing back, as if whatever they did in that room would somehow not be counted in the world because the world couldn't see them; as if there was a big wall between what he did and what pain Lucy might feel; as if, because he was making one other person happy, there could be nothing wrong with what he was doing. As if he could easily and rightfully be husband to a world of abandoned women and father to all their children.

They made love on top of the bedspread with their clothes on, quickly, carelessly, Carmellina saying his name over and over again, and then weeping and squeezing him against her very hard as if she could hold him in place and stop time.

Afterwards, he couldn't look at her. He knew that hurt her, but he couldn't make himself look. His hat had fallen over the side of the bed but he didn't reach down to pick it up. He couldn't remember what he said then, or what she said, only that he took his toolbox without fixing the window and went downstairs and out the door and across their yards, a hypnotized man, a fallen man, *rotto*, making a new trail of boot prints there in the snow and sleet where the other trail had been covered over.

He turned on the windshield wipers, but so much ice had accumulated that he had to turn them off again and get out and clean the glass, the icy air cutting into his bare hands in a way that seemed right, like a penance.

Fifteen

A gust of wind whipped Joanna's hair against her face. She leaned back, slid the glass door shut, stripped off her clothes, walked naked into the bedroom, pulled the sheet and the quilt up over her and eventually drifted off into a restless sleep.

She dreamed that her brother was still living close by, still gambling, still in debt to Eddie Crevine. In the dream, Peter was pounding on the door of her apartment and calling her name, telling her and half the neighbors on the floor that Eddie was going to kill him this time, really, if he didn't pay the debt, pleading with her to lend him eighty thousand dollars. Now. Tonight. This minute. Eighty thousand.

She was awakened by the sound of someone trying the handle of the hallway door. Leslie had the security code. If it was Leslie, why would she be wrestling with the doorknob? She thought she could hear a finger punching at the security panel, trying different combinations. She reached into the nightstand drawer, pushed aside the gift box and took the new pistol into her hand.

She seemed to be breathing abnormally loudly. She was half-propped against the pillows and holding the new gun in front of her, between her legs, beneath the quilt.

The handle in the entranceway shook again, then clicked. She could hear the soft scraping sound the bottom of the door made against the carpet. The door bumped closed, there were footsteps in the dining room. Beneath the quilt she pointed the gun at the door, and when Leslie appeared there and switched the light on, Joanna had a fleeting urge, just a thousandth of a second of an urge, to squeeze the trigger.

She pressed her eyes closed against the sudden brightness, relaxed her hand and let the gun rest on the fabric between her thighs. In another moment, Leslie was standing next to the bed, then sitting on its edge, caressing her knee through the bedclothes. She was wearing a white cableknit sweater. The shoulders of the sweater were wet with melted ice, as was her hair. Her eyes shone like gems.

"You're high."

Leslie's laugh was a tinkling, golden warble, an utterly careless laugh, it seemed to her now, though at one time it had sounded like the tone of love itself. "Only a little bit." She squeezed Joanna's knee and ran her hand down along the blanketed shin.

It was like making eye contact through three layers of cellophane. Everything was almost clear, almost the same, almost right. It was like being touched by a lover through a blanket.

"Hey, shift the covers out of the way so I can have access, would you?"

Joanna shook her head. "Have you been home?"

"Home is here tonight, what's wrong?"

"You're high."

"Just a little after-work partying. I called you to see if you wanted to come, there was no answer."

"Don't lie to me, Les."

She smirked. "Oh, it's a fib, not a lie. I was thinking of calling. I almost called. Someone came by my office at the end of the day—"

"Someone who?"

"Someone Jeanette. We thought we'd go out and have a quick beer. There were a couple of trips to the bathroom, the

54

music seemed so nice, the dancing—"

"Go."

"What? It's bad out there. Move over, slide over." Leslie started to pull her sweater up over her head, but partly lost her balance and put a hand down on the bed to catch herself. "What's this?" She was smiling expectantly, dreamily, pulling the quilt back. "Whoa! What the hell? What's going on, Jo?"

"Go home."

"What's going on? Are you going to shoot yourself or something?"

"Go home."

"Jeanette and I danced, we didn't do anything, for God's sake. What's the gun for?"

"For Eddie Crevine. In case he comes, in case one of his men breaks in. I bought one for my father, too."

Leslie tilted her head to one side in a gesture of disdain, one half-inch shy of pity. "Oh, Joanna. A gun in bed with you? A pistol? It's really too much now."

"We'll talk when you're in a normal state of mind."

She'd tried to adopt a mature, even tone, but Leslie was immune to it, bulletproof. The last sweet wisps of the drug made for a sort of glitter around the edges of her face, a beautiful, utterly confident face clouded with pity.

"You're not a police officer, Joanna. You're not an FBI agent. No one's coming to kill you or hurt you or break in or screw with your tender family. For Christ's sake you have an alarm system that's like the Pentagon War Room. It's too really . . . It's too much, really. It's beneath dignity."

"Go home."

"It's this Italian melodrama thing. Me! My family! The Mafia! I've seen the movie, you know, I'm tired of it. I . . . Look, you had your famous brush with death—"

"Go. I made us a special meal. It's . . . today is . . ."

55

Leslie stared at her, shaking her head. "Sorry," she said, but it sounded nothing like an apology. She patted her on the knee and stood, found her balance, walked out through the door and then reached back in and snapped off the light.

Joanna listened to the front door open and close. For the better part of half an hour she sat propped against the pillows, naked under the sheet, touching the pistol with two fingers, listening to the gusts of wind, ghostly breaths, slam against the windows.

Sixteen

On Broadway again, little rain now mixing in, Vito peered through the windshield, riding the brake, studying the skin of snow on the slick street. He made the turn onto Proctor Avenue at four miles an hour, but the plows hadn't reached this part of the city yet, and the wheels of his car spun several times on the uphill grade. After he passed the old hospital—turned into a nursing home now—the road reached a plateau, and left him only another hundred slick, flat yards before he was turning into his own driveway.

There was the wide-open storm door in the car port, snow and rain and ice blowing in. For one instant the sight of it offered the illusion that another person was living in the house with him again—Lucy or Peter or Joanie. But there were no lights in the windows. He parked the Pontiac and got out. There was a cardboard box, small, against the bottom of the inside door, so maybe it wasn't him left it open. On top of the box was a note, Joanie's writing.

For you, Papa. We'll talk.
Love, Joanna

He carried the box inside and opened it and looked a minute at what was there. Then he changed into the galoshes and work clothes, heavy sweater and coat, and he went outside and topped off the birdfeeders on the porch.

Three inches had fallen on the porch steps before it turned to sleet. If he didn't clean it off now, tomorrow it would be like cement. Away from the shelter of the house the sleet knocked sharply against his eyes and cheeks and clung to the sleeves of his plain gray coat. A blanket of silence had been thrown over the Avenue, music of another world, and he set to work in it as if it were an embrace.

He worked in a steady rhythm, the way people work who have done manual labor their whole lives. Once, thinking he heard two knocks, an old signal, he looked up at the picture window. But there was no Lucy there now, waving him in for a rest, making him hot chocolate, asking about the storm, reminding him that, since the DiRuzzas were out, he should go across and shovel the end of their driveway, too, so it would be easier for Joe and Mary to drive their car back in later on. He thought he heard the knocking again, a few minutes later. He didn't look.

By the time a car pulled to a stop in front of the house and parked—on the no-parking side of the street—he'd finished only about a quarter of the task he'd set for himself. A man stood up out of the driver's side and Vito could immediately tell who it was by the way the man held his shoulders. A soldier's posture, a policeman's.

"Where's the other shovel, Uncle?" Alfonse said.

They worked together in silence for the better part of an hour. By the time the driveway and the walk had been cleared, by the time the edges of the carport had been shoveled clean and the berm of wet snow at the end of the driveway broken down and thrown onto the lawn, the daylight had gone, the air had turned colder again, and big, wet flakes were sailing down through the streetlight. "She's supposed to stop soon," Vito said, as if to convince himself. "She'll be a little easier for me now in the morning." But it almost seemed to him, with the driveway covered in a thin, glistening carpet of white again, that all their work would go for nothing.

They crossed the street together and in ten more minutes cleared away the ridge of snow the plow had made at the base of the DiRuzzas' driveway.

Alfonse pulled his car in off the street. They leaned the shovels against the house and kicked their boots against the riser of the bottom step and took them off in the entranceway, by the phone. Vito set the coffeepot on the gas stove, and reached up into the shelf on top of the broom closet for the bottle of anisette. While the coffee was making, he buttered four pieces of bread and set them on the tray of the toaster oven Joanie had given Lucy and him, lightly browned them there, put two pieces each on two plates, dribbled olive oil over them—shoelaces of tomato-stalk green—added a few chips of garlic, grated a layer of cheese over everything, put the slices back in the toaster just long enough for the cheese to melt, then served Alfonse at the kitchen table. Everything just right. The pieces of bread, the coffee, black, with a splash of anisette inside, the blue cloth napkin and a fork and knife in case Alfonse wanted not to eat with his fingers. Everything the way it was supposed to be now, Alfonse in this house, eating his food. *Tutto a posto.*

"How's your back been feeling, Uncle?"

"Strong, like always."

"No pain?"

"Zero now."

"You're keeping in shape?"

"I walk. To the cemetery. Sometimes down Broadway and back, two, three times in a day. Some days down the beach if it's not too cold. And I work in the shop down cellar for the arms."

"What are you making there?"

"The tables. Small ones. Five so far, I have. Maple, oak, whatever you want. If you need one, say."

They ate and drank, the city plow rumbled past in the street. Vito fetched the coffeepot from the stove and refilled both cups.

"Something's bothering you, Uncle."

"No, nothing."

Alfonse finished the second piece of bread, and ran the tip of a finger around the plate to collect the last of the oil and sesame seeds. Vito turned the bottle of anisette so that it faced him and he studied the picture on the label, scene of some imaginary land with sun shining over a gray cliffside and a river. Trees in the foreground. A man and a woman walking. Italy, it was supposed to be. Sometimes he thought that he and his family should have stayed. There was a faint steady ringing in his ears these days, all the time. Beyond it, he could hear snow ticking quickly against the windows.

"I have some news, Uncle." Alfonse said at last. "Nice news."

"We could use some."

"There's a woman I've been seeing for a while, since not long after Aunt Lucy died. We just decided last night to get married."

Vito nodded, his eyes on Alfonse's eyes, a little stretch of happy silence between them now. He said: "I'm a pay for the wedding."

Alfonse laughed a two-note nervous laugh and shook his head. "We don't want that. We have plenty of money between the two of us—she works, her name is Lily—we have plenty of money."

"I pay anyway, I don't care how much money you have."

Alfonse was shaking his head. "We don't want that. We want something else as a gift, a special favor."

"Say."

"I'm selling my mother's house."

"Why?"

"Because I don't want to live with the memories there, Uncle, to tell you the truth. I'm selling it to a guy who works with me, it's all set. Lily and I bought the last lot of open land on Herter Street."

"When?"

"Three days ago. It's only a mile from here."

"That's a good lot, one of the only open ones left."

"Right." Alfonse paused, kept his eyes on Vito, said, "We want you to build us a place to live there."

Vito looked, at first, as if he didn't understand, or was pretending not to. His face bore the expression a child's face bears when the child is given a gift he might have hoped for had he been brave enough to let himself imagine it. "I'm too old for that now," he said, with no conviction. "I'm a retired."

"We'll hire people to help you—anybody you need. Young guys with strong backs. But we want you to run the project."

"Why?"

"Because I want your mark on the house I'm going to live in the rest of my life."

Vito stared across at Alfonse for another half minute or so, then opened his mouth and worked the jaw and tongue. No sound came. He put his right hand flat on the tablecloth and tensed the muscles of his arm to brace himself. He opened his mouth and tried a second time. Nothing. He stood up, went over to the sink, cupped his hands under the faucet and splashed cold water against his face. One time, two time, three. Alfonse sat at the table fingering the tasseled hem of the tablecloth. His father's face-washing went on so long that at last he got up and took two small glasses from the cupboards. He brought the glasses to the table and poured an inch of the clear syrupy drink into each of them, and he waited.

After a time, Vito turned off the water. He wiped his face with a blue-checkered dishcloth, and stood with his back to the room. A minute passed. At last he returned to the seat and took the glass in his fingers, but still wouldn't raise his eyes. "What kind of father I been to you?" he said, almost inaudibly. He appeared to be talking to the glass of anisette.

"That doesn't matter now, Uncle."

"What kind of man does what I done?"

"You gave my mother money every month until I was twenty-one. You made sure friends who owed you favors came by to fix the roof and fix the plumbing. You sent me a thousand dollars when I graduated high school, and told my mother to tell people it was from her husband, who she hadn't seen in twenty years and would never see again."

"Lucy said for me to do that."

"You never once drove past me in the city without stopping, not once, no matter how busy you were. Stopping to talk to me from your truck for a few minutes, or to take me into Rosa's to get me something to eat. Not one birthday and not one Christmas went by without basketball shoes from Uncle Vito, or skates from Uncle Vito, or a shirt or tickets to go see the Red Sox. When I was in the service, you wrote me every week."

Vito remained unconvinced, frowning at this litany, an ounce of water caught and trembling in the corner of one eye. He twirled the glass between his thumb and middle finger. The plow rumbled past in the street again, going the other way now, and he looked at the picture window, and then back into Alfonse's face.

"It's past now, Uncle. Way past."

Vito kept looking, kept trying. Alfonse watched him, waiting for what he had to say. Nothing came.

"Uncle—"

"Don't call me that no more," Vito said, at last.

"Alright."

"*Babbo* is what they call in Italy the father."

"Alright, Uncle."

"I'm a fix it up if I can, what I been doin all these years to you."

"There's nothing to fix, Uncle."

"I'm a fix it up."

Having made this promise, this pledging of the future against the past, Vito seemed to regain some small measure of peace. After another few seconds he drank from the glass, one sip, held the liquid in his mouth a moment then swallowed. After stretch of awkward silence, like a man who'd changed into the uniform of a second profession, a former life, nearly forgotten, he said, "How big a house you talkin?"

Seventeen

It was a little confusing, driving again. For all those years, first Pitchie Luglio and then Xavier drove him where he needed to go. Down here, the few times he left the house, Alicia drove because she was afraid he'd get in a fight with somebody who cut him off, or that he'd run a red light and the police would recognize him. "No chance," he liked to say. "The new nose, the different color hair, the license and the other I.D., the fake registration. There's no fucking chance they could catch me that way, but go head and drive if you want to. I never liked it anyway."

That part was true. All the switches and dials made him confused. He could remember the names of everybody from the guy who managed the delivery trucks at the airport (Joseph "Joey Manicotti" Moulder), to the woman who drove the shrink-wrapped stacks of porno books from Providence to the Adult Pleasure shops on the North Shore (Katrina DiSilva) to the five other underbosses who used to meet with him at Patriarca's or Angiulo's and who ran Springfield and Worcester and New Haven and southern New Hampshire (Aldo Bags, The Fish, Paul D. DeAngelis, Mimsi Frontina). As if it had all been written down in a notebook and the notebook was open in front of him, he could bring to mind their quirks and strengths and weaknesses—that Katrina liked Klonopins, that The Fish never cheated on his wife, that Joey stole only when it was sports equipment, and that he had a storage unit rented in

Peabody, in a place run by another guy whose name he remembered, Carlos Rintera. In his mind, he had files on all these people; he and Xavier used to like to talk about the ways they could put pressure on this guy or that guy if they ever needed to.

But when it came to figuring out how to turn the wipers on high, or dial the radio, or dim the dashboard lights, he was like a little kid. He could drive okay—smart, careful, never too fast—but he didn't like the feeling of people in other cars that close to him. You couldn't look at them if you were driving. You couldn't pay attention to the road and know if they were following you, watching you, pointing a gun at you. One time when he was very little he'd gone skating with a friend at the M.D.C. rink and he fell hard, on his ass, and never went back. Driving was like that to him: the ground wasn't solid no more; anything could happen.

So he told himself take it slow. Out of the garage, down the driveway, over the bridge across the river they lived on and then onto Collins Avenue, which led north up the beach. North was really the only thing he had to remember. Just keep going north and you'd get there. Wednesday, Washington. He had the name and address of the hotel, and phone numbers on a piece of paper in his wallet. All set. But Collins Avenue was too much stop-and-go and when he found the turn to the highway he had to travel through Little Haiti, where every face was black, and the music was loud, and there were nigger women waiting at the bus stops, and now, what the fuck was this, a guy selling bottles of water in the middle of the street. On impulse, and because the light was going yellow, he pulled up next to the guy, who had three bottles in each hand and was swinging them around like he was palming a basketball and showing off for his friends.

"Gimme six of them," Eddie said.

"Six for five dolla," the guy said, handing them through the open window as carefully as if they were glass statuettes.

While Eddie had a hand in his pocket the light turned green again, the guy behind him leaned on the horn. Eddie made a show for a minute of not having the money, and could feel the water guy getting nervous, and the guy behind him pulling around and flipping him off. "Geez I thought I had—" he said, just playing with the water guy, and then he pulled out a hundred and handed it across and got a little kick out of the nigger's face, the surprise, the gratitude, and then he gunned the gas and nearly tore the guy's arm off. Wouldn't it be funny, he thought, if the hundred was phony?

He went up the ramp onto 95, happy for a few seconds, but it was wild there, cars and trucks and motorcycles flying past and cutting back and forth from one lane to the other. It was hard to merge, but he did it. He held the wheel with both hands and took it slow and in a little while, once he was up past Fort Lauderdale, things calmed down. The radio was going. His mind was okay now, not that bad. He'd always had the ability to put things behind him and not think about them too much if he didn't want to. Pretty soon there were orange trees and a little open land and then his thoughts started to spin again in a way he didn't like. Maybe it hadn't been the best thing, doing Alicia that way. Maybe she could have come with him.

"And what?" he said aloud. "Go shopping in Manhattan holding hands?"

It was like there were two voices in his head now, two distinct voices. And it was like he could see that dark thing waiting for him, north, past Washington, past whatever it was he was going to do when he got to Revere. There was nothing to look forward to no more, that was the thing. There was just the idea of revenge, like a piece of candy or a drink, the settling scores, putting his name back on the map. And then after that . . . this other thing.

Thinking about it, he maybe wasn't paying as much attention as he should have. He didn't notice the car pulling up behind him. Green cruiser with a white roof. Florida Highway Patrol. The prick had his lights flashing. Keeping one hand on the wheel and edging the car into the breakdown lane, Eddie dropped the Sauer gently onto the floor and used the back of his left heel to nudge it under the seat. There was nothing to worry about. Zero. If he heard the words, "Can you please step out of the car, sir," he'd reach down and blow a nice hole in the trooper's belly—his father had been arrested by a trooper— then drive as far as he could with the gun in one hand and if it looked like they were going to catch him, he'd do what he had to do.

He pulled the car to a stop and put it in Park. Behind him he could feel the trooper looking at his computer, checking the license plate against his records. Nothing would show, Eddie knew that, not unless Leon had fucked up. Edward Ronald Echeverria had a clean driving record, had never once been to court. The trooper got out, dressed like a soldier in a puke-green army, like fucking Hitler, and sneaked up the fender of the car like that would save him from a guy who knew how to use a gun.

"Good afternoon, officer," Eddie said with a big smile. His mind had suddenly gone quiet and clean. It was like shifting into his old self.

"License and registration."

"Not a problem. Why the stop?"

"You were weaving. Been drinking?"

"I don't drink," Eddie said. "Just tired, I guess. Up late at the girlfriend's, then had to go back home to do a little business."

The trooper checked his eyes, looked at the empty seat, the

67

water bottles, suits hanging in the back. He took the documents into his hands. He had a fucking round cowboy hat on, two little tassels. "What line of work are you in Mr. Echeverria."

"It's pronounced "Eckeverria, Eck, not Etch. I'm mostly retired. I was in real estate up north. Still have a few properties there."

The trooper stared at him too long, almost seemed to maybe recognize him, then took the license and registration and marched back to his vehicle to see what he could find out.

Eighteen

When Alfonse drove away, Vito stood at the porch door and watched the snow falling through the circle of light around the telephone pole. It fell and fell, covering all the work they'd done, falling and falling and kicking sideways in gusts of wind. Every surface he could see had been rounded off and whitened now—the porch railing, the top of the birdfeeder, even the points of the pickets on the back fence between his yard and the Antonellis'—so that the world seemed a softer place, a place in which the consequences of a mistake might turn out to be not as sharp and lasting as they had once seemed.

He drew a bath and soaked his old bones. In the bath he turned his hands over and studied them, as if they'd been away for a few years and had just returned for his inspection. The skin was rough and callused, even now, the fingers and palms marked with small scars. Little monuments to instants of inattention. A Sheetrock knife, a saw blade, sharp corner of a Formica countertop.

He put on his pajamas and got into bed. So many months had passed, so many nights, but the mattress still seemed grotesquely oversized. Even with the curtains closed, the room was filled with the pale glow of the storm, and even with the closet empty and the untouched half of the bed beside him, the house was full of Lucy.

Joanie's package sat on the table beside the bed. Though it was very late for him—the latest he'd gone to sleep since the days when he'd been nursing Lucy through her pain—he took the gun out of the box and held it in his fingers. He wasn't mad on her for giving it—even though he'd told her not to, five times. He wasn't mad. But the gun, to him, felt like a heavy piece of sin, something God wouldn't want in the world. It made him think of the night they killed the Ollanno boy in front of this house, a night you wanted to forget forever. He put the gun back and took Peter's letter from the drawer in the table and read it over again, as he'd done every night for the past week. Near the end of the letter there were three lines that caught him. He read them over several times: "Life is okay here, Pa. I'm not gambling now. Elsie and Austin are happy. I'm sorry for all the trouble I gave you over the years, and if I can ever make up for it I will. Give my brother and sister a kiss for me when you see them."

He folded the letter into its plain envelope with no post-mark on it, no return address, no stamp, and set it on the white lace cloth Lucy had made for the night table. *My brother and sister*, Peter had written, even though they never once talked about it. As he reached to turn out the light he noticed there was dust on the uncovered margins of the table top he'd cleaned a week ago, and it seemed to him that not much in life stayed the same, not even for one minute. God had to always keep moving, maybe. You had a big job like that, you couldn't rest.

Nineteen

By car, at nine o'clock on a weekday morning, Boston's most dangerous neighborhood was fourteen minutes from Joanna's office. Though she'd been there a half dozen times in the past eight years, it had always been on station business, with a camera crew, in a WSBT van, someone else driving. So it took her several extra minutes to find the street she was looking for, and several minutes after that to find what seemed to be a safe place to park—one long block down from the address in her purse, near the corner of a main thoroughfare.

As if to celebrate her arrival, when she stepped into the raw air two rats scuttled out from beneath the next car at the curb, scrambled over each other for a moment in the middle of the street, then ran off in single file up the driveway of the house opposite. Joanna turned her eyes from them and took in the broken window on the first floor, and the broken railings of the front steps, and the asphalt-shingle siding that had fallen off in patches, leaving black tar-paper scars the size of kitchen appliances on the first floor of the house. On two of these blank spaces graffiti had been sprayed, bright orange hieroglyphs of fury and desperation. She saw a movement just above, in a second-story window. Curtains. A face. An elderly black woman, six generations into the dream of freedom, watching her. Joanna waved, then pushed the button on the black plastic end of her key, so that her BMW locked itself and beeped.

The spring sun had already taken care of most of Saturday's

snow, but there were slippery patches here and there so she walked in the street, through thin streams of melt. Rusted chain link fences protected the yards to her right and left. The houses behind them were not so different from those in certain sections of Revere—two and three-story wood-frame houses with porches and dormers—but built even closer together, as if some clause in the State Building Code dictated that the distance between lives must be proportional to the distance between those lives and the heart of the city. Some of the roofs were peaked, some flat. Some of the windows were broken, some boarded-up, some of the cars in the short cement driveways and along the curb wore thin jackets of ice and looked as if they hadn't been driven since the Vietnam war. When she was a girl, this neighborhood had been a safe, stable, working-class part of town, similar to the one she'd grown up in, though with a greater degree of racial mix. Thirty years of drugs, gangs, bad politics, and neglect, and it went now, in media circles and on the street, by the name Little Hell.

There was no one else on the streets of Little Hell at that hour. Here and there on the steep block, like a flotsam of hope on a sea of hopelessness, stood monuments to the neighborhood's better days: houses with trimmed shrubbery and painted window sashes, upright antennas or satellite dishes on the roof, birdfeeders, neatly shoveled driveways. One of these, probably the best-kept house on the block, showed the number 248 over its front door, and a banner in one window sporting Chinese calligraphy. HOUSE OF THE DEVIL she thought the characters might mean. She stepped across the sidewalk there, lifted the clasp of the chain-link gate, strode up a walk that had been carefully shoveled and sanded, climbed five steps, and knocked. The inner door opened immediately, and then the storm door. Before her stood a motherly black woman, twenty years her senior.

The woman greeted her as if she were a neighbor bringing over homemade cake, but the kindliness was edged with something else, the businesslike air of an administrative assistant or professional hostess, someone used to extending a warm welcome to her boss's clients—friends and enemies alike, but acting as a filter, too. She was wearing a pair of lavender pumps, a calf-length lavender skirt, and a pleated white silk blouse with a necklace—Joanna winced—of what seemed to be onyx showing at the collar. Once Joanna was safely inside, the woman closed the door on Little Hell, and ushered her famous visitor down a carpeted hallway that smelled of aftershave.

With its lightly worn leather chairs and framed photos on the walls, and its tidy oriental rug, the room to which she led Joanna might well have been a psychiatrist's waiting room—except for the faint scent, an oversized television standing on a table, and the man sitting peacefully in a leather recliner opposite it. The man, as famous and accomplished in his world as Joanna Imbesalacqua was in hers, was seventy-three, looked to be in his late fifties, and might have passed for a retired professional football player. Neck, shoulders, belly, hands—everything two sizes larger than the ordinary model. He had the skin and hair of a black man, but there was a distinctly Asiatic cast to his face. China Louis, people called him. Second or third or fourth in line for the throne of the Boston underworld, no one knew, exactly, except that he controlled certain sections of the city, certain kinds of business, and did not control others.

He clicked the television into silence, and gestured for her to sit.

"I'm off to church, China," the woman called from the doorway. "Anything you need?"

"Just the coffee for Miss Imbesalacqua before you go, Sweet. She's a coffee addict, people say. We wouldn't want to make her uncomfortable while she's here."

Joanna sat, folded her hands, and turned a waxy, TV smile at him. "You've been checking up on me."

A resonant chuckle leaked out of China Louis' throat. His eyes did not move from her. He seemed never to blink. "A small amount of cream, no sugar," he called into the kitchen, and, after a short delay, the woman, wearing a black cashmere sweater now, carried in a blue-edged cup and saucer with a blue cloth napkin beneath it, and settled them on the coffee table at Joanna's knee. She kissed the man on his forehead, smiled at Joanna in what seemed a genuinely empathetic way, and went down the hall and out the back door. In another minute a car murmured past beneath the curtained windows. Joanna sipped her coffee and said nothing. Eyes still fastened upon her, China Louis shifted his weight in the seat.

"Sure I've been checking up on you," he said, quite pleasantly. "You wouldn't have put the toe of your pretty black boot inside that front door if I hadn't been checking up on you. You wouldn't have made it three steps up this block."

"I'm sure."

"You're sure?" He chuckled again, but one note of the kindness had gone out of the sound and, with the older woman's departure, out of the house. "Full of sass, aren't you? But I know that, too. I know where your apartment is—what building, what floor, which side. I know you drive a brand new BMW, green, license tag SBT-ANCH . . . I hope you drove a company car into this neighborhood, by the way, and not that."

"You told me *not* to drive a company car, remember?"

"Did I?"

"It has the best security system available . . . like my apartment."

China Louis paused, appraising her, puzzling over her as one would puzzle over a conceited child who'd just said something foolish. And then: "I know you have an old father over there in Revere. Nice man. And a little brother who used to have a money problem until he went to work for the government."

"That was in the papers during Xavier Manzo's trial. We reported it ourselves."

China Louis waved one large hand around in front of him, as if stirring a soup he was making in air. "I know you like girls not boys in bed with you. I know who the particular girl of the season is, too. Pretty woman. Works in what they call the world of finance. Kind of a shame from a man's point of view—the pretty part, I mean."

Joanna's steady expression, perfected over years of presenting a pleasing and businesslike personality to a camera lens, did not waver. It had been days now and no apologetic phone call from Leslie. Gold-edged wine glasses every time she opened the cupboard, the photo in her desk drawer at work, onyx necklaces—the world of objects whispered Leslie, Leslie, Leslie like a taunt.

"I know that for the last eight or ten months or so you been dragging your cute ass all over the city, asking about Eddie Crevine, pretending it's part of some investigation you're doing at the TV station, when what it's really about is getting Eddie caught and put in jail, and baby brother out of harm's way, and letting Papa and you sleep a little better at night."

"Finished?" Joanna pushed the word into a brief pause. She set her coffee cup on top of the polished table. Mahogany, with a maple filigree. Her father would be proud that she knew.

"Time being."

"I know that you spent nine years at the Federal Penitentiary in Danbury in your thirties and never want to go back."

"Hard to figure why—"

"That for the last two decades, since Shirlen Abrams was shot, you've pretty much controlled the drugs that move through this side of Boston—with the exception of the North End. The gambling. At least a piece of the prostitution."

"No money in that anymore, sad to say. But I deny all this in any case, in case you're going your brother's route and wearing a wire."

"I'm not."

"I'll have to take your word for that, or feel you up . . . I'll take your word, I guess. For now."

"I know that you've poisoned, or helped poison, your own people with it. Brought your own neighborhood to ruin."

"Something the guineas never managed in their best day, isn't that right? Just other people's neighborhoods."

"That you choose to live here and hardly ever go out, when you have the resources—"

"Money."

"The resources to travel or to live anywhere you like, but that the only thing that really matters to you is power, control, and not going back to prison."

"My wife matters to me. That wonderful woman you just met. That woman can walk anywhere in this neighborhood at any hour and no one will dare say so much as a nasty word in her presence."

"That you lost a son ten years ago, a son who was addicted to the very sub—"

"Careful now, Miss," China Louis said, giving her a glimpse of another face, a brute's face beneath satin. "Sass is one thing. I almost admire it in you, finding out who my people are, calling them, coming alone to Little Hell. You could be wearing a wire under that dress, after all, and trying to get me upset. But you might have the good manners to keep clear of certain subjects in my home."

"Addicted to the very substance," Joanna said, the instant he finished, "which you help import and distribute. And that the only reason you even began to entertain the thought of letting me get within three blocks of this house is because you'd like nothing better than to make sure Eddie Crevine is permanently gone so you can move in on what's left of his territory, and you think I might be able to contribute to that in some small way."

When she stopped speaking the room was quiet but for a lazy tapping of heating pipes near the floor. One knock, another, a squeal of old wood. Then only the quiet gauzy curtains and quiet carpet, China Louis's unblinking attention. His hands drooped down over the arms of the chair like animals hanging from branches in their sleep. "No manners," he said at last.

"It's not a social visit, Mister Louis. I came here for whatever you could tell me about Eddie Crevine. It helps me, and it helps you, and you know it."

"Sure it does. It's business. But there's different ways of going about business. There's the blunt, crude way, like yours, and there's something with a little more class to it. I expected the class part for some reason. I see now that I was mistaken."

"You expected the class part? After the greeting you offered me?"

The eyebrows went up and down once. China Louis seemed as if he might concede the point. He hit the remote button, turned the television on for a moment, then snapped it off again. Joanna, who could not see the screen, had the sense he was checking stock prices.

"Now Eddie Crevine is an interesting case," China Louis said, turning his eyes from the TV and into the air, half sunlit, in the middle of the room. "The whole way things were organized in this part of the country is interesting. You're interested. I can see you are. This whole underneath world turns you on, doesn't it?"

"It disgusts me."

"Sure. I bet. But there's something about it that just calls out to you, too. It has its own rules and laws, and you're smart, and you believe you can figure them out. The people who run it don't walk around all day carrying big heavy sacks of doubt and guilt on their backs like you do, and you want to understand why that is."

"Whatever you can tell me I'll listen to."

China Louis blinked, holding his eyelids down for two seconds before raising them again. "Oh I could tell you things you'd lie awake all night thinking about, Miss. Horrible things. Things to make you question the existence of any kind of God whatsoever. Children murdered, men tortured in imaginative ways, women bought and sold like pieces of cloth and then used up and cast away. I could solve crimes that haven't been solved in years by the city of Boston's finest detectives. I could give you all the excitement and blackness of a neighborhood like this—which is part of what you want, too, isn't it? There's something about Little Hell that has a hold on people like yourself. You almost wonder some days, when you're not feeling sorry for them, when the rich little life you've made for yourself is disappointing you yet again, you almost wonder if the people here aren't just a little bit better off than you and your friends are, somehow, in spite of the fact that they have nothing now and nothing ever to look forward to. You listen to them laugh and you wonder if maybe they feel something you can't feel. With each other. Inside themselves. You wonder sometimes if God likes them better than he likes you."

"You speak as if you spent all your time and energies making life better for them."

China Louis grunted. "I don't spend all my time and energy making life better for myself. With my fancy clothes, my fancy place to live, my fancy car, my second and third and fourth houses. Do I now?" He shifted his weight again, seemed, as these words were spoken, to remember something, then pushed himself up and out of the chair. For a moment Joanna thought the interview was over, or that China Louis had prepared materials for demonstrating his points and was setting off to fetch them. But he smiled down at her, the low table between them. "You'll excuse me a minute. Just remembered something. Need to make one quick call in private."

Without him, the room had no character of its own. Still as the interior of a cave, recently cleaned, silent—it had the feeling of a half-paralyzed pet waiting upon its master's return. Chair, sofa, tables, lamp, TV—every item Joanna laid eyes on seemed to have turned itself to sleep mode. Listening intently, she heard the light scrape of his slippers fading into the far reaches of the house, then one car passing in the street, then the radiator pipes, then quiet. She touched a finger to her saucer. She ran her eyes across every surface in the room, but it was sterile and staid, offering nothing in the way of helpful clues. The framed pictures were neutral prints that might have hung in any hospital hallway—mountain scenes, woodland scenes, men fishing beside a meadow—China Louis was said to leave this house only rarely; perhaps these pictures were his sole link to the world of the out of doors. There was a phone next to the chair in which he'd been sitting, and a bookshelf with See-No-Evil, Hear-No-Evil glass figurines and a dozen video tapes, titles penciled on, unreadable from this distance.

Several minutes passed before China Louis came back through the door, looking refreshed. He took up his former place, shifted his weight until it settled comfortably against the cushions, picked a piece of lint from his black shirt, then went on as though the presentation hadn't been interrupted: "You want to understand Eddie, you have to see things in terms of money. Not power, you see, though the two things are connected. Not evil and good. Not Eye-talian or Black or Chinese or Irish. Money. You have to understand there are certain rules to the way the underneath world works. If it's a hot day, a person sweats, see? He doesn't decide to sweat. No God makes him sweat. He just sweats, natural as water going downhill instead of up. And it's that same way with money. Money is like blood in the world's body, see? It flows from this part to that part, wherever it most needs to be at any given time. You can make anything happen with enough money, anything. Your lady friend understands this, I'm sure, but only in her world, not in this world we're talking about now, not in the world of the street. If you understood this what I'm telling you, you'd understand the whole system, the whole underneath system of how the world works. But you don't."

"I nev—"

"And the other thing you don't understand is that a person's type determines what he does. You can count on that, depend on it. You can look at the type and predict just what will happen, see? Now you said something a minute ago about my son. It wasn't true what you said. But there are people it would be true about. People have been addicted since the beginning of time—drugs, liquor, sex, gambling, work, power. That's just one type of human person, see? Your little brother, for example. He's just of a certain type, that's all. That's the way he is." China Louis turned his eyes to the middle of the room and back. "Like a maple tree is maple and a oak is oak. He'll go on borrowing money and taking foolish risks, Eddie Crevine or no Eddie Crevine, and he'll go on gambling or wanting to gamble, in one way or another, until the day he leaves this earth. And in just the same way, Eddie will go on doing the things he did until somebody puts a bullet in his brain."

"And people can't change?"

"Change," Louis scoffed. "Religious types are all about changing things—themselves, you, the way the world is. But things don't change, not really. When I was a little kid I used to go to church, you see, and in church I used to hear the stories from the Bible. I remember those stories. Say Jesus Christ was sent from God. Say he was. He came into a world with killers and gamblers and whores in it. Done his thing. And then went back out of the world, and you know what? Two thousand years later, still killers and gamblers and whores.

"Now, of course, I don't hold it against my wife even in the smallest way for being a religious person. I don't respect her a drop less for it. That's her type. That's what is. You're like a religious type in your own way, as a matter of fact."

"There you are dead wrong."

"In your own way, I said. You going to change it all, fix it all. It shows right there on your face every night on the news, even though you try not to let it. One of these types not satisfied with what is, has to fix it, absolutely must fix it. Well, let's see, year or so down the road, what you end up fixing, and what you break. Come talk to me then. I'd like that."

"And Eddie?"

Louis drank from a glass of water and waved the glass in the air as he swallowed. "Man of the past. All the Eye-talians are men of the past now. Even in those days when they ran all the money—they were like the heart in the body, see, in those days, pushing the money this way and that way, wherever it needed to go—even in those days Eddie would never make it all the way to boss. Now, though, with Raymond P. dead and Angiulo in jail, the Eyetalians only have their used-to-be, little pieces of power here and there, old power, old sections of things that haven't been broken down yet, although they will be in not too many more years. A lot of the trucking, for example. They still have that. A lot of the gambling, though not all of it."

"Not the drugs, though."

"Some of the drugs, sure, not all. You need to watch the

Russians now, the Vietnamese, the bike gangs. It's all small now, just the opposite of the way the rest of the world is going. Out there," Louis gestured at the TV, "companies getting bigger and bigger. Here it's just the other way. But your Eddie wasn't smart enough to figure that out. Eddie was stuck in a place from twenty years ago. Eddie climbed up this ladder, see, longest, hardest ladder in the world, too. Blood all over it, all these guys up top of him that he has to cut off their legs or put a bullet in their heads so they fall off, all kinds of dark and terrible things in his world, disloyal people, evil people. He killed his own wife, did you know that about Eddie?"

"His first wife?"

"His boys' own mother. Beat her to death with a two-by-four and then told everybody she walked out on him. Hah! Nobody walks out on Eddie, nobody except Pitch Luglio, and that's still an open case, a mystery."

"Is that your opinion or—"

"The wife? I have it from a person who heard it from a guy who saw it with his own eyes . . . Eddie does things like that, see, he carries things like that on his conscience. And carrying all those things on his conscience, he climbs this awful, horrible, bloody ladder thinking he's gonna make it to the top, see, and at the top is everything he wants, all the power, all the safety and money, all the peace. A kind of heaven, see. And you have to give him credit, too, because he did get most of the way to that top place without having too much in the brains department. But then what happens? Then it turns out somebody moved the ladder in the meantime, or somebody moved the ground that ladder stood on. The law of loyalty don't hold no more the way it used to. Guys don't keep quiet now. Eddie's still climbing, looking up, but now he makes one little mistake with your brother—doing something in person he shouldn't have done—and all of a sudden the real ladder is over to the other side of the building, and the one he's standing on is all air and old wood."

"He's still dangerous, though, isn't he?"

"You bet."

"Where is he?"

"I don't know that, Miss. No idea."

"Where would a type like him go?"

For the first time China Louis smiled a true smile. His teeth were cluttered and uncared-for, a sour surprise against the shine of his skin. He held the smile on her like a light, then switched it off. "A type like him," he said, in an approving tone.

"To Italy?"

"Not unless he took a boat."

"Meaning what?"

"Afraid to fly, Eddie. You didn't know that? After all your looking around? Afraid about airplanes like a baby about a vacuum cleaner."

"Would he stay around here?"

Louis shook his head. "His pals would have a place for him just like the U.S. Marshals have a place for your brother. Just as secret, too. Down south someplace, maybe. Offshore. Cuba, in the old days."

"Would he be satisfied to just stay there and leave things as they are?"

"He might be, he might not. I'm curious about that myself."

"If he were dead or in prison would my family be safe?"

"Safer than it is now."

"My brother, my father?"

"Your brother, your dad, you—if you'd stop poking around. Who would care about you all then?"

"It's my job to poke around."

"No it ain't. It's your type. The ladder was moved on you, too, a little bit, woman your age. You're near the top, maybe, holding on tight in the wind. But some younger person is down there making the ground shake, like always."

"Would anyone else be out to hurt us if Eddie were in prison?"

"Only Johnny Cut—who's on his way to a concrete cell now, looks like—and the big fella, Eddie's legbreaker in the old days."

"Xavier."

"Xavier. Although Xavier won't be out of jail for what, eight years? And Xavier never in his life did anything somebody didn't tell him to. The others—what's left of the others—Billy Cheeks, the guys on Winter Hill, they might be happy for what your brother did—sending Eddie away— though it would be hard for him to get a loan anywhere in that crowd."

"What about his sons?"

"Eddie's? Jimmy's a gentle boy, you'd like him. And Johnny the plumber, well, you could have a little problem there someday, though maybe he learned something from seeing his father go away. Hard to tell."

"Would Xavier talk to me?"

China Louis had been appraising her while he spoke, calmly, amused. At this question he looked into the middle of the room again and hummed two slow notes, then went quiet. A siren wailed in the distance, swung closer, faded out entirely. The sound did not seem to reach him. "Xavier's the type I'd have working for me if I did the things you say I do. That's why I have such a peaceful life, Miss. Because I know people. I can spot a type. Xavier would be the type for me, the type who'd let people pull his eyeballs out and never say his boss's name . . . But, maybe, you know, maybe go talk to him if you want to, give it a try. He might be more open to the idea than you think."

"The type for you," Joanna said. "Meaning he's a paid killer.

The taking of life means nothing to you, then."

"Overrated, that taking of life business."

"I expected something like that from you."

"Gets taken eventually, don't it? People would rather hang on and hang on and get old and ugly and have everything stop working inside them, and lay in some bed in some nursing home someplace for years and years rather than be shot in the head and just die. What that is is just more making up the world to be what you want instead of what it really is. There's a little part of people thinks they won't die if they hold on long enough, that's all, that some miracle will come along and they'll be young again. Some little secret part thinks that. No, you don't take a life, you just move things up ahead of schedule a little bit, you just take away that piece of fake belief."

"It's not our place to change the schedule."

He smiled at her again, a blink of a smile. "Whose place is it then? That God you don't believe in?"

"I don't know whose place it is. I know whose place it isn't, though. I know that it's pure evil to make a living purveying death, the way you do, poisoning people."

"I don't do that, Miss. And it's not poisoning, in any case. It's giving them a hour of happiness now and again, in a life where there's nothing else. Where everything else, every other chance for happiness has been taken away. And by who? Think about it. Who sets up the world in such a way that, if these people can find a job . . . IF . . . then that job is the most pitiful trade-off: selling their life, their time on this earth, for just barely enough money to pay for food and heat. No car, probably, or some dumb old car more trouble than it's worth. No golf club membership, no vacation home down south, no vacation at all most of the time. And what do you do in your business? You spend all your energy showing these very same people beautiful cars, and beautiful vacation homes, and white people on the

85

golf course who've made all their money from investments, which means from somebody else's sweat. That helps the people here in Little Hell? That makes them feel better about their lives?"

"It encour—"

"No, no, you see, what that does is make them even more miserable, twice miserable—once because you take away any chance of them ever having those things, and twice because then you go and dangle those things in front of their eyes all day and night. It's like cutting out a man's tongue and showing him pictures of food."

The effort of this speech showed in China Louis' breathing. He waved the glass across in front of him again in the strange gesture, clearing away smoke, clearing away the words themselves.

"I have the feeling you don't appreciate what I'm trying to tell you. I have the feeling it's too hard to understand for a person in your position."

"You haven't the remotest clue what I understand and don't understand."

"Maybe not. But you could seem a little more appreciative for the gift of my hard-earned wisdom. I don't do this a whole hell of a lot."

"I'm waiting for you to ask me for money."

China Louis exposed to her for another moment his decrepit smile. "Money is not something I particularly need," he said. "Just my privacy, is all."

"I won't attribute anything to you—in any forum. You'll be "a source", and in a way that no one will be able to trace you."

"That's friendly."

"It has nothing to do with friendship, it's professional ethics. I loathe you and everything you stand for."

"Smart then, if you want, instead of friendly. I've always

thought of trust as kind of a dumb way of . . . a putting of a soft pillow around what's-in-it-for-me. What's-in-it-for-me you can always count on. Always. Trust is like making a loan to somebody you've never met."

"Your theories on life are fascinating."

China Louis stared at her for a moment, something close to pity showing in his eyes. "It's better to just be afraid and admit it, Miss, I think, than to go around always being sassy like that to prove to yourself that you ain't."

"Thank you. I'll remember that. But I'm not afraid in the slightest."

He laughed. "If that's true, you know why it's true? Because you live in a world where you don't believe—not really, not deep down—that anything bad could ever be done to you personally in a place like this, in a situation like this. Your brother maybe, your daddy, but not you. You have the protection of the TV station, you're a celebrity, and you're quite rich. But, you know, people like you die too, and sometimes they die in ways that are horrible to think about."

"I'll keep that in mind."

"Do that."

"And if you think of anything else you can tell me about Eddie Crevine, you know how to get in touch."

"Well, I do have one more thing I wanted to give you."

"I'm listening."

"It would seem to me that if I was Eddie Crevine I'd be disappointed in this Xavier Manzo character, wouldn't I? It was Xavier's job to be sure your brother wasn't wearing something when he had that meeting with Eddie, and somehow he messed up there, didn't he. That little wire your brother was wearing—"

"It was a tape recorder."

"That little tape recorder ruined Eddie's life. I don't imagine he's too happy about that. Now there's something you might use if you're smart."

"Yes, I—"

"Listen to me," China Louis said, with a sudden ferocity that pushed Joanna's head back an inch. "Don't be so quick to say "I know, I know." Listen to what I just told you. Eddie is not happy with Xavier. Think about what that means. This is the person he trusted more than his mother, and this person screwed up, big. What does that make you think about Eddie's mindset right about now?"

"You said he was on a yacht someplace, and—"

"I said that, right, Miss. I didn't say what his mindset might be on that yacht. I didn't say anything about how pissed off he might be at the way things turned out. Pissed off at Xavier, at you, and your brother and father. How it might drive him a little bit crazy all day and all night. What he might be thinking about life, about people, about trust. And, notice, by the way, I didn't have somebody here to check you in that way."

"I'm not—"

"I could trust you on that. You don't seem the type to. But then your brother made everybody a little extra careful these days. And Eddie's situation made everybody a little more careful. And those devices are so small and sophisticated now."

"I wouldn't be that foolish," Joanna said. "We're at risk enough as it is, all of us, my whole family."

"That's right. I'm sorry. But I ought to check to be sure."

"Fine, are you asking to feel me up? Or would you rather I strip?"

"Either of those."

"Not a chance." Joanna stared him down for a few seconds, then got to her feet and retraced her steps, without looking back and without saying another word. Unescorted, she went out of the room, turned left along the hallway, toward the same door she'd come through half an hour earlier. Now, though, two young men slouched there against the wood, grinning at her, plainly blocking the way. She turned and marched back into the TV room, the smallest tingle of fear running along the back of her neck. China Louis still hadn't moved. "Tell your two bodyguards or whoever they are to let me leave."

"I surely will," Louis agreed, but he said nothing else, and seemed as relaxed and comfortable in the chair as when she'd walked in.

"I'm not taping anything. I turned off my cell phone, see? I bought a small pistol last week. I left that in the office on purpose."

China Louis, looking intently at the linen curtains now, seemed not to hear her.

"Look." Joanna emptied her handbag onto the bare coffee table between them and held up each item in turn: make-up compact, roll of mints, two tampons in their paper wrappers, some change and folded bills, a small notebook and a small gold pen, a paper clip, a few squares of tissue in a plastic wrapper, a bottle of prescription pills. Louis barely ran his eyes over them.

"There will be six kinds of hell to pay if you don't let me out of here."

"Will there?" he said.

"I am *not* stripping for you or anyone. Let me out!"

At the raised voice, one of the young men appeared at the door. With an agility not to be guessed at from his reclining form or his previous movements, China Louis flexed his legs and was on his feet, facing her. Joanna's eyes were at the level of his breastbone. "Miss", he said. "I have never in my life had any much of a sex interest in the white woman, you see. Pretty as you are, you're no exception. But you have to be smart enough to know that I couldn't possibly let you leave here with my words on tape. Not that I think you'd do such a thing. I

89

don't think so. Really. I'm almost sure you wouldn't. But almost sure is just one step short of sure enough for a person like me. And if Eddie was somehow to hear those things I said about him, and where he might be, and how you might find out where he might be, then he or people connected to him could make my days unpleasant. So, I could either ask my two employees to make completely sure my words don't leave this house. Or we could do that here in a dignified way. You're outside of the world you're used to now. The eye of that world can't reach you here, can't protect you, see?"

Joanna turned on her heel as if to leave the room, but didn't step forward. When the hand touched her, she flinched, pressed her teeth together, but did not move.

Slowly, almost tenderly, China Louis ran the backs of two fingers up under her hair and down the back of her sweater, feeling, through the woven cloth, every square inch of her skin. Down the backs of her legs, up the insides of her legs. Front of the thighs, around inside the waistband of her slacks, up across her abdomen, collarbones, places where she couldn't possibly be hiding anything.

"Boots off for a second, please," he said, and peered into them. Joanna put them back on, and with one hand he turned her to face him. "Just move the sides of that sweater away and open up your shirt please now."

"Never. It will never happen. I'll sue you into the gutter."

He laughed, seemed genuinely pleased. "I'll look forward to that," he said. "'Anchorwoman Sues Black Mob King For Sex Harassment. Claims He Put His Hands on Her Breasts.'" That will be a nice story for the people in your little world. Will you report it yourself?"

"You're never going to touch me there."

"Michael. Emmanuel," Louis called softly. The two young men were immediately in the room. Professional as doctors with a patient, they stood one on either side of her, each holding an arm and pressing a foot down firmly on the top of a boot. Joanna fought with them a moment then went rigid. Louis unbuttoned her blouse, peered in to one side and the next, felt the material of her bra between thumb and forefinger, lifted the cups an inch, then slowly refastened the buttons, and tugged the lapels of the sweater together. The men had let go and stepped toward the door when Joanna swung a roundhouse right, open handed, which caught China Louis on the shoulder. The young men leapt toward her, Louis waved them away.

"I'll pretend you didn't do that, Miss."

She swung again, and this time he raised his left arm, almost lazily, caught her by the forearm and twisted very slightly, so that a bolt of pain shot into her shoulder for an instant, then passed. Still holding the arm, he turned her gently in the direction of the door.

"Now, Miss," he said into her ear. "It was such a nice visit. Why, every time I see you on that TV news from now on I'll think of your nice little pink nipples, that pouty look on your face. Let's just leave it at that."

He gave her a gentle push and she went through the door and strode down the hallway, purse in hand, China Louis half a step behind. The two young men leaned just far enough to either side to allow the front door to open. They had the faces of boys, and the posture of adolescents, that strange combination of languor and energy that lives only in the two or three-year moment before the heaviness of full adulthood finds a soul. And they seemed to live in a perfect symbiosis with the man at her heels, as if he'd rescued them from their little hell, and the only possible repayment for a gift of that magnitude was a lifetime of absolute loyalty. They were the cleanerfish swimming a foot away from the shark's teeth: deferential, attendant, gliding alongside the monster in their lethal sea. Safe while he lived.

China Louis reached past Joanna's left elbow and twisted the bolt back, opened the door for her with the same familiar courtliness as his wife. Coatless in the winter air, he stood on the porch while she hurried down the steps, as if it wouldn't be proper to end such a visit without a wave and a last couplet of kind words. "There's a little rib place, Jo-Jo's," he called out as she reached the gate. Joanna didn't turn her head. "Keep going to the end of the street and take a left. He'll let you stand in out of the cold until the taxi comes."

With that, Louis turned into the house and closed both doors between them.

On the way back down the block, burning, furious, overlapping the sweater lapels against her breast, already figuring her revenge, Joanna walked through a knot of children just off the schoolbus and headed home. Second or third-graders. Three pretty girls in pigtails and a boy with a bright red backpack. They parted to let her pass, turning up to her their curious, somber faces, not recognizing her, accepting the trembling smile she offered as if it were the gift of an unknown aunt. Once she was beyond them and they could no longer see her face, she had to fight back an urge to weep—for their lives and for her own.

But the urge to weep lasted only until she reached the place where her BMW had been parked. No evidence of the car now, only a stretch of empty curb with matted leaves in the gutter, a lottery scratch ticket bent in half, some shards of glass and a half-full bottle of Rolling Rock standing like a victorious chess piece where her left front tire should have been.

Twenty

From a dream of the craps tables—the dice, the felt, the watching eyes—Peter awoke to a cold Montana morning. It was as if he'd slept all night in a bath filled with the warm syrup of nostalgia, and awakened to a frosted-window present. For a short while the dream had given him back his faith that a life could be totally altered in twenty minutes. That a person—ordinary, imperfect, wrestling with a thousand forms of failure—could, with a few lucky rolls of the dice, with one slapping, clicking spin of a roulette wheel, one lottery ticket or illicit bet, one thoroughbred or greyhound crossing the finish line, be catapulted into another orbit in which there were no patches of boredom, no worry, no debt. Gambling was the sex of the mental world. The heart slammed in its cage, the lips tingled; for a little while before, during, and after, you could convince yourself that thrill and pleasure were a day's regular diet; that it was possible to sculpt for yourself an existence composed entirely of succulent moments; that you could swing through a starlit space, beyond the reach of the gravitational pull of pain.

He lay in the sheets, listening—the scrape of Elsie's slippers on the kitchen linoleum, the whir of the microwave cooking Austin's oatmeal, a newswoman's voice on their little TV—and it seemed absolutely true and perfectly apparent to him that a few hours of gambling could in no way harm him now. He and Elsie had a stable financial life—three different incomes, guaranteed, if you counted the U.S. Marshals stipend. They had an excellent marriage. A side trip to Reno or Vegas on his way to Revere would be no more ruinous than a piece of chocolate cake at the end of a Lenten fast.

He showered, shaved, pulled on pants, shirt, and sweater, peeking out the bedroom window once to assess the day. Against the soothing background of kitchen sounds, his temptation faded away like a full warm tide slipping back down a line of shore. It was just a thought, he told himself. An idea. Nothing he would ever actually do, and nothing, obviously, that he could mention to Elsie.

She hugged and kissed him when he came into the kitchen, but it seemed to him there was something different in the feel of it, something dutiful and forced. Austin sent his usual, "Hi, Pete," up from his oatmeal bowl, eyes on a music magazine, ear pierced, wrist and hand caught and released by the band of yellow-gold light angling in through the window.

Peter poured his cereal at the counter, poured his coffee, carried them to the table and doused them both with sugar.

"Little bit of Cheerios with your sugar today, Pete?" Austin's mouth wrinkled into his shy smile. He glanced up from the magazine for all of two seconds. Everything was Rap and Hip-Hop now, Peter noticed. Rap, Hip-Hop, Michael Jordan. This new golf star, Tiger Woods. Even for white kids, all the heroes now were black. Their own lives seemed boring and flat and safe to them; they wanted the Gangsta life, South Central LA, the gold, the girls, the yelling out of a big Fuck You to the working world. It probably wasn't so different from the way he'd felt, years ago, seeing Jerry Angiulo drive along Revere Beach Boulevard in his long black limo, the mob king in back behind tinted glass, untouchable. As his father had told him again and again and again, the mob guys gave Italians a lousy name. All the warmth, the generosity, the love and class and honest hard work—all of it was like a white shirt stained in

94

front with big splashes of MAFIA! True, absolutely. And Peter despised them as much as his father did. But at the same time it tickled everybody's little weird fantasy of being Boss. Untouchable. Bigger than Life.

"I'm forty-one," he said, turning his mind away from it. "You na-know how many fillings I have in my mouth? Three. How-how many crowns? Zero. How many ra-root canals? Zero. Joanie got my mother's good looks, Alfonse got my father's arms and shoulders. I got the old man's teeth and na-nose and good sense with ma-ma-ma-money."

The corners of Austin's mouth curled up a quarter of an inch, but Elsie didn't seem to hear. She finished her poached egg and wheat toast and went to take her shower.

"I have an errand to ra-run in Bridgeman this morning," Peter said across the corner of the table. "I'll drive you over if y-you want a break from the b-bus routine."

"Sure." Austin clanked the spoon down into his empty bowl, slapped the magazine closed and disappeared into his room, leaving Peter alone in the tidy kitchen with its view of snowfields and foothills and a chip of jagged bluish mountain in the distance. On the little TV the anchorwoman was chirping through a story about a flood in a city to the south of them. Blocks of ice and snow appeared on the screen, piled against a bridge abutment like the tilting white floors of a hospital in Armenia or someplace after an earthquake. For some reason, watching it, Peter was presented with an image of himself as an old man: a stooped old bald guy making change for somebody in his little video shop in Maddles, Montana, thousands of miles from anyplace that mattered to him. A non-life in nowhere. A waste.

Teeth brushed, TV turned off, dishes put into the sink to soak, textbooks gathered up, jackets and gloves and hats located and put on—they moved around the house like silent actors in a play about the modern American morning. At the door, as Elsie was hugging and kissing Austin, asking about his lunch, his after-school schedule, his homework, Peter pulled down the earflaps on the fur-lined hat she'd given him, raised the collar of his leather jacket, and wrapped one arm around Austin's shoulders in an exaggerated embrace. "Moun-moun-mountain men go out now to get the m-moose meat for supper." It wasn't exactly the royal flush of comedy routines, but it drew a pair of smiles, flexed the pale freckles around Elsie's beautiful mouth, seemed to him to break up some of the bad air left over from their conversation the night before. She touched his arm in a certain loving way she had and he went out into the cold morning, forgiven.

The car the government had given them was, to Peter's mind, almost criminally plain—plain dark blue, nothing to play music with, no real spare tire, nothing of beauty in its lines or interior. He'd had a T-Bird at home, and this shitbox had never seemed to him a proper reward for someone who'd tricked the master trickster, who'd enabled the FBI to get an indictment on Eddie Crevine, something they'd been trying to do for a decade. The day the car was delivered, he'd hung a Saint Christopher medal over the rear-view mirror, patron saint of safe travel. For Christmas, Elsie had fitted out the front seats with sheepskin covers. Other than those two personal touches—one to remind them of their old home, one to make them feel they were part of their new—the car was as bland and uninspiring as the architecture on the edge-of-town cul-de-sac where they now lived.

He turned on the motor and while the car warmed up, he and Austin scraped the windows front and back, chuffing out spumes of frozen vapor, waving to Elsie as she drove out of the garage and away.

"Ev-ev-ever wish you had a brother or a sister?" Peter

96

asked, when they were sitting on their sheepskins, waiting for the last frost to clear from the windows. He was thinking of Joanie just then, he didn't know why.

Austin nodded. Peter put the car into reverse, backed out, made the loop of their half-developed cul-de-sac, and turned right, onto the two-lane road that led to Maddles.

To the north, the foothills of the Western Brayton Basin rolled off toward the bigger peaks, gently ascending backs of sleeping beasts, coated in fir trees, dotted with mountain houses whose windows glinted in the sun, the meadows and hillsides veined with quick cold streams. Between the foothills and the town lay a slanted plain speckled with boulders and grazing cattle in the warmer months, blanketed with snow from Halloween to Mother's Day. A river cut across it in a thick, restless diagonal, then turned due south and ran in a concrete sluiceway through the eastern edge of Maddles' commercial district. A dozen miles to the south, this same river was pushing up over its banks. He and Austin crossed it on a four-lane metal bridge, with the horns of prize bulls mounted on the rusty superstructure at either end. Along the riverbank lay blocks of broken-up ice.

At the far end Austin said: "What's going on with you and Mom?"

"You picked up on that, I ga-guess."

"You usually talk like a radio at breakfast. Mom's usually got her hands all over you when she says good-bye."

"Like the radio, huh?"

"Did you have a fight, skiing?"

"A fa-fight? Are you kidding me? We were kiss-kissing like sixteen-year-olds on the chairlift."

"Is she pregnant?"

"Pr-pregnant? You d-d-d-do want a little brother or sister, don't you. B-be the big man around the house. Sh-show somebody the ropes." He stopped at a red light and looked across the seat. Unwavering blue eyes and thin shoulders. A nice-enough-looking face inherited from his dad, with a mouth and eyes that could turn instantly serious at times like these, as if the smallest domestic disruption loaded him instantly with all the freight of adulthood, everything his biological father had refused to carry. It had gotten worse since they left Revere, since Austin turned eighteen. They'd torn him away from the only girl he'd ever slept with, and Peter wondered, at times, if he would ever really be forgiven for that, if Austin only pretended to like him, if secretly the boy looked at him and thought: Loser Number Two.

"Your Mom and I are fine. Don't worry about it. No fight. No pregnancy in the f-foreseeable future."

"What's going on, then?"

They passed into the town itself, six blocks of wood-frame houses and an enormous lumberyard with stacks of planks and plywood under metal roofs, and carpenters in workboots climbing out of cold pickup trucks to make their morning purchase.

"I'm ga-going to sneak b-back to Revere to see my f-f-father. Your Mom isn't crazy about the idea."

"They'll let you do that?"

"That's where the sn-sneak part comes in. And th-this is strictly between me and you."

Austin looked away and began flicking his thumbnail against the cover of one of the textbooks in his lap. After another block they turned onto the broad commercial strip of Main Street, Maddles, Montana: more pickups, loaded logging trucks, storefronts of weathered clapboard and cut gray stone. Though there were parking meters at the curb, and two stoplights, and the same sense of weekday-morning bustle found in any modern place, the town had preserved, without especially

trying to, a somewhat diluted sense of the old west. It might
have come from the men in cowboy boots and Stetson hats, or
the faded advertisements for cattle feed on the sides of buildings, or the remaining stretches of wooden sidewalk in front of
old saloons. It might have been the expression on the faces of
certain black-haired women who walked there as their ances-
tors had walked, twenty thousand years before: seeming to
sense the mountains without looking up at them; seeming to
feel in their bones a certain obvious spoilage, lost on everyone
else.

Peter felt the old west, too—he'd sensed it from his first
glimpse of the place—but, for him, that chapter of American
history was as moving and relevant as an out-of-date TV sit-
com. Not ethnic, not urban, that world had nothing to do with
a person like him, a guy from a tribe of newcomers; he came
from people to whom this land had never really belonged
and—it seemed on certain days—never really would. The Irish,
the Jews, even the descendents of African slaves—they were
men and women with a drama something like his own. But
people like that were rare species here, and their absence
drummed out a constant nagging undertone of alienation. Being sent away to a place like this was more punishment than
reward. An exile. A type of house arrest. The injustice of it
worked against his skin like dry wool.

Drinkwater's Video squatted in the middle of a stretch of
small shops on the last block, its washed windows sporting
posters for *Lethal Weapon 4* and *The Horse Whisperer;* a six-space
parking lot out back. Inside stood a few dozen shelves of
boxed, All-American fantasies of improbable romance and ad-
venture that, along with the U.S. Marshals stipend and Elsie's
part-time job at the elementary school, had enabled him to put
more money in the bank in eight months than in his previous
forty years combined. He could not pass the shop without ex-

periencing a twinge of pride. Not because of the business—it wasn't much of a business, really, he hadn't exactly sweated through a drawer full of shirts setting it up, and he didn't expect it would last very long: people were finding new ways to get their movies—but because of the life it represented. The life of a married, sober, unaddicted man who took his wife skiing on weekends and drove his adopted son to school to save him a bus ride, a man who put money aside every week, sacrificing present-day indulgences for the sake of some solid, predictable, modest future . . . that might never come.

As far as lives like that were concerned, he'd always been an outsider looking in. For years he'd told himself and his married Revere friends and Elsie that all he really wanted was a house and happy family, a few ordinary pleasures—baseball game on the TV, barbecue in the backyard. Today though, thoughts of his married friends evoked only a sparkle of pity in him. Terrible as his days and nights had been when he was gambling and running from creditors, there had been a gasflame of life and energy in him then. He'd always felt and looked younger than his years. Now, some nights, closing up his little shop in the early winter darkness and climbing into his plain car and driving home to his unsurprising house with its plastic trash barrels lined up neatly inside the garage, he felt as though it had been raining in his soul since the hour he'd been handed his new identity papers and been escorted out of Massachusetts.

Austin stopped chipping away at the cover of his book, but by the time they reached the on-ramp to the Interstate, he was locked solid in a mountain funk. Peter worried some days that the dullness, the foreignness of their new life was going to take what was left of the spark out of Austin, too. And it would be his fault. The kid would end up managing a fast-food chicken place somewhere in Idaho, wearing a ridiculous green uniform and a little hat and checking the time to the second on his waitress's lunch breaks.

"Feel like ta-taking the wheel? While there's st-still time for me to pull over?"

"Not today, Pete."

What kind of eighteen-year-old refused an opportunity to drive?

"Want me to bring th-this la-little crapbox up to a hun-hun-hundred like the rest of the cow-cowboys on the road?"

Austin shrugged, fiddled with the small new loop in his right ear. He turned his eyes out the side window, where Peter couldn't see them.

Once they were on the highway, Peter kept the speedometer at seventy-eight miles an hour, a small shadow of guilt rushing after him on the Interstate, the memory of his gambling fantasy and of Elsie's cool good-bye. Pickups rocketed past in the fast lane. Toward Bridgeman the mountains receded and the land turned flat and soulless. Ranchland, rangeland, hayfield and fir—the territory spoke no language he knew, though it did, in places, remind him of a less-arid version of the land between Las Vegas and Reno. Once, in Vegas, he'd won eighteen thousand, four hundred dollars in the course of a single night, playing thirteen-card Chinese poker, and, on impulse, had rented a Cadillac—silver with a leather interior, he could still remember it—and driven to Reno, pouring coffee into himself to stay awake, stopping once for steak and eggs and the slot machines, staring out at the bombing ranges and the whorehouses beside the road, the memory of his triumph and the vast emptiness of the desert opening out into space like endless possibility.

"You think I'm n-nuts, right. For going back?"

The boy shook his head, still not turning.

"I la-la-la-love your m-mom more than anybody could ever love anybody, okay Austin? Your m-mom saved me. She-she-

101

she m-makes life worth going through for me, okay? But I have this little itch lately."

"For another woman?" Austin turned to face at him now, somber as a policeman.

"Wh-what? Are ya-you ab-absolutely crazy? Another woman? Do you na-know me after all this time, or what? Not that kind of itch! I meant an itch f-f-for some-something other than this." Peter waved his hand in a horizontal sweep just above the dashboard. "Mon-Mon-Montana. The quiet la-life. It ain't me, pal." He concentrated on the road for a few seconds. "Besides, I ma-miss my father. I ma-miss seeing him, talking to him. It seems like a s-sin not to be seeing him at his age."

"I don't think you're nuts for going," Austin said to the window. He paused a few seconds and added, "I just want to go with you."

"You want to go with me."

"Yeah," Austin said, a small spurt of anger in him now.

"Right, great. Let's ca-call your mother and run that idea by her. She'll meet both of us at the door with a shotgun."

A logging truck drew up so close behind them that all Peter could see of it when he glanced in the mirror was the chrome grill and headlights. For a moment all of the American West seemed represented there: too big, too clean, cowboy rednecks pushing at him from all sides. He lifted his foot back off the accelerator and watched the speedometer needle fall—seventy-six, seventy-four, seventy-two. The driver of the logging truck was forced to downshift, wait for an opening in the inside lane. He blasted his air horn as he pulled alongside. Peter held a finger against the window but didn't turn to look. As the truck passed, he sped up and rode alongside it for several miles, fender to wheel, eyes fixed forward, pulling ahead a few car lengths, easily, and then dropping back. Austin was watching him.

On a slight downhill grade, the truck pulled ahead and Peter let it go, the sawed ends of the logs fading into the distance like shrinking coins.

"I don't expect you to take me. I'm just being honest, the way we said we always would. If there was any way I could go I'd want to, that's all."

"Because of Darcy?"

Austin looked out the window and said nothing.

"Are you mis-miserable here? Tell me."

"No."

"The k-kids giving you a hard time? Because of the way you talk or anything?"

"The kids are cool."

"Any de-decent looking girls in the pic-picture?"

Austin shook his head. Peter slowed for the exit and curled around and down onto a strip of chain motels and fast-food restaurants—flat and featureless as a cemetery plot—that brought them into and then through the heart of a larger, busier, fundamentally unattractive city that boasted a new brick high school on its western perimeter. At first glance the high school might have been mistaken for a prison. A line of yellow buses had formed near the end of the front walk, and hatless inmates wearing Walkmans and running shoes were stepping down somberly and sleepily and congregating in loose knots near the door. He could see clouds of breath and bulky maroon-and-gold football jackets, and fifteen-year-olds holding hands. He pulled up to the opposite curb and put three fingers on Austin's arm.

"Aus-Austin, look at me."

The boy ran a sleeve across his eyes and turned. A tear rolled into the corner of his mouth. He swept it away.

"La-listen. I'll ga-give you two hun-hundred bucks when we get home tonight, you ba-buy Darcy something—and I'll sn-

103

sneak down to her house when I'm in Revere and giv-give it to her. How-how's that sound?"

The boy studied Peter's eyes for a few seconds like someone who wanted to judge whether his own pain was being reflected accurately there, or whether it was only some kind of trick, a gimmick, another scrap of the shabby treachery of adults. And then, almost as if he'd mastered already the terse ways of the tribe of men who surrounded him, he gave one short nod and went to join his nation.

The nod could have meant anything on a continuum from gratitude to disdain. Peter took it as a compliment, a vote of faith. Comforted, he made an illegal U-turn directly in front of the crowd of kids—as if to assure them they wouldn't be in prison forever—then pointed the plain car off in the direction of his latest dream.

Twenty-One

She did not go to Jo-Jo's. If she were starving and Jo-Jo's was the last place on earth serving food; if she were desperate to call someone—and her phone wouldn't work—and Jo-Jo's offered the only telephone within eleven miles; if she were terrified at being a white woman, alone, on the streets of Little Hell and Jo-Jo's seemed like the only secure refuge, she wouldn't have gone there. The feeling of China Louis's hands stayed on her skin like an ink stain and her mind circled a bitter memory. Her roommate at Cornell had been raped, on a first date. Thrown down against the armrest in the front seat of a Buick and nearly choked to death with the sleeve of a Cornell Wrestling jacket while, body and mind, she was torn open. They were freshmen. The young woman—Amelia—was black, the wrestler a white senior. She remembered holding Amelia as she wept and bled, rocking her back and forth on the floor in their dormitory room. She remembered skipping classes for days afterwards and serving Amelia soup and wrapping her up in a blanket of words—that she should go to the hospital, go to the police, that she was to blame for nothing, absolutely nothing, that the horror would eventually stop replaying itself in her mind's eye. She remembered prying the boy's name out of her and marching across campus and pounding on the door of his room and spitting empty threats up into his blank, angelic face. He stood absolutely still, watching her, looking down and through her, and when she finished he made the smallest little satanic smile at the corners of his mouth and said: "She loved it," and slammed the door between them with such force that it echoed in the corridor like a shot.

She remembered her roommate lying still as death on the bed and saying "Such a fool, such a fool, such a fool," and one night sneaking away and taking a bus back to South Carolina, never to be heard from again.

China Louis's touch had not been sexual at all, but the humiliation of it had summoned forth every buried, awful voice, an encyclopedia of self-hate. She stood on the corner of Dayner Avenue, dialing her cell phone with frozen fingers. A man sitting against the base of a building with a tattered blanket wrapped around his legs and a bottle in a greasy paper bag at his elbow; a woman walking two children by the hand, laces dripping, on their backs the cheapest, thinnest coats, shiny with wear; sheets of newspapers, stirring, sliding, opening, drifting in a comical slow motion along the gutter. Everywhere she looked she saw the humiliation of poverty—Pawn Shop, Checks Cashed, We Buy Gold, Instant Loans—bits of plastic litter knocking helplessly against the metal hull of someone else's wealth. To be poor meant to be awash in humiliation every waking moment. Even after all the reports she had done, she'd never felt it before, never understood it like this. Two men in a polished blue Lexus drove slowly past, eyeing her, rap lyrics blasting out of their windows like cannons firing at any standing thing. She pressed the phone to her ear. She was cold. A man in minister's clothes walked past and nodded in a friendly way.

"Precinct B-2, Sergeant MacNamara."

She wanted, shingle and brick, to tear down the walls of China Louis' world. "Sergeant," she said, "my car was just stolen and I think I know who did it."

"Who's calling?"

"Joanna Imbesalacqua . . . from Channel 8."

"Your personal car?"

"That's right. A new BMW i780. Green. License plate SBT-ANCH—"

"Whereabouts, ma'am?"

"The corner of Dayner and Liberty."

There was a slight pause. "What in God's name are you doing there?"

"I was interviewing China Louis. He had someone steal it, I'm sure. I—"

"And you're alone?"

"Yes."

"Stay put then. Stay on the phone. Listen for the siren."

Twenty Two

Darcy Salamone sat in her Revere High School English class, half-listening to Ms. Pederson ramble on about the big essay they were supposed to write and fingering the edge of the letter Austin had sent her. It came in a plain envelope, as always—no stamp, no return address, nothing to give her any idea where he was. She'd put it in her notebook so just the top of edge of it showed. *I'm not forgetting you,* Austin had written. *Don't forget me.* There was nothing in it about seeing other people, and she wondered, turning her eyes to the big map in the front left corner of the room, if he was sleeping with somebody else already. She tried to imagine where he might be. Hawaii, she guessed. Being taught surfing by some cute Hawaiian girl in a bikini. Staying out late with her. Making love with her on the beach.

"What you have to do to write a great essay," Ms. Pederson was saying, "is to go down deep into your feelings. Sometimes that's hard. Sometimes you don't want to go there, but if you're going to really reach your reader, that's what you have to do."

David Donald sat behind her. Hockey star, redhead, owner of a two-year-old Mustang his father or uncle had given him. When Ms. Pederson starting talking about deep feelings, David reached his leg forward and kicked the back of her right boot. This was his idea of a sexy suggestion. She ignored him and, in her mind, wrote an imaginary letter to Austin.

108

Twenty Three

Saint Cecelia's Catholic Church occupied a parcel of not-so-choice real estate between Bridgeman's flat commercial strip and its bland exurbs. Close beside the church stood the six-room white house that served as a rectory. It was linked to the church by a closed-in walkway—clapboarded also, and also painted white—so the priests wouldn't be required to step out into the minus-sixty-degree air on a Montana winter morning

The temperature now, in the first days of spring, often climbed above freezing. For a few hours in the middle of the day the snow melted, and the melt pooled in the low places, and turned to ice overnight on stretches of sidewalk and road.

Going toward the three stone steps that led from the sidewalk to church property, Peter slipped on a patch of ice and landed hard on his left side, against a bank of crusted snow. He broke some of the impact with his wrist and forearm but most of the force of the fall was borne by his left shoulder. He lay there for a few seconds, letting the pain subside. No one appeared at the rectory door. A car passed in the street without stopping. He got slowly to his feet, cursed again, brushed grit and granules of snow from his coat with his right hand, tried to lift his left arm and couldn't. After another few seconds he went forward along the walk and pressed the bell beside the rectory door.

There was no response. He massaged his shoulder and waited, turning once to glance at the street with its silent bungalows and empty driveways. When a minute had passed he rapped his knuckles against the wood of the storm door, rang the bell again, cupped his right hand to the glass and pressed his face close. He was in pain.

After another minute he heard footsteps in the house, someone fumbling with the door handle, and then with the hook that held the storm door tight. Father Pettibone opened the door a foot and peered out as if giving his visitor an opportunity to make a very brief and hopeless sales pitch. The priest shifted a mint from one side of his mouth to the other and squinted through black-rimmed glasses.

"Father, it's me. Pe-Pe-Peter Drinkwater."

The priest raised his left hand and coughed into his fist.

"D-do you have a couple minutes?"

For several seconds longer than Peter would have expected, Father Pettibone stared back at him. They stood there eye-to-eye, Father Pettibone blinking behind the glasses, beneath overgrown gray eyebrows, and frowning, Peter leaning forward with his left arm held against his side.

"Di-did I wa-wake you up? If this isn't the greatest time. . ."

"No, no. Come in, son."

Peter moved his left hand to take the door, and the pain shot through his shoulder again. When it passed he was standing in a dim parlor that smelled of old carpet and boiled meat. The priest was facing him, perplexed.

"Pe-Pe-Peter Drinkwater, Father. We came to see you when we-we first moved here. M-my wife, El-Elsie, and me. We have a son. Austin."

"Yes. Yes, of course."

"We've been meaning to get to mass, you know, but the wa-winters here, we we're not used to them yet."

The priest was wearing black pants and a black shirt. The shades were pulled on the parlor's two front windows and there were no lights on in the room.

"I wo-woke you up, didn't I."

"No, son. Not really, no. Marjorie the housekeeper called in this morning—her child is ill you see—and I've just said Mass to an empty house, and . . . have you injured yourself somehow?"

"I fe-fell coming up your walk."

"Good Lord. Where is it, the clavicle? The collar bone? Could you have broken it?"

"I don't think so. I broke it once when I was a kid, it didn't feel like this."

"Marjorie, you see, usually puts down sand. Do you need me to call someone? Do you need a drink for it? Whiskey and aspirin, you see, is the greatest thing for pain. Good Lord."

"I'm not that much of a drinker, Father."

"For the pain only. How severe is the pain?"

In a moment they were sitting in the rectory kitchen, where the smell of meat was stronger and the refrigerator hummed. Father Pettibone had poured him a small glass of Glenalister, and, complaining of arthritis and the cold, meted out a similar portion for himself. A bronze crucifix hung on the wall over the Formica-topped table. The chairs were vintage 1950, chrome-backed, with red vinyl cushions held by brass buttons at their edges. Peter remembered chairs very much like them in the kitchen of his parents' house on Proctor Avenue. He took it as a sign from God.

"I need a fa-favor, Father."

"Ask, son. That's why we're here. Drink up."

"I nee-need to bor-borrow, if I ca-can, some priest's clothes."

Father Pettibone concentrated on sipping his whiskey. He pressed his lips in against each other and squeezed them out again with a slight squeaking noise. He looked up, began to nod, then seemed to be hit by the question as if it had bounced around against the walls of the room for a minute before reaching him.

"I'm not sure I understand, Paul."

"Peter, Father. You-you and ma-me, we're about the same size. I remembered that from meeting you. I need to b-borrow a priest's sh-shirt and pants and ev-everything, the collar and so on, for about three days. Or buy-buy-buy it from you if you have an extra. And I n-need you na-not to tell anyone."

"Is it some kind of costume party you're going to?"

"No, Father."

The priest finished his drink and looked around the room, giving each wall his attention for a two-count. "I'm perplexed at this," he said.

"All the churches in M-Maddles are Protestant, I didn't feel right going there. You couldn't just give me a sa-suit of clothes and trust me enough not to na-know why?"

"No, I'm afraid I cannot, son. You see, it's more than some kind of uniform. There's a certain sanctity to the objects of the religious life. And I barely know you."

"What if it was for a ca-cause, you know, th-that could be considered something that was a little un-unusual, but really a ga-good deed?"

Father Pettibone looked at the telephone and then back at Peter. He shook his head. "You're not . . . involved in any kind of Black Mass or anything of that nature, are you?"

"No, Father. I don't even know what th-that is."

"Do you take your host in the mouth or in your hand?"

"In my mouth. The old fashioned way. I n-never thought it was right to have God's body in ma-my hand."

"And you swallow it immediately?"

"As im-mediately as I can, sure. Sometimes it sta-sticks."

The priest seemed to relax one half of one degree.

"La-look, Father. I'm-I'm not who people think I am. I've da-done some things in the past . . . I had a ba-bad gambling problem at one time."

"You're not from this area originally, are you."

"No Father."

"Can you say where you are from?"

"N-no, Father, n-not really. N-not unless you absolutely have to know."

"Why is that?" Father Pettibone poured himself another portion, without offering to do the same for his guest.

Peter watched him drink, looked over the priest's shoulder at the hands of the clock. Fifty-two minutes until the shop was scheduled to open, and it was a twenty-minute drive back. "You can't tell anybody what some-someone says to you in the c-confession, ca-can you."

"No, son. It's under the seal."

"Then I'd-I'd like you to hear my confession."

"When?"

"Na-now."

Twenty Four

Vito awoke to the sound of rain against the windows, a cold spring rain, stirring in gusts against the glass. He washed, shaved, combed what was left of his hair, then sat on the sofa, in the place where Lucy used to sit, a thin pillow behind to keep his spine straight, hands folded in his lap, raindrops knocking. Sixty-five years ago, his mother had taught him a type of prayer with no words to it, no pleas, not even any particular image of God.

He sat with his eyes closed, and the little travel clock—that had never traveled anywhere—on the maple table not far from his arm, and he tried to open his mind to God and God's will and God's presence. Not to think about anything if he could help it, not to plan, not to worry, not to hope. All kinds of thoughts assaulted him—images of Lucy and Carmellina, pieces of his conversation with Alfonse, the idea of building a house, the fact that Joanie hadn't called in three days, the worry that someone might come through the door at night and try to hurt him. Peter's letter . . . He let all of them go by. "Like clouds in the sky," his mother had told him. He tried.

When thirty minutes had passed, he heard the minute-hand click once against the unset alarm, and he opened his eyes. *"Alla fine, non mantenere la pace per te,"* his mother had said. At the end, don't keep the peace for yourself. So what little peace he'd been given he offered up for the soul of his wife, for his three children and the people close to them, for his friends—here
114

and passed on, and even for his enemies, as God said you were supposed to do, though he'd discovered that it was impossible to pray for Eddie Crevine with any amount of sincerity so he no longer bothered. Finished at last, he stood up and set about his day. A big one, it was gonna be. He hoped he wouldn't mess it up.

The first thing was take the pieces of chicken out of the refrigerator and put them on the counter to warm up while he brought out his pans, spices, and cutting boards. When the chicken wasn't cold anymore to the touch he sliced off a one-inch pat of butter, and with the fingers of both hands massaged it into the pieces of meat. He crushed a clove of garlic and stirred it into a glass bowl with a teaspoon of olive oil, some pepper and salt, some oregano, then massaged this, too, into the meat. He greased a flat pan with this mixture and more butter, put the pieces of chicken in the pan, washed and dried his hands and then set the pan in the oven to broil. While the meat cooked he put a pot on the stove, and into the pot went canned plum tomatoes and tomato paste, olive oil, garlic, a shot of red wine and a sprinkling each of sugar, salt, pepper and oregano. He washed his hands and poured himself a glass of water and stood away from the stove for a few minutes, watching a small fog rise from what was left of the snow in the yard, and listening to the rain drumming on the boards of the back porch and on the little aluminum roof over the door there. The first part of April now, it was, not the best time for weather. A few more weeks it would be Easter. Holidays were sad for him now—no wife, no children; maybe he'd go have Easter dinner with Dommy at the rectory.

He decided to practice what he was going to say to his guests. He looked at the front and back doors to make sure nobody was there to see him—Roberta Antonelli was always coming over now with food, like he couldn't cook for himself, or with the questions about the leak on her roof—he didn't go on roofs no more, didn't do work for single women neighbors. Once in a while she was holding a letter she said the mailman delivered wrong, but he thought she'd really just taken it from his front porch mailbox herself and was using it as an excuse. Since Patsy, her husband, had the heart attack and died, Vito thought he could feel the loneliness coming out of her house like smoke out of the chimney. He could see it on her face like makeup. He understood the loneliness, and was sorry she had to carry it, but girlfriends were finished for him now, in this life, and how did you say that to somebody?

Neither Roberta nor anybody else was watching him through the door window. "Nice to see you," he said to the empty kitchen. "I'm Vito Imbesalacqua . . . I'm Vito . . . I'm Alfonse's Uncle Vito . . . I'm his father. I'm Victor Bones, how are you? I'm not the best cook like my wife she used to be but let's eat. I'm Vito. I don't speak that good English, but . . ."

The pot of gravy began to bubble. The chicken hissed and snapped. He kept a radio on top of the refrigerator, tuned to a station that played opera on Saturday mornings, and he added that now to the mix of sounds. He set a frying pan on the stove, one of Lucy's old iron pans, black and heavy like two crowbars. Olive oil, sliced onion, sliced green pepper, mushrooms, garlic and salt on the low gas. The smell of the garlic and onions filled the room. The rain drummed outside, the music whirled and soared. For a moment—a rare moment now, since Lucy died and Peter left and his old life was smashed up and swept away like a favorite dish you broke—Vito felt happy.

By noontime the gravy had been simmering three hours, the peppers, mushrooms and onions added in; the chicken, three-quarters cooked, was set aside in a flat pan. He'd prepared an antipasto and a large bowl of salad and he'd set the table in the parlor the best he could. He kept a regular watch on the puddled driveway. When he saw Alfonse's car he poured the gravy into the flat pan and placed it into the oven again.

By the time he finished with that, somebody was knocking at the back door. He hurried over to open it. A short, dark-haired woman stood in front of him, drops of rain on her face. A pretty woman, not Italian, not white. Behind her on the small porch stood a younger woman, little bit taller, black-haired too, not white either. And behind them, Alfonse with an umbrella and a shaky smile. Trying not to let the smallest wrinkle of surprise show on his face, Vito opened the door wide and gestured for them to come in.

"Uncle," Alfonse said, "*Babbo* . . . this is Lily, who I told you about. And this is Lily's daughter, Estelle."

Vito made a nervous bow to the women, took hold of their hands for a moment each in turn, and recited a version of the short speech he'd practiced. "I'm Vito Imbesalacqua, Alfonse's real father. But my whole life people called me Victor Bones, or Vito. You welcome in my house."

There was a bit more stamping and scraping of feet, a few comments about how the rain had been sleet early on and so the sidewalks were still slippery in places. Alfonse had brought a loaf of bread in a waxed white paper bag, and a cardboard bakery box tied with string. Vito told him to bring them into the kitchen; he carried his guests' coats into the back bedroom and, even though they were wet, he laid them carefully on the bedspread. For a moment, alone there, he looked at Lucy's picture on the bureau, then he went back out to tend to his guests. He asked them to sit, and brought out the bread and butter and glasses of water. He opened the wine and brought it into the parlor, too—though it turned out that Lily wasn't drinking wine—then he carried in the antipasto: olives, anchovies, half-

117

slices of rolled mortadella, white beans in vinegar, small ivory rings of cooked squid, mushrooms—set it among them, started the pasta cooking, and sat down.

They ate the antipasto and the bread and talked some more about the weather. First the snow they had, then now the rain. That was how April came in, you couldn't ever know what you'd be getting. Though sometimes it was sun now. The summers, probably, they were getting hotter. The woman and the girl were nice, he liked them, but mainly he was worrying did they like him.

For the second course, they had the ziti with one ladle of gravy to a portion, and the cheese he grated over each plate to order. When they'd eaten the pasta—Vito sneaked a look at their faces the whole time—he stood up again and brought the *cacciatore* to the table in a serving dish he and Lucy had been given as a wedding gift fifty years before. The young woman— Stella was the name, he thought—let out a moan and said, "Oh, God, I thought we were just having macaroni. I ate so much of it, I'm sorry, I can't."

But it turned out that she could. And that she could manage, even, most of the salad that followed, and another slice of the bread that had been baked only a few hours before and only a few miles away, soft and white as cotton. Vito refused to let anyone help him clear the plates, or help pour coffee into the fifty-year-old china cups with red lilies on them that Lucy used to get mad about when somebody broke one by an accident. He served them with a steady hand, going around the table in his white shirt with the cuffs unbuttoned and rolled up over his wrists, and he set out the macaroon cookies Alfonse had brought. And then—it was the wine, maybe, he relaxed a little bit.

"Never, ever in my life have I had such a wonderful meal," Lily pronounced, over the coffee.

"Never, Mom," Estelle agreed. "Not in my life either."

Vito said he was sure they'd had many meals that were better, and that, if his wife were alive, they would have seen what a real cookin was like, and that, in Italy, this was only an ordinary meal, nothing that special. *"Cacciatore,"* he told them. "It comes from the word that means "the hunter". This is only what the hunter's wife she makes for him when she doesn't have so much time."

"Now I'm definitely going to live in Italy," Estelle said.

"You'd like it, Miss, in Italy, when you go."

"She's a painter," Lily said. "She talks about Italy constantly."

"What year did Joanie and Peter send you, *Babbo?*"

"Nineteen eighty-five, when we were married forty years," he said and for a little while he entertained them with stories of what he'd seen there, descriptions of Venice, the buildings, the canals, the way all the people went on one street but if you spoke Italian or you weren't afraid you could go down a side street and it was like a secret world with the shops and the bridges, the small, crooked alleys; then the boys on motor scooters in Rome, crazy, and the paintings in the museums and on the walls of the churches; then the Vatican with a church so big you got lost from the other person; then the village where he came from, in the hills near Naples where you had to rent a car with a driver to go and how the people there would let you into their house and cook for you, just because they knew your last name, and used to know your mother or your grandfather fifty or a hundred years ago. He went on and on, teaching them Italian words, watching their faces, nervous in three different ways. And when he finally stopped he felt what a fool he'd made for himself, talking so much. *Chiacchierone*, was the word for it.

"I'm definitely going to go now, Mom," the girl said to her

mother.

Maybe Estelle now the name was, he thought, not Stella. She had the eyes a little bit pointed, and skin like a walnut, and a face you wanted to look at all the time. "And where are you from, Miss," he said to the girl's mother, "if it's not bad to ask?"

"Cambodia. A place called Kampong Cham. Estelle was born there."

"What was things like there, Cambodia? You see a lot of Cambodia people in Revere now, you don't ask them."

"Before the war it was like paradise. You could take food from the trees—bananas, papayas, mangoes, coconuts, something called a pomelo, which you don't have here but which is like a combination of a pear and an orange. We had all kinds of fish, shrimp, rice, nuts, noodles. People were kind to each other. It was a very religious place."

"Catholic people?"

"We were very devout Buddhists. Estelle still is."

"And then there was a war?"

"It's next to Vietnam, *Babbo*."

"A war, and then after the war, other things, worse things. Estelle was tiny and very sick and we escaped on a boat and we thought she would die. Estelle's father was left there and eventually starved to death. Both my parents were killed and two of my sisters were raped and killed . . . Two million people were killed. Soldiers went into hospitals and killed the patients according to their illness. If they had been burned, the soldiers burned them to death; if they had stomach cancer the soldiers cut open their stomachs. They killed every old person, every teacher, every doctor, anyone who wore glasses, anyone with soft hands, anyone educated."

As Lily spoke, Vito stared across the table at her, blinking and blinking, caught in a cloud of bad air, as if the woman was opening a door into another part of life he didn't know, and the smell was so terrible you wanted to close the door again and run the other way. His eyes moved for a moment to the younger of the two women, Stella, he was gonna call her if that was all right, and then back, squinting slightly now, as if the explanation for such horror might be spied out there, in the face opposite him. "Why did God let this happen?" he said, at last.

No one seemed to know. For a short time, half a minute, a vapor of the Southeast Asian holocaust seemed to hang in the air around them. Alfonse shifted in his seat. Vito said, "I'm sorry that happened to you. I don't know nobody that something like that happened. I'm . . . when the first minute I saw your face I saw what a sadness was there. When I went in to put the coats I was saying to myself: where could such a sadness come from in a woman like this? Young, pretty. What could make?"

"It seems like a long time ago now. I have a wonderful daughter, a wonderful man."

"Sure you do," Vito said. "Two of the best."

"And Alfonse says we're going to have a famous carpenter build us a house."

"Who?" Vito turned to his son. He was caught by the hard grip of disappointment because Alfonse hadn't mentioned the house to him a second time, and he was sure now that they'd found somebody else, a younger carpenter, and now they were going to tell him and he was going to have to pretend not to be upset. "Who'd you get?"

Alfonse made a dramatic pause, took a long sip from his coffee up, then said, "Imbesalacqua," and paused again, watching his father's face. "'Vito'", people call him, or sometimes "'Victor Bones'."

"Oh," Vito said, but maybe he didn't understand right. The jealousy still had him around the neck, a little anger maybe mixed in, a little hope, too. It was as if he were hearing the words, really hearing them, but a few seconds after they'd been spoken. "Who'd you say?"

"Imbesalacqua."

Alfonse was looking at him funny now, smiling.

"Me?"

"I told you, *Babbo*, remember?."

Another pause. He nodded. The jealousy had let go of him, but he felt a little water in the eyes.

"Is he any good, this guy, *Babbo*?"

Vito looked around him. Three faces smiling. "So-so," he said, because he could get a joke once in a while, too. He had the napkin in his hands without knowing it. He squeezed and let go. "Old now," he said. "But at one time he could do a job for you."

"You look the same," Estelle said.

"What?"

"Look. You're sitting exactly the same way and for one second there your faces, the light on your faces, was the same."

With identical gestures, Alfonse and Vito looked down. They'd crossed their arms over their chests in a particular way, left hand tucked into right armpit, right hand on the outside of the left upper arm. Each looked up at the other. Alfonse laughed. The phone rang in the kitchen and Vito went to answer it—the usual—and he stood in the kitchen a minute so nobody would know.

"Who was it, *Babbo*?"

"Nothing. I'm making more coffee," he said "These cookies you have to eat while they're fresh."

During the meal the rain had lessened to a gusty drizzle. Now it stopped altogether. They could hear the wind knocking the storm windows back and forth in their metal tracks, and the hollow metal rolling of a neighbor's trash barrel blown into the street, but now and again a flash of sunlight found its way between the clouds and lit the room like the first payment on the new season's promissory note.

"We have all the permits," Alfonse said. "They poured the foundation yesterday. Ground was a little wet, but—"

"Who done it?"

"Capone and Lewey."

"Good. Nice work they do. What about money—not for me, I'm doing this job no pay. But what about for the lumber, the helpers?"

"Lily is an executive with a big computer company, *Babbo*. I have a captain's salary, no mortgage, no kids all these years. We paid cash for the land, and the bank financed most of the rest. We could probably have paid cash for the whole thing."

"And the bank, by the way," Lily said, "has budgeted fifty-five dollars an hour for the general contractor."

"Who is he?" Vito asked. "It's too much."

"Imbesalacqua," Estelle said. "Vito. He's supposed to be pretty good."

Vito looked at her and had the strange and unsettling feeling that he had known her for all of his life. From before everything happened, before Lucy and Peter and Joanie, before Revere, before the village. For a hundred years and more he'd known this face looking across the table at him—the brown, brown eyes, the black hair, the skin like cinnamon. Something about the insides of this girl he knew already.

They talked another little while about the house—architectural plans, sub-contractors, a broad-backed heavy-lifter called Julian Manzo who would serve as Vito's helper.

"To the other one he's related, Manzo?" Vito asked.

Alfonse nodded. "Same father, different mother. He looks like Xavier but he's a good kid, hard worker, and he needed a break. I thought it would be okay."

"Sure, fine," Vito said, but he wasn't sure how fine it was. The half-brother was a killer. The memories were bad. And then again, as if the words had reached him at a delay, he heard "*same father different mother,*" and he understood something, and he shut up.

The women, this time, wouldn't let him argue them away from clearing the table, at least, putting a few things back in the refrigerator, rinsing a dish or two. When Vito went back to fetch the three coats, Alfonse followed, and Vito told him that, for a wife, he couldn't see a better one than Lily. Alfonse nodded, plucked at the damp spot on the bed, said: "Are you getting phone calls, *Babbo*?"

"Sure, sometimes."

"How often."

"Once in the night, late. Maybe once, two times, in the day."

"Does the person talk?"

"Nothing. Five seconds on the line, then the hang-up."

"When did this start?"

"Since months ago."

"And you didn't tell anyone?"

Vito shook his head. "I *want* that he calls, Alfonse. I *want* that he comes here, in this house, Eddie. I have the crowbar next to the door." He thought of telling Alfonse about the new gun, then decided not to. "I'll fix him up."

"When he calls again, see if you can make him talk for a little while, alright? We'll get the phone tapped by Tuesday night. All we need to do is find out where he is and he goes to jail."

"I'll send him someplace else before jail, Alfonse. He was gonna kill Joanie and Peter both if you didn't stop him. I'll fix him up good."

"He'll kill anybody he thinks he has to, *Babbo*. That's who Eddie is. Make him angry. Try to get him to talk."

"God lets them kill the people over there for wearing the

glasses," Vito said. "Eddie Creviniello he lets stay alive."

The scene at the back door was repeated in reverse, coats going on, water evaporating from the porch boards instead of falling on them. Lily and Estelle kissed Vito this time instead of shaking hands. "This house for you should be like a father's house," he said to Lily. "If that's alright." And to her daughter: "I'm gonna teach you the Italian language, so when you go over there you know what to say to people."

"Can you teach me carpentry? Can I be your helper on the house?"

"You're a girl . . . the young woman now."

She pursed her lips. "I'm strong. I'm smart."

"You're almost finished with the college. Look at all the jobs you can get then."

"She's a painter," Lily said.

"An artist, *Babbo*."

"I want to know how to work with my hands, though. I'll work for apprentice wages."

"It's work for men, the carpentry," Vito told her.

Her eyes were almost even with his, brown lens to brown, unblinking. "Not now," she said. "Not anymore."

Lily put a hand on her daughter's arm, Vito looked at his son. The loose strands of the conversation floated in the air for a moment before a hard gust of wind pushed the storm door against Alfonse's shoulder, blew two damp, dead maple leaves into the house, and the visit was over.

It seemed to him, when they had gone down the steps and into the car, and the car was backing out, and he was standing on the porch watching them go, that it had been a good day, a good Saturday meal, one bitter taste of coffee in the cup at the very end: a look in the girl's eyes like he'd hurt her a little bit, or made her mad on him. Two sons he had, nobody never wanted to learn the carpentry. And now in the family a girl finally, and she wanted.

Twenty Five

It had never made much sense to James Crellin why people—his father and his father's friends, among them—decided to make money illegally. Bending the rules a bit on taxes was understandable: the rules could be open to interpretation, the risk of being caught was small and the punishment rarely severe. But making an entire career on the far side of the iron fence of the law, risking prison and even death . . . there was no logic to it, as far as he could see. Of course, he'd never said anything like that to his father or to his brother John. From the day in fifth grade when he'd first become something more than vaguely aware of what his father did to earn his living, he'd adopted a policy of respectful avoidance of any discussion that had anything to do with Daddy's work. His father—uneducated but devilishly people-smart—had seemed to sense his feelings, and—in perfect contrast to what he'd done with his brother— never once talked about bringing his second son into the family business. "You're goin' to school," was the old man's mantra and, dutiful son that he was, James had gone to school for accounting, earned his C.P.A., then—on his father's suggestion— legally changed his name and set himself up as tax consultant and financial advisor, thirty miles west of Eddie Crevine's territorial center. His father liked to send him what he called "legitimate clients". They saw each other once a month for lunch, and sometimes on holidays. They talked about the weather, sports, politics—all of this with the two giant elephants—his father's work and his own love life—grazing silently at the edges of the room.

In twenty-eight years there had been two exceptions. First, in the grand old tradition, on his fifteenth birthday his father had brought him to a high-class prostitute: one of three times in his life he'd had sex with a woman. Second, four years ago, his father took him to an expensive steak house on Newbury Street for lunch, table for two in a private dining room and said, "Jimmy, I never asked you to do nothing for me, you know, work-wise, right?" And he'd felt a sudden eruption of dread. His business, his reputation, his freedom, maybe even his life seemed to lie there like the slab of rare beef on his father's plate, a sharp knife and fork poised above it.

"Right, Dad," he said, mouthing a silent prayer.

"Well, you don't got to worry. I never will."

He smiled a great huge smile of relief. His father watched him intently, smiled himself, then said, "Except for one time." And then, "Ha, you should see your face. You went green. Need to puke?"

"I'm okay, Dad."

"Nothin' big," his father went on, stabbing the fork into a corner of his steak and slicing the knife through it, then turning the meat so he could see how it had been cooked, frowning, jabbing it into his mouth, chewing, swallowing, looking up like a mastiff in mid-meal. "One day," he said, "one time, and I mean once, and I hope it never happens, but one time if I'm in a jam I'm gonna need you to do one tiny favor for your father."

"Anything," he croaked out.

His father lifted his eyebrows and chuckled. "I'm gonna need you, if I ever say to you "Right now I feel like a *Philly cheese steak*"—that's the code, I'm gonna need you to drive over to your brother's house and say that to him, Philly cheese steak, okay? And then he'll tell you what to do. Too much to ask?"

"No, Dad."

"You sure?"

"I just . . . I have a nice business set up. If it could at all be avoided I'd want not to do anything patently illegal."

Another too-large chunk of steak cut, chewed, swallowed. His father gulped from a glass of beer and looked up at him and James understood, only then, that everything that had ever been written about the man, and most of what had been said about him, was true. There was one word for the smile on Chelsea Eddie's square face: murderous.

His father watched him, let a few seconds pass like a stage actor milking a pause, then said, "Fucking boys is illegal, you know . . . patently, or whatever."

It had suddenly become impossible to speak. "Not boys," he wanted to say, but he couldn't.

The victorious smile again. The waiter stopped by and was rudely chased away. "Everything I done for you, all the guys I sent to you for work . . . this is one small favor and the chances of you getting in trouble for it are about nil."

"Okay, Dad," he croaked and it was as if his father had taken hold of his intestines in one hand and was squeezing as he spoke.

"You get the phone call from me and you hear me say "Philly cheese steak" and you hang up that second, understand? Then you drive over to Johnny's and you make sure nobody else is around and you say, "Pa called. Philly cheese steak." And he tells you what to do. Deal?"

"Deal," James said.

"Good." And then, as if bestowing an enormous favor, his father added, "And about the other shit, you know, the queer stuff. I'll never mention it again as long as I live."

Twenty Six

Peter paused for a moment, unsure whether or not Father Pettibone had passed out there on the other side of the screen. The pain in his shoulder had started pushing up through the soft quilt of whiskey, and his knees were so sore—it had been years since he'd knelt like this—that he was forced to shift his weight from one to the other as he went on with his story. "Bu-but I did-didn't have the money, Father. Seventeen th-thousand it was. And with somebody like Eddie the mon-money itself wasn't so important as him keep-keep-keeping up his reputation, sa-saving face, if you na-know what I mean. So when I met with him th-th-that night I carried this tiny ta-tape recorder in a cigar in the pocket of my suit coat . . . Are you st-still there?"

"Of course, Paul. Go on."

"His bodyguard, Xavier, pat-patted me down beforehand, ba-but I talked to him a little to dis-distract him, and con-conned him a little bit when he thought he felt something, and we'd been sort-sort-sort of acquaintances in a weird way, growing up. So I had the recorder on when I got into Eddie's limousine, with-with-without anybody knowing it. We took a drive. Eddie threatened to ki-kill me, tr-tried to talk me into bur-burning down a house. I got that on the ta-tape, and got-got-got away. Do you understand, Father? Eddie was in-indicted because of that tape—loansharking, conspiracy to arson— he ra-ran. The U.S. Marshals had me testify to a grand jury then

130

they sent me away, here, Mon-Montana. No off-offense, Father, ba-but it's driv-driving me crazy, Montana. I use-use-used to think about ga-gambling every day, every fa-free minute. Na-now I think about going back to Revere, about seeing my fa-father and my sister and my best friend. Do you understand?"

"Of course, Paul. You've been through a spiritual trial that even—"

"You think you can do me just this one little favor, then?"

Twenty Seven

The noon broadcast had gone smoothly—the traveling pope, Red Sox opening day, more rain in the forecast—and now Joanna had some quiet time, an hour and a half before the latest in a series of meetings with the marketing people. As she sometimes did, she stood against one wall of the newsroom, sipping coffee and running her eyes over the jovial commotion.

The newsroom was alive with the ordinary bustle of early afternoon: reporters talking into telephones, production assistants swinging down the rows of cubicles with a sheaf of AP bulletins in one hand and a mug of coffee in the other, stopping to relay the latest joke, to flirt, to finish off a piece of business, check a fact, a phone number, a sports score. No one but the secretaries ever seemed to be still for more than a minute at a time. Keyboards clicked, printers printed, copiers copied. Into the room poured a dozen little streams, electrical burps and blinks and babble, as if the passion and terror of millions of lives needed to flow through these cubicles first, to be suitably processed, before being passed on, through her and through the frail confidence of Marty Lincoln, to the people of eastern New England. As if news were a nutrient. As if the human animal would wither and die if it wasn't constantly drinking at the information trough.

She'd always loved it. Intern at Cornell, roving reporter, special features reporter, anchor for a year or two years in places like Boise, Omaha, and Knoxville—the closer the studio was

132

to Manhattan, the more sweetly the pulse of the planet tapped in her chest.

In her mid-thirties it had seemed for a while that she'd be summoned to New York by the network. She was anchoring the CBS affiliate in Birmingham, Alabama—a place she loved in spite of herself—and, after her own broadcast ended at six-thirty, she'd sit and watch Dan Rather for half an hour, and it would feel as though the screen were a magnetic force and her chest and throat and eyes were pure steel. I can do better, she'd think; I can do better than that. She had never wanted any-thing—not a true love, not even children—the way she wanted to sit in front of a camera and say to America: "I'm Joanna Imbesalacqua and this is what the world is doing tonight."

The executive producer, a man they called D.T., walked past her and winked. She turned the corners of her lips down an eighth of an inch and averted her eyes. All evidence, all re-cent history to the contrary, D.T. seemed buoyed by the fantasy that she'd be swept into bed some night by his sex jokes and lingering pats on the forearm, his power ties and squeaky voice. All evidence to the contrary, she floated along on her own fan-tasy, too, of being summoned to CBS or ABC or NBC or down to Atlanta for a CNN interview. A weekend or holiday anchor, to begin with. And then, one of those rare creatures: a middle-aged woman allowed to show her face to all of America at the dinner hour and say, into thirty million living rooms: "Good evening. I'm Joanna Imbesalacqua and this is what's happening in our world tonight."

Her sex, her age, her too-long name—they all counted against her. Still, even now, there were rumors, whispers, subtle signals that it might not be too late. Which was part—a small part—of her obsession with Eddie Crevine. Tracking him down would surely call her to the attention of the powers that be. Having sent Eddie away, she'd be able to leave her father without guilt. Leslie wasn't holding her now. Peter wasn't holding her here.

She took refuge in her office and closed the door on the lively circus, musing, dreaming. For a little while she stood at the window, looking down on Oxford Street, watching taxicabs dart through the intersection and fingering the frayed satiny hem of her own ambition. The city she stared out at, and reported on, had been filled up by impossible dreamers, built by them. English, Irish, Jewish, Neapolitan—some version of a fantasy had carried all of them onto this shore. There was nothing at all wrong with it.

Marjorie knocked once and put her head into the room. "There's a man downstairs who says he's your father. Sally keeps telling him you're in a meeting, that you don't entertain people during business hours, and so on, but he won't leave. I told her to tell him your real father has the number of your private line, but this guy insists. He's been sitting there for over an hour already, do you want to go down in elevator two and just have a peek? A handsome old man in a suit, she said. Big nose, half bald. Doesn't seem like the usual nutcase, she says. She's been up here three times already."

The elevator doors opened onto the capacious lobby, with ten-foot plate-glass windows offering a street-level view, the receptionist talking into a headphone at her bare desk, and an expanse of gray carpet adorned with a geometric arrangement of rose-colored couches, on one of which her father sat. He was dressed in his best suit, brown wool with a blood-red stripe. His shoes were newly polished. His gray felt hat—thirty years out of style—rested on a topcoat that was folded over one arm. Shaven cheeks and good posture, a certain tension gathered in the muscles around his mouth, he resembled nothing so much as a man come looking for a job he had very little hope of being offered.

Joanna was sure, at first, that he'd come to tell her Peter had been killed.

"Papa," she said, when she was still several feet away. His face turned toward her. "What happened, what's wrong? Why didn't you call?"

He had some trouble pushing himself forward and up from the soft cushion. She reached down both arms to help. He frowned, ignored her hands, got to his feet by himself, and she moved the hands to his shoulders and kissed him dutifully on the cheek. "What's wrong?"

"Nothing happened bad. Is it a trouble, me coming to where you work?"

"No. Of course not." She felt the smallest line of anger running in her voice—not anger exactly but a very old frustration, the friction of two worlds rubbing. An irregular stream of workers passed through the room, snatches of conversation floating, the elevator light going on and off with a sound like thick glasses being touched in a toast. "But why didn't you call me? You have my number. They would have let you right up."

"I took out the number to be sure I brought it. She's on the table now, at home, sitting there."

"You should keep it with you in your wallet. I told you that."

His eyes looked steadily across at her. Something flickered there—anger, hurt—and she felt an answering spark snap across behind her own eyes. History to history they were standing, forty years of argument and reconciliation swirling through a yard of silent air.

"I never been here before, since your office moved. I asked people on the street."

"Is everything okay? Nothing's happened to Peter?"

He shook his head without taking his eyes from her eyes. She looked away, at the receptionist, and made a small wave.

"I had one thing I had to look in your face and tell you. Nothing too bad."

"Have you eaten?"

"Breakfast I had."

"We'll go downstairs then. Come with me, Papa."

She ushered him down a set of rubber-coated stairs and along a line of wrapped salads, hot dishes, and cartons of Hood milk on ice. They sat at a table in the farthest corner of the room, two other parties of diners not far from them, the plastic and paper ruins of a few other meals on the white tabletops. Her father had taken a plate of beef tips in mushroom gravy, a roll, and a miniature bottle of some pinkish wine she knew he would not be able to drink. "Eat first and then we'll talk," she said, unwrapping her salad. His face had grown suddenly serious; when he swallowed, his throat worked against the collar of his shirt. After two bites he looked down at the food on his plate with a sort of pity, and set his fork to one side.

"If I'd known you were coming we could have made reservations and gone out to someplace nice. You should have called me from home."

The spark in his eyes again. He turned his attention to the roll, buttered it carefully, took a bite leaning his head forward over the plate, poured out the portion of wine, sipped it, made a face.

"You have now a few minutes?"

"Of course, Papa."

"I know sometimes now you don't have so much business at work this time on the day."

"It's quiet. I have an hour. Papa, what happened?"

"I came to tell you, I came to ask . . ." He held the buttered roll halfway between the table and his mouth as if he'd forgot-

136

ten about it in mid-flight. Joanna reached out and took it from him and set it on the napkin beside his dish. "You know," he said, "why Mama yelled so much that night Alfonse called you up for the date?"

She nodded, made herself keep looking at him. This was so perfectly her father: he'd dressed up and come all this way in the middle of the work day to talk with her about a phone call from twenty-five years ago.

"You know why, you sure?"

"Yes."

"Who told you that you know? Mama?"

"Alfonse."

"When?"

"One night last summer. A few days before Mama died. We were sitting out in his yard looking over at the house on Tapley Avenue and he told me everything." She stared across the table until her father looked down.

He picked up his fork and touched the tines to the edge of the pool of mushroom gravy, which had already started to congeal. He made some kind of pattern there as if writing himself a reminder: neat, geometric, the angle of rafter and wall, then lay the fork down again and looked resolutely up. "She wasn't yelling like that for no reason."

"I know it."

"She wasn't crazy."

Joanna nodded, though she wasn't sure she agreed. An adultery that had produced a bastard child was an excellent reason. But good reason or not, there had been, to her mother's tirades, something that went a few steps beyond the border of sanity.

"Five years it went on like that and then one day she stopped and never started again."

"Papa, I was there. I know this."

He didn't seem to quite hear. He was presenting his case now, carefully, methodically, assembling one wall, then another, boxing in his version of reality so that it fit neatly there in his sunny Revere, with Jesus looking down upon it, blessing it as the truth. She put her hands beneath the edge of the table and squeezed them hard together.

"It was because of what Alfonse told you that she made a little crazy on us like that."

"I know Papa."

"It was because of me, what I did."

Joanna looked at him. The nose and ears, the thinning hair and brown eyes and the delicate mole to one side of his mouth that he had trouble shaving around now so that it was ringed by small white irregular bristles. That this figure before her, this old man in a nicely tailored suit that fit him like an apology . . . that he could have walked across their backyard with his God staring down at him and made love to another woman, while his pregnant wife and two-year-old daughter were shopping for Christmas presents a few miles away . . . the image could not, by any force of will or imagination, be squeezed into the rest of her picture of him . . . that he had kept the secret for forty years, that Carmellina and her mother had kept it, three of them leaning over the child Alfonse and spreading out their coats to shield him from the eye of the neighborhood, to shield their own collective shame. She couldn't picture it. Even though she could see that Alfonse clearly bore her father's face, he'd had to work hard to make her believe it on that first night. "In certain men," he'd said, "at a certain age, the urge for sex runs over everything else. Logic, morals, love, the law. You might as well hold up your hand and stop a train."

She shook her head as if to shake the idea of it from the earth. And people talked about women . . . their hormones and heats and middle-aged ravings . . . It was a sadistic chemist who'd fashioned the world. They were, all of them, an experiment gone ridiculously wrong.

"I'm sorry," her father said now.

The words were like two polished pieces of coal set in front of her as an offering. She looked away.

"I'm asking now for you to forgive me what I done."

She ran her eyes across the empty tables, the two Guatemalan servers idly stirring soup and polishing apples. For a moment she felt herself pulled back again into the woman she was in this building, the person she would have been with no Revere in her past, no Proctor Avenue echoes, no vein of craziness running through the family saga. For a moment she wanted to get up and just walk away.

"Joanie," he said.

Joanna, she thought. She turned her eyes back to him. "I need time, Papa. You knew for forty years and didn't say anything, you and Mama both."

"Your Mama didn't want me to say."

"What would you have done if she'd wanted you to?"

"Take him into my house and give him my name. Raise him like I raised you and Peter."

"He turned out better than either Peter or I, though. Growing up the way he did he turned out better. Eat, Papa."

But he made no move to eat. His eyes held her in place, pinned her against the church wall in some sun-baked village fifty miles east of Naples. "This is what you do," he said. "You talk about your life like you grew up in the fire in purgatory. It used to hurt your mother like you don't know. Was it that bad, the way we were to you?"

"It came out harsher than I meant it. Eat now. Please."

"You don't say it like you feel."

"I don't know what you want, Papa." She pressed her lips together and ran her eyes almost desperately around the room.

139

A trill of laughter leaked out of the kitchen, the Guatemalan women turned toward it expectantly. "I call you every week. I give you money. I've helped you out that way, you and Mama and Peter, for years and years. I risk my life to try and catch Eddie, to track him down, so Peter might have some hope of coming back, so you won't have to be afraid for your life every night. I went out and bought you a gun. You come to see me unexpectedly, at my office, in the middle of the working day, to tell me something I already know, and I buy you lunch and sit with you and listen. What do you want?"

"I want you to do those things not like they're a job for you."

"I'm sorry, Papa. I *am* sorry. But I did not have the beautiful childhood you think I had, that you and Mama wanted me to have. The secret you and Mama and Carmellina kept tore our family to pieces, can't you see that? You being perennially guilty, Mama's unexplained tirades, Peter's gambling addiction and the way you both kept enabling him. Think of what all that was like for me . . . Forty years! And now you come to see me and want me to forget about it in two minutes."

"If you come to see me, I want you to come because you want to."

"You said that. I understand. I've been tremendously busy lately. I've been trying, among a thousand other things, to track down Eddie Crevine so we can put that chapter of our life behind us."

"He calls me."

"Who does?"

"Creviniello. He calls me every night and doesn't say nothing."

"How do you know it's him?"

"Who else it's gonna be?"

"Have you told anyone? Alfonse?"

"Just the other day, I told."

"Why don't you disconnect the phone, or have the number unlisted?"

"Because what if Peter calls me up?"

She couldn't keep herself from letting out an exasperated breath. "Papa, listen to me. Peter isn't going to call. He isn't coming back. If Eddie is caught, maybe, possibly. Failing that, we'll never see him again."

But her father—wrinkled skin and yellowed teeth—was staring at her right through the smoke and drama of Eddie Crevine. Until he spoke again she believed that all he was interested in doing was staring her back into childhood so he could rearrange her life to suit his vision of it. He was, she thought, not for the first time, a man crippled by some Old World sentimental vision of family life.

"You keep your own secret too," he said.

She felt a quick surge of something very close to fear, blinked it away, willed herself to look straight back at him. He was leaning slightly forward now, his forearms on either side of the uneaten meal.

"Everyone has private aspects to their life," she said calmly, rationally. "That's part of being an adult. But I have nothing as big as . . ." The words seemed to be limping out of her. She stopped.

"Pretty big I think it is, this one."

She couldn't stop her eyes from traveling once, quickly, over the empty room. She feebly shook her head. For once, she could not seem to will the muscles of her face to obey her, and so she kept it turned a quarter-turn to the right and felt her father's steady gaze burning the bones of her cheek.

A silence swelled between them. She considered and rejected a dozen different ways of puncturing it.

"Look at me, Joanie."

Joanna.

"Look at me."

"Papa, this is neither the time nor the place for this particular discussion."

"Look at me now, I'm askin'. In the eyes."

Her eyes seemed to be weighted. With a great effort she swung them in the direction of her father's face.

"I don't care now that you don't tell me about you life. You have secrets, too, that's all. That's what people do, they keep secrets from other people. They keep their own little house inside them and they close the doors and pull down the shades in the windows, and they think the other people and God don't see. Adam and Eve, they did it. That's the original sin, keepin secrets like that from who loves you."

A sound escaped her, a half-cough of derision. He didn't notice.

"I love you just the same, no matter what. Like I loved your brother all these years when he was going all around Revere making the name Imbesalacqua mean the same thing as "in trouble" in people's minds."

"And that's the main thing," she said quietly.

"What."

"What people think. What people in Revere might think of us. The truth, the emotional health of the family—everything takes a back seat to what people might think of us. Don't you see how much damage that has done?"

"The family comes first. There's nothing I wouldn't do for you and Peter now, nothing."

"But what people think is what you care about."

"Sure I care. Revere is my world for me like this is your world for you. You don't care who sees us now, who hears? You don't care if God sees?"

"I don't believe in God, Papa," she said. She thought of

142

Leslie with her professor-father and college-graduate/political-activist mother and two siblings for whom a homosexual sister was about as shameful as a passion for milk chocolate candy bars. Leslie sailed through the world unfettered, while she herself lived in a cage of fame and Old World judgments, held there by melodrama, twisted logic, unbreakable blood ties. "I don't believe someone is watching me day and night to make sure I behave a certain way."

"He doesn't care whether you believe on him or no. You think somebody who made the sun come up—"

"But if I believed in God, your kind of God, a God who's always giving you lessons that work out neatly in the end, then I'd worry that he'd set you up so something would happen to break you of caring so much what the people in Revere think, caring so much about being so good, so right."

"He already done it, Joanie. Two times."

"It doesn't seem to have worked."

She looked down at her uneaten salad, at her watch, then away, feeling that she'd lost hold of the rein on herself again, with him, gone too far. He would leave now—already he was reaching for his hat—and she'd bite back on an apology and slog around for days in a swamp of guilt.

"Maybe so," her father said, still looking straight at her, the hat and folded coat in his lap now. "I'm not the smartest person God ever made. Maybe it takes me three, four times to learn what I gotta learn."

"Papa, don't be hurt. It doesn't—"

"But I didn't come here to fight. I came to tell you you don't have to give me no money now, anymore."

"Oh, Papa. I don't care about the money, really. I have more money than I know what to do with. I shouldn't have said that."

"I'm goin now back to work."

"Papa, you're seventy-one."

"Seventy-two. I'm goin back to work buildin the house."

"That's ridiculous."

"Alfonse asked me. He's getting marry and he asked me and I decided yes. I wanted to come say to you first I'm sorry. I never built a house for you and never for Peter, but this one I'm gonna built. I decided."

"And what? Go lift heavy boards all day? Climb around on a roof?"

"I decided, that's all. There's gonna be a helper."

Joanna lifted her eyes away from him. The beeper at her belt sounded. She glanced at it and switched it off. Alfonse had caught the disease now. Alfonse, Peter, her father. They lived as if a logical life were some kind of enemy. She remembered driving home from Cornell, March of her senior year, in a snowstorm, in a borrowed car, driving into Revere and turning from Broadway onto Park Avenue and coming upon a familiar figure there. Her mother plodded straight ahead in the driving wet snow, shopping bags filled with groceries held straight down in each hand so they nearly scuffed the top of the snow. An old hat on, bare-handed, too stubborn or too stingy to call a taxi, too proud to call her husband or son and ask for a ride. Joanna skidded to the curb just in front of her, got out, lifted the bags into the back seat, settled her mother in front. Her mother turned her face across the seat for a kiss—red cheeks, bright eyes, cold lips—and there was a quiet triumph about her. I'm not afraid of pain, that expression seemed to say. See, I'm not afraid of work, of pain, of death. God will protect me, God will provide.

Her father had slid halfway out of the booth, but she could tell there was something else he wanted to say. Her own private life, her own secret, seemed to be teetering there at the top of the tall windows, tilting and wobbling like a glass that had slid to the edge of a desk; one word would bring it crashing down.

"I want to say," her father began. He was squeezing the brim of the felt hat in his hands. "That after I built this one, for Alfonse, for his girl, after that, if you wanted, if I stayed healthy, I could built one for you. For you and . . . for you and another person you loved I could built it."

At that instant the elevator doors opened not twenty feet from their booth and her new co-anchor stepped out like a rooster in a blue necktie. Shoulders back, chin tilted up slightly, the white shirt as stiffly starched as if it was meant to serve a secondary purpose as a bullet-proof vest. Marty Lincoln beamed a smile at her and said, too loudly, "Greetings, oh Gorgeous One!" and made a fake little bow. Though she wished with all her strength that he'd keep on strutting toward the salad bar, he stopped at their table and put his hands on his hips.

"Hi, Marty. Things going okay?"

"Over all over the city over," he said, beaming.

"This is my father, Vito. Papa, this is Marty Lincoln, my co-anchor."

Marty thrust out his hand. "Vito is a name we don't hear often enough these days," he said, pumping her father's hand and smiling with such force that his ears moved. "Your daughter is a goddess. I'm honored to sit beside her."

"Yes," her father said. He had started to get to his feet but Marty was standing too close and he hit his legs up against the table, lost his balance, and sat down again with a thump. He winced, still looking up. "Yes, she's-a nice girl. The bess there is."

Mike hesitated for a second as if he might be missing a joke, then he put a hand on her shoulder and squeezed, already turning away. "Ooh, that's-a spicey meat-a-ball," he said, and he was gone.

Twenty Eight

Eddie reached down and slid the safety off then leaned back and watched in the rear view mirror. He let his left arm hang out the window so he would seem as unconcerned and unthreatening as possible. The officer kept the cruiser door open and one booted foot flat on the asphalt. His face was turned toward his computer screen.

Eddie could feel his heart going—bang, bang—and a small change in his breathing, but he kept his right hand in his lap. It was a simple thing, really, a simple black or white, no extra thinking necessary. The instant he heard, "Could you step out of the car please, sir," he'd say, "Sure, officer," and open the door with his left hand at the same time he was reaching down with his right. One shot would do it, anywhere in the chest or belly. Then you drive away and see how far you get. Simple.

But as he was thinking this, the dark place—it was like a pool of black water—appeared there in front of him. He'd seen so many people die, in so many different ways, and felt, a dozen times at least, that he was close to death himself. This was different, though, cold and real like nothing he'd ever felt. So after he shot the cop, how far would he get? A mile, five miles, a day up the highway? One thing would never happen, black pool or no: he would never die in jail. His father had died in jail, in a shitty metal bed at Devens, with a shitty male nurse taking his sweet time bringing the pain medicine, and Eddie next to his bed, and bars on the windows, and a cold metal nothing-feeling in the air, and his father's face twisted up like he was absolutely scared shitless. That would never happen to him.

Now he saw the trooper get out of his cruiser and walk toward him, the license and registration squeezed between his left thumb and fingers. Eddie looked to see if his holster had been unbuttoned. It had not.

"All set, Mr. Echeverria," the trooper said, standing more normally at the open window now, face-on. "Stop and have a coffee or something. Stay alert."

"Thank you, officer," Eddie said. "Have a good day, alright?"

The officer turned without answering and Eddie took his time replacing the registration in the glove compartment. Before he started up the car again he sent a small word of thanks in the direction of China Louis and Louis' good pal, Leon the Plan-Man.

Twenty Nine

It was late afternoon, Austin had come home from school and gone to shoot baskets with Renny Mitchum, the only real friend he'd made since they moved here, the steaks were marinating on top of the stove, and Elsie was having what she thought of as a "Montana moment."

She checked the potatoes, turned the burner down one notch, grabbed her coat off the hook and went out the back door. To the southwest the sun had dropped behind the hills, casting the house and icy yard into shadow and sending streams of cool breezes running down off the snowfields. North and east of their yard the tops of the mountains were still lit. The light on them was dull gold, the forested foothills a dark, shimmering lavender, the sky behind and above them a delicate pink. From where she stood she could see only one house on the hillside; it seemed a tiny thing, yellow windows and dark roof, a few living souls huddled in a warm box on a spinning stone ball that swung round and round through something huge beyond imagining.

She took a few steps into the yard, the thin coating of ice crackling beneath her boots, and she stood there with her bare hands in her pockets. The pink sky seemed to be bleeding down onto the face of the mountains now. The lavender hills went to rust, to charcoal, and a star or a planet—Venus, she guessed—winked into view.

She felt that the essence of her had been sent out into the

air in a way that made her feel totally at peace. Her skin no longer quite contained her. The past—a drug-haunted ex-husband, a mother and father swept away from each other and away from her in separate orbits of poverty and lunacy, Peter's years of gambling, those horrible last days with Eddie and Xavier, all the press coverage and then the legal stuff that followed—the pain of those memories could find no resting place in her now. It was a Montana moment, pure space, blissfully large. She would have given anything to hold it, to be able to tell someone about it. But she could not tell Austin because, in a way she only half understood, it was Austin who pulled her back into the world of people, who reminded her what she'd been through and why she'd ended up here in this place. And she could not tell Peter because this love of solitude, quiet, and nature was exactly the place where they didn't fit together at all. Every cell of Peter's being was locked into the peopled world. He had to have that other person there, to reflect him, to sparkle in the light of his personality. He had to talk, to plan, to be surrounded by drama and busyness and noise. She loved him in spite of that, because of that; she nursed her small loneliness in private.

The moment fled with the light, leaving only a small sweet mark in her. In the time it took to draw two breaths, the air went from cool to cold. She heard a car come along the street, turn into their driveway and go silent, and she walked around the side of the house to greet her husband.

The car was there in the drive, Peter standing in the protection of the recessed doorway, invisible to her, knocking, for some reason, instead of using his key. It was dusk now. When she called out his name the syllables floated away on a blanket of cold air.

A man stepped out of the doorway enclosure, but it wasn't Peter. It was a black man—she hadn't seen a black person in

149

months. For a moment she thought Peter would appear behind him: it would be just like her husband to meet a black man in his little shop and invite the man and his family home for dinner, just because he thought no one else would. And then he'd tell the story of it for the rest of his life: how fine black people were, how they had always been the underdog, same as the Italians, always treated wrong, how, when he lived in Montana years ago, he'd been the only one in that half of the state to invite a black man to dinner and treat him like a human being.

But no, the man was alone. Maybe Peter had gone into the house and was looking for her . . . but then why leave the guest outside? Now the man was coming down the steps—he limped, he used a cane—and turning towards her, not speaking. "Hi, I'm Elsie Drinkwater, Peter's wife," she said across the distance that separated them, but he kept hobbling toward her, not speaking still, slightly hunched over. In the twilight she saw the lapels of his topcoat fall open, a flash of white cloth at his throat. He was a priest, or a minister. She stopped dead still and words flew out of her mouth. "Austin . . . hurt?"

The man continued walking toward her, silently, chasing up a dark dustcloud of fear. He stopped six feet away. They stood staring at each other. She heard a basketball bouncing on the tar street behind her, getting closer, and the first knot of worry in her chest dissolved. "Is Peter all right?" she asked, but her voice wasn't working the way it was supposed to work; the words creaked out of her. Austin's ball bounced closer, stopped. "Hi Mom. Hi, I'm Austin Drinkwater. Everything okay?" He was standing right beside her, he had a hand on her shoulder. The black man only stared and stared, then reached out his cane and tapped her gently on the hip.

"Fa-fa-fa-fooled ya, di-didn't I, honey," he said.

Thirty

By dusk that first day, Eddie had made it as far as the northern part of Florida. He'd never been good at reading maps—there never used to be any need for it: where was he gonna go, Everett? He had people who could find Everett if need be, or New York City, or Jersey, or Philly. When he had to make his escape from Boston there were favors he could call in and guys he could count on—thank you, Leon the Plan-Man—as far down the coast as Virginia. Alicia had taken over from there and gotten them to Miami. And what good were maps to him there? What, you needed a fucking map to find your way from the bedroom downstairs? Out into the fucking yard?

But the first thing he'd done after leaving the kitchen bloodbath was to find a drug store and buy a Rand McNally and sit in the parking lot for twenty minutes trying to figure it out. It turned out to be not that hard. You had Florida and you had Washington, D.C., and you had Massachusetts and you had the purplish line of I-95 connecting them; any moron could see that. So he would just keep following 95, pulling over at rest areas to piss and eat their ratty food. It would be like a vacation. So far—one day on the road—and there had been the interesting encounter with the highway patrolman, and this dark stain or pool or swamp that keep appearing at the end of his thoughts, and now there was something else, too, flashes of Alicia's face the way it looked half blown away. The pain would

151

come for a few minutes and then disappear and his mind was going a little twisty. He wondered if he'd given Jimmy's secretary the right fucking code words. Philly cheese steak, that's what it was. But had that been what he said? Stupid fucking thing, anyway. "It's childish, Eddie," he heard Alicia say next to him and he swiveled his head around fast to shut her up but she wasn't there. He wasn't going to start talking to her either. He was on vacation. He was going back to kill one of the Imbesalacquas, he didn't know which one yet, and he was going to maybe kill somebody in Xavier's family, too, to pay him back for his huge fuck-up, and then . . . then he didn't know. A bullet in his own brain, maybe. Or a doctor who would treat him and keep his mouth shut. He still had favors to call in. Pitchie Luglio, for one. Maybe Pitchie could make him into another person and he could start all over again someplace else.

He tried to get his thoughts back in one straight line. Just drive for now, he told himself. You can handle later, later. Stay on the highway and just keep going, and when you get back to Boston you find the old man, or his bitch daughter, or you find the both of them and finish the story . . . and then we'll see. Then the dark place would be closer, he knew that. He'd figure it out then.

The problem was mostly when you had to stop. All the way up through Stuart and Melbourne and Jacksonville he'd been seeing billboards for hotels, but the idea of getting off the highway then getting back on again made him nervous. Except for Vegas, he'd never liked staying in hotels. You didn't know who else was there, that was the problem, what kind of scumbag might be on the other side of the wall. Still, there was no way he was going to drive all the way to Washington without sleeping.

By Jacksonville—mad traffic there—he was feeling tired and he kept telling himself he should pull off before he attracted the attention of another trooper, pull off and get something half-decent to eat, sleep, leave early in the morning and head north again. But he procrastinated. Sometimes he'd tell himself he was going to get off at the next exit, but then, just as he came to the next exit he'd change his mind and decide to go another few miles.

North of Jacksonville, though, after he'd gone over a high bridge he didn't much like, and then past another exit where there were supposed to be places to stay, he could feel a bad drowsiness pulling down at his eyes. And so, without checking to be sure if motels had been advertised there, he took the next exit and found himself on a four-lane commercial strip with malls to either side. He was going east, maybe. Restaurants. Stores. No motels. He thought he could hear Alicia's voice again; she was giving him a hard time about it. That he couldn't even read a map. That he should have paid attention to the signs. He could hear her voice in the car.

"Keep it up," he said aloud. "We'll see where it gets you." And that made him feel foolish, too.

He just kept going, what else were you supposed to do? As long as he kept going straight he was pretty sure he could find his way back. A gas station. A Bar-B-Q joint. No motels. He kept going. Another few minutes and he was in no-man's land, the fucking jungle, no businesses at all just little shit houses to both sides with palm trees around them and pickup trucks up on concrete blocks. Nigger-ville, it looked like, too. Perfect.

Another few miles, and the houses, if anything, got shittier. It was starting to look like the road would just end someplace in the palm trees and weeds, and he was tired, and it seemed to him it was starting to get dark, in which case he'd really be screwed. He took a right turn on what seemed like a fairly big side street, thinking there had to be a motel someplace in here. These people had to have someplace to go get laid in the middle of the afternoon, didn't they? At this point he'd take any little shit place as long as it had a bed.

But pretty soon the line in the middle of the road wasn't there anymore. There were houses every once in a while but mostly trees, maybe a little broken-down shack or a rusted-out pickup truck with vines growing over the roof, then a roadside stand that said they were selling tomatoes, with a little old *molignan* sitting in a chair, knitting or something. Railroad tracks in the trees behind her. He thought maybe he should turn around, but the farther he went the more the roads behind him became a jumble of rights and lefts in his mind. He wasn't sure anymore where the highway was, exactly. Off to the right, probably, but you couldn't tell anymore.

Good place to get lost, she said. Nice going.

The road was shadowy. He blinked his eyes hard to keep them open. Pretty soon there weren't even any houses and he felt his heart starting to go too fast, and then the familiar pain shooting up through the middle of him. He'd never been much for saying prayers but it was starting to seem to him that once in a while you had to ask for things. It couldn't hurt. He waited a few minutes, though, listening for what Alicia might say about it, then he realized how stupid that was. "God," he said out loud, and the word echoed weirdly in the car. "God Almighty, Jesus F. Christ," he said, smiling now, trying to make it a joke. "How about a little help here before I drive into a fucking swamp or something and the alligators eat me? How about letting me die someplace other than this?"

A joke, but for a time there was nothing except more shadows. And then, a hundred yards in front of him, like an answer to his prayer, like a ghost, he saw a guy standing beside the road with his thumb out. Bent shoulders, black as the ace of spades. Not a chance in a million Eddie Crevine was stopping to pick up a nigger. He had nothing against them, not really, but nothing to do with them, either. He'd always left that to China Louis and his Roxbury boys. Sure, lately, even in Revere you were starting to see more of them, but his policy had always been to stay clear.

As he got closer he could see that the guy was old—their hair went gray, too—and a little bent over, one big thumb sticking out and a pitiful suitcase on the ground at his feet. Eddie went past about a hundred yards then jammed on the brakes and skidded to the side of the road in a cloud of dust. It was the suitcase that made him stop. Maybe the nigger knew a hotel. He watched in the mirror as the old guy came toward the car at a shuffling trot, the suitcase banging against his knee and the other hand waving like, "Wait! Wait! I'm coming!" It was funny. He could have backed up the car and made it easier for the old bastard but he was having too much fun watching him trot. Just as the guy reached the back of the car Eddie pulled it forward a few feet like he was driving away, and the guy yelled out something in a panicky voice. Eddie stopped, the old guy opened the door and leaned his face in—out of breath, yellow eyes all bloodshot like a drunk, a longsleeve shirt in this heat and it was all worn away around the top of the collar.

"Yes suh, thank you," the nigger said.

"Where ya going?"

"Up ahaid a few miles. Wife's meeting me. We goin' to our dawta's fer two nights."

"You know a hotel around here?"

"No suh," he said, and then, "yes suh. Up past where I'm goin' then back toward nahnty fahv."

"Get in."

The nigger smelled. Eddie had expected as much. Cheap booze, cigarettes, something else like sweat.

"Put your seat belt on so the cops don't stop us."

"Yes, suh, and I thank ya."

Eddie rolled down his window and started to drive. After a few seconds he remembered that he'd never taken the pistol out from under his seat so he pushed his foot back against it to keep it from sliding into view. Alicia would have had a shit fit if she'd been in the car and he'd stopped to pick up a black guy. It would have been a great joke to play on her. He wasn't worried anymore, though, even with the sun sinking behind the trees to his right because it seemed like God was maybe listening to him. He'd never asked for anything all these years; he was owed a favor or two. It was kind of funny, even, the situation. Maybe the nigger could tell him where he could get a blow job.

"There's water bottles there, if you want one."

"No suh, thank you."

"You live around here?"

"Mahl beck."

"A mahl, huh?"

"Yes, suh."

"I'm drivin' up from Miami to see my daughter, too. She lives in Virginia."

"Whereabouts?"

There was a dead animal in the road, gray, bloody, long skinny tail. "Huh?"

"What town?"

"Chelsea," Eddie said.

"Doan know it."

"Small town. Lot of assholes."

The man said nothing. The swear seemed to make him uncomfortable. He had the tattered suitcase across his lap and he adjusted it an inch, looked out at the trees.

"How old's your daughter?"

"Thirty-foh."

"And you?"

"Fitty some."

Eddie grunted. The guy looked like he was hundred and fifty-some. "You married young, huh?'

"Yes, suh."

"Lot of crime around here? People get shot and shit like that?"

"No, suh. Jesus watches ovah us heahbouts."

"You're lucky."

"Yes, suh, that's true."

"He watches over my wife, too. Jesus."

"I imagine she a good woman."

"Quiet type . . . You miss your daughter?"

"Yes, suh."

"Hard to be away from your kids, ain't it?"

Eddie was just starting to enjoy the conversation when the man said, "Raht heah. They's ma wahf." Eddie pulled to the side of the road next to a heavy woman with a blue bandana around her head.

"Pretty woman."

"Most thank you for the rahd."

"Welcome. See ya."

"You a man of God, suh. I kin tale that."

"Takes one to know one," Eddie said, and the man, halfway out of the car, smiled, showing a mouth of gums and scattered teeth.

The door closed, Eddie was driving away, smiling, happy for some reason, amused, when he saw the man waving crazily in the mirror and running toward him. He looked to his right to see if the old guy had forgotten the suitcase, but no, the guy had it and was running. Eddie stopped and waited so the nigger could come up to the driver's side window. He reached down and lifted the pistol with his right hand and turned so he could press it against the inside of the door without the guy seeing it. Maybe his face was on the TV. A reward or something. Maybe the old guy had recognized him.

The guy hustled up to the driver's door and leaned his smelly face close. "Mo-tell's that-a-way," he said, pointing right. "You git to the end heah, one mo mahl, you go that-a-way. Jesus watch ovah you."

"You, too," Eddie said, and he left the man in the dust and drove and when he'd gone another little ways he rolled up the window and broke into a long peal of rat-a-tat laughter that nobody else could hear. A good sleep now, he thought, when the laughing was finished. A good sleep, no trouble. Washington, D.C. by day after tomorrow.

Thirty One

Vito woke from a sound sleep at five o'clock on Monday morning, after a night in which there had been three calls. He sat on the edge of the bed and said a Hail Mary for Lucy's soul, one for Joanie, an Our Father for each of his two sons. He washed and dressed—long johns, old scarred workboots, overalls, a flannel shirt. He went into the kitchen and made himself a breakfast of scrambled eggs and coffee, washed and dried his dishes, sat on the sofa and made his silent prayer for half an hour, and still it was only ten past six. In the old days, when there had been a business to nurture, a reputation, he'd always observed an unwritten rule: no work before seven a.m.. It wasn't right to make noise too early when you had neighbors close to the job.

His tools were already packed into the car—he'd spent the previous day preparing, had even carried the deWalt radial arm saw up from his basement shop and out into the back seat, to prove to himself that he was still capable of heavy lifting.

The tools were ready, the architect's blueprints read and re-read, practically memorized, rolled up with a rubber band. A good job they'd done with the drawings. One or two little things needed to be fixed, but it was a good-looking house, big, not too complicated. For a few minutes he walked back and forth in the hallway, checking the bedroom and kitchen clocks against each other, and working through the plan for the day.

In the time since he'd last built a house, there had been new provisions added to the state building code and new materials developed. He'd spent a couple of days calling up old carpenter friends and telling them the news, then going to the lumberyard and pestering the people there with questions, talking to the building inspector at City Hall. The building inspector had told him the code now required that the sill be made of pressure-treated lumber, and a strip of insulation laid down between it and the top of the concrete foundation wall. In his day there had been no such a thing as pressure-treated lumber—they'd used native pine against insects and rot, sometimes coating it with creosote. And they hadn't worried so much about a few breaths of cold air leaking into the cellar every winter. The new rules worried him. What if he made a big mistake on Alfonse and Lily's house?

At six-twenty-five he turned on Channel Eight to get the weather. Joanie's friend was saying it. Curious George, she called him. No bad weather today until California.

Once the forecast ended, there was nothing left to fill the time, so he turned off the television and drove to the site. He'd work quietly for the first half hour or so, checking the foundation, putting the two-by-fours into different piles: straight, so-so, and crooked. None of the neighbors would hear.

But as soon as he turned onto Herter Street it was clear to him that something wasn't right. Three cars and a truck were already parked at the curb where Alfonse's house was gonna be. He could see—he could sense—a commotion there that more closely resembled a commercial construction site than a two-man house job, and he was sure then that Alfonse and Lily had hired a whole company. The workers didn't care so much about the Revere neighbors and had showed up at five in the morning, and now his "big job" would turn out to be standing around like a tired old man and giving people advice they didn't need. For fifty-five dollars an hour.

When he opened the door of his car he heard hammering. And as he approached the front of the lot, someone there yelled out, "Coffee break. Boss is here," in a voice he recognized. He walked across the dirt with the cold sun shining on his face, and saw somebody he'd known since ninth grade. The somebody had a hand out in front of him.

"Gus," Vito said to him, "*Come va?*"

"Word got around," Gus said. He had a strong handshake still. He was wearing a baseball cap with REVERE ITAM LODGE 630 on the front, and standing so that he and Vito both faced the site.

Vito was afraid Gus would start in on his storytelling— talking about his grandchildren—which was, among other things, what Gus Pallione was known for: nice guy, but you said hi to him and spent the next half hour listening.

"You can't have four retired carpenters know Imbesalacqua's starting a house and not have them come over to help instead of going crazy at home, doing nothing," Gus said. "Two Italians, a Jew, and an Irish. Plus the giant Alfonse hired, who seems like somebody forgot to turn his lights on, if you know what I mean."

Vito looked around at the small piles of crusted snow in the shadows, the stacks of new lumber, the churned-up, muddy earth, and wondered why Alfonse and Lily hadn't waited until warmer weather, until the ground dried out at least. What was the big rush? In the old days people waited two, three years to get marry. Near the back fence he saw an enormous young man, showing them his wide back, and pissing in the weeds.

"A Manzo," Gus said.

"Alfonse put him on the job."

"Cousin to Eddie Crevine's legbreaker. Julian, his name is."

"Half-a-brother, not cousin," Vito said. It wasn't a subject he wanted to reopen. As it was—since Xavier Manzo's trial,

161

since all the stories in the paper after Eddie was indicted—he felt that everywhere in the city all his life's mistakes had been put out in the street for people to look at and talk about: he'd raised a son who'd gotten involved with Eddie Crevine; he hadn't raised his other son, who had a different mother; he'd been going to the Holy Name meetings all these years, ushering at the church, taking communion, with that kind of sin on his soul. He left his storm door open at night now, for hours at a time, in snowstorms, because he was too old to remember. His daughter, who everybody saw every night on the TV, never visited. She went with other girls. "Your wife's here," he said, to move Gus onto another subject.

"My wife and Ben's wife, Ruthie. They made coffee and pastry. We were here when the sun came up. The lumber's all sorted. Ben and Frankie have the saw table all built. See?"

"I have the radial arm in my car."

"Who carried it?"

"Me."

"Yourself?" Gus reached out and squeezed Vito's upper arm with one hand. "Bob Murph and me we're just about done making a shed for the tools. I brought a padlock in case you didn't have one. The foundation looks good, but there's a little water inside still. We figure we can make it as far as lunchtime every day without any heart attacks. And we want a little time in the afternoon for our grandchildren."

"Good," Vito said quickly. But the word "grandchildren" had hit him like a little punch.

With Gus still going on and on at his elbow, he walked over to inspect the foundation. It was in the shape of an L, already waterproofed with tar, and backfilled. The inch or two of muddy water lying along the floor carried a small cargo of beer cans and sandwich wrappers, legacy of the concrete crew. Some things, at least, hadn't changed.

162

"She's level?"

"A quarter inch off in a couple places—we marked them."

"All right. Finish the coffee break quick, if you're workin then. I'm the saw man. You give me the measure for the sill—you and Bobby Murph. Pressure-treated that's gotta be."

"The green?"

Vito nodded. "It's a hard pine. The green is the chemicals they put in to keep out the bugs and the water."

"Who told you this?"

"I studied. Last week. Let Benny and Frankie cut the insulation for underneath."

"Insulation now they put?"

"And then make a mark for the holes the bolts go in. Then you check the level, and shim it up."

"Good, Boss. We'll bring you a coffee."

When he was done pissing, Julian Manzo made his way across the muddy lot and stood at the coffee urn that had been set up on a makeshift table of sawhorses and planks, and plugged in, with an extension cord, to the temporary power supply. Vito watched him accept a Styrofoam cup and a piece of pastry from Gus' wife, Eleonora, and stand there, not saying anything, eating and drinking with the patient concentration of a bear. After a time he saw Gus hand him a second coffee, say a few words, point. Julian set his cup down on the table and came walking over. He stopped in front of Vito and held out the cup in a hand the size of a first baseman's mitt. Vito's eyes were even with the pocket in his work shirt.

"I'm Julian, Vito."

Vito took the coffee and shook Julian's hand. "What can you do?"

"I can work, Vito."

"Alright. Can you use the circle saw?"

"If you show me. I can lift wood. I can dig. I can paint."

163

"The paint she comes later. Can you measure?"

"If you show me."

Vito studied his face a moment—a handsome, square face with dark hair and a fleshy cleft chin. There seemed to be a curtain between their eyes, Julian standing on the wrong side of it, trying to see through to the light. "Alright. You bring me the boards, then carry them back to Gus when I cut them. He'll show you the ones you bring, okay?"

"Alright, Vito."

"Right now, go over in my car and take out the big saw there, careful, and carry it over to that table and I'll show you how we set him up."

Dressed in housedresses and woolen sweaters, the two wives walked around the site picking up scraps of wood and litter and leaving them in a pile near the sidewalk. Their old men worked slowly, deliberately, checking and leveling the foundation, putting the last touches on the saw table and the outhouse-sized shed they'd already built for storing tools, gradually bringing order out of the weedy, stony square of ground that had been one of the last open lots in the city.

The saw table was itself a small monument to the carpenter's craft. Built at the height of Vito's belt, it consisted of two sixteen-foot two-by-tens to the left of where Julian set the deWalt saw, and two to the right, and a two-by-four frame, diagonally braced and nailed with double-headed staging nails so it could be easily taken apart at the end of the project.

Once the saw was in place—Julian had carried it like it was a lunchbox—Vito took his framing square from the toolbox and set the saw so it would make even cuts, ninety-degrees both ways. With his four-foot level, he checked the table. He took his chalk line and checked the straightness of the back board. Among them, the four old men had a hundred and seventy-five years of house-making in their hands. Ten million mistakes, he figured they'd made in those two centuries—bad cuts, bad measurements, misread plans, poorly-driven nails, Bennie Waxman's two missing fingers. Ten million lessons. You didn't have to tell them how to build a table for the big saw.

But, *bella Madonna*, they moved slow. In their dungarees, sweatshirts, and old muddy boots they hobbled across the soft backfilled dirt like a platoon of old warriors recruited from the veterans' hospital. Arthritis, prostate cancer, two back surgeries, diabetes, heart attacks—it seemed to him he could read his friends' medical histories in the way they walked. They didn't bend from the waist no more, but half-squatted like getting ready to go on a toilet, and then had a hard time standing up again. Their hands shook when they held the measuring tape; under the wool hats their heads were bald or gray or both. But, first thing, they'd sorted the framing lumber into piles, and Gus and Frankie Pallione were going around now with their hammers and knocking off the little chips of concrete that might set the sill a quarter inch off level. How many healthy twenty-five-year-old carpenters would think to do those things, would understand that any mistake now, any small unevenness, would echo through the whole structure, causing the plywood sheathing to fit together unevenly, the window frames and screens to buckle slightly, the Sheetrock ceilings—weeks or months or years down the road—to pop a nail or show a small white wave? There was, Vito supposed, one or two things to be said for getting old.

He wondered what they'd expect to be paid.

For the next hour he stood at the saw table, squaring and cutting the pressure-treated two-by-sixes that Julian Manzo carried over to him, and then starting in on the spruce two-by-twelves that would serve as the band joist. At ten o'clock, he called another break, so the old men could pee in the trees if they needed to. The women had the coffee urn set up again, pastries on paper plates. They were putting on jackets and rubbing their hands together against the chill. At this rate, Vito thought, they'd finish the house in five years, they'd all weigh three hundred pounds, and the plants around the edge of the yard would stay dead forever.

As he stood watching, blowing on his coffee to cool it, Eleonora Pallione, Gus' wife, came walking over to him with two biscotti balanced on a paper plate.

She set the plate down on the saw table, took hold of his elbow, and said: "Eat something while you have the time, with your coffee." He thanked her, dipped one of the biscotti into his coffee, and took a bite on the side where his teeth were still strong. "What are you thinking, Vittorio?" she said.

Vito looked at her, then back at the men. "Nobody in a long time asked me that."

"Well, give the person an answer then."

He looked more closely at her and could see, still, the muted glow of her youthful beauty, in spite of the two or three stiff gray hairs springing out above her upper lip, and the nests of wrinkles in which her blue eyes now sat. She'd been born in America, like Gus, and spoke, like him, without the mark of the Old Country on his voice. She'd made the Tuesday Novena with Lucy every week for thirty-five years, and when Lucy died, she stood in their kitchen and cooked for six hours instead of going to the funeral, so there would be food for the mourners who came back to the house afterwards. She'd raised four sons and two daughters who never had their names in the paper except when they got marry.

"I was thinkin about mistakes," he said to her. "How if you make one at the start, she's gonna be trouble for you all the way up. The house is gonna be done, painted, people livin in, and still you gonna see that mistake if you know how to look for."

He could see Julian Manzo carrying a sixteen-foot length of two-by-twelve over to him now, in one hand, like it was a piece of bamboo. After he'd taken a dozen steps, he stopped, turned, and walked back to Gus again, so Gus could repeat the measurement.

"Like a family," Eleonora suggested.

Vito looked at her, then away. A sadness came up like blood through his throat and face. To his great shame he felt a lens of water form between himself and the world.

Eleonora put a hand on his arm. "No one who knows anything believes what they see from the street, Vittorio, understand me?"

He nodded.

"I've been married to a carpenter fifty-six years. Six kids we had, starting when I was seventeen and Gus was eighteen. You know a house in the city that's made perfect, you know a marriage that has no mistakes in it, a family with no trouble, you tell me and I'll go over and take a picture and hang it in the bedroom next to the cross." She patted his arm. She was looking at him square and straight as a sister. "*Capisci?*" she said, with a small American accent.

Vito was about to answer her that it was one thing to understand it in your mind, and something very different to feel it, to live it; one thing to have the trouble inside your house and another thing to have it in the papers, when Julian Manzo came up, bumped him accidentally in the hip with the end of the board, and said: "Fifteen feet, ten inches and a half, Vito. Gus says to minus it one cunt hair."

For the rest of the morning his time was split between the saw table and the foundation. As sometimes happened, the smells that surrounded him—fresh sawdust, the breathing lumber, the metal and oil smell of a box of new nails—seemed to reach his brain like a big ship carrying a cargo of memory: for moments at a time he almost forgot that he was old and retired, forgot his family troubles, forgot about Eddie Crevine. He was just a carpenter again. He was doing the work he'd been born to do, the work that had earned him his very small portion of renown in this small place. He was out in the air again—a damp, raw, wonderful air—like a living creature, instead of slowly shrinking inside his clothes, in a dry, dead house with the TV going and the phone ready to ring.

Julian brought him the two-by-twelves that would support the house's first floor, and smoothly, effortlessly, as if he hadn't been away from the work for a weekend, Vito squared one end, let Julian flip it end-to-end so the square cut was at the far end of the table to his left, measured from the square cut, marked his V, lined up the edge of the blade against the mark, pushed the blade back an inch away from the board, squeezed the trigger and, holding the board down firmly with his left hand, drew the spinning saw through with his right. When enough two-by-twelves were cut to give the boys work for a while, he left his post and walked once around the foundation, eyeing the way the box joist sat on the sill, the way it was nailed at the corners. There was no advice to give. Except for the occasional calling out of a number, the men had no need to speak to each other but seemed, instead, to be listening with one ear to the whispered grammar of a language they'd memorized decades ago, his language too, perfectly without accent. If a joist was slightly crowned they knew it merely by eyeing it once along its length, and they marked the edge with three Xs, and set it into place crown-up, so that the weight of the house would gradually straighten it. They didn't drive nails into knots. They didn't split the joists at their ends because they knew enough to turn the head of the nail sideways and smack it once with the hammer, denting the grain of the wood first. They swung their hammers not with their hands and wrists but with their whole bodies, driving in the three-and-a-half-inch sixteen-penny nails with two rhythmic bangs and a final tap. Bob Murph whistled Sinatra through his teeth, Gus talked constantly under his breath, Benny Waxman and Paul Pallione would work silently for half an hour before starting in on each other.

"Butt that joist in there tight, you Jew bastard," Vito heard on one of his passes.

"Who you saying has a tight butt?"

"Not you. You gained there over the years."

"You wish you'd gained, you got a tusch like the two elbows of a chicken. I thought you Italians ate."

"We eat, you wish you ate like we eat. Is it in there tight, can I nail?"

"It's in there alright."

"You wish you were in there."

"Later I'll be in there. You'll be home, eating."

"You wish you could eat like I eat."

"I ate not so bad in my day."

"Sure, I bet. In your dreams."

"And some dreams I had not so bad, too."

"Nail it then, if she's butted in good."

Since Vito seemed disinclined to do so, the women called another break at a quarter to eleven, and stood with their husbands sipping coffee, then cleaned up the cups, plates, and pastry scraps and went off in one car. The men worked until the noon whistle sounded at the fire station, then packed up their tools and stood looking at what they had managed in a senior citizens' morning—a neat grid of two-by-twelves on edge over the foundation hole, each board set precisely sixteen inches on center. The smell of mud, the fingerprints in nail-oil ink on pale pieces of spruce, the beautiful saffron symmetry of it against the spring day.

Gus took off his tool apron and held the two ends of the belt in his left hand, dangling against his leg. "If we did this part right, Boss, the house will sit solid for four hundred years."

"You did it right."

"Tomorrow we lay the deck. Then watch how fast she goes."

Other than to repeat numbers and call out Vito's name, Julian Manzo hadn't spoken a word all morning, but now the camaraderie and satisfaction of the moment seemed to inspire him. "I didn't know you built the deck first on a house," he said.

Ben Waxman turned his head sideways and looked up at him. The others stared straight ahead. "'Deck'", in this case, means the plywood we're gonna put down over the joists," Ben said. "Subfloor" is another name for it. It goes under the floor you walk on when the house is finished. It's different than the kind of deck you sit out on drinking a beer on a summer night."

"Oh."

"It's carpenter talk. You'll catch on after a while."

"I'll catch on."

"These other guys here ain't exactly geniuses, you know."

"I know."

"Now you're catching on."

They hung their aprons on nails in the makeshift tool shed, promised to return early the next morning, and drove off to their lunches and their naps.

Vito had brought a tunafish sandwich and an apple in a paper bag. Like the old days. Julian had two cold-cut sub sandwiches the size of small torpedoes. They laid a sheet of plywood over one corner of the two-by-twelve grid, tacked it down, and sat facing the weak April sun.

"My brother is Xavier, you know," Julian said. "We have Manzo, the same last name, but our mothers aren't the same."

Vito said that he knew.

"In Italy, Manzo means "beef"".

Vito said he knew that as well, and they poured from their separate thermoses and stared out at the street. A white Ford van went slowly past, the driver—a woman with blond blond hair—glanced at them, then made the corner and disappeared. Vito wondered where Gus had left the padlock to the little tool shed. He could hear young children singing the alphabet in the next yard over. His fingers were already sore.

"Xavier has the bad blood. From the other mother."

Vito turned and examined the blank, open face, the wide mouth and curtained eyes and the nose that looked like it had been broken once from either side and had decided to squat in neutral ground.

"He has the bad seed," Julian went on.

"Maybe the jail will straighten him out."

"The devil has him in his hand."

"It's hard to know sometimes who the devil has and who he doesn't have."

"He's not afraid of God," Julian persisted.

It sounded to Vito as if he was repeating phrases he'd been hearing all his life, simple explanations for things that could never be explained.

"He's not afraid of anyone. He used to live with us when we were little. He used to put out cigarettes on my arm." Julian rolled up his left sleeve and turned over his bare forearm, wide as the bottom of a quart bottle. The pale flesh there was freckled with two dozen shiny pink scars, the size of peas.

"God will take care of him someday. God will fix him up."

"When Vito?"

"After he dies."

"Why doesn't God fix him up now?"

"Nobody knows why. You can't ask."

The white van passed by the site again, just as slowly, going the opposite way. Vito turned his head left, to watch it go, and saw there, walking onto the damp dirt at the edge of the lot, Alfonse's wife's girl, the one who painted pictures and wanted to go to Italy, whose name he couldn't remember now. She was dressed in dungarees and work boots and a heavy brown sweater. It made him a surprise how happy he was to see her.

Thirty Two

It was probably the easiest job she ever had, Janine thought, easier than taking her clothes off in front of a hundred horny creeps or turning tricks in the back room at the club, though she was too old for that now in any case probably. Girls got booed sometimes once they had a little fat or, God forbid, some cellulite or stretch marks or something, because what the creeps—and they weren't all of them creeps—wanted was some perfect picture in their mind they could go home and jerk off to, or pretend they were with instead of their wife underneath them. It made them feel young and, even though it was almost impossible to believe grown men could be so stupid, if the girl looked at them with no clothes on it made them think they were super-hot and all the girl wanted, really, all she thought about when she went back to the changing room, was getting together with the creep who didn't ever smile and glued his eyes to your pussy and had a dollar bill in his hand. Right. But hey, it made the world go round and babies be born and it let people like her have a nice car when she was in her twenties and get high as much as she wanted without worrying about it.

She still had the same car now and it wasn't so nice, and she wasn't in her twenties or even her thirties anymore practically and getting high had almost turned into the kind of thing that was about as fun as brushing your hair, and this job, for a girl like her, wasn't by a long shot the worst thing you could do to get the necessary cash. For a few hours in the morning and at night she drove different color vans around the streets of Revere, going by the old guy's house and seeing if there was any activity there, and then stopping at different pay phones and dialing the number and waiting five seconds before she hung up. She was up most of the night anyway, it didn't matter, and she liked to drive, and she could still be back when Chrissy got home from school, and as Johnny told her there was nothing illegal in it so even if she got caught, which wasn't too likely, there wasn't anything they could do. Let them try squeezing her to tell who paid for it. Like she was stupid enough to say, "Johnny Crevine pays. He told me to drive by the old guy's house on Proctor Avenue and see if anybody was showing up there who didn't live there, and then dial the number from a pay phone a couple of times in the day and night, whenever I wanted to basically, and wait a few seconds and hang up."

Right. That was gonna happen. Next thing after that Johnny himself would get in the other front seat of the van at a stoplight, or he'd call you over to the plumbing shop in Melrose and he'd have a pipe in his hand and after a little while you'd have no face.

They were nicer than people said though, Johnny and his old man. Look, they were giving her a job, weren't they, knowing she needed it for her little habit and to pay for food for her kid and gas for her car and so on. Lots of guys wouldn't do that for a retired dancer from the club, the kind of girl who most of the time would fade away without anybody noticing, take her money one day and go out to Reno and try to make it in one of the whorehouses, or start making jerk-off phone calls from home, or shack up with somebody and sell milk and smokes at the convenient store, or just die. But the Crevine family was taking care of her pretty good and every couple of days she'd drive over to the plumbing shop just before it closed and if Johnny needed a BJ she'd give him one and she'd give him the report on the old guy and get her cash.

The old guy was building a house now with a bunch of other old guys and it was really the first time she'd been able to really see him other than just walking around or shoveling snow or taking the car to church or the cemetery and she had just the smallest little nick of bad feeling. But if there was one thing she knew about Eddie and his son it was that they didn't just randomly pick on somebody if the person didn't do something to piss them off. In this case the guy's son was a rat, everybody on the street knew about that, and Eddie had to go away and hide because of it, and the cops and the feds were all over Johnny because of it, probably videoing the BJs and everything else. So it wasn't anything wrong she was doing just checking on the old guy and waking him up once in a while, nothing too wrong really.

And she couldn't think about that now, anyway, because she had a living to make.

Thirty Three

She saw Vito before he saw her. He was sitting on the edge of the foundation with his back very straight and his hands resting, fingers spread, on the tops of his thighs. He was wearing a black wool hat over the bald top of his head, jeans, workboots, and a brown wool sweater, and he looked so much like an old Italian Buddha there that she had a sudden urge to paint a portrait of him, in those clothes, in that place, in thick oils on a large canvas. Sitting next to Vito was a huge guy about her own age, finishing the last bite of a sandwich. Neat piles of lumber stood here and there, some of them half-covered with plastic sheets the color of a clear sky just before dark. The yard was muddy and torn up, but she could see how nice it would someday be—with the buffer of tall bushes and trees between it and the pretty big houses to either side, and the view of a shallow, busy valley to the north. Maybe, after all her mother's suffering, this would be her reward: a good man, a new house, a kind father-in-law. And maybe, after all her own suffering—the nightmare beginning to life, the death of her father, the long illness, the things her first American boyfriend had done to her—things she had never told a soul, maybe, after all that, there would be some peace for her now, too.

When Vito saw her he stood up and came towards her across the mud. The big man followed as if connected by a string.

"I'm Estelle. Do you remember me?"

"Sure I remember, Miss."

He came and stood close to her and seemed not to know what to do next, so she hugged him, tight, kissed his cheek, and stepped back. "Don't be embarrassed. I kissed you good-bye at your house, remember?"

"I'm not embarrass, Miss. But I'm sawdust all over me. All morning we been working. Look."

There was sawdust on the front of his sweater. She looked down and saw that the embrace had transferred a hundred yellow crumbs of it to her sweatshirt. For some reason the sight pleased her. When she looked up again the younger man was standing at Vito's side, a few inches behind, staring down at her as if he'd grown up in a nation without women. She stuck out her hand. "Estelle."

"My name is Julian," he said, "Manzo," and it felt as if his hand wrapped all the way around hers and then overlapped itself. "I have the same last name as Xavier. He's my brother, partly. He's in jail. Walpole. He has the bad seed but I don't."

"Okay," she said. "I'm glad."

"Even from when he was little the devil had him in his hand. But not me."

"Excellent," Estelle said.

He blinked, once, but the eyes didn't move from her face.

"They had to lock him up inside the jail to keep him from hurting people."

"I've known guys like that."

"You did?"

"Sure. I can see right away you're not like them."

"You can?"

"Sure. It's a good thing, too, because you're about the strongest guy I've ever seen."

"I am?"

"I bet you're a big help to Vito, I can see it."

"Vito's the boss on this job. We're gonna put up the deck now and sit out on it on chairs on a summer night with the carpenters talking and having beers, except some of them aren't so smart."

"Excellent. I came to ask Vito if I could help, too."

"You did?" Julian turned his eyes away from her at last, and attached them, with the same dull intensity, to Vito.

Vito took hold of his elbow in one hand. "Lunch is over now," he said. "You see that stack of the plywood next to the saw table? Go take two more of them, one at the time, and put them flat on the boards we made this morning, just like that other one. Watch out you don't fall in. You know how to lift them?"

"Like the other one, Vito, on my shoulder and my arm, sideways."

"Okay, go head."

Julian turned his wide back to them and marched off. Before Vito could say anything to her, Estelle took hold of his right forearm with both hands and squeezed it as hard as she could. It was not an old man's arm. "See," she said. "I'm pretty strong for somebody my size. I'll work for free. I don't think it's right that I should have to be a guy to learn carpentry because I'm going to have a house someday, with a painting studio in it, and what if—"

Vito held up his free hand and stopped her. "Alright, Miss."

"Estelle."

"Alright, you're hired on the job."

"I am?"

"Every day when you don't have the college I want you to come right after lunch like today."

"You do? At your house you seemed like you'd never let me. What happened?"

"He happened," Vito said. Just as he turned to indicate Julian, there was a clatter and crash at the foundation. Instead of carrying one sheet of plywood at a time, Julian had carried two, and instead of setting them down flat on the grid of two-by-twelves, he'd shrugged them off his shoulder, and since he'd been carrying them at an angle, with one hand cupped outward at his hip and the wood leaning against his shoulder, and since he'd climbed up onto the place where he and Vito had been eating lunch, the wood went edge-first, both pieces, straight down between the parallel two-by-twelves, fell eight feet, and crashed into the damp basement. Julian gazed down at them a moment as if puzzling out the mystery of gravity, and then turned his large head over his shoulder to see what the boss made of it. His eyes shifted to Estelle, and then back to Vito. "Is there gonna be a deck in the cellar, Boss?"

Vito shook his head, no.

Estelle kept a straight face, and then, when Julian started back for more plywood, she said, so only Vito could hear, "Who is this Xavier person anyway?"

Thirty Four

There was a fifteen-foot chain-link fence with a double strand of razor wire on top, a dry moat beyond it edged with ridges of old snow, then a twenty-foot concrete wall with glassed-in guard towers set at the yard's four corners. From the street, except for an occasional figure moving about in the guard towers, it appeared to be a place devoid of human presence, as if only the idea of evil were imprisoned there—bad air, bad thoughts—or as if the people in the surrounding neighborhood had somehow managed to collect all their own dark impulses and deposit them inside this horrifying structure, out of the public eye.

Joanna went through the door of the Main Administration Building, and felt as though she'd stepped straight from a drizzly April morning in Massachusetts into an outer circle of hell. Hell, in this case, consisted of dull linoleum and uniformed men and one woman standing in front of locked metal doors.

She signed in, filled out a form asserting she had no criminal history, put her personal items into a small metal locker, submitted herself to a body search—mechanical, official, nothing like the touch of China Louis—then had her hand stamped with ink that could be read only under ultra violet light. She passed through a ten-foot-square steel door, then a series of checkpoints like a ship passing through locks in a canal, each slow stage dropping her another foot or two nearer to the bottom of the malarial jungle. At one point she was in something

180

called "the man trap", a terrifying steel box with a machine-gun-toting guard above her, watching. Then she crossed a small distance through the open air and through a gate in a razor-wire-topped fence and into a stone corridor. The walls seemed to send her own sweaty-palmed fear echoing back against her. An armed guard waited for her at another door, which slid open left to right and admitted them into a visiting room. There were vending machines, rows of folding chairs and some family visits going on, and another guard sitting at a desk raised at head-height above the floor. She handed him her pass. He checked her name and I.D. and spoke into a walkie-talkie to call the prisoner. Beyond the chairs, beneath the awful fluorescent lights, there was a floor-to-ceiling barrier—brick and glass—that separated the family visits—face to face, no touching—from visitors there to speak with criminals who were thought to be a threat. There were guards on both sides, a cigarette butt in the corner. Six chairs, set eight feet apart, faced six sheets of inch-thick glass with six holes in them the size of the top of a coffee mug, covered in a thin, strong mesh. At the nearest place, a woman sat balancing a squirming two-year-old on her lap and conversing in what sounded like Portuguese with a slight, mustachioed man who seemed to Joanna like he could not possibly have broken any law of any kind, ever.

The guard indicated the farthest chair. Joanna passed at a discreet distance behind the woman and child, crossed the room, and sat facing the glass. A moment later a door opened on the other side and a figure stepped out of her nightmares and into the guarded room beyond the glass. Xavier Manzo was not handcuffed or shackled, and he was wearing khakis and a pale orange shirt. From the instant he passed through the door he locked his eyes onto her face and held them there. The guard led him to the chair and he sat with his hands in his lap, leaning slightly forward, sending thin beams of hatred through

181

the glass. Joanna had to take a breath before she was able to deliver the speech she'd rehearsed.

"Listen," she said through the screened circle. "I know you hate me. I know you would hurt me or kill me if you thought you could get away with it. I don't particularly want to see you back out on the street, but you're eventually going to get out anyway, and I don't think you'd come after me or my family because they'd send you right back in again. I came here with a straightforward proposal."

She paused. Xavier seemed not to blink or breathe. Every few seconds he shifted his clasped hands to the right or left between his knees, and when he did so the enormous muscles of his upper arms and shoulders jumped beneath the fabric of his prison shirt. Twice, he snorted, as if suffering from a cold. If it hadn't been for the dull malice, Joanna thought, he might almost have been handsome.

"I'm going to be perfectly honest with you. The most important thing in the world for me now is to see Eddie Crevine caught and put in prison for the rest of his life. If you give me any information about where he might have gone, and if it leads to his arrest, I'll do everything I can to see that you get into an early-release program. I have connections in the prison system, I can pull a few strings."

She paused again, struggled to keep her eyes on his eyes. She glanced away, then back. Xavier snorted, stared, worked his closed lips in a way that made her believe he might be getting ready to say something. But he did not.

"I'm not going to come driving out here a second time."

Still nothing.

"Fine. I should tell you, though, that I paid a visit to China Louis not long ago. It was his idea that I come and talk to you, and do you know why? He said that of all the people Eddie would be furious at, you'd be on top of the list. You screwed up, after all. If you'd checked my brother that night the way you were supposed to, the way you were paid to, the way Eddie counted on you to do, then Eddie wouldn't be in hiding now. You're keeping silent to protect him. Do you think he's as interested in protecting you?"

This information seemed to register in the muscles of Xavier's face. The lips worked, he snorted again. With his eyes still fixed on her he leaned closer to the screened opening in the posture of someone ready to divulge a secret. Joanna leaned in too. The air around him seemed to vibrate with an invisible violence, as if the molecules themselves were racing and shivering in a desperate attempt escape his reach. The thick glass between them seemed suddenly as flimsy as cellophane. She leaned her face in close, into the fear. Xavier parted his lips slightly, showing the tip of his tongue, and with great force spat a heavy mouthful of mucous that slapped against the screened opening and reached the skin of her face in a few drops of sticky spray.

Thirty Five

Late afternoon and, if Eddie had the map figured right, he was just now in North Carolina. There was a bitter taste in his teeth. The mood had started last night in the motel, because he was feeling a little bit horny. Not horny like the old days when you had a fire going inside you and you couldn't think straight about anything else. This was a sixty-year-old's horniness. This was a little warm buzzy feeling down below, the difference between a house on fire and a cigarette lighter. This was where Alicia could have come in handy, because Alicia had never said no to him in her life, not once, even when she was nine months pregnant, even after they'd had a fight. It was part of the deal: she cooked, she fucked; he paid for the clothes and manicures and hairdos and cars.

It wasn't like he missed her, not really. It wasn't even exactly like he wished he hadn't done what he did—though from time to time now, maybe every ten minutes, he caught himself looking over at the passenger seat because he thought he heard her voice, or saw her leg move, or her arm with all the bracelets reach over and turn the radio dial; and from time to time, less often, he wondered what he was going to say when Jimmy asked where she was. He'd called Jimmy's office today, this morning, pay phone, too quick to trace, and told the secretary the code words, then hung up. No problem. If the kid asked about Alicia when he saw him, Eddie would say, "She's home, cleaning the kitchen floor." Or maybe, "She's in heaven with

184

your mother . . . She went to the big hairdresser's in the sky" Or, "She's givin blood." There were a lot of good answers.

It wasn't that. It was more like a feeling he used to have sometimes when he was at the plumbing shop, in a back room that was scoured every morning for wires and bugs, talking for half the day to Johnny Cut and his own Johnny and two or three of the guys. It was something he could never tell anybody: he didn't like being in a world with just men. Pain in the fucking ass that women could be, when they weren't around everything was a bad smell and hairy faces. Like jail. After a while it got to you. He'd been that way since about ninth grade, because he remembered telling his old man about it one day, and remembered the way his old man had laughed at him, and told his uncle, and the two of them had taken him to a house in the South End and let him get laid the first time and afterwards his uncle said, "You liked it, right? Good. This is how we keep you from going queer."

So he'd done the same thing with his own son, Jimmy, eleventh grade, when the kid started to seem a little . . . fluffy. That had turned out real good.

"Jimmy's a sweetheart," he thought he heard Alicia say.

And he opened up the window and spit into the air and said, "Exactly," and speeded up the car.

Probably this was partly why he'd started the Leopard Club, so there would always be a place that wasn't just men. Johnny Cut said he didn't like the idea of starting a club when he first came up with it, but the guys over him—Pags, Shirlen, Raymond, Angelo—helped him with it from the start, and even though they took their piece of the profits, there was still tons left over, and, later, it was a place you could do other business from, selling this and that, a place to keep your employees happy. Xavier, Billy Ollanno—guys like that practically wanted to live there full-time.

He missed it now. Bad days he could always go down to the Club and even if all he did was take a peek at the stage as he walked through, even just sitting in his office and listening to the beat from the music, it had a kind of comfort in it for him. Like a drink for another guy. A cigar. Most of the girls would do anything he asked them, and some were on the stuff, that was the reason, and some even weren't. It was the way he'd started doing more business with China Louis, because Louis knew where to get the girls, white and black and Chinese all of them, and how to keep them supplied, and told him how much money was involved in that part of it, and how easy it was, not much risk. He never even talked to the street dealers, or even the guys who sold to the street dealers. There were layers of protection between him and the stuff itself.

"And look how that worked out," Alicia said, so Eddie slammed his arm hard against the passenger seat, as if she was really there.

He drove on. He was thinking about that now, the nice life he used to have, and how one little stuttering bullshit artist had come along and ruined the whole thing, single-handed. Not that he could forgive Xavier either. He couldn't. But Xavier was in Walpole now, paying for his stupid mistakes, and he'd always known Xavier had a brain like a fucking potato anyway, and so it was his own fault, really: he should have kept some levels between the little prick and himself, he should never have met in person with the stuttering shithead Imbesalacqua, and he wouldn't have, either, except that the kid's sister had gotten involved with her series on so-called "organized crime", then the old man came to his house, and somehow he wanted to see in person the little shit-weed they were all so worried about. Who would've guessed the shit-weed had the balls to wear a wire? Who would've guessed Xavier would miss it? One stupid little mistake and lookit the price he was paying. It turned his mood bad.

But then, like another sign from God, as he was going up the highway, careful now, he saw way way up on like a telephone pole one nice word:

TOPLESS

How could you not take the exit? Another little side-highway with malls and stores and places to eat all along it. He drove right past the club, checking it out, then made a U-turn in a mall parking lot and drove back and parked between two trucks. After thinking about it for a minute, he left the gun in the car, under the seat. Risky, sure, but what were the chances he'd need it in there? What, a cop was going to be next to him at the bar and recognize him? And if they had a detector the gun would attract attention.

He got out and walked toward the door and even from ten feet away he felt at home. Just the sound of the bass made him feel at home, then just the lights inside, then just the bouncer—always wearing black, always with a nice looking girl standing next to him so you got two messages: come in; don't cause trouble. He knew the rules in a place like this the same as he knew his own real name.

A two-dollar cover. He almost laughed, then peeled it off the roll in his pocket and gave the girl a five besides. Inside, the place was shabby, old crap on the walls, mirrors, a bar at one end and a stage at the other. Just now getting off the stage was a girl who looked like she was fifteen. Not his thing, young, but she was cute enough, pulling her black stockings back on after the end of her act. He looked closer and saw that she had one regular arm and one that ended halfway between her wrist and elbow. No hand. It would work out good then, because he was always called Eddie Three-Hands. He had an extra.

It made him interested. She looked at him and smiled and he smiled back and walked to the bar and ordered a beer and when the bartender, older broad, said "Four ninety-five," he almost laughed again and gave her a twenty and told her to keep it.

She made a little signal to the girl who was getting off. Eddie knew how it went. The signal meant: Money in town, go to work. The girl came right over like he knew she would and he told her she looked beautiful, and she smiled, and he told her to order what she wanted and she nodded at the bartender and got cranberry juice and ginger ale and it was eight bucks and Eddie could have cared less if it was eighty. The girl—she looked a little older now, college kid—stood close against his knee, rubbing herself there a little bit, and they started talking.

"Florida," he said, when she asked where he was from. "Miami Beach."

"I want to go there some day. Like, so bad."

"I'd take ya, but your boyfriend would get pissed."

"Who said anything about a boyfriend?"

"Here," Eddie said. He peeled a hundred dollar bill off his roll and tucked it into the top of her shirt.

"What's this for? We don't do lap dances."

"For I missed your dance, that's all. Stay and talk to me. What happened to your hand?"

The smile disappeared. Wrong question. "I don't talk about that," she said.

"Yeah, lots of things I don't talk about, too. That's smart. You look smarter than the other girls here."

"You're a college professor?"

"Plumbing company," he said, stupidly. And then, "Real estate, too. Mostly real estate now. Big stuff."

"Can I sit on your lap?"

Like he would say no. She sat more or less on his lap, mostly on his leg. She asked him about real estate and he made shit up: that he'd sold a house to Sinatra when he was alive. That he'd gotten to know all the stars in Florida."

"Chaka Khan?"

"Sure. Sold him a huge house last year."

She laughed like he was making a joke.

"You're from here?" he asked. She was wiggling around on his leg. It made him think of Alicia.

"Georgia."

"Nice there, ain't it?"

"Nicer than here."

"Why'd you move?"

"Aren't we Mister Question today," she said, squirming. She'd drained the drink and asked if he'd buy her another one. Why wouldn't he?

"No laps, huh?"

She shook her head, smiling a little devil's smile.

"No back room or nothing?"

Another shake of the head. She leaned in. He could see the little freckles above her cleavages, where he'd put the money. He took out another hundred and squeezed it in there.

"I like a generous man."

"Well I like a generous girl. No place we can go?"

"I'm done for the day."

"Pick the best hotel around," he said. "The president's suite. Jacuzzi. Whatever you want."

"Whatever?'

"Anything that costs less than a car," he said. It was an old line that had used to work.

She raised her eyebrows and took the bill and folded it up tight and slipped it someplace into the top of her panties. "Five minutes," she said, and he watched the stump of her skinny arm swinging as she walked away. A nice skinny little ass, too.

He sipped his beer and waited, feeling young. On the stage a bigger, older, blonder dancer was moving like she was on

Klonopins, like she was rolling around with her legs up in the air getting away from a very old mouse. His eyes moved left and he saw that the bouncer was staring at him in a way he didn't like. He stared back a minute then looked away, sipped his beer. He'd kill the fucking guy. Watered down beer. So the joke was on him, for four ninety-five. So he'd left the gun in the car. Alicia said: Real smart.

He waited, nervous now, not at home after all. Everybody talked funny. The bartender woman was looking at him like he was drinking too slow. He flicked his eyes up into the mirror and saw that the bouncer was watching him and pretending not to. A feeling went over the skin of his arms and neck. The gun was in the car. The five minutes had went by a long time ago. He finished the beer, put a ten dollar tip on the bar.

"Another one?"

"I'm good."

Another minute he waited. Nothing. The bar was getting crowded, the woman was sending him little looks. The bouncer wasn't at the front door anymore. He decided he'd count to a hundred and watch the back entrance with the curtain over it and if the little one-handed cunt didn't come, he was gone. He made it only as far as fifty, hands sweating now, and stood up. He watched for another few seconds, still hoping, but then he had it figured out and he walked to the entrance in a way no one with a brain was going to try to stop and he hit the parking lot and kept going at a steady pace, calm-like, had a little trouble opening the car door and then put the gun right on the seat beside him, and backed out careful as could be, like the ninety-year-olds you saw on Collins Avenue. What you didn't want now was an accident. He looked at the door once and saw the bouncer's face, just quick. The little one-arm must have recognized him close up like that, seen the fake hair color, seen the work on his nose, went into the back room with dreams of the half-million dollar reward. Smart, Eddie, he heard Alicia say again. Nice going.

This, he thought, driving out of the lot and into the street and heading back to the highway with one eye in the mirror, this is why you kill them.

Thirty Six

The sun was out, finally, and James arrived at the office in an upbeat mood. Yes, it was the beginning of April, which meant he was working seven days a week from nine in the morning until ten or eleven at night. But, even with the late filers, all that would be over soon, a month at the very most, and it meant a lot of money coming in, and Sean was very understanding about it. They were both healthy—which was more than they could say for a number of their friends—both very much in love. They had tickets for a Caribbean cruise, leaving May 1. Life was good.

Coffee in one hand, bulging briefcase in the other, he stepped through his office door and was greeted by the smiling face of a woman who had to be the best executive assistant in all New England. Grace's desk was a study in neatness. She arrived an hour early in filing season, always in good spirits. Single, early fifties, unfailingly professional with clients, warm as a sister with Sean, utterly loyal to him—she was more partner than secretary and he made a mental note to give her some kind of gift or bonus before heading off on vacation.

"Long day ahead of us, Boss," she said. "More coffee brewing and I stopped at Whole Foods for chocolate croissants. I figured we'd need some fortification for the battle."

"You're an angel, Gracie."

She smiled, blushed. It seemed to be what she lived for—a little praise now and again, the sense of pleasing someone.

Lucky, lucky, lucky, he thought, going into the inner office. He settled himself behind the desk, the humming computer screen, coffee safely off to one side, six different client folders in a line on the side table. He opened the first one and set to work, and, except for coffee and a brief snack, didn't look up for several hours. It was late morning when he heard the phone ring in the outer office and then, not five seconds later, saw Grace take hold of the door jamb and lean her head and shoulders into view the way she always did. But something wasn't right. In place of the usual smile—dancing blue eyes, braces at her advanced age—her lips were flexed in a way that made dimples form on her cheeks. Her eyebrows were pinched in.

"Everything okay?"

"Just had a weird call. I said "Crellin Accounting" the way I always do and a man with a very rough voice said something odd and immediately hung up."

"A crank," James said. "Don't let it upset you."

"I know. *Very* odd, though. He said, "Tell Jimmy Philly cheese steak. Day after tomorrow." And then he yelled, "Tell him! Now!" in a nasty way and slammed down the phone."

When Gracie returned to her desk James stood up and went to the window. There was a view of Sudbury's meager downtown—pharmacy, bank, Congregational church—everything white and neat with Volvos parked in front of the cafe and a pair of new moms with fur-lined jackets, walking their children in strollers. His office was on the third floor. He had a sudden urge to open the window and dive out. He had an image of himself landing on the sidewalk, head-first, his neck snapping, everything going black. Sean weeping, Gracie in shock, the newspapers spilling everything he'd worked so hard to hide all these years, clients and anonymous readers alike marveling at the place James Crellin had come from and the place he'd ended up.

This was so perfectly like his father that he wanted to smash a fist through the glass. He could see the man everyone else called Chelsea Eddie and he called Dad, sitting across from him in his favorite restaurant on Newbury Street, chewing his steak with a vengeance and saying, "Only one thing I'm ever gonna ask from you and I probably won't ever need to." One thing. Right. And at exactly the worst possible moment. A lineup of work on his desk. More work on Gracie's desk—she was doing the prep for another four clients. A meeting this afternoon. He'd be here until nine or ten or eleven and now he was going to lose at least a precious hour and a half on some kind of ridiculous child's game. Philly Cheese Steak!

Except that he knew, by some instinct, that it wasn't a game. His father had been gone seven months. In all that time he hadn't once called or contacted him, and now—Philly Cheese Steak! The big, secret code! Yay!

It disgusted him. It made him want to drive to the airport and fly to the Bahamas and go into hiding himself. A giant filthy wave seemed to have broken over the building, over his life, crashing through the neat levees he'd built, flooding his brain, knocking down the little house of happiness he'd worked so hard to create—the career, the relationship. He was a Revere kid, son of a big Mafia boss, with a bully for an older brother and an erotic reaction to other men's bodies that made him a pariah in this society, made him do constant battle with the voice of shame, made him hide things, tell little lies, pretend. And in the face of that, brick by brick, board by board, he'd built a clean life—education, work, love, treating other people well. And all the time, every minute of that time, in the deepest recesses of his thoughts he knew his father could call him like this one day and put everything in jeopardy, and he knew there was nothing he could do about it. What were the options? Go to the police and say, "My father's Eddie Crevine, and I know

he's in hiding and I know he's done bad things, but I'm innocent, really, and he just called me and asked me to do him a favor that I believe might be illegal and I wanted to let you know?
Go see his brother and ask him to use the secure line he was
never allowed to use, so he could call Alicia and whine and beg?
It was wreckage, all of it. With the exception of Sean and
Gracie—neither of whom he had ever let his father meet—all
the primary relationships in his life were wrecked, and his father was the cause of it all, and now he was being asked to help
the man out and risk going to jail himself. Or go to the police
and turn him in and probably be kidnapped and tortured and
shot.

He hesitated. He stared out the window, tried to rope in his
thoughts. Two hours wasn't the end of the world. His father
had promised it wouldn't put him in danger, but it was aiding a
fugitive, he knew that much. It was a crime, and if he got
caught the business would evaporate, he'd go to court, to jail.
He turned around at looked at the telephone. If he called the
FBI he was almost certain his brother would find out—hell, the
FBI would probably be the ones to pass on the news to him . . .
He took a deep breath and went into the outer office. He told
Gracie he'd forgotten something at home and he'd be back.

"Want me to go and fetch it?"

"No, it requires a small search, and Sean's not feeling well.
I'll be back in half an hour. Hold the fort."

She promised she would do that.

Like a robot, like a man walking in a dream, he went to his
car and started it and backed out of his parking space and
headed into downtown Boston. He did not turn on the radio.
He did not look right or left. It was a kind of spell, a hypnosis,
almost as if his father's fingers were wrapped around his throat.
He did what his brother Johnny told him he should do if the
code ever came. He wanted to call the plumbing shop now, but

calling there for something like this would be absolutely taboo. Johnny had repeated it to him every month since their father's disappearance, like a regular present, like brainwashing: The Turnpike, the Allston exit, the parking garage in Harvard Square. The numbered space, 565, on the top floor. He parked there and got out and locked his car—all according to the memorized instructions, and he'd taken exactly one step toward the elevator when he was grabbed from behind and shoved into the open door of a van and pushed down onto the floor there. Someone heavy on top of him. His face was pressed into the gritty carpet of the back seat. His chest hurt, his arms were pinned at his hips. "Go!" he heard the heavy someone say. Man's voice.

"Off me, off me," he was grunting, but the man on top of him was a hundred pounds heavier, a thousand times stronger. The van had started to move. He assumed he was being arrested. It had all been a trick, all of it. Or the cops had wired the plumbing shop or his house or Johnny's house and heard Johnny giving him the instructions, testing him on it like some spy about to be sent behind enemy lines. The parking garage. Harvard Square. 565. His ribs hurt, he was babbling—"My lawyer, you'll see . . . Wrong person . . . Nothing wrong." Whatever came to his mind just bubbled out in a stream of fear.

He felt the van turning, this way, that way, a pause at the exit. "Get off me," he said, but it came out in a pleading, warbling voice, a little boy's voice that commanded no response.

The man lay still on top of him for ten minutes, twenty minutes. A sharp pain in his ribs, the filthy carpet, the sickening sense that his life had just been ripped out of his hands. "95 South," he heard the man tell the driver. So they were taking him directly to Walpole State Prison, a walled-in hell on earth. They were going to lock him in a cell with Xavier Manzo or Johnny Denok, or some other animal. They were going to force him to talk.

"I don't know anything," he said, his lips against the carpet.

No response.

Another ten minutes and he felt the body above him shift, and then the weight slowly lift off him. "You can get up. Sorry."

James spit the dirt away from his lips, tried to push himself up and couldn't. A hand reached down and pulled him, in a polite way, and he settled himself in the seat and tried to clean himself off, and looked. A face he didn't know. Unshaven. Late thirties, he guessed. Black hair in bangs, one wandering eye. In front of him in the driver's seat, a black man with a gold loop in his right ear. They did not look anything like policemen.

"I don't know anything," he said.

"You got that right," the man beside him said.

"You're arresting me?"

A terrible laugh.

"Not likely. We work for your dad, kind of. You're going to Philadelphia, that's all we know. We have an address, and we have Philadelphia. That's it. Sorry, but it's not like we coulda stood around in the garage, talking."

"You're not the police?"

Another mean laugh.

"Look, it's April 9th. I have twenty clients who need to—"

The man looked out the opposite side window.

"I can't go, don't you see?"

"What the fuck?" the man said, exasperated, turning back. "Are you really Eddie's kid? Are you stupid? Do you have any idea what kind of people you're dealing with?"

"It's a terrible time. I really can't right now. Could somebody else . . . I was supposed to just drive to Cambridge and pass the message on. That was it, that was the deal."

"Unbelievable," the man said, looking forward, shaking his

head like a disappointed parent.

"Listen, I'd be happy to pay you for your time."

The man laughed. "Now," he said, meeting James' eyes again. "Now, I think, would be a real good time to just do what Daddy wants you to do and shut up about it."

Thirty Seven

Even four old men didn't need much more than two hours to finish laying down a plywood skin over the skeleton of two-by-twelves they'd nailed in place the day before. By the ten o'clock coffee break, twenty sheets of four-foot by eight-foot, five-eighths-inch plywood (two of them retrieved from the basement) had been tacked into place, a nail's width of space left between sheets to allow the wood to swell on wet days without buckling. The crew spent the last part of the morning on its knees, nailing plywood to joist, all of Herter Street echoing with the staccato of hammer blows. Except for Julian, the men knelt on folded sweatshirts or small rubber pads. Every quarter hour or so they sat, stretched out their legs and massaged their kneecaps for a minute, or stood and limped through what would be Lily and Alfonse's living room or kitchen, letting the ache seep out of their joints. By the time the noon whistle blew, the deck was nailed down tight, giving them a flat clean surface on which to begin building walls the next day.

When Gus and Frankie, Ben Waxman and Bob Murph packed up and drove away, Vito and Julian brought their brown paper bags to the edge of the deck and sat there with their legs dangling over the side, unwrapping sandwiches and twisting the tops off of thermoses of warm coffee. The day was typical of April in Boston: gusts of wind crossing the worksite in an unpredictable rhythm; a scudding thin blanket of clouds, gray with the promise of rain.

199

"My mother says this is a holy week," Julian said through half a mouthful of cold cuts and bread. "She says Easter is Sunday, and the week before Easter is always a holy week."

Vito nodded, looking out at the street. He'd made himself a tunafish sandwich again, on Italian bread, with lettuce. He swallowed a bite of it, took a mouthful of coffee from the red plastic cup. "Friday, no work after lunch."

"Why Vito?"

"Good Friday."

"Why is it so good, Vito?"

"Because Jesus Crise they crucified him on the cross that day."

They chewed their food and sipped their coffee and looked up to watch a car or delivery truck pass in the street.

"Why did they do that Vito?"

"Because he was tellin the people things they didn't like to hear."

"Why?"

"That's what God sent him to do."

"Why didn't the people want to hear it?"

"I don't know."

"Maybe it made them feel bad."

"Probly it did."

"Why don't they call it Bad Friday, then?"

"I don't know."

When Julian finished his line of questioning and his meal he folded the wax paper wrapping into a neat square and set it under the edge of his thigh to keep it from being carried away on the wind. He seemed, for some minutes, to lose himself in thought, staring up at the sailing clouds. At last, he pushed himself down off the deck and walked over to the cardboard boxes where the different sizes of nails were kept. He rummaged around there. Vito had to catch the folded-up square of

200

paper as the wind was lifting it, and put it and his own paper bag beneath his thermos. Julian returned with a sixteen-penny nail, took his place again beside his boss, and pressed the sharp point of the spike against the palm of his left hand until the skin puckered and broke, squeezing one drop of bright blood out into the day.

Vito put a hand on his arm to stop him. The wind rustled the plastic tarpaulin that had been pulled back from the stack of two-by-fours. Vito looked at Julian, then away, and heard him say, "There comes the pretty girl."

Thirty Eight

It was five and a half hours from Boston to Philadelphia. They stopped once at a rest area and the black man and the white man followed him into the bathroom and then bought him coffee and a sandwich and marched him back into the van, one on either side of him. They switched the radio compulsively from one music station to the next and said nothing. Once, in northern New Jersey, James tried to ask a question, and the man beside him twisted his head on a thick neck and, almost kindly, said, "Look, Jimmy, don't make life hard for me and don't make it hard for you, alright? We know zero about it. We're just doing what somebody told us to do. You should do the same."

He shut up. He stared out the window. Trucks, trees, small cities with normal people living normal lives. The man was right. He was going to do what they asked, do whatever errand it was his father needed. And then he was going to go back and finish his work and give Gracie a bonus and take Sean on a cruise and then they were going to get absolutely as far away from his father and his brother and their business associates as he possibly could. Sudbury had been a mistake. He should have gone to Los Angeles, Bimini, Costa Rica. He told himself he would put together a plan next week for relocating the business.

When they left the highway and turned down the exit into Philadelphia the man told him to get on the floor.

"Fine," he said, "just don't get on top of me."

"Who wants to?"

He lay on the floor, ribs throbbing, face on the backs of his hands. In another ten minutes he felt the van slow nearly to a complete stop and make a ninety-degree right turn. The light coming through the windows changed. He heard the sound of an automatic garage door closing, and then he was being helped up and taken out of the van, along a short hallway, and into the kitchen of what appeared to be a fairly luxurious house. A tiled corridor. Granite countertops and the kind of stove you saw in the homes of professional chefs. An expansive living room with long couches, an empty aquarium, and a huge TV. They went past the couches, through another door, and into a room that felt like the library of a men's club: a bar, a writing desk, leather chairs, walls covered with full bookshelves, floor-to-ceiling. One gilded title caught his eye: HOLY BIBLE.

The men told him to sit and wait. He did so. Ten seconds after they left the room another stranger entered. This man was overweight nearly to the point of obesity and he was dressed like some kind of European actor gone to seed—silk trousers held up by suspenders, a white dress shirt and yellow silk cravat. Lifeless eyes. James started to get to his feet but the man made a gesture for him to stay seated and then held out a soft, fat hand. "Leon," he said. "Glass of something?"

James shook his head, then changed his mind and asked for water.

Leon busied himself at a small bar at the side of the room and returned with a tall glass of ice water and, for himself, what seemed to be a shot of whiskey. He settled his bulk in the chair at right angles to James, took a delicate sip, and set the glass on a table at his elbow.

"Let me first apologize for any rough treatment," he said. His eyes were unreadable, pinched in pouches of flesh above chubby cheeks. He might have been forty and he might have been sixty-five—the light in the room was not good. "Some of the men in my employ are not the most cultured of creatures and I believe they made the assumption that you wouldn't join us voluntarily."

"I'm tremendously busy," James said. "I'm an accountant. This is *the* busiest week of the year for me and what happened was tantamount to kidnapping."

Leon pursed his lips in what might have been a sympathetic way and took another small sip from his glass. Each time he leaned forward to replace it a grunt escaped from his round mouth. He tugged once at the crease of his right pantleg. "These things have a timing all their own," he said.

"What things? Am I being held hostage? Is there some errand I can perform and get back to my own work? I'd appreciate it if I had some information."

Leon nodded agreeably. "Your father is a client of mine," he said. "Albeit indirectly. I am a species of specialized travel agent. However, instead of arranging trips for actual dates, vacations and so on, I make open-ended arrangements for certain types of eventualities. Your father engaged my services years ago and now, so to speak, the note has come due."

"No one knows where my father is. If you're taping me or something, if you work for the police, or one of his enemies, believe me, I know absolutely nothing about where he is or what he's doing. We're not on good terms. We never were."

The tiny eyes watched him carefully until he'd finished, then Leon took a slightly larger dose of the whiskey and smacked his lips in a decorous way. There was another quick "unh" as he set the glass on the coaster. "We have a car for you," was all he said. "A car that cannot be traced. We've created a driver's license with your photo—"

"How on earth did you get my photo?"

Leon went on as if he hadn't been interrupted. "Your photo and a different name, a registration. In the unlikely event that you are stopped, the license and registration will turn up a person in the State of Maryland files, a person with a perfect driving record, no criminal background. A person who does not actually exist. These are the kinds of services I provide. I've been at it a long time and never had the slightest bit of trouble. Your part in this is really very simple. You are to take this car to Washington, D.C., to the Carlyle Hotel on 19th Street Northwest."

Making another small grunt, Leon leaned forward and lifted from the table a black leather envelope like the ones that hold a check at restaurants. He handed it to James. "There's seven hundred dollars inside. Tens, twenties, fifties. We don't want you using credit cards or ATMs. Absolutely forbidden. And it's best, just for an extra measure of safety, to try to avoid places that have a security camera—though that is getting more difficult these days. You are to go to the hotel—not tonight, tomorrow at noon—and walk up to the front desk and tell the clerk there that there's a car waiting for a Mr. Edward Echeverria, which is your father's alias. They'll call up to your father's room. He'll come down, and for all intents and purposes my job will be finished. You're welcome to leave the car pretty much anyplace you'd like, or hand it over to your father, whatever he asks of you. It will eventually be towed and the towing company will be unable to track down the owner. Your father has compensated me in advance for all of this. Questions?"

"He's at the hotel?"

"He'll be there tonight and will be ready to check out by noon, as he requested. You should find someplace to stay tonight, not with friends, preferably close enough to D.C. to allow for any traffic delays in the morning."

"How did you arrange all this? He called you?"

Instead of answering, Leon sipped his whiskey and smacked his lips and ran his eyes over the curtained window.

"Can you dial the number and hand me the phone? Can I talk to him?"

"Impossible. Your father's name, as I'm certain you realize, is on a certain list. His photograph is in every police station in America and half the newspapers."

"Why would he do this, then? Why risk being caught?"

"You might ask him that when you see him. That question is outside the parameters of our relationship."

"And I'm supposed to just get in the car and drive to a hotel and ask for this man I've never heard of and trust everything will be fine? While I have a list of clients as long as my leg waiting for their returns by April 15th?"

"They could file extensions," Leon said. He stretched out an arm and consulted a ten-thousand-dollar watch. "You'll be accompanied and blindfolded for the first little ways, then you'll have the car to yourself. If you leave now, you might miss the afternoon rush. Keep to the speed limit, of course. Pay for everything in cash." He adjusted the cravat and ran a hand through the side of his hair. "Questions?"

James shook his head.

Leon pushed himself forward and, before standing, extended the soft hand again. James thought he wanted to shake, but he said, "Your cell phone, please."

"You're kidding," James said.

"Hardly. It will be mailed to your office within an hour after you leave here."

"I need it. It's essential."

"An unnecessary risk," Leon said, hand still out.

"And if I refuse?"

Leon's fat cheeks flexed. "It was such an honor meeting you," he said. "It would be a shame to end our association with an unpleasantry."

James handed over his phone and Leon allowed himself a small smile—a one-second twitch of his facial muscles—and waddled out of the room.

The door was left open. The two men stepped through it. They escorted James back along the same route, through the living room and down the hallway, but when he stepped into the garage a different vehicle was sitting there, facing outward. A gray Chevrolet with Maryland plates, new and clean but as bland as a the back side of a strip mall. One of the men wrapped a blindfold around his eyes and helped him into the car. They drove—rights and lefts, stop and go—for probably ten minutes before he felt the car being pulled to the curb. The engine was turned off, blindfold removed, and James saw that they were on a quiet side street, city neighborhood, two black, grade-school brothers walking past and looking at him.

"Know where you're going?" one of his escorts asked.

He nodded.

"Left at the end of this street, left again at the first light, straight a half mile and you'll see signs for 95."

The man handed him a single key.

James's hands were shaking when he sat behind the wheel. Anger, fear, frustration—he didn't want to know what it was. He set the leather envelope on the passenger seat and opened it. There was a stack of new bills. He jabbed the key forward three times before it slipped into its slot. The men were out of the car, watching him. Left at the end of the street, left at the first light. Another minute and a half and he saw the sign and drove up the ramp and onto the Interstate.

Thirty Nine

Leon waited at a front window until the car was out of sight. He was pleased with himself on that day, pleased at the contribution he made, professionally, to the terrible world in which they all tried to survive. For as long as he could remember he'd thought of himself as a kind of modern-day philosopher, a man who considered the big picture, who had a perspective that most ordinary people did not have. The earth, if you stepped back and studied it, was a system in which all of its creatures fed off each other. Cows ate grasses and grains; humans ate cows. In the seas, as he understood it, there was a whole ladder of killing: small fish eaten by larger fish, who were then eaten by sharks, and so on. Life was built from the bricks of death, clearly.

He did not know if there was any kind of God behind this system of murder and survival. It wasn't a subject he often pondered. But if some God did exist, then He would need assistance from people like Leon Tisch. In the human realm, especially, there would have to be men who saw the larger picture, and these men would act as facilitators, ensuring the survival of the fittest, pulling a string here, setting up a consequence there, seeing to it that, when their time came, the weaker members of the species were dispatched with some efficiency.

How fortunate I am, Leon thought, to be able to do this work. How lucky the world is to have me.

Satisfied that everything was in its proper place, he chose from his collection of disposable cell phones and dialed a certain number. "China," he said, "Leon calling. Here is the make, model, and plate number you asked for."

Forty

He went like a robot. For the first hour he looked in the mirror every few seconds to see if someone was following him. His mind was a circus of conflicting voices—that he should go to the police, that he should abandon the car and call Sean and they should run. That he should at least call Gracie and explain. It was three o'clock in the afternoon, he'd told her he'd be back in half an hour. She'd wait and worry, try his cell phone. She'd call home. Sean would worry. By the end of the day they'd be thinking of calling the police, and then what?

He stopped at the first rest area, changed some of the bills, pumped money into the pay phone and called the office.

"Where are you?" Gracie said. He could hear the worry in her voice.

"Just a little change in plans. I'm fine. Call Sean and tell him I'm fine and I'll explain it tomorrow. Family emergency, okay?"

"Okay, but . . . the work. Mr. Blakesly was here for the meeting. He was a little frantic."

"I'll explain when I get back. Don't worry. It's a . . . just a strange family thing, an emergency. Call Sean and tell him not to worry and not to try to call me, and don't you worry either. I'll work overtime and make it all up. Don't worry."

After he hung up he walked back to the car and sat there for a few minutes, breathing. He expected, any second, that someone with an FBI badge would come and handcuff him and take him away and he half-wanted that. Sean would think he was cheating on him. Gracie would ask a dozen questions. He'd be so far behind he'd have to go without sleep for a week to make the filing deadlines. The Blakesley account would go elsewhere. One call now. Go back inside, he told himself, call the FBI, tell them everything . . . "Sure," he said aloud, "and spend the rest of your life wondering when your brother or one of his "associates", or Leon or Leon's men will come and shoot you in the back of the head."

He started the car and drove. He'd get through this day, and the next day, and then he'd get through tax season, and then they would leave.

Forty One

Without precisely knowing why—more and more now he acted on intuition, blindly following what seemed to him a bit of Divine road instructions—Father Dominic Bucci had decided to write a book. Well, not a book, exactly. He didn't expect it would ever be published and didn't really want that, at least not while the subjects of the book—the Imbesalacqua family—were alive. But it seemed to him important that he put the story on the page, a latter-day Book of Job. Vito, after all, was his closest friend on earth. He'd watched Peter and Joanie grow up. He'd counseled Lucy through her crisis and until the last day of her life. He'd known Alfonse's actual paternity from the first, from a certain tortured hour with Vito in the confessional.

But it was more than that. What impelled him was a larger story, the idea that behind the multifarious faces of human life, beyond addiction, adultery, love, greed, sacrifice, jealousy and murder, lay a mystery composed of threads as fine as a spider's silk, a Divine architecture a million times more complex than the inner workings of an atom. The older he grew, the more time he spent in prayer and meditation, the calmer his mind became and the clearer it was to him that the entire human drama masked the simplest of spiritual laws: if you injured another soul, that pain reverberated through God's creation. For studying this eternal law, the family was the finest laboratory, a cauldron of love and acted-out imperfection, a theater either monstrous or sublime, with a million variations between. He
212

had known, for example, Eddie Creviniello's father, a man so crude and bereft of compassion that it was almost an untruth to call him human. Creviniello had ordered people tortured and killed for the slightest infraction of some savage, made-up code. For instance, his brother had been involved in an auto accident at Bell Circle—no doubt, the brother's fault—and a week later the other driver had been found floating face-down in one of the irrigation canals of the Lynn marsh. What chance did the children of a man like Matteo Creviniello have?

But even less extreme examples proved the point. With his momentary lapse, his one adultery, Vito had hurt Lucy, a terrible wound. The disturbance this caused in Lucy's mind reverberated in their household, spawned her tirades and inconstancy: she frosted hand-made cakes for her children's birthdays and then screamed at them, for nothing, in broad daylight in front of the house. This, in turn, had echoed in Peter's spirit, and he'd sought some confirmation of his worthlessness in the shame of compulsion. His troubles then bounced back against his mother and father, raising a dust storm of guilt and confusion, more shame, a cascade of illogical, well-meant, but ultimately unhelpful responses. Joanie had spent much of her life trying to clear this bad air and, for her troubles, had gotten only lungful after lungful of dirt. It had hardened her in a way that caused trouble in her own love relationships.

What a cancerous circle it all was! And how did one go about escaping? He believed he knew the answer now, at last. It was so simple. You prayed, you cleared the mind; you worked against your baser instincts and tried, to the degree humanly possible, not to injure another soul in any way. You bore your suffering with courage. You worked your own garden, weeding and weeding, watering and watering, keeping the insects and animals away. And with God's blessing that small plot bore the fruit of understanding. But what a sour fruit this could be! And what agony it involved, especially when you were forced to watch the confusion of people you deeply loved.

He tried with every sermon, every confession, every act of his waking life—sometimes against the grain of the Church's harsher dictums—to spread this understanding to the people of his parish. He struggled mightily against his own egotism and frailties, his own pettiness and wants. In the end, though, you had to simply stand back and watch and let things work themselves out across the endless film reel of eternity.

For months now he'd been writing the story in his journal, imagining his way into the minds of the Imbesalacquas and the others involved, drilling down and down into the mystery in the hopes of hitting its core. What good it would ever do anyone, he did not know. None, he suspected. But, if nothing else, it helped him see through the smokescreen of pain. That had to be, he told himself, in the fullness of time, of some benefit to someone.

Forty Two

By the time James reached the outskirts of Washington it was 8:45 p.m. and he was hungry and tired and wrung out and so angry at his father that he wanted to strangle him, shoot him, club him over the head and watch him bleed to death. How on earth his stepmother had lived like this for all these years and not killed the man, he didn't know. Maybe she'd be with him tomorrow and he'd at least have that, her company, a little semi-sanity. They'd have a nice lunch, a talk. His father would explain what was going on and he'd be free to grab a shuttle to Logan and be back home in time to get a few hours' sleep before heading back to the office.

Just on the outskirts of the city James found a hotel and paid in cash, making up some story that he'd left his wallet and I.D. at a rest area on the highway. The clerk hesitated, wondered aloud about "incidentals", so James left him a $200 deposit and went upstairs to his room. No bags. No change of clothing. No toothbrush. Thanks, Dad. It occurred to him that his father might be turning himself in, but that would be crazy. He could have turned himself in anyplace. Why come back to Boston? To turn himself into a particular agent? Had some kind of plea deal been arranged? If there was a deal, he thought, then maybe his father would go to jail for a few years and get out, reform himself, lead a more or less normal life. Was it too much to hope for? Could he risk a call to Sean from the hotel room? Of course he could. Why shouldn't he? What was the worst that could happen?

Forty Three

Alfonse and Joanie had a lunch of steak tips and salad at the New Bridge Cafe and talked in a circular way about the house and Lily and Estelle and how happy their father seemed to be, working again. After the meal they drove in separate cars to the beach, as if compelled by some unspoken agreement that the beach was the only place they could have this particular conversation. It was a windy day, rain threatening again, but they lifted their coat collars and walked on the firm damp sand where the tide had receded. Alfonse kept his hands down in his raincoat pockets, Joanna wore gloves and swung her arms to stay warm. The air tasted of salt.

"You know when you asked me at lunch how everything was going in my life and I said it was all going fine? Well, I lied. Last week I arranged to interview China Louis—it was months of work, getting to see him, and during the interview he arranged to have my car stolen."

Alfonse was looking down at the sand as he walked. When he didn't respond she went on. "Yesterday when you called I had just managed an interview with Xavier Manzo, after weeks of lying to him, telling him I might be able to help him . . . and he spit at me through the screen in the visitors' room." She hesitated again, Alfonse didn't look up. "Yesterday also, Leslie— my girlfriend, my lover—wrote me a note on her work letterhead telling me that she's tired of all this, quote, "sentimental Italian intrigue and working-class melodrama", that she thinks

I've lost my mind over trying to catch Eddie Crevine, and that, basically, she never wants to see me again."

Alfonse gave no sign of having heard her. Joanna glanced at him, saw a younger version of her father's face in profile, then lowered her head slightly, leaning into the wind. As they were passing the concrete condominiums that had been built behind Ocean Avenue, he took one hand out of his pocket, put the hand on her shoulder, squeezed her through the coat, and went back to his original posture, as if the metal-blue mussel shells at his feet spelled out a code he was determined to decipher. A moment later he looked up at her, then shifted his eyes forward.

"I knew about the car and the visit to Xavier, Joanie. I'm sorry about Leslie."

"You knew?"

"I know people at the prison. I have friends in the Boston P.D."

"The old-boys' network."

"Something like that. Though the person I know at the prison is a woman I used to date. But I knew anyway, it's part of the reason I called you to have lunch."

"To tell me to calm down, back off, stick to my own business, right?"

"To see if you've been able to find anything we haven't been able to find."

"What was the other part?"

"Turn around here?" Alfonse suggested. "We can go look at the house, if you want."

"Not today."

They'd reached the bathhouse opposite the Wonderland subway station, not far from where Peter used to live, and as they turned, the wind pushed their coats against their backs, a hand urging them in the other direction.

"The other part of it," Alfonse said, "is two parts. Part one: I got a call at my house last night threatening your life. A woman's voice. We traced the call to a phone booth in Jamaica Plain. It sounded like she was high and reading something somebody else had written."

Joanna shrugged. "It could be anybody. It could be some woman whose husband was arrested and whose face was shown on the evening news. It could be somebody who just stepped out of a mental hospital and saw me on TV in a coffeeshop. It could be a Red Sox fan, angry that I seemed to smile after the report of a loss to the Yankees last week. You wouldn't believe the calls we get at the station. Our weatherman wears a bullet-proof vest, for God's sake, when he drives home from work. The whole country's crazy . . . and Leslie thinks I was foolish to buy a pistol!"

Alfonse let the wind carry her words down the beach. When he was sure she was finished he said: "This person didn't call the station, Joanie. She called me. At home. About you."

A siren sounded on the Boulevard. Alfonse glanced up long enough to see the blue lights flash past. On the sand to their left lay a thin skin of silver water and broken shells, and, beyond that, rows of small breakers running ashore like an army of white tufted troops.

"It could be anybody," Joanna said. "People call me at home, I have to change the number every few months. Twice in the last month alone, someone came right up and knocked on the door.

"You don't have a doorman in that building?"

"Sure. But you can walk into the garage and ride the elevator right up. I bought a pistol. I had an expensive alarm system installed. What else can I do, live in a fortress? Move every two weeks? Retire and buy an apartment in Rome?"

They went another hundred yards in silence. Seagulls strut-

ted away as they approached, circling, turning an eye to measure them, the more timid among them flapping into the air and
riding the wind toward Winthrop.

"Really," Joanna said . . . "Honestly, I'm moving rapidly toward the point where I wouldn't mind so much if someone
killed me, as long as they were efficient about it."

Alfonse looked up at her. A compassion, she thought, that
Peter, locked as he was in his own melodrama, had never
shown.

"Since my mother died I don't seem to be anchored anywhere. Leslie dumps me. At work, they're showing signs of replacing me with a handsome twenty-eight-year-old man who
practically bites off his own tongue at least once a broadcast.
He's saying the news tonight without me. The station manager
says they want him to get his own "sea legs." At least when Peter was around I could distract myself from my own life by
worrying about his. I think sometimes that if Eddie *is* ever
caught my life will be totally without purpose . . . Sorry, I'm
whining, I know."

"We might be half a step closer to catching him. That's the
other part of what I wanted to tell you."

"We are?"

"Eddie has two sons, John and James, from his first wife."

"After the disciples, no doubt."

"John runs the plumbing shop in Melrose and was as involved as Eddie was in the Leopard Club and, as far as we
know, Eddie's other business ventures. Jimmy is more complicated. I knew him a little bit when he was a kid and I did some
work in the schools. He only grew to be about five feet five.
Smartest kid you ever saw, but it almost seemed like he was
living under a blanket half the time."

"With Eddie for a father, no wonder."

"Right. He went to college and for a while I thought he was

219

going to get completely away from here, from his family. But he was drawn back here somehow, for some reason. A boyfriend, I think. He does a little work—accounting work, strictly legal—for his father and brother now and then. But he inherited something from Eddie. He's another Three-Hands in his own way. You'll be talking to him and talking to him and thinking how smart he is, how polite, how nice, and then, later on, he'll do something that makes you see this other side to him, a mean side, a hurt little boy getting back at you. He'll go and tell somebody you said something you didn't say. It's happened to me, and to a few of the other guys who know him. Schizophrenic, maybe, I don't know. Or just a broken-up mind from all the shit he lived with, growing up. One of our neighbors had a dog like that. The neighbor would yell at the dog and scream at him, and the dog would be wagging its tail in this beaten-down way, whining, looking up with these pathetic eyes. The neighbor would turn and walk away and the dog would jump up, nip him on the ass, and run like hell. This Jimmy is a little bit like that, another Billy Ollanno almost, only smarter. No record."

"And look how Billy Ollanno ended up. Shot dead on the street after a lifetime of kissing ass."

"Right. Jimmy runs a CPA business now out in the suburbs, Sudbury, and as far as anybody can tell he's stayed clear of his dad's business."

"You've heard something from him?"

"No. The FBI guys are all over Johnny and the Melrose plumbing shop, hoping Eddie will try to get in touch, but I doubt they're very interested in Jimmy. By now, wherever he is, Eddie knows the Leopard Club has been shut down. He knows Xavier's in Walpole for eleven years, and probably that Johnny Cut had his bail denied. Whatever contact he maintained with his operation is slipping away, though I'd bet he's still owed a few favors. These aren't the kind of people who'll keep from moving in on the territory out of respect, though, most of them."

"So what's the half step closer?"

"Just little bits of traffic on the wiretaps that maybe Eddie's upset about all this. Just hints and suggestions. My FBI friend said they had something recently, Johnny saying something about his brother and his father. It could be nothing."

"But what you're saying is that Eddie knows he's being put out to pasture. The business, his old territory, it's all being taken away from him in his absence. His son Johnny senses as much."

"Exactly. Only Eddie's not the pasture type. Other guys would just let it go. Eddie . . . I don't think so."

"Which means, if he possibly can, he'll try to do something to show he's still in charge here."

"Exactly."

"Such as what?" Joanna said.

"If we knew that," Alfonse said, "we'd be more than half a step closer."

Forty Four

After lunch, Vito had Estelle stand next to him at the saw table while Julian carried over armfuls of two by four studs, and he held each piece of wood in his scarred hands and showed her how to sight down its length to see that it was straight, and then turn it to make sure it was flat, how to make your cut a little distance from the knots so the end-nailing would be easier. "Every piece has his own little problems," he said. "One, maybe, he's straight alla way but he goes a little crooked on the end. So you cut that little crooked part off. Some, they're crooked all the way from the start, and if you put those inside your wall, you gonna have trouble all the rest of the way: the plywood she's not gonna fit the right way on top; if there's a window there the window's not gonna go in easy; you won't be able to check her right with your square; the screen might not go smooth in his track. In the old days they used to only make wood from trees that grew slow, so the wood was almost always pretty straight. Now the lumber they have they grow it fast, on purpose, so they can make the money, and she's more of the time crooked, see, look at this here. This one you have to save and cut up in little pieces and we'll use the pieces later on where it doesn't matter if they're straight. I'll show you."

By the time Alfonse and Joanna started their talk on the beach, all the pieces for the north wall had been cut and set out on the deck like a puzzle, the sole and top plates marked with lines and "X's" where the studs would go. Vito had Julian hold the studs on their edge on the plywood deck, while he drove the sixteen-penny nails through the sole plate into them, letting Estelle use his spare hammer to knock in the final inch or so. But the girl she had strong hands and arms, and soon she was asking to drive the nails from start to finish—bending some, missing the nailhead once or twice and making what carpenters call "a ding" in the plate—but putting them in pretty solid. By late afternoon, the studs, windows jacks, headers, and sills had all been fastened tight and true, and the wall was ready to raise.

Vito started four nails into the sole plate, evenly spaced, then he and Julian stood near either end and Estelle in the middle and they hoisted the wall to vertical. With the toes of their boots they moved it into place at the edge of the deck, drove the spikes down through the plywood and into the band joist the old guys had set just so, braced it at both ends and the middle, and stood back.

Julian had his arms held out away from his body and his eyebrows were raising and lowering like black ribs over breathing eyes.

"Vito!" he called loudly, though Vito was standing eight feet to his left. "A house came out of the air!" He climbed down off the deck and walked back and forth in the mud, assessing the afternoon's work from several angles, then hoisting himself back up on the plywood and making lines of muddy tracks there. He'd admire the even two-by-fours, the thick, neat headers, then he'd look at Estelle as if checking to see that she saw the miracle, too. A space carved out of spaciousness.

Forty Five

Once he'd found his way into NW Washington, James stopped twice to ask directions to the hotel, found a parking space outside it, and buoyed by a small gust of impossible hope, went in to the front desk and told the clerk to tell Mr. Echeverria that his ride was here. Nervous, again, wondering if he was being set up, James retreated to the car and watched through the passenger window. Fifteen minutes later, his father appeared. Even with the sunglasses and the hair colored a ridiculous light brown, James recognized him the instant he saw him step out of the front door. The small, thick body, the I-own-the-world walk—here came the famous Chelsea Eddie Crevine, sauntering toward the gray Chevy, carrying a suitcase in one hand and a suiter over the other shoulder like any businessman headed toward a flight home, a meeting, a deal.

James stepped out of the car and went to give him the obligatory hug. By an instinct that had been planted in him since grade school, he understood that it was important not to mention the hair, the glasses, the nose job, to pretend that everything was normal and fine. You did not say things that would upset Daddy. He took the bag from his father's hand like some kind of paid driver.

"Hi," his father said and James understood instantly that something was wrong. Something in the face, the voice.

"You alright, Dad?" he said quietly.

"Yeah, let's go."

He started to put the suitcase in the trunk but his father said, "Back seat." So he did that. Took the suits and hung them on the other side, behind him. They got in and his father slapped him on top of the thigh in a congratulatory way and said, "How do I look?'

"Good, fine."

"Recognize me?"

"By the walk. Nobody else would."

"Hah!" his father said. "Drive. Let's go."

"Where?"

"New York. Manhattan. Go."

Something wasn't right. He couldn't put his finger on it, but there was something in the too-casual greeting—after seven months—in the voice, the face. It had nothing to do with the ridiculous disguise, it was something else. He concentrated, at first, on finding his way back to the highway, but they got momentarily lost and drove by the Capitol. His father didn't seem to see it, or if he saw it he didn't seem to care. He was facing straight ahead, sitting stiffly. They were two frozen men.

Once they were on 95 his father took the glasses off.

"How's Alicia? I thought maybe she'd be with you."

"On a cruise," his father said. "Bahamas."

"We . . . I'm going on one. You okay, Dad?"

His father didn't seem to hear.

"She's okay," he said. "Been giving me a fucking hard time, like always."

"It's not risky for you, doing this? Going to New York for a meeting?"

"She's on me all the time," his father said.

James looked across at him and wondered if his father was taking some kind of anti-anxiety drug or something. He seemed almost catatonic. It occurred to him, for just the quickest moment, that his father was uncomfortable in his presence, maybe

225

even intimidated. Could that possibly be true?

"Aren't the police looking for you?" James asked weakly. He felt his father turn to him and for an instant he thought he'd be struck.

"Did you call anybody?"

"No, of course not."

"Nobody?"

"Of course not, Dad."

"Nobody knows you're picking me up?"

"Leon . . . His guys were a little—"

His father turned forward again and grunted.

"What's going on? Something's wrong? What's the matter, Dad?"

"Your brother call you?"

"A month ago."

"Johnny Cut call?"

"Johnny Cut's been arrested. I assumed you—"

"WHAT!"

It was an explosion, the old familiar explosion. James raised his right shoulder to protect himself from a slap, a punch, worse.

"What did you fucking just say?"

This was the father he remembered.

"I assumed you knew."

"When? How? What the fuck?" His father was practically screaming. He'd turned to face him across the shift and when James glanced sideways he saw a roadmap of veins in the forehead and neck.

"I don't know, a few days, a week ago. I heard it on the news."

"Out on bail?"

"No bail."

"What the FUCK!" his father screamed, and he began

slamming his fist down against the dashboard like a madman. "Why didn't you fucking CALL ME!!"

"I didn't have a number, remember?"

"Why didn't your fucking brother CALL ME!"

"I assumed he did. I'm out of the loop, remember?"

Slam, slam, slam, the small soft fist on the dashboard. A string of curses. Familiar territory. This was the stuff he'd grown up with, as normal to him as fatherly hugs to another child. The voice, the curses, the slaps and kicks and punches. His father controlled things, that was his job. He controlled things, and the instant he ran into something he couldn't control—an empty toothpaste tube, a slightly overcooked dish of pasta, a subordinate who messed up—this was the response, half an hour of this. Then he'd go calm, disappear into a deadly silence, make a phone call, leave for a meeting, no doubt have someone brought to him, tortured, killed . . . until he felt like he was in control again. It had been exactly like this—a blind tantrum—the day before he went out to meet with Peter Imbesalacqua. James had been at the house with Alicia then. Alicia had advised him not to go.

James waited.

The dashboard-thumping eventually stopped. The curses dissolved into muttering. A day, James was thinking. One day of this and then he'd be back at work and his father could have his meeting, or turn himself in, or curse at or torment or kill someone else, and then go back into hiding wherever he'd been. One time, he'd said. One favor. That was the agreement. This one time, and then he'd be left alone.

After almost an hour of silence on the crowded gray stripe of the New Jersey Turnpike, James risked a question. "Where in New York, Dad?"

"What?"

"Where in New York?"

"Manhattan. I told you."

"Where in Manhattan?"

"The fucking Waldorf Astoria."

"We're staying the night?"

"I'm staying the night. You take the car and go."

"Go where?"

"Home. They can't trace the car. Take it and leave it some-place. Don't leave nothing in it. No receipts, no sunglasses, not even a fucking coffee cup. Park it anywhere you want, not Boston. Providence. Wherever you want. Get yourself home and go back to your fucking life."

"You're welcome."

"Huh?"

"You're welcome. You call me away from work for two days in the busiest time of year. Barely say hello, after seven months of no contact. I get my news through Johnny, in a kind of code. I say hello to Alicia through Johnny. I'm like a slave."

"A slave?" his father said, and there it was again, the odd note, almost as if he were on something, or sick, half there.

James could feel the anger bubbling up in him. "I get thrown down on the floor of a van, probably break a rib, I get taken away—"

His father swung his left arm and smashed it back-handed into his mouth. James swerved into the next lane, someone leaned on the horn. He regained control of the car, shook his head to clear it, tasted blood. His hands and arms were shaking. The pain in his lips and teeth radiated up into the bones of his face. His father slumped back, breathing hard. James wiped a sleeve across his lips. "Shut the fuck up then, slave," his father mumbled.

So he did.

Forty Six

Vito had them cover the deck with blue plastic tarps ("tops", he called them), weighting the edges down with pieces of scrap lumber and stones they pulled from the mud of what would be her mother and Alfonse's yard. Even now it seemed impossible to her, a kind of American fairy tale. Impossible to believe that, after the various layers of hell her mother had known, she would end up with a sort of dream life: the wonderful job, the wonderful man, the built-to-order house on a quiet street in a city that felt, on certain days, in certain neighborhoods, like the mythical old-world Cambodia she'd heard about, only with snow and pizza shops.

She could feel Julian's eyes on her as they worked, and she noticed that he'd sometimes pick up especially heavy stones and carry them across the yard when he knew she was watching, as if she required any more evidence of his strength. As if it mattered to her.

"Julie," Vito said to him at one point, "She's maybe a wind comin tonight, not the hurricane. A rock like the bocce ball is big enough, you don't need the half a mountain size, okay?"

"Okay Vito."

But then Vito himself went over and carried the big saw from the cutting table to the tool shed with one hand, when it would have been a simple thing, asking for help. It would be an education, working with two men, she could see that already.

When they'd finished covering the deck and the stacks of

lumber, and had locked up the tools in the little shed, they stood around for another few minutes, scraping mud off their boots with scraps of wood and admiring the walls again from the vantage point of the sidewalk. She could sense Julian was trying to find something to say to her because he stood there like the trunk of an old bo tree, peeking down at her every few seconds as if she were a spirit from another world and might vanish into air if he didn't keep checking. At last, he made a small noise, and she looked at him and saw that he was holding a hand out for her to shake. She shook it. Satisfied, pleased, Julian climbed into his pickup truck, a blue Ford as oversized as he was, revved the engine half a dozen times—apparently an essential part of the mating dance of the American male—and disappeared in a cloud of exhaust.

She and Vito watched him go. "It's a hard thing for the man if he likes a girl and can't say it," Vito said. " I remember from when I was young."

"It's a hard thing for the woman if he says it and you wish he didn't."

"Sure, Miss. I bet."

"What's "sure" in Italian?"

"*Certo*".

"Chair-toe. It sounds surer than "sure". In Cambodian it's "*piht*".

"I'll drive you home, Miss, so you don't have to walk. We're gonna be two carpenters out in the dark here, another few minutes."

"I want to take you to dinner."

"What, Miss?"

"Please stop calling me "Miss". It's Estelle. Or Stella, if you want. I'd like to take you to dinner tonight as a way of thanking you for letting me work on the house. We need some time for the Italian practice anyway."

"I can't, Miss."

"Stella. Why not? I know a little Cambodian place in Chelsea I want to take you to."

"I can't, Stella."

"I'll be offended. I'll be hurt."

He leaned away from her slightly, his eyes opened a bit wider. She could see from his face and posture that this idea threw him into a small pool of confusion, as if he believed that offending someone would stain his soul forever. A white boy came up the sidewalk bouncing a basketball. They stepped apart to let him pass.

"In my culture it's a serious insult to refuse an offer of a meal."

"But I'm all dirty from the work."

"This place is totally informal, Vito."

"But look—boots . . . dungarees . . . you can't go in a restaurant lookin like this."

"Then we can go back to your house and you can change and wash up if you really want to. But you'll see when we get there how unfancy a place it is."

Outside the door to his house she brushed off her pants and sweater, took off her boots at the threshold, and waited in the kitchen, drinking a glass of water, while Vito washed up and changed clothes. She didn't like the house any more this time than she had on their Saturday visit. It had a sterile, overly tidy feeling to it, as if all the roughness and naturalness of life had been chased into the cellar. A perfectly clean counter and perfectly clean sink, beige curtains on the window, neatly tied back, a four-inch-high plastic saint on the windowsill next to a photograph of a young, dark-haired woman in a wedding gown. His wife, she supposed. Absolutely beautiful. The only refreshing aspect was an old-fashioned black telephone that squatted on a table in the entranceway. As she stood there looking at the telephone, studying the slivers of silver light on the curved black surface, it rang. She could hear water running in the bathroom behind the closed door. The phone rang again. A third ring. On the fourth ring she lifted the heavy receiver and said hello. There was an awkward second or two of silence—she supposed the person on the other end was surprised to have heard a woman's voice, and she was about to explain the situation and say that this was, in fact, the Imbesalacqua household, when a man's voice said, "Eddie Crevine's coming back to kill you. He'll be there in two more days."

"What?" she said. "I'm not—" But the line had already gone dead.

She put the phone down and stood there without moving, the words "kill you", running along the surfaces of her bones. Vito came out of the bathroom. His shoes were shined and his pants were creased and he was wearing a light brown V-neck sweater over a white shirt. His face had gotten lightly burned by the wind. With the bald spot on top and the carefully combed white hair to the sides, he looked like a man dressed for a date, carrying a small cargo of embarrassment and expectation in the muscles of his face. On the short ride from the construction site, he'd asked her twice if she was sure it wouldn't be better to have him cook a meal for them at his home, and the second time she'd said, "I'm *certo*," and he'd laughed his shy nervous laugh.

Looking at him now, wondering what to do about the phone message, she could sense that any shift of wind, any hesitation, would wash the shine from his eyes and make him change his mind. It seemed clear to her then that she had taken on this old man's happiness as her new duty in this life, and so, though the "kill you" still reverberated in her, she told herself she'd wait until they were safely in the car before letting Vito know about the call. She wanted to lift the veil of worry from the bones of his face.

In the car, she told herself she'd wait until they reached the end of Proctor Avenue. At the end of Proctor Avenue, she told herself she'd wait until they'd traveled a little ways down Broadway, as if, at some point, there would be a flashing sign saying: Too Late to Turn Back Now, Vito, and she could safely let him know that his daughter's life had just been threatened. He drove with both hands on the wheel and his upper body lifted slightly forward off the seatback.

Broadway was busy at that hour, ribbons of headlights and taillights, parked cars, storefronts marked by splashes of neon sign. The city was still new enough to her that she noticed everything: men standing on the corners even on such a damp night, looking as if they were waiting for someone or something—a delivery, a friend, a Messiah of the streets; girls her own age, barely swinging their arms as they walked, looking left and right, laughing in what seemed to her a mean way; a young couple in rain jackets pushing a stroller, stopping so the woman could squat down and rearrange the blanket on her sleeping child.

Broadway climbed a slight rise, almost unnoticeable, reached a plateau at City Hall, and descended gently past the American Legion Hall, past a restaurant called China Roma, a bakery with a CAPPUCCINO sign in the window, a bar, another bar, a Dunkin Donuts. They passed beneath an overpass made of stone, then crossed a small river into the city of Chelsea, where her one American ex-boyfriend had lived for a time, and where some of the signs said things like: "Bodega Dominicana" and "Loteria", and tenement-lined side streets sloped off into the shadows. A mile of this and the road bent right and then left into a tighter, messier commercial area. Mu-

sic with a Caribbean beat played loudly from the car beside
them, and there were a few dark-haired women with shopping
bags and a shivering, skeletal, dark-skinned man waiting at the
covered bus stop. They found a parking space. It took Vito
three tries to back into it. She told herself she would say something about the telephone call as soon as they sat down and
ordered.

The restaurant was called, unoriginally enough, the Phnom
Penh, and the owners had hung cheap pictures of the Ankor
Wat and the Old Market section of Siem Reap on the walls, as
if they might recreate the nation they had once known, and, in
doing so, wash the torrents of blood from its recent history.
There were nine tables squeezed into the narrow room, with a
kitchen at one end and, at the other, windows facing out onto
the shadows and bustle of Bellingham Square. The only empty
table stood in a window alcove next to a couple with four small
sons. "They're eating Ve Thon Laksa," Estelle said, once they
were seated. "Noodles and squid and crab. You'd like it."

"Squid a lot of Italians eat. Calamari, we call."

"*Certo*, calamari."

Vito smiled, but from his rigid posture and the shifting of
his eyes she could see the restaurant was making him uncomfortable. He was a different man from the man she'd worked
with all afternoon, as though his good clothes kept him at some
distance from his own body, or as if the worksite was the only
territory where he could be truly himself. She was reminded of
her mother when they'd first come to America—the fearful
posture and little-girl look in her eyes, a new crackle in her
voice. Small to begin with, she had seemed to shrink to the size
of a tiny brown bird the moment they'd stepped off the plane
in New York. It had taken her five or six years to stand up
straight again, to look people in the face. Another five years
and she was an executive in a software company, going to char-

ity events in heels and pearls. She wondered what her mother would do if someone called the house and said, "Your daughter will be killed in two days."

She opened her mouth, intending to tell Vito about the call, but said, "I'd like to paint you sometime, if you wouldn't object."

"Excuse me, Miss?"

"Stella. I'd like to have you sit for me in my studio so we could do a portrait. You have one of the most expressive faces I've ever seen. It's like everyone in the world can see exactly what you're feeling, second by second."

"All my life I wanted it not to be that way."

"Why? It's wonderful. The person with you feels right away that you aren't playing any games, that you don't want anything from them."

Vito shrugged his powerful shoulders and ran his eyes around the little room, noisy now with the sounds of scraping chair legs, voices, the touch of porcelain spoon to porcelain bowl. The youngest of the four boys sitting to Vito's left was staring up at him, three pale noodles caught in chopstick tips and held there, dripping, above his bowl. The boy's eyes were polished discs of onyx. "*Nham,*" his mother said to him. Eat. But the boy's attention held to Vito like a magnet to metal. His father reached over and touched the small wrist, gently, with two fingers, and the boy shifted his eyes to him and said: "*Chitea mean chramouh thom,*" which earned him a stern look from each parent and his brother's giggles.

Vito looked at Estelle for a translation.

"The grandfather has a big nose."

Vito looked back at the boy, took his nose between thumb and forefinger and wiggled it back and forth. The parents squirmed and scolded, the oldest brother laughed. Into this happy commotion floated the white-shirted waiter, who took

235

the order from Estelle without benefit of pencil and pad, then disappeared again in the direction of the kitchen.

"Peter got this nose, too. Alfonse got some of it. I'm glad only that Joanie got the nose from her mother."

"It's a nice nose."

"Nice and big. A man's face she can carry it. On a girl it would be a trouble."

"Did Alfonse tell you about the baby?"

"What baby, Miss?"

"Oops."

Vito was staring at her now, across the table, with an innocent, steady attention not very different from the little boy's. Another impossibility, this simple sincerity in a grown American man, in someone this age. The eyes held to her as if there were nothing else in the room, nothing else in the world worth looking at, and for a moment she found herself thinking of the photo on the kitchen wall, and what it must feel like to live all your life with a man who looked at you this way when you spoke.

"My mother's forty-two, they didn't want to wait. That's why they're in such hurry with the house."

"You mother, she's . . ."

"I'm sorry. I thought Alfonse had told you. He must be embarrassed in front of you because they're not married."

"Alfonse . . . by Alfonse you mother is . . ."

"Well, I hope so, don't you?"

An enormous smile broke over Vito's face, lighting the skin there as if you'd turned a crumpled sheet of forty-weight drawing paper to the window, and the noon sunlight had caught against it on a dozen different planes.

"That's the face I want to paint, that smile. Will you sit for me?"

"Sure, Miss. *Certo.* Now, this minute, anything you ask me

I'll do."

"How about a big raise, since I'm an experienced wall-builder now."

"Okay, Miss."

"How about calling me Stella."

"Okay."

"How about sitting for me Friday after work."

"Friday's Good Friday. A Holy Day for Catholics."

"Next week then."

"If you want. But what about the big grandfather's nose?"

She laughed, the waiter brought two bowls of Ve Thon Laksa on a tray, the telephone message caught her again. The strange thing was that it had sounded more like a warning than a threat, as if the man on the other end of the line had been trying to help Vito and his family, save them, keep the cold ripple of fear out of his voice rather than pass it on. He'd passed it on anyway, planted it in her. Again.

Vito ate as if he'd been eating Ve Thon soup all his life, and she watched him to see if he was just being polite, and couldn't tell. The boy at the next table watched him, too, despite his mother's half-hearted reprimands. Grandfathers, it seemed, were in short supply in the Cambodian Diaspora. When he and his brothers and parents at last stood up to leave, they all pushed their chairs in tight to the table as they might do in the home of a relative. The little boy put his hands together and bowed toward Vito, slowly, with a dignity beyond his years. His father watched him, glanced at the bald white man sitting straight-backed before his bowl, and led his family to the door.

"My son Peter, he reminds me of a little bit, that boy."

"Alfonse told me how much you miss him."

"Always when we went out someplace he would get up and go around talkin to people. All his life he was like that, and Joanie was always the other way, quiet, staying next to her mother and me all the time."

"More like Alfonse."

"That's right, Miss."

"Stella . . . So do you see Joanie much? I haven't met her yet."

"Not so much, not since her mother . . . not since Lucy . . ."

She waited, but Vito couldn't seem to say the word. "I watched the series she did on organized crime. It took a lot of courage to do that. She seems like a strong woman."

"That's right, Miss."

"Stella."

"Stella."

"Eddie Crevine, especially, she seemed pretty tough on."

"Creviniello is the real name. An Italian name, but he's the devil. I used to think he was only another person like me or like you, only gone bad. I used even to pray for him, that he would change, that God would forgive him for what he done in this world. No more now. Now I know he's only a devil in a man's body, somebody who breaks a family apart, and if I could kill him now I would. He calls my house now, him or his people."

"What time does he call?"

"Anytime. In the night, in the day."

"Does he ever threaten you or anyone?"

"No. He don't say nothing, just the call, the hang-up."

"Then how do you know it's him?"

"Who else it's gonna be?"

She watched the pain play on his face, and thought she would paint that, too, put it into the smile, somehow, etch it into the lines around his eyes and mouth. She would tell Alfonse about the phone call, she decided, instead of telling Vito. She'd call Alfonse the minute she got home and tell him.

The waiter appeared and took their empty bowls.

"Did you really like that soup, Vito, or were you just being polite?"

"I can't eat food I don't like, Miss."

"Stella."

"Stella."

"Now we're getting someplace. You said for me to think of you as a grandfather. Well, not many grandfathers call their granddaughters "Miss". The waiter's going to bring shrimp on rice next. In a coconut milk sauce. I thought we'd stay with seafood."

"*I frutti di mare.*"

"*I frutti di mare.* Fruits of the sea. I like that. You're teaching me Italian, you're teaching me carpentry, sitting for a portrait. What can I give you in return?"

The eyes on her again, somber and clear as rain, that boyish spark of joy chasing the old-man pain away. "You mother she's gonna give me somethin I been waitin my whole life. Until ten minutes ago today I was pretty sure I was never gonna get it."

"It's nice, isn't it."

"Better than nice."

"Peter's married, he could still have a child."

"If he had one, who's gonna see it?"

"Joanie looks like she's still young enough."

Vito nodded in what seemed to her a sad way. The food arrived and they both began to eat.

"There's some trouble between you and Joanie, isn't there. I can see it on your face."

"No trouble."

"That's the first thing you said to me since I've known you that wasn't true."

Vito moved a shrimp along the edge of the plate of rice and would not look up at her.

"I'm sorry if I'm being pushy."

"It's alright," Vito said, but he was depriving her still of his

239

full attention. It seemed almost a punishment.

"It's a problem I have with people. It's just that, from that first meal we had at your house, from the first minute you met us at the door, I felt like I was part of your family. Alfonse is like a younger you, exactly, and I love Alfonse almost as much as my mother does. We haven't had a lot of family connection in our lives, you know. So when we finally met people like Alfonse, like you . . . the world started to look like a world again for us instead of a dirty, inside-out jacket."

"I'm sorry . . . Stella," Vito said, and now he raised his face to her again. "I'm sorry that what happened to you mother it happened. And to you. A lot of the time now I think about why things like that happen to people, why the world is the way it is. I talked to my friend the priest about it, Dommy Bucci, I looked for the answer in the Bible, I look at people—the other carpenters on the job, Julian, I look at everything and I say in a whisper in my mind to God: why do you make it like this?"

"The main question."

"For me, now, even though my Lucy died not that long ago, Joanie is what I ask God about, Joanie and my family.

"Why, because she doesn't go out with men?"

Another splash against the skin of Vito's face. He winced, looked away, then back.

"Alfonse told us. You don't have to talk with me about it if you don't want to, but it's not such a big deal these days. And she could still have a baby, you know."

Rain began to fall, softly, against the window. Vito was looking down at his plate. Eat, she wanted to say to him. Let the happiness come back with the food. But the polite little veneer that kept people from feeling through to the rough center of another person had been broken open now, she had cracked it and broken it open, that was her payment to him. She waited, forcing herself not to look away, not to talk, not to cover over what was raw.

"Joanie," he said, looking up. "If Joanie brought over my house one of her girlfriends to have dinner, I would hug the girlfriend just like anybody. If she wanted it I would walk her up the church in her wedding and give her over to another girl in front of everybody if that other girl was making her happy. Just like Peter I was gonna pay a debt for him to Eddie Crevine. Just like Alfonse I'm gonna build him now a house. For me, the family is more important than any thing in life. I went back to Italy by myself on the boat to take my mother and father and my sister and bring them over here to a better place. I was thirteen years when I went and there was a war comin. If somebody said to me to make you daughter happy, Vito, to make you family happy go down Broadway and lay down underneath the bus, I'd do it now. Any father would."

"Not any father I ever knew."

"For a father, especially, if a daughter doesn't show she loves him, it's like a stone in your throat."

"Some fathers deserve a stone on the head."

"But I wasn't like that with Joanie."

"I believe you."

"I never once raised my hand to her, or to Lucy."

"I know."

"I never once came home drinking."

"I believe you."

"Lucy's gone seven months now and a half and Joanie came over the house three times. Two of those times to take her mother's clothes and bring them over to the poor house."

"What is it then?"

Vito looked down at his hands and then back up. "What I did with Alfonse's mother. My big sin. It ruined my family what I did. It was the same thing as building up a whole house then you go around and cut holes in it in winter with the circle saw."

"I can't imagine a man like you. . . Did you ever tell Joanie you were sorry?"

"Sixteen times. Peter I could shoot with a gun and say I'm sorry and he'd say me back, 'Okay, Pa, no problem'. Alfonse— look what I did, forty-one years I let him go around the city calling me "Uncle"— he comes by every two days. Lucy was mad on me only a year—and look what it did in Lucy's life. It was a sin, nobody knows better than me, but how much do you pay for a sin, how long?"

"Joanie just found out a little while ago, though, didn't she?"

"Just before Lucy died. Alfonse told her. I kept it a secret all my life because Lucy wanted it that way. She's mad on me for that too."

"She's a woman, so it's worse for her what you did. It must seem worse."

"Worse than for Lucy?"

"No."

"You tell me something I can do, another way to say I'm sorry, a way for a woman, and I'll do it in one second."

"I don't know any good advice for things like that. It just takes time, I think."

"Time is what I don't have so much of no more."

They began to eat, though it seemed to Estelle that the rest of the conversation, unspoken as it was, floated and shifted in the air between them, and that the phone call floated there, too. It seemed to her that the unspoken things always climbed up between people and hung curtains of shame and guilt and anger, and that that was why Joanie didn't visit her own father. It seemed so clear to her, but how did you find the words? How did you say it to someone three times your age? How did you involve yourself in the problems of a different family without sounding like a short little know-it-all from another country?

242

Vito ate with a fork. He tasted the shrimp, gingerly at first, not looking at her, then the cooked slices of carrot in the spiced coconut milk, then he stirred the rice and vegetables together and began to eat with more enthusiasm. Another family finished its meal and left, and then, as if to fill up with sound the small quiet place they'd created at the table, the rain began to strike with more force against the plate glass window.

"Good thing we covered over the plywood," Estelle said.

Vito looked up at her, nodded as if he hadn't heard. After he'd swallowed another mouthful and taken another sip of the milky, lukewarm tea, he fixed his eyes on her and said: "You're not a Catholic."

"Buddhist."

"What do they think happens when you die, the Buddhist?"

"That you're born again, that you go into another body, another life, and you learn what you have to learn there, and eventually, after thousands of lives, you, well, you would say you begin to see the world the way God sees it. We believe everything teaches you—even when someone harms you or hates you, it's another lesson, even if you're born with a deformity or into a family of evil people, or if you're terribly sick, it all has some teaching in it. Even what happened in Cambodia."

"So you have Buddha for God instead of Jesus?"

"Not instead. Buddha was a sort of teacher, and we believe Jesus was too. Didn't they call him "teacher" in your Bible? But you still have to do the work for yourself, learn the lessons yourself. We believe, or I believe anyway, that you're put together with certain people for a particular reason, that some souls stay with each other, lifetime after lifetime until they get it right."

"Lucy and me."

"You and Lucy. You and Alfonse, Peter, Joanie, Alfonse's mother, me, Julian, even Eddie Crevine."

"And it leads to what, in the end?"

"Enlightenment. Though even that isn't really an end."

"Like a heaven?"

"In a way, yes."

"That's a harder heaven you people have than our heaven. Our heaven you only have to live one life good, or go to a good confession at the end, and you're all set."

"You have purgatory or something though, don't you?"

Vito nodded, finished off the last forkful of rice, the last shrimp.

"And don't you suffer in purgatory for a certain amount of time before you move up to heaven?"

"That's right."

"Well that's when the Buddhists are living all their next life-times. They would say this is purgatory, right now, right here. It's the same basic plan."

"And there's no hell?"

"Hell is here, this life, for some people."

"Here is not so bad."

"For some people it is. For my mother and her family it was."

"Our hell goes on forever."

"Ours only feels like it does."

"It never seemed to me right that a God would make it go on forever. It never seemed to me like something God would do."

"Not even for Eddie Crevine, for the people who did those things in Cambodia?"

"Maybe an exception, He'll make."

They practically went into hand-to-hand combat over who would pay the check—which came to all of eighteen dollars—

Vito trying to grab the piece of paper from her hand, then taking out a roll of bills and trying to force twenty dollars on the waiter, then, when the waiter walked away with Estelle's money, saying, "No, no, you have to let me, Miss. It isn't right. Fifty-five dollars every hour you mother and Alfonse are payin me, you have to . . ." Until the deed was done, the tip handed over, the plates cleared away, at which point she was finally able to calm him by saying: "One, if you keep calling me "Miss" instead of "Stella", I'll arrange for you to be born into a lousy lifetime next time around. And two, if you absolutely have to, you can buy me dessert and coffee at that Italian bakery on Broadway, on the way home."

Forty Seven

Joanna hugged Alfonse good-bye on Revere Beach Boulevard just as a gray cottony dusk was settling over the ocean. The forecast was calling for rain again—this was April in Boston, after all—and the air felt heavy and cool against her face. As she was fitting her key into the car door she heard the sound of running shoes slapping the pavement, then a man's laboring breath, and she glanced up over the top of her rented Buick and saw a pair of bare, heavy, hairy legs, a blue sweatshirt with RHS on the chest, a broad, unhandsome, unfamiliar face with dark eyes looking straight at her. Her breath caught in her chest but the man called out: "Revere is proud of you!" and she smiled her professional smile, waved, stood a moment listening to his footsteps fade away in the direction of Winthrop.

She sat behind the wheel with the motor running and watched as the gray dusk turned black. Her father would be finished with his day's work now and would no doubt be back at Proctor Avenue, washing up, changing out of his work clothes, going through a routine he'd gone through six days a week for forty years. Now, though, there would be no wife standing at the stove in a cotton apron, calling him to the table, no children to pry from the TV. And his body would have changed beneath him, as if directed by some slow-working, evil magician, into an old man's body: strong still, and capable, but singing out its gradual failure in a chorus of stiffness and ache. It did not seem like much to look forward to.

246

She drove up Revere Street, past the two funeral parlors and Saint Anthony's church, past the modest, mostly well-kept homes where the Italians had settled when they first came to this city, a hundred years ago. Instead of driving down Broadway—a tangle of fenders and headlights at this hour—she took the back way to her father's house, up over the rise of Cushman Avenue, down through the housing projects, up again to Proctor.

There were no lights on in the house. She stepped out into a cool soft rain and looked down the car port: no car. Unlike him to be out at this hour. Maybe a friend had died and he was at the wake; or maybe he'd decided to break up his solitary routine and go see Father Bucci for an early supper.

The rain began to fall somewhat harder. She'd taken two steps back toward the car when the house seemed to summon her. She climbed the steps and used her key in the lock, and another key to open the deadbolt. Moved by some odd urge, she did not turn on any lights, but stood in the entranceway next to the telephone table until her eyes adjusted. She went through the kitchen and along the carpeted hall, feeling her way by memory, step by step, resting a hand on the doorframe of the room where she'd slept as a girl, then her brother's room, then pushing open the door to her parents' bedroom.

She knocked a knee against the footboard of the bed, sat on the near side, lay back and stretched out in the place where her mother had died.

It had been many years since she had prayed, and she did not pray now. Not unless prayer meant a blind reaching out toward the possibility of some long-lost hope, some spirit that wanted the best for you on the road from innocence to decrepitude. All you had for comfort on that trip was a handful of people—the family you'd been born into, a mate and children if you were lucky, two or three real friends. She'd known for a long time that if you were slightly outside the common mold—a working class soul in an upper class world, a lesbian, an immigrant, a prisoner of fame—then there was a special loneliness reserved for you, and you were forced to find a few of your own kind and try to stick close. But it occurred to her now for the first time, lying where her mother had lain, that old age carried with it the promise of that loneliness, too, a sadistic bonus for those unlucky enough to outlive their mates. For the first time she believed she could imagine what her father must feel. No wife, no grandchildren. His siblings and half of his many friends in the grave. How easy it would be for him to blame all his pain on Eddie Crevine; how easy for her to do the same thing. As if all life's troubles could be set there, on Eddie's small shoulders, as if Eddie, not Peter's gambling addiction, not the merciless sweep of time, had broken up their family. She and her father were linked, then, by their separate solitudes, if nothing else.

She sat up and switched on the light. There was paper next to the telephone but she had to go into her purse for a pen. *"Dear Papa,"* she wrote, and as soon as the words were on the page she believed she could hear Leslie telling her how sentimental she was, childishly sentimental, how maudlin, how Italian. She squeezed the pen more tightly.

> *I came by to visit, but you were out. I'll come again soon.*
> *Love you, Joanna*

She slipped the paper under the phone and had just snapped her purse closed when she thought she heard a noise in the back yard, someone or something at the windows to her father's basement shop. For a full minute she sat there, perfectly still, listening, but the noise did not repeat itself.

Forty Eight

Elsie's way of getting angry was to go silent. In the time they'd been together—four and a half years—Peter could count on the fingers of one hand the times she'd raised her voice to him, or to Austin. Usually, if she was upset, she'd start with a question—*Why are you acting like this, Peter?* Or: *Austin, what made you say that?*—and try to have a talk. But if the talk didn't go where she wanted it to go, which had been the situation in bed last night, she'd pull back into a hard turtle shell and turn quiet, and it would be a few hours, or a day, an apology or a box of candy or a night out, before they'd really be on speaking terms again.

She was in the shell now. They'd watched Austin get on the school bus and were making the two-hour drive to the Bozeman airport. The empty highway, the snow-covered cattle ranches and the blue mountains in the distance—it was a landscape from a bad movie and the truth was, Peter thought, much as he'd miss Elsie and Austin, he couldn't wait to get on the plane and get the hell out of there for a couple of days.

"I'm na-not going to gamble, in c-case you're thinking that."

Nothing. Silence of the dead. Elsie kept her hands on the wheel and her eyes straight forward. The last thing she'd said to him, at breakfast, was that she was taking him to the airport, no argument.

"I wa-wanted t-to. I was thinking about it, to be-be-be honest. But I'm not stupid. I na-know how much better things are.

249

If you're thinking I'm ga-going to ga-gamble, I'm na-not."

The little muscles around her mouth moved. Peter looked down at the dark skin of his hands. It was some kind internal die, Carol had told him. Two little pills and you wake up a light-skinned black man. Lasted a week. No side effects. Most of the work she'd done had been on his hair, a cut, a permanent, and a little clay-like stuff to try to make the nose look different. That part needed a touch-up once a day. It occurred to him, a little late, that his father would be shocked to see a black man at the door, and maybe even it wouldn't be quite the same to have his son there, not looking like his son. But the priest disguise had been his idea, and the black skin had been Carol's idea, and he just couldn't resist putting the two of them together for a little added security.

"Gambling with your life," Elsie said in a flat tone, eyes forward, "is still gambling."

What she didn't understand was that the disguise was so perfect he wasn't gambling at all. He knew Eddie would be bullshit about what had happened—who wouldn't be?—and he knew there were still guys loyal to the Crevine operation, and he guessed Eddie had some way of staying in touch with them—through Johnny Denok, probably, before the arrest—and he knew there was a chance one or more of these guys—Eddie's son, Johnny, most likely—was watching his sister and maybe his father's house. The FBI might be monitoring the phone at 299 Proctor. That would be the type of thing Alfonse would have arranged. So there would be no smart way to contact his father in advance and risk tipping off either the bad guys or the good guys. Really, it would be nuts to show up there, Elsie was right . . . except that he looked so amazingly different that even if Eddie himself was parked in a car across the street he wouldn't ever guess. Limping black priest with a cane? It was just about the last thing in the world anybody would ever connect with the former Prince of Revere Beach Boulevard, Peter Amadeo Imbesalacqua.

He'd said all that to Elsie the night before, lying beside her with a foot of air between their bodies and the slight smell of the hair stuff in the room. She wasn't buying.

"Ev-everything is a gamble with your life," he said now, trying a different approach. "Driving a ca-car, going outside the house. You can have-have-have a heart attack in the sh-shower and drop dead."

"Says Mister Percentage," Elsie said, in a tone so bitter Peter couldn't believe it. She never talked to him this way. "You're always the one calculating the odds, playing the percentages. Tell me doing this doesn't up the odds of something bad happening by about a thousand times."

She turned to look at him and her eyes were brimming over. It killed him to see someone cry. Anybody, a teenage girl on the street, a little kid with his mom in the store. Drove him right over the edge.

"It's wa-once," he said. "Wa-once before my f-father dies."

Silence.

"If you wait till they catch Eddie, you could go back, we could all go back. You know that as well as I do."

"Ra-right. But what I know better than you is that they'll nev-never catch Eddie. He's Ed-Ed-Eddie Three-Hands. The Boss. The King. You th-think you get to that point in that vicious world by getting ca-caught? You think he'd risk coming back to Revere?"

"His wife's picture was on the TV last night, Peter. In Montana. On a national show. If we saw it, that means everybody in America saw it. And there's a half a million dollar reward. You don't think there's a good chance somebody will turn him in for that? You don't think Johnny Denok, or whatever his name is, will talk?"

Peter couldn't keep a short, bad laugh from escaping into the air. "They could c-cut out Denok's intes-intes-intestines with a steak knife and he wa-wouldn't talk."

Silence. Almost another whole hour of silence, the two of them looking straight ahead now like crash-dolls, waiting for the impact, the engineers standing by to see how fast the neck snapped. There were signs for the airport. Twenty miles. Ten miles. Peter wracked his brain to find something else to say. It was like having his heart ripped out, fighting with Elsie, but if he didn't go now he'd never go, never see his father again before the old guy passed on, and it would be the pinnacle of embarrassment to turn around here and go back and show Austin that he'd chickened out. He had a necklace in his briefcase. The kid had written up a little card for Darcy to go with it, and sealed it and put it in the box, and then wrapped it up for her himself.

He was still trying to find something to say when Elsie steered the car into the airport. He expected her to pull into the parking area, but she went right instead of left and pulled up to the curb in front of the half-assed terminal with the blue mountains in the distance.

"Na-not coming in?" he asked.

She shook her head and the movement caused one tear to track down along her cheek onto her jawbone. It turned sideways there and ran toward her chin and he reached out and brushed it away and she let him.

"Will you ba-be here when I ga-get back?"

She couldn't talk, he could tell, even if she wanted to. She nodded, not looking at him.

"K-k-k-kiss?"

She half-turned her mouth toward him and he planted a kiss there, held it as long as he could, squeezed her arm, and got out. Just before he closed the door he said, "Sa-sorry." But now he was a little angry himself. She should have understood. She should have said, "I love you" or something there, at the end. If the plane crashed or something and she never saw him again she'd feel bad forever. Halfway across the sidewalk he turned to look and she was staring at him through the windshield, tears down both cheeks. He waved. She raised her eyebrows. And he was through the door and in the terminal, carrying the cane in one hand and the small suitcase in the other, having forgotten that he was supposed to be limping.

Forty Nine

Luberto's Bakery stood near the corner of Fenno Street and Broadway, a square large room with five tables and plate-glass windows looking out on the street. The room smelled of baking bread and coffee. There were glass counters on two sides, and glassed-in shelves on which stood an array of cookies and Italian pastries—all cream and fluff and the occasional strawberry.

At this hour on a rainy Wednesday night the tables stood unoccupied. Estelle found one to her liking, and sat looking out at the shapes and shadows of the night while Vito ordered at the counter: coffee and an apple turnover for him, decaffeinated cappuccino and a cannoli for her, a pound of macaroon cookies—said to be the best thing for pregnant women—to be taken home as a gift for Lily.

"I was just thinking," Estelle said, when Vito set the paper plates on the table and sat opposite her, "You came to America when you were eleven, and so did I."

Vito nodded, swallowed, fixed upon her his full-bodied attention. "But my time is almost done with now, your time is just getting going."

"You're pretty strong for somebody whose time is almost done with."

"My whole family was always that way. Seventy-nine, my brother Carmine was when he died. And till the last day of his life he could lift Peter and Joanie up and hold them in his two arms and they were ten and eight. In our village in Italy when they needed a stone moved or somebody to carry the dead people in their caskets they would always say, *"Chiama un Imbesalacqua."*

"Call an Imbesalacqua?"

"That's right. Not so many brains maybe we got, but a little bit extra with the muscles."

"Should I live in your village when I go to Italy?"

Vito swallowed, shook his head, took another sip of his coffee. "Venice you should live."

"Want to come with me?"

"Sure, that's what you want. An old man with you in Venice, a pretty young girl like you."

A tall, thin, white-haired man came through the door, drops of rain shining on his cheeks. He put a hand on Vito's shoulder as he went past, and said, "Victor Bones." Vito put a hand over the hand for a moment, and the friend paused for a beat, then went to the counter buy his bread.

"Why did you leave?"

"Why? Because in Italy the way it was set up there were big bosses."

"Mafia?"

Vito shook his head. "Just bosses. The land belonged to them, the work all belonged to them. The rest of the people they were so poor they used to think they weren't even people. They lived in the caves, some of them, like animals. And my parents, they knew what Mussolini was gonna do, with the other one."

"Hitler?"

Vito nodded.

"And it was better here?"

"After thirty years working it got to be here about half what you dream of it was when you first come over. But that half was pretty good."

"Do you ever wish you stayed?"

He shrugged, turned down the outer edges of his lips. "Once in a while now I go down the beach and I stop the car and I look out past the ocean and I think what it would be like over there."

"My mother still thinks about Cambodia, even after everything that happened to her there."

"You always will. When you were a little boy or a little girl in a place, you always have that place inside your mind—good or bad. Let me get you another cappuccino?"

She shook her head and took the paper dishes to the wastebasket and then she and Vito went side-by-side out to the car. Every minute now she was debating with herself whether to tell him about the call or not. Maybe Alfonse would be visiting when she got home; if not, she'd call him the second she walked in the door. But all during the ride from Broadway to their apartment at the end of Beach Street, she thought about it.

"Want to come in and say congratulations to my mom in person?"

Vito pressed his lips together and shook his head.

"How do you say "too shy" in Italian.

"Troppo timido".

He was watching her now. She had the strange sense then, a weird intuition, that it would be the last time she would ever see him, and so she decided and opened her mouth and it came out, finally.

"When you were washing up and getting changed, the phone rang and I picked it up."

He watched her, waiting.

"A man's voice. He said, "Eddie Crevine's coming back to kill you. Two days." Then he hung up.

She expected to see a fear reflex on Vito's face, but he just kept looking at her calmly, unsurprised.

"I didn't . . . I was worried about telling you. I was going to tell Alfonse and let him . . ."

"It's okay, Miss," Vito said. "Joanie left me the gun. He comes now I'll shoot him, then I'll call up Alfonse to come get."

"You don't think you should go live with Alfonse or something, just for a while?"

Another stubborn shake of the head.

"Just a couple of days? If you're going to have a grandchild, you know, it's not really fair to let Eddie kill you first, is it?" She watched his face and it seemed to her—maybe it was just what she wanted to see—that the grandchild argument had made the stubbornness break apart a little bit.

"I'll take care of him," Vito said, in a certain tone that made her feel she'd pushed as much as she could. She leaned across the front seat of the car and kissed him on the cheek, and he thanked her again for the dinner.

"See you tomorrow," she said hopefully, and she got out and stood in front of the house, in the rain, watching the car until it made the corner onto Ocean Avenue.

Fifty

It was almost nine o'clock by the time Vito turned into his driveway, and he wondered at first if the light he saw burning in the bedroom was God's way of telling him old men weren't supposed to do so much in one day. Like Lucy knocking on the window that night when he was shoveling snow. A signal not to forget you weren't young no more. But being old was a surprise to him still, every day, a thing you wanted to say no to, and couldn't.

A grandson, he was thinking. A granddaughter. Either way it would be good. He would take him to the beach in the summer, take her out for ice cream every day after school. If he lived long enough maybe he could teach a little carpentry. It would be like a chance to do better.

He went in through the hard rain and unlocked both locks on the back door and, instead of turning on the overhead light in the kitchen, he took off his shoes and walked down the hallway in the shadows cast from the bedroom light. Years ago, when the children were small, one night every week he would stay out playing whist and eating cold cuts at one of his brother's houses. Friday night, usually, sometimes Saturday. He'd come home a little later than this even, and sometimes he would see the light on in the bedroom and know it was Lucy's way of saying she wanted to make love. He would have a little ritual then: looking in on Joanie and Peter in their sleep, saying a prayer over them, pulling up the covers, then brushing his teeth in the bathroom. He'd make a small noise, closing the bathroom door. Lucy would click off the light. And he'd go down the dark hall and get into bed beside her and they would make love, and then lie beside each other not saying a word, holding hands or touching just at the ankles. On those nights, in thanks for the love of his brothers and sisters and his wife, in gratitude for the fact of his sleeping children in the house, he would say the Hail Mary prayer to himself, slow, over and over again, riding the familiar phrases toward sleep. He remembered those days now. The light on in the bedroom had made him remember.

Barefoot, carrying a peace he'd almost forgotten was possible to have inside you, he went into the bedroom and saw the note on the table by the phone. He read the note, closed the light, and lay back for just a minute on the too-big bed, fully dressed, and fell asleep.

Fifty One

On the way north from D.C., his father had insisted they stop for a steak dinner, then stop again for coffee, and then, approaching New York, that they avoid the George Washington Bridge. Because of the traffic, he said, but James knew it was a fear of heights. Another thing not to be mentioned. The anger, the fear of heights and airplanes, the reason for coming north, the punch in the face, his father's health, his own work, his feelings, his relationship with brother John, their mother, Sean. Instead of pushing them apart, each unmentionable subject was like a strand of cable tying them tight to each other, because all those secrets were composed of the fibers of fear—his fear, not his father's. Never in his life had he been able to stand up to the man, not even in the smallest way, and it ate away at him now like acid on his skin. As a child it had been physical fear, a feeling so pure and cold it was like standing mouth-deep in a pool of freezing water. Later, it mutated into something else, some way his father had of making him feel ashamed and disloyal for not having gone into the family business, for not matching him as a man. "Change your name," his father had suggested on the day he graduated from college. But it was fake, a trick, a setup; behind those words—even though his father had changed his own last name—was the sense that James should have said, "No, Dad, never. I'm not ashamed to be related to you. I don't care if it's bad for my career."

But, of course, he *was* ashamed. Another thing he could

260

never say out loud. His refusal to say it, his inability to cut the cables and tell his father that what he did in his life was wrong, evil, hurtful, foolish—somehow his father used that to control him. To keep him as a slave. In the irony of ironies, his brother John, who'd gone into the business so eagerly, who hadn't changed his name, John could say anything at all to their father and never be struck or mocked. John was free, and for a while then, as James drove and checked the mirror, a strange, evil dream of freedom seemed to float along in front of the hood of the car, taunting him.

His face hurt where his father had hit him. There would be a mark. He'd have to make up a story for Grace. He'd have to explain to Sean why he let these things happen and didn't fight back.

It was after seven p.m. by the time they went through the tunnel and into Manhattan. Taxis, a few pedestrians with umbrellas held overhead against a light rain, the office buildings dark, the side streets half-lit, Park Avenue quiet except for a few garbage trucks and taxis and the occasional hired car. His mouth had stopped bleeding but it had not stopped aching. His father had gone into some kind of a trance, silent and still as a stone, brooding, calculating, feeling sorry for himself, lost in his mean little world. Fine. He'd drop him at the hotel and be done with him forever. Forget the secrets and cables and imaginary conversations. Forget it all. A punch in the face, a wasted day of work. Small price to pray for getting away from the man for all eternity . . . or maybe there was another answer.

"Fiftieth Street," his father said. "Pull up in front."

Caught up in a small eddy of thought, a tantalizing dream, James did not reply. Somewhere so deep inside him it was like a tiny spider moving back and forth in the darkest corner of a damp basement, there was a new idea in his blood. It made his lips curl up an eighth of an inch. Not an idea, really, not even a

Roland Merullo

fully-formed thought, just the first twitch of something that hadn't been there, or hadn't been visible at least, before his father hit him. Hit him! He was twenty-nine-years-old and his father had hit him! He was tired of the humiliation and tired of burying the anger under a blanket of fear. Tired to death of his father's definition of the world, of manhood, of loyalty, of everything.

"Pull right up, Jimmy."

It was like nothing had happened. As far as his father was concerned, his son's feelings weren't on the visible spectrum of light. He wasn't even a slave, he was invisible.

"Listen," his father said, turning to him. "I'm sorry I smacked you. This here's a bad time for me. Listen, here's a few thousand bucks for what you did." His father had been fiddling around in his pocket with one hand and now he pressed some bills between the bottom of James' thigh and the seat. "Now go, take the car and leave it someplace. And don't say a word to nobody."

James looked across the seat and had to use every ounce of willpower not to laugh at the light-brown hair and the sunglasses . . . at night! The word "small" came into his mind. His father was small, a small man physically and a tiny man inside. He managed not to laugh, but he couldn't stop himself from asking, in his dutiful-son voice: "What are you going to do?"

"Check in. Figure things out. Let me get out and then go. No fucking umbrella."

James felt the spider crawling along in the dark, and he had the thought, for two seconds, that if his father had said "thank you" or "I love you" then maybe he'd just let it go. Chalk it up to an old, sick, insecure man acting out. But his father was busy putting the roll of bills back into his pocket, taking off his sunglasses and hooking them over the front of his shirt, reaching for the door handle. The front door closed, the back door

262

opened. James sat still and watched his father struggle with the suitcase, place it on the ground at his feet, hand it to the doorman and reach in for his suits. James waited, eyes forward. The twitch of a shadow of a thought. A vision of violence and revenge. One thread of his inheritance.

"Bye," his father said, and the back door closed between them.

James sat a minute, watched his father following the doorman toward the entrance. In his sixties now, but he still had the walk, the aura of ownership; he was still The Boss. James put the Chevy in gear and waited for a cab to pass, then moved into the middle lane. The money fell off the front of the seat onto the floor and lay there looking almost alive. When he was safely away from the hotel he smiled in a mean way, another self rising up in him. He glanced one last time in the rear view mirror, and said, "Bye, Daddy," in a voice that was a little too loud.

Fifty Two

As she stepped out of the elevator Joanna could hear the telephone ringing in her apartment. It was still ringing when she punched the code into the alarm system and opened the door. By the time she reached it, the answering machine had picked up, so she stood next to the table in her raincoat and waited, thinking it might be Leslie. A click, a woman's voice: "Miss Imbesalacqua are you there? Miss Imbesalacqua? Please pick up the phone if you're there, this is an emergency. This is Alicia Crevine, Eddie Crevine's wife. I can't talk for more than a few seconds. I have some information for you, please, if you're there—"

Joanna hesitated, looked at the phone, picked it up. "Hello."

"Oh, thank God," the voice said, and for a moment it seemed as if the woman on the other end of the line would burst into tears.   "This is Alicia, Eddie Crevine's wife. I'm running away from him, can you help me? Please?"

Joanna gauged the voice, waited.

"Please, I can't talk long, please help me."

"How did you get this number?"

"Eddie had it."

"Where is he?"

"I'll tell you that, I will, but please meet with me. Please. I need help now."

"Why not go to the police if you need help?"

"I'm running away. I'm Eddie's legal wife. I can't testify against him. I don't trust the police, I trust you. Meet with me, please."

"I'm not available now," Joanna said, and she was about to take the phone from her ear when the woman began to sob in what seemed an absolutely sincere way, loudly, terribly, coughing and hiccupping like someone in the throes of psychological agony. "Please . . . This isn't a trick. I would never do . . . to you. Please. I'll kill myself if I have to worry about running from him for the rest of my life, please, I beg you. I'm at a phone booth at the corner of Broadway and Protection Avenue in South Boston. I'm getting soaked in the rain. Can you meet me here? The police would make me help them, I know they would, and Eddie would have somebody kill me before it ever got to that, I know he would. I'll tell you where he is but help me, please."

"I'll meet you at the L Street diner in twenty minutes."

"But I don't have a car. I ran . . . I took a bus . . . my sister is in New Hampshire . . . "

"A public place or no place."

"Alright, I—"

The line went dead as if the caller's twenty-five cents worth of time had run out.

Joanna set the telephone back in its cradle and stood still, staring out at the city. She tried Alfonse's home number. It rang twelve times without answer or answering machine. She tried his cell phone and got the recording. She called the Revere Police Station and was told he was in a meeting at the moment and couldn't get out.

"I'm his sister," she heard herself say. "Joanie."

"Sorry, Ma'am. Is this an emergency?"

"No. Important . . . not an emergency."

"Leave a number where you can be reached and I'll have him call you the second he's free."

"He has the number," she said. "It's Joanie, his sister. Half-sister. He'll know."

She hung up and waited. A minute, five minutes. She had her coat on and was at the door when she decided to call Mike McGowan.

"Where are you meeting her?" was the first thing he said.

"I won't tell you unless you promise to send only an un-marked car and keep people outside until I'm finished talking with her."

"Where are you now?"

"Home. Michael, I have only a few seconds. I want your word or I'm going there alone."

"It's a trick, Joanna."

"I'll take that chance. I have to hang up now."

"Alright . . . where is she?"

"Your word first."

"You have it."

"L Street Diner."

"When?"

"Twenty minutes."

She broke the connection and hurried out into the hall. It seemed to take the elevator ten minutes to arrive. She rode it down to the lower garage level. She'd parked the rented car in her reserved space, a few yards from the corner of the building. Her footsteps echoed as she went toward it, almost running. She noticed that the ceiling light near the corner wasn't work-ing, and, even in her haste, made a mental note to talk to the superintendent, who leased the garage to some Chinatown group. The car sat in shadow. It had no alarm system. She un-locked it quickly, opened the door and was already swinging

266

herself down into the seat when she realized that the interior lights had not gone on. She saw the large leg, then the torso, then the face of China Louis, his hair almost touching the roof of the car. A scream caught in her throat.

"Close the door," he said, very calmly. She couldn't move. Someone pushed against the door from outside and she turned and saw only the back of a leather jacket pressed against the glass. She tried to speak. She held her knees together instinctively, tried to reach down inside herself for one strong, fearless word. But something in China Louis' presence rendered her mute.

"The people who run your garage," he said, in a very quiet voice. "I helped them get their license. Nice deal for them."

She was leaning away from him, but even so, his huge face was only four feet from hers. He turned his body slightly toward her. This skin of his cheeks and forehead had a leathery sheen, as if it had been polished.

"Kid-kidnapping," she said, but the word squeaked and broke and seemed to cringe as it left her mouth.

China Louis's lips spread slightly, a miniature smile.

"No, just a visit. I came to give the newslady some news. As a favor. Because I like her so much. Because she cares so much about fixing up this broken world. The news is this: Eddie Crevine's wife is dead."

"She . . . she called me ten minutes ago."

"According to my sources she's been dead a day or two . . . That was a friend of mine who called you. Actress friend. All that crying and so on. Broadway in South Boston, the bus, her sister in New Hampshire and so on."

"You killed her."

"Me? What would have been in it for me? I never yet killed a woman or had a woman killed. There was even a woman once, white woman, pretty smart, famous, who went to visit a new friend of mine in prison and tried to really do me harm. I haven't even killed her yet."

China Louis reached down and took her handbag as if it belonged to him, and she didn't try to stop him. As he opened the clasp her cell phone rang. He ignored it, moved his fingers through the bag the way someone would shuffle through a bowl of change looking for a quarter. It took him two seconds to find the gun. With the phone still ringing he held the pistol up as if it was a prize. "Nice," he said. "Expensive." He took the clip out of it expertly. As if phone and pistol were connected, the ringing stopped. "It turned out," he said, "that Eddie was staying in a house in some undisclosed location and I have it on good authority that he killed his wife there in that house, left the body in plain view and drove away."

Louis put the gun back into the purse, took the phone out, looked at the screen, and slipped it into his pocket. He closed the purse and set it on the seat against her thigh: "Now what's so interesting is not that Eddie killed his wife . . . again . . . but that he left her body in plain view, don't you think?"

Joanna started to speak, to ask for the phone, but China Louis silenced her by touching one finger to her shoulder.

"I would take that to be the act of a desperate man, now, wouldn't you? Desperate or crazy, one or both. This desperate man drove away from a house where he was absolutely safe, you see. Now it seems to me a fair bet that this man might be going to pay your brother a visit, if he happened somehow to find out where he lives."

"No one knows where Peter is. Not me, not my father, no one."

"Probably not. Then you see, chances are this desperate man is coming to pay *you* a visit. You or your daddy, or both."

"How do you know this?"

"Wish I could say. But if you think I've come all the way

over here to make up a story for you, see your pretty face again, look down your shirt, well, then you're not as smart as I think you are."

"Why didn't you just have him killed if you knew all along where he was? Or tell the police and let them go arrest him?"

Louis looked at her as one might look at a foolish child, and spoke to her the same way. He shifted his weight in the too-small seat, as if her naiveté were causing him a bit of physical pain. "In your world, see, everything is two and two and it always adds up to four. Am I right? Have someone killed, call the police, take it to the courts. But in the real world, the world you'll never understand because your mind has taken over the territory where your heart and body are supposed to be, sometimes two and two makes five, or three, or eight. There's ways to do things and ways not to do them. There's other parties to consider, relationships between the Guineas and the Chinese, for instance, the Chinese and the Blacks and the Micks and a few old Hebrews, and that happens on another level entirely than Eddie and me. A half-Chinaman like me has an Eye-talian killed, what does that do on those other levels? See? That makes two and a half, say. A black man like me goes to the police, when the police have had nothing but enmity toward the black man since the beginning of time, then what does that make me in the eyes of my people? That's two and a quarter, say. So now all of a sudden your neat little two plus two comes out to equal four and three quarters. See?"

"So you came to me to do me a favor? Save my life?"

China Louis was shaking his massive head, keeping a tiny smile at the corners of his lips. "Well, I like you for some reason. And I like your old father. But this visit is pure self-interest."

"Like everything else you do."

"Exactly. Besides, you're a natural for the job. Spunky,

269

looking to fix things, looking to take an aspirin for that little pain you have inside you, that little guilt about being a nice Eye-talian girl who never did right by her family. I know the Eye-talians a little bit, see. The Chinese and the Guineas have a sort of mutual understanding. The blacks, too, though neither one of them would be caught dead admitting it. That guilt in you goes back two thousand years. Your daddy's sadness about his boy and you, that goes back two thousand years, too. Your brothers'—both of them—connection to their daddy and to you . . . same thing. It's all tribal, you see, the Sicilians, the Africans, they're not that far apart. All tribal. So I'm giving you quite a gift here."

"You stole my car. And give me back my phone, please."

"Too flashy for you, that car. Separated you from your people. Get a plain car, see, like this one."

At first, Joanna thought he was referring to the car in which they sat. But China Louis was holding something out to her. Not her phone. A business card. It had a name on the front side, a masseuse it seemed to be. She didn't understand.

"Other side," China Louis told her.

She turned it over and tilted it back and forth in the frail light.

"Eddie's car and license," China Louis said. "Gray Chevrolet Impala, new, 1998. Maryland plates. Being delivered to him even as we speak. Maybe he already has it . . . You don't have to thank me." He opened the door two inches, then turned and looked at her. "Very bad for you if you use my name in this, by the way. Very dangerous thing to do."

"You have my word that I won't do that, as I said before."

"Kind of you," Louis said. "You know, if you're alive when this is all over, you should think about moving back to Revere, visit your father some more, like you did today. Take that guilt out of you before it causes any more trouble."

She nodded, lips pressed tight together, not guilt now but fear running in her blood, fear and a strange, hot desire for revenge. She'd had enough humiliation at the hands of this man. She'd find a way to pay him back for it. She'd end up visiting him in Walpole Prison. She said, "My phone," but by then he was gone, and she was sitting alone in the dark car, holding the business card. For a few seconds, the black leather jacket stayed pressed against her window, then that man, too, disappeared, soundlessly. Still, she didn't move. When she was sure it was safe to do so, she got out of the car and went back upstairs and called Alfonse again, at the station.

Fifty Three

Peter found the ticket counter without any trouble and decided not to check the leather briefcase filled with gifts: Austin's package for Darcy, wrapped in gold-banded paper and tied
with a gold ribbon; a classy dress shirt for his father; fleece-
lined kid-leather gloves for Alfonse; for Joanie, a wool scarf in
blues and blacks from the Native American store just down the
block from Drinkwater's Video. Folded in around the gifts was
a change of underclothes and socks. On top was his tooth-
brush, and some make-up accessories for retouching the disguise.

His flight wasn't scheduled to depart until 12:50, an hour
and a half. He wandered up and down the terminal for a while,
just another black man in the halls of white America. He found
a restaurant, sat at a corner table, ordered lunch. The menu, the
restaurant, the building itself—everything he saw seemed to
have been set in place to remind him how plain this Montana
life was, how decent and orderly and plain. How middle-
American, how country-western, how wrong for a person like
him. Despite the risk—a very small risk, he knew—and despite
the difficulty it had caused between him and Elsie, he believed
he was more than justified in making the trip. For the past sev-
en months he'd been living the life other people wanted him to
live. Alfonse had wanted him to wear a wire to the meeting
with Eddie Crevine, and he had done so, even though he knew
it would mean either being put into a tree shredder if Eddie

caught him, or leaving Revere forever if Eddie didn't. Joanie had always wanted him to give up gambling, and he had done so, even though it was clear to him more and more lately that gambling had filled his life with as much excitement as trouble, all things taken into account. Elsie had hated it when he smoked . . . so out went the cigarettes. His father had always wanted him to turn into a stable, ordinary, responsible, middle-class man, and he had done that, too. He was a good father himself now, a good husband, a member of the Maddles Rotary club, and there was some real satisfaction to be found there, he had to admit.

But the price for all these compromises was an awful watering-down of what he thought of as his real self. He'd gone from custom tailored suits to J.C. Penney sportcoats, from a T-Bird to a Chevy Cavalier, from a profession in which he might make twenty thousand dollars in a single sale, to a daily grind of ninety cents profit per rented film, a dollar-thirty on new releases, a slow drip-drip of cash that filled the well nicely enough, sure, but made you a little bit crazy in the meantime. Waiting for his burger and Coors, he studied the people walking by the door, carrying suitcases, pulling luggage carts. One little electronic malfunction up there and their lives would end in a matter of seconds, and what would they have done in the world? Traded fifty years of clock-punching for a little house and a little car? Traded their lives away in exchange for not dying yet?

The TV over the bar showed an advertisement for a casino in Las Vegas: a happy guy playing craps with a beautiful woman at his elbow, a roulette wheel spinning in the glittering lights. He turned his eyes away from it, finished the hamburger, rewarded himself with a dessert—slice of cheesecake in a plastic box with one pink strawberry on top. $4.95.

His plane took off thirty minutes late. Caught in a steel and plastic airborne melancholy, he stared out the window for the first half hour, watching the puckered mountain landscape turn gradually tamer and flatter, the blanket of snow receding to the west, the cities cupped in webs of highway and sprawl with wide, still rivers meandering through. Somewhere over the northern Midwest he lay back in his chair and drifted into a dream: his mother scolding him, shouting at him. She was standing at the kitchen sink washing dishes and he was behind her, trying to explain, to plead his case. But, though he struggled and struggled, he could not make the words come out of his mouth in a straight smooth line, and his mother's anger rained down on him with the force of artillery rounds. *Disgrace, quitter, embarrassment, no son of hers.* He looked around to see if his father was home, but she didn't do this when he was home. It felt, in the dream, as if there were some kind of structure in his abdomen, a house or a building or a tower of some sort, and artillery rounds were breaking it down, word by word by word, and it was somehow clear to him that when the house was completely flattened, he would no longer be alive.

He woke to the sound of the flight attendant announcing their approach to Detroit International, seatbacks in the upright position, tray tables, and so on, but the dream haunted him as they landed, making the day sour, leaving him to limp through a larger, brighter, busier terminal with the word "disgrace" ringing faintly in his ears. It began to seem to him that his father might not be so happy to see him come strolling back into Revere, that the name "Imbesalacqua", once associated with a solid carpentry business and a famous anchorwoman, might have other associations in the minds of his neighbors now.

There were other black people in this airport. The sight of them made Peter less comfortable, rather than more. In Bozeman he'd been completely confident in his disguise; here, he limped into the men's' room and stared at himself in the mirror, checking the skin of his throat and hands, the strange hair and priest's collar, trying to see himself through a stranger's eyes. It took him a minute to be convinced. "Bulletproof", he said aloud when he was sure no one else was in the room. "Pa-perfect." But he didn't quite believe it.

There was a long and unexplained delay during which he wandered past the food and souvenir shops, practicing different degrees of his imperfect gait and imagining for himself an ancestry of slaves. It began to seem to him that he'd been a black man his entire life—isolated somehow from the entitlements of middle America, different, suspect, carrying beneath his soulfulness and charm a long history of hurt. What must it be like, he thought, to be set apart by something as immediate as skin color? It would be worse than stuttering. It would make you wonder all the time what people were thinking, whether they were calibrating their tone of voice to sound kinder than they actually felt. He thought of his sister—the word *lesbian* ringing in his ears like a taunt—and it suddenly seemed to him that everybody was always trying to find a way to divide humanity into competing segments. Maybe he did that, too. The Montanans were mountain people, hicks, not Italian, not warm—hadn't he said stuff like that to Elsie a hundred times? Men did it to women and women did it to men and young people did it to old people and northern Italians did it to southern Italians, who did it to Sicilians, who did it to Africans, who did it to other Africans. Straight and gay, educated and not, rich, poor, conservative, liberal . . . If you carried this tendency out to the last degree, you ended up with somebody like Eddie Crevine, who eventually turned the world into two big groups—himself, and everybody else. His "I" was a giant thing, some kind of massive puddle of oily water that spread out and out away from him. All you had to do was look at the puddle wrong, or step in the edge of it with the toe of your shoe and you became his sworn enemy. Of course, in his own case, he'd gone running right into the middle of the puddle and taken a piss there, so it probably made sense for him to be on the enemies' list. Badge of honor as far as he was concerned.

Buoyed by this small new understanding of the human condition, Peter stood at the floor-to-ceiling plate-glass window and offered up a silent prayer. He wanted to make sure God understood that he wasn't trying to be disrespectful, wearing the priest's outfit and pretending to be a man of the cloth. "Get me as far as my dad's house and back," he said to the overcast sky, in a respectful interior tone, "and I won't complain anymore about the Montana lifestyle. That's a promise."

Boarding the plane for Boston, still cruising along in an upbeat mood, he made a point of engaging in a little smalltalk with the gate attendants and watching their reaction. All was well.

He found his place—another window seat—and sidestepped in, settling the cane between his leg and the fuselage. People bumped down the aisle in an unruly stream, overhead compartments knocking, excuse-mes tossed about, the engines whining and roaring outside and the hatches of the luggage compartment being slammed closed. Just when he was sure he'd have both seats to himself for the last, three-hour leg of the trip, a man about his own age came backtracking up the aisle, bumping the seats with his carry-on and checking his boarding pass against the numbers above.

"Hi, this is me," he said, apologetically. Peter looked up at him and tried to keep the disappointment from showing. For once in his life, he wanted to be alone and look what happens. Chinos and a cashmere sweater over a pressed, button-down shirt, wire-rimmed glasses, the guy looked like he'd stepped out of an Audi ad. He stowed his gear above, sat, and immediately

276

put on his seatbelt. He plucked at the seams of his trousers, adjusted himself in the seat, glanced out the window, swung his eyes to Peter, smiled, held out a hand and said: "Graham Willis."

"Fa-fa-fa-father Pe-Peter Dr-drinkwater."

"Catholic?"

When Peter nodded the man seemed to smirk. For reasons he could not fathom, this Graham Willis raised an instinctive dislike in him, enough to make him forget, instantly, his theory of the divisiveness of human psychology. The guy was yuppified to the max, as they would have said in Revere: too neat, too sure of all the wrong things. The kind of guy who'd always lived the way he was supposed to, and had been rewarded for it by never having to worry about money, jail, sickness, family troubles, or anything else. In protest, Peter remained sitting on his seatbelt until the attendant came by and reminded him.

"I used to be Catholic," his neighbor said as they were taxiing onto the runway. A light rain had begun to fall against the windows.

Who, Peter had an urge to say, gives a shit.

The jet revved its engines a couple of times, a metal rooster showing off for nearby metal hens, then went racing and bumping down the runway. It seemed to take an unusually long time before the nose wheel lifted off. Peter felt himself pushed gently back in his seat—he'd always liked this part, the first rush, the gunning of the engines, the little flip-flop of the wings as the plane got used to being airborne after its boring hours on the tar. The jet climbed and climbed, leveled off, the landing gear groaned and bumped up into its housing. Graham Willis had fallen silent. He clutched the arms of his chair until the seatback light blinked on and then he let go gradually, like a first-time skater at the side of the rink.

When they reached cruising altitude, Graham wiggled around nervously in the seat for a second, then started to talk. "I suppose I should confess—no pun intended—that I've left the Church now. I'm lapsed. Too much bad history there for me."

Peter realized it was too late to pretend to be asleep. "You're n-not alone," he said, keeping his eyes forward, sending signals for the guy to zip the yap.

"Actually, as long as I'm confessing, I should say that I came to the conclusion a while ago that white men have been responsible for pretty much all the trouble in the world." He peeked at Peter's eyes, looked forward again. "You've probably heard all this before, but I have to say that when I saw you sitting here I was glad, at first, then I felt this sort of wash of guilt, you know? "

"Don't wa-wa-wa-worry ab-about it," Peter said. He was thinking: Idi Amin. Ho Chi Minh. Mata Hari.

"Sure, of course. But still, you know, my father would have an absolute fit if he heard me saying this, but sometimes I think we should all just give up everything we have and start over again from nothing."

"You ca-can't just p-pay attention to a person's skin. You nev-never know what's un-un-underneath."

"Right. I understand you perfectly. At the same time there *is* the political dimension, isn't there? History is still the story of humankind. One can't ignore it."

"N-no way."

"I mean, you do something evil and it breeds anger, and that anger is bound to reverberate, generation after generation, in funny ways, don't you think? It's why I can't be a Catholic, do you see? I'm sure you do. I mean no disrespect, Father, and nothing against you personally."

"I un-understand."

"It's just that sometimes I think of what men have done to women, what whites have done to people of color, the Crusades, the Inquisition, and I wish I could go back in time and be born somewhere else, in some culture with less of the lie and bad history to it. We're sort of built on a foundation of genocide, aren't we? And then we go and criticize other cultures for it. Genocide and slavery, really. And the Church just seems part of that to me, perhaps that's illogical."

"Only a la-little."

"And the woman question, you know. The Church doesn't exactly have a good record where women are concerned."

"I'd la-like to see that ch-ch-changed."

"Would you?"

"Ab-absolutely. B-but what can one pr-priest do?"

"Exactly, you see. You need to find others like yourself and organize."

"Ri-right."

The flight attendant came by with juice and pretzels. Graham Willis sighed and leaned his head back against the seat. He remained in that position for a few seconds then said, "I was a Dostoevsky scholar in graduate school," and gave a short laugh. "Thought I wanted to be a writer. Ended up in my father's little financial services business, which I've built up into something pretty solid, if I can boast a bit. But, you know, I think my study of Dostoevsky infuses that work, really gives me a moral compass in what I do. He was a big gambler, you know, Dostoevsky."

Peter choked on his cranberry juice and coughed for so long Graham turned to ask if he was okay and he had to nod and wipe his mouth carefully with a napkin. A little of the lip stuff came off on the paper.

"His wife finally cured him."

"Aw-aw-awful habit," Peter said.

"There's worse, I suppose. But what I meant when I brought up Dostoevsky was that he had this idea that, while the individual could improve and, you know, find *salvation*, society will always be the way it is. Good people and bad, saints and killers. You can see it in all his books."

Peter did not know what to say. He'd heard of Dostoevsky, maybe read something in high school once. He didn't remember.

Graham didn't seem to need any encouragement. "I'm not sure I agree with the great man. I like to think we can do better than that."

"Sh-sure we can."

"You don't have children so this might not mean anything to you but I have two, boy and a girl, and I believe that everything my wife and I do, every word, every decision, every mood, is going to ripple through their lives for as long as they're alive. Drives you crazy sometimes."

"Ca-ca-ca-cut yourself a little sl-slack," Peter said, and his neighbor laughed heartily.

"If there were more priests like you in my childhood I'd probably still be going to mass every Sunday."

"The Church's d-door is always open," Peter said.

He was hoping for the opportunity to pretend he was falling asleep, but Graham Willis was looking at him now, so closely he started to worry that something in the disguise was giving him away.

"I think about dying, some days," his new friend admitted. "I don't know if there's anything beyond that door, but at the moment I step through it I don't want to feel I could have done things better. I don't want to be taking my last breath and having a lot of regrets."

"I'm sure you won't," Peter said. "I can see in-in your f-face that you'll be fa-fine. You have a sh-shining soul."

"Really? Nice to hear that, coming from a priest. I'll tell my wife. She'll be shocked. She won't believe a priest said that to me. You made my day."

"Wh-what we're here for," Peter said. "I'll ka-keep you in my prayers."

Graham thanked him and closed his eyes and at last seemed to have said all he wanted to say. Peter looked out the window again—a blanket of clouds now—and thought about Father Bucci, and remembered that Easter was coming up, and wondered if he could squeeze in a side visit to St. Anthony's for a quick hello. He hadn't written Dommy the way he'd promised to do, though in letters to his father he'd at least asked him to pass on his regards. He wondered what a life like that was like. Talk about plain! No women, no fun that he could see. No wonder the guy liked to eat so much; what else was left to him? And that was supposed to be the route to God? Giving up everything and helping out other people all your life? Dying alone in a bed in the Old Priests' Home in Scituate surrounded by a bunch of other old guys with a history of celibacy and a unicolor wardrobe? That was God's idea of a good life?

Sunlight glinted on the wing. It was funny: down below, people believed it was raining. It was all a matter of perspective, he told himself, of seeing the world the way it really was. This Dostoevsky guy, it seemed to him, probably had it right: the world was the world, always the same. Bad guys. Good guys. It was like a movie. You had a role to play and you just had to drop the self-consciousness and play the scene out as best you could. This Graham Willis loved his kids at least, you could hear it in his voice . . . But he needed to stop putting people in boxes.

Fifty Four

Eddie followed the bellman as far as the revolving door and halfway across the lobby then told him to stop. "Listen," he said, holding out a hand with a folded fifty-dollar bill concealed in the palm. "I just changed my mind. Go grab me a taxi, will ya? I need to see my wife."

The bellman, who was Chinese or something, needed about a second and a half to cover his surprise and then he had the money in his pocket and was carrying the suitcase and suiter back in the direction of the street as if it was the most natural thing in the world to have a guest arrive and depart within a few seconds. He signaled a cab, opened the back door for Eddie, thanked him, bade him good-night. Eddie settled himself in, wondering why the Christ he'd bought two suits with him. The cabbie—another fucking *niwhita*—looked at him in the mirror.

"Boston," Eddie said through the partition.

The driver made a face. "Cahn't do, mahn," he said. "I'm off at four a.m. I'll never make it bahk."

Eddie had ten hundreds folded in his left hand. "Here," he said, pushing the money through the slot in the thick plastic divider. "Going to see my girlfriend and I'm horny as a bastard. This is to make up for your inconvenient, and I'll give you another grand at the end. Just don't tell nobody, don't write it in your log, okay? In case the wife takes me to court or something. If you don't wanna go, say so and I'll give it to the next guy in line."

The driver looked at the bills in his hand and said, "Mahn, de powa of women."

"Yeah," Eddie said. "Amazing, huh?"

"Dey rahn da worl, doan dey?"

"You know, that there's a fact," Eddie said. "Which is why it's so fucked up."

The cabbie laughed and asked Eddie to put on his seatbelt. Eddie said he didn't want to, and settled in for the long ride home.

Fifty Five

When he finished listening to what Joanie had to tell him, Alfonse asked her three times if she would give him the source of the information, and three times she told him she couldn't.

"Protecting your sources?" he said, with just the smallest edge in his voice.

"Alfonse, I just can't. I'm sorry. It wouldn't make a bit of difference in any case."

He took a breath and let it out. "Do you have someplace other than your apartment where you could spend the night. Even a hotel would be better at this point."

"I'm staying here," she said.

He squeezed the phone. "Not a time to be stubborn, Jo. Estelle—my fiancée's daughter—was at Vito's house today. She's working with him on our new house. She said there was a call saying Eddie's coming to kill him and kill you and that he'd be here in two days. That's why I keep asking you about the source, because if these two pieces of information came from the same—"

"I'm ninety per cent sure this source is accurate, Alfonse. And I'm staying right here. I have a gun, extra ammunition, an alarm system. I'll call and have a car take me to the station in the morning. I'll be fine."

"You can come stay at my house if you want. I can have some men—"

"I'll be fine, Alfonse."

"All right," he said. Her tone of voice gave him a little sting. The refusal to divulge her source was stupid. There had been so many false alarms about Eddie over the past months . . . "All right. I'll call and get the BPD to put somebody on you, though, so don't be surprised about that. He'll be in uniform. I'm going over to . . . to Proctor Avenue now to make sure Vito's not just sitting around there waiting to get shot. We'll have to act as if the information is right this time, and if it is, if Eddie left his hiding place to come back here and get revenge or something, then this isn't a sane man we're dealing with now. Either this is a trick, or bad information, or he's losing his mind. You don't just come out of hiding for no reason."

Alfonse was irritated when he hung up. Joanie, it seemed to him, was making the classic mistake of confusing courage with foolishness, setting up her journalistic ethics against the morals of a mad killer . . . but he couldn't change that at the moment. It was entirely possible that Eddie's people were toying with her, and toying with Vito, too, but, after thinking about it for a minute he called his FBI and State Police contacts and passed on the information, called an old friend on the Boston Police Department and suggested they watch Joanna's building, the garage, her office. Uniformed officer so there wasn't any confusion. "She has a handgun," he said. "We wouldn't want the wrong person getting shot."

Everyone was more than happy to oblige. Since the disappearance of another giant Boston underworld figure a few years earlier, and the revelation that an FBI agent had been the one who'd tipped him off, relations between the Bureau and their counterparts in the state and local forces hadn't been exactly harmonious. Based on an anonymous phone call and the word of Joanie's anonymous tipster, it wasn't likely the feds would send anyone to watch out for her or Vito. It wasn't their job, really. Their job was to catch Eddie, but Alfonse could sense—

285

it came from years of police work—that a competition would be set in motion now. If it turned out to be true that Eddie had left his hiding place, then every agent, every beat cop, every supervisor and ambitious lieutenant, would want to be the one to catch him. A real mess, it could turn out to be. And if it turned out he'd had the license plate and *not* passed it on, then he'd be Patrolman Romano again . . . if he was lucky.

He got into his car and drove to Proctor Avenue, assaulted by small demons of doubt at every streetcorner. Better safe than sorry, he kept telling himself. Better wake his father up and make the phone calls he'd made, than have it be good information and not act on it. By the time he arrived it was past eleven o'clock and the house was dark and closed-up, the shrubs along the front windows laden with berets of frozen snow. Vito, he knew, had gone to bed hours ago and would be up at five for prayers and then work. For a moment or two, sitting in his own car on the other side of the street, he thought he might just let the man sleep and give him the bad news in the morning. But it was too risky. He went and rang the bell and after two minutes a hallway light went on and his father showed his face on the other side of the glass. He had a crowbar in one hand and a pistol in the other, and a look of the purest fear on his face.

"It's me," Alfonse said. "*Babbo*, it's me. Alfonse."

He heard the lock turn and the door open. He took the gun gently from his father's hand. "Sorry to wake you," he said. "But you're staying at my house tonight."

"What, for what?" Vito said sleepily. He was wearing long johns and a pajama shirt and the sleep-creases in his face made him look eighty-five.

"We had a tip that Eddie might be coming here. You had a call, didn't you?"

"Who told?"

"Estelle. But we had another tip, too, same thing. Could be it's just a game he's playing but I think we should take some precautions this time."

"I got the gun now," Vito said. "I'm waitin here."

"I don't think that's wise, *Babbo*. There could be more than one guy, front door, back door, windows. A gun wouldn't help you then."

Vito had not let go of the crowbar; it was hanging at his side. He was shaking his head in small movements.

Alfonse had a moment in which he pondered the stubbornness that ran through all of them—Vito, Peter, Joanie, even Lucy. Certainly himself. There had to be a gene for that. "Pa," he said. The word had seemed to stick in his mouth for a second on the way out. "I'm asking you, as a favor to me." He could see the force of the word reflected in his father's eyes. *Babbo* was one thing, the Italian version, only a notch or two better than "Uncle". *Pa* was a syllable that carried a different weight.

Vito watched him for a few seconds, eyes steady, decades of secrets and small lies there, forty years of guilt and longing. Alfonse could see him breathing. His father nodded finally, and went to the back part of the house to get dressed, and Alfonse found a drawer for the pistol and stood in the hallway with the photos of Lucy there, and Peter and Joanie, and it occurred to him for the first time that it was his brother Peter who'd brought their whole house of shame and secrets crashing to the ground. Without Peter's gambling debt, without his crazy courage in carrying the tape recorder to his meeting with a killer, without all that, he and Vito and Joanie would have gone the rest of their lives stepping through a choreography of deceit. They owed the guy a word of thanks.

While he waited, Alfonse called the station and told them to get someone to sit in an unmarked car on the other side of the street and keep a watch on the house. It turned out there was a fire on Shirley Avenue, two patrol cars tied up there. Captain Silovsky said he'd send Robson, the rookie, and Alfonse didn't see how that would be a problem. Even a rookie, even Robson could watch an empty house and make a radio call in the event he saw something suspicious.

Another two minutes and he had his father in the car and was driving him back to Ambrose Street, and it was only then that he realized it might be uncomfortable for Vito to spend the night there, a few feet down the hall from the upstairs bedroom where he'd committed his one great sin.

Fifty Six

For the first hour after leaving his father in Manhattan, James watched the rear view mirror almost as much as he watched the road. Boxer in college, rock climber now, he wasn't a particularly fearful man, but—and he knew he wasn't alone in this—he harbored a tremendous terror of going to jail. Two or three times over the years he'd heard his dad talk about his own father—who'd spent the last decade of his life in federal prison—and while his grandfather's reputation and contacts had protected him from physical harm, the idea of being caged in like that, surrounded by shouting, screaming, deranged men, was, for James, the exact equivalent of hell on earth. He'd spent not a small portion of his adult life worrying that his father would coerce him into doing something illegal. And he knew—it was just the way things worked—that the first time he crossed the line he'd pay a price for it. His father and his father's friends spent their entire lives breaking one law after the next and, for long stretches of time, living free and unworried. His father would ask him one favor—cheating on a tax return for a big friend of his—and he'd be wearing an orange jumpsuit for years because of it.

But all through the northern outskirts of New York City and then the Connecticut countryside there were only passenger cars and trucks in the rear-view. This was it, then; it was over. The big favor had been called in. One time. That was the agreement. Now he could go back to his life.

But as he drove—he couldn't help himself—he tried to puzzle out the reason why his father had come north again. James supposed there was some high-level mob meeting in Queens or Brooklyn, and his father either had to show up or risk losing hold completely on his Boston operation. Even that made little sense to him, though. His father had been safe in hiding someplace. He had Alicia for company and sex, all the money he could ever need. The cancer scare of a few years ago seemed to have given him a little perspective on appreciating life more and worrying less about power and murder and money. Why take the risk, then, of leaving his exile and making the call and venturing into the part of the world where he was, among law enforcement officials at least, a household name? Was the addiction to power that all-consuming? Was his father just the kind of person who needed to live on the edge all the time or feel bored to death? He had a couple of clients like that; Sean called them "risk-addicted". They had a few friends like that, too, so sure they wouldn't get sick that they cruised the minefield of the sexual underworld with about as much concern as kids risking a kiss on prom night.

Maybe his father had simply lost his mind, like the old Mafioso who used to walk around Manhattan in his bathrobe. What had they called him? The Oddfather. Perfect.

It didn't matter now. He decided not to think about it. Long ago Alicia had advised him to let his father live his life the way he wanted to, and concentrate on his own. She'd been right, of course. Let it go, he told himself. Let it go. But some little devil was whispering to him now; he could almost make out the words.

All the way through Connecticut—Greenwich, Bridgeport, New Haven, New London—he was fine. He saw signs for Providence. He crossed the Massachusetts State line. It was 8:30, he'd be back in time for dinner and a nice bottle of wine.

He'd talk about his father as little as possible, put cream or something over the bruise on his face, make up some story for Sean and Gracie and the client—Blakesley, it was—whose meeting he'd blown off. Let it go, he kept telling himself. You're all right now, home free. Let it go.

The thought gave him a measure of peace, and the peace carried him along Interstate 95 very nicely until he saw a sparkle of flashing blue lights in the mirror. It suddenly occurred to him that he should have ditched the car, and it suddenly felt like the darkness was alive with hands grasping at his neck. He pulled into the right lane, hoping the cruiser would go flying past, but it stayed on his bumper. Siren going now, lights splitting the highway darkness. James had a sudden urge to jam his foot down on the accelerator and drive Leon's plain Chevrolet into a bridge abutment, but he fought it, pulled into the breakdown lane, put the car in Park, reached for the fake papers as calmly as he could.

Nothing happened. The flashing lights stayed behind him—it was a Massachusetts State Trooper—but no one got out. He waited, palms sweating, pulse going. "Thanks, Dad," he said out loud. "Many thanks."

Another three minutes and a second state police car pulled up behind the first, and then there were three men walking toward him, two of them in uniform. One stood behind the car. One went to either side. He rolled down his window. He had the registration in his lap. "Going a little too fast, officer?" he tried, but the face was over his left shoulder, unimpressed, unforgiving, and there was another face at the passenger window. They'd drawn their guns.

"Step out, please," the trooper said.

James obeyed and, as if the position had been taught to him since first grade, a kind of Creviniello family yoga, he leaned straight-armed against the car with his legs spread and stood still while the trooper felt for a weapon. "Can I ask what this is about?"

Nothing, at first, no answer. And then the plainclothes cop said, "We think you know what it's about, Jimmy."

"If I'm being arrested for something, I'd want to speak with a lawyer."

"No arrest at this point," the man said. He had a particularly calm, unnervingly quiet way about him, a square face, a short haircut with a two-inch scar in the hairline at the top of his forehead. The lights from the two police cars flashed against the skin of his face, strobes at an 80's party.

"No Miranda rights?"

"Not at this point. If you want to, though, we can go that route. We'll be more than happy to arrest you and book you . . . Or you can just come to the barracks voluntarily and we can have a little conversation and let you go. No lawyer. Your choice, Jimmy."

"James," he said. "What's this about?"

"Your choice," the man repeated, a little impatiently. "Cuffs or conversation. You got five seconds to decide."

"Conversation, of course," he said, and he was surprised at the calm way the words came to him. His father, he thought bitterly, would be proud.

"This your car?" one of the troopers asked, as if he knew the answer to the question.

"Borrowed . . . a friend's."

"We'll tow it to the barracks for you. Just a little ways up the road here."

"Fine."

No cuffs. No rough handling. They escorted him almost politely into the back seat of the second cruiser, a trooper at the wheel, the mysterious square-faced man in the passenger seat, eyes forward. It was, as they'd promised, only about ten minutes to the State Police barracks, but during that time not a word was spoken. The uniformed trooper drove around back, parked beneath a streetlight, and opened the door for him like a bellman. The two men walked on either side of him up the wide back steps and into a hallway and then motioned him into what he recognized, from a dozen TV shows, as an interrogation room. No window. A mirror that was obviously two-way. Plain table and four chairs. Next, he thought, they'll offer me coffee in a Styrofoam cup.

"Coffee?"

"Sure."

They took their time about it, one of the uniformed troopers fetching the cup and placing it in front of him, thoughtfully, with two creamers and two sugars, a stirring stick and a small pile of brown napkins. As if they knew how he took it.

The square-faced man sat down directly opposite him. Big, muscular arms, James noticed. Slight twitch to his right eye. "Okay," he said. "I'm agent Phillip Savoy with the FBI. We have reason to think that you might have some information about the whereabouts of your dad, Eddie Crevine."

"What makes you think that?"

Agent Savoy smirked with one side of his mouth. "I'm a psychic," he said. "A palm reader. Let's not play games, Jimmy."

"Fine. I have no idea at all where he is right now. And that's true."

"*Right now*," the agent said. "Cute."

There was a knock at the door. A uniformed officer stepped into the room, handed him a manila envelope, and left. "Let me rephrase this then: We have reason to believe you drove your father someplace tonight."

"I'm on the verge," James said, though it felt like his intestines were crawling up through his throat to accompany the words, "of asking for an attorney."

"As we told you, you have every right to an attorney at any time during this conversation. I probably should also tell you that we're perfectly willing to let you walk out of here and not arrest you. The charge would be, and I say *would be*, abetting a fugitive. Not any ordinary fugitive either, I might add. Not the kind of fugitive a D.A. is liable to look the other way about." He opened the clasp on the envelope and glanced inside without removing the contents. "But we'd be willing to overlook that in exchange for a little cooperation, as long as that cooperation happens right now."

James pressed his mouth closed, thoughts racing. It seemed to him he should ask for a lawyer. In fact, he *knew* he should. At the same time, if they'd let him go . . .

"We know it's a busy time for you," Agent Savoy said in a kinder tone, "in your line of work . . . And we want to keep you here for as little time as possible. But it's a big moment for us, as I'm sure you'll understand. We've been looking for your father, the whole law enforcement world has been looking for him, for what, six, seven months now? A million tips and leads and every one of them as cold as an ice cube in Antartica. Now, just today, we have something that's more . . . promising. We didn't just accidentally pull you over, as I'm sure you can guess. We had the make and model, color, license plate. Even the approximate time of arrival back in our fine commonwealth." He paused, giving James a moment to speak.

James watched him and waited. His father's so-called friend, he thought, Leon. Leon with the aquarium and the dead eyes. They'd set him up from the start.

"Have some coffee," the agent said. "Give it a minute's thought."

James took a sip and nearly spit it out.

"Nothing personal, James, but your father is not a nice

man. Murder, extortion, prostitution, drug peddling, threats, arson, intimidating witnesses. This isn't exactly the type of behavior we turn a blind eye to. We think maybe you're not keen on that stuff, either."

"You've never proved any of this," James said. It was all twisted up. He wanted to kill his father, not defend him. He was doing this for himself now, trying to find the route out. Once they formally arrested him, he knew, it would set in motion an unstoppable series of events—press coverage to begin with, lawyers, court appearances. The end of his career, his relationship . . .

"That's right," Agent Savoy went on. There was just a touch of impatience in his voice. "We believe we could prove at least some of the charges now though, if we could find him. And your dad knows that, which is why he ran in the first place. Like I was saying, we don't think this is your style, all this stuff. In fact, we think you're more or less blameless and just got asked to do Daddy a favor. Under pressure, I'm sure. That's the kind of thing we might overlook, with a bit of cooperation at a key moment. If you read me."

"I read you." James gulped, he couldn't help himself. He felt like a ball of twine that was being unraveled. He touched the coffee cup then took his hand away. "But I can't help you right now."

"That's fine," Agent Savoy said. "We're still going to let you walk."

"You are?"

"For now we are, sure. Just a couple more questions and then you can get back on the road if you want to. Your dad's married to Alicia Bentley, isn't he? Girl who used to work at his club years ago?"

"He calls her his wife," James said, hoping to sound cooperative now, to show he had nothing to hide, "but they're not legally married as far as I know, just living together."

"In sin, as they used to say."

James broke eye contact and had a sip of coffee. The liquid was almost poisonous; it went down into his belly like ink, or oil. He shrugged and looked up again.

"Nice woman?"

"Very nice."

"You're close to her?"

"Yes."

"Almost a second mom, in some ways, though she's what, four years older than you are? A sister, then, maybe? Yes?"

"She's a good soul," he said.

Agent Savoy was looking at him steadily now. Before he said the next word James somehow had an intuition of what it would be. Somehow he knew.

"Was," the captain said.

"What do you mean?"

"*Was* a good soul." The captain reached into the envelope and slid out a photograph. For a second, two seconds, he held it up in such a way that James couldn't see it. And then he placed it on the table between them, spun it around, and slid it across. "We got this a half hour ago."

It was a photograph, horrible scene, of a woman lying on the floor of what seemed to be a kitchen. Blood everywhere. Her face ripped apart around the left eye and cheekbone as if she'd been hit by a tank shell. Though it shouldn't have, though, even before the picture had been taken out of the envelope he'd had an idea where the captain was going, it took James a second, one beat, one last gasp of denial, to realize who the woman was. A second later he'd turned sideways and was vomiting on the floor.

"It's okay," the State Policeman, who'd been silent to that moment, said now in a fake-kind voice. "We'll clean that up in a minute. You're not the first guy who's ever done that here."

"It's a shock," Agent Savoy chimed in. "We understand. We're sorry for your loss." He waited, eyes unmoving. "I'd say we're about ninety per cent sure at this point that this is your father's handiwork. This photo was taken in the house where it turns out he'd been living. Nice home. On a tidal river about half a mile from Miami Beach. The guys who were cleaning his pool today happened to need to ask him something. He forgot to pay them, I guess. They looked in through the sliding door and saw some blood and they called the local cops. Alicia's picture's been everywhere lately, and so, even with her face all ruined like this it didn't take the cops more than a few minutes to figure it out. They found evidence in the house that Eddie had been living there. Car was gone. We heard all this, naturally, pretty much right away, which would have been about several hours ago. And then, a short while ago, we had the tip I mentioned, about the car you turned out to be driving, and I have to say it just seemed like too much of a coincidence for us to let it pass. I wanted you to see the photo just in case it changed your mind about talking to us."

James was wiping his lips with one of the paper napkins. He slid his chair sideways away from the small puddle of vomit. He looked down, reflexively, to see if any of it had gotten onto his shoes. He looked up into Agent Savoy's eyes, glanced at the photo again. And then it was as if a door opened to a room where he'd kept all the things he'd heard over the years about his own mother. She'd run away, his father had always told them. She didn't like the life. She'd gone to the bank one day and taken out a shitload of money, and never come home, and he'd let her go. Never even looked for her, his father had said. And then, "That's love."

That's love. All these years he'd let himself believe it. Once, one time, he'd asked his brother John about it, and John had confirmed their father's story with such unwavering confidence that James had been happy enough to set it aside. He barely had memories of his mother, anyway. He'd been two when she left. He remembered maids, babysitters, so-called "aunts", and then, when he was almost finished with high school, Alicia. She was the first person he'd come out to, the first person he'd told about Sean. The captain was right—a sister, a mother, a friend, a mix of all three. He glanced at the photo again. He felt the air pressing against him from all sides, like a swarm of hornets just released from long captivity, angry, hungry. He looked at the wall to the left of the captain's face and he said, very clearly, from out of the center of a hot pool of hate, "I dropped my father at the Waldorf Astoria hotel in New York City." He looked at his watch. "Three hours ago, a little more."

"He say where he was going?"

James shook his head. "He checked in. I waited for him to go through the doors. This was the one favor he said he'd ever ask of me, that I drive him. That's all I did. I swear it."

There was a terrible smell in the room now. The State Trooper and Agent Savoy seemed not to notice. They asked where he'd gotten the car, how he'd known where to go, what the various men had looked like, what names they'd used—the questions piling up like bricks building a cell. Answering them, one after the next, James felt that his fear was being replaced, word by word, with a fury that had been living inside him for twenty years. At some point the state trooper left the room, already going after his father, he supposed. It didn't matter to him now. He just wanted out. He wanted his father dead or in jail, alone, unvisited, helpless. He wanted to leave this building and get Sean and get on a plane and make another life somewhere else entirely. He wanted to chop off his past as if it were a gangrenous limb and leave it . . . and go. And then, beneath all that, he realized he wanted something more. He pushed it down and back, behind the other thoughts; it peeked back out at him.

The questions, it seemed, were finally finished. Agent Savoy said, "We really appreciate all this. You're free to go. Car's outside."

"Sure," James said. "And then, tomorrow or the next day you'll come and arrest me, right?"

"I don't think so," he said. "Really, I don't. Probably now, though, tonight at least, you should go stay someplace you don't usually stay. Your brother might be unhappy with you if he finds out we had this meeting. Your father will definitely be unhappy."

James couldn't stop a bitter laugh from flying out of his mouth, one syllable, half spit, half cough. "Witness protection," he said, with all the sarcasm he could muster.

The agent shook his head and, for the first time, smiled. "I think," he said, "in your case . . . probably not."

Fifty Seven

The jet circled and circled, providing Peter with an aerial tour of Greater Boston at night. He had never been at good at maps and geography, but he recognized the sixty-five-story John Hancock Tower—Boston's tallest building—in the heart of the Back Bay and he was able to take a reading off that and more or less figure out where the plane was—way south of the city, and then west, and then north. Hours late taking off from Detroit, the plane circled and dawdled for so long he was ready to find a parachute and jump. At last the pilot announced their final approach. This final loop took them out over the Atlantic, somewhere near Gloucester he guessed, then they turned south and came swinging in low right over Marblehead—where he'd had his famous last ride with Eddie Crevine—and Nahant—where he'd once lost eleven thousand dollars in a poker game—and then, as if it were a tour arranged specially for him, directly over the three-mile crescent that marked the shoreline of Revere Beach. A bump of excitement went through his face and hands; it was extremely hard to sit still. "That's where I grew up," he wanted to say to his seatmate. "That beach right down there, that's my territory." But he decided it wouldn't be wise and he squeezed his hands together and tried—unsuccessfully—to catch a glimpse of Proctor Avenue before the plane dropped over the triple-deckers of Beachmont and Orient Heights, so close he felt he could reach out and grab a glass of wine off a top-floor tenant's table.

Once they were on the ground, finally, two and a half hours behind schedule, Graham let out a sigh of relief and shook Peter's hand warmly.

"That conversation meant more to me than you will ever know, Father," he said.

"Noth-nothing," Peter said. "R-really." But Graham thanked him again, and told him people often failed to realize what good they did in the world, and he took out a business card and said that if he ever needed investment advice . . . yes, priests didn't make much, but if he ever inherited some family money or something like that, he should please call. "Strictly *pro bono*," Graham said, and Peter nodded as if he knew what that meant. He stalled a bit so Graham would get out ahead in the line of passengers and not invite him to share a cab or have dinner or something. He waited until the last stragglers passed his row, then he got to his feet, glad he hadn't checked his briefcase, and headed for the door. On his way out a pretty flight attendant apologized for the delay and wished him a good night and Peter couldn't resist saying, "Bless you."

Staying in character, he told himself. Making people smile wherever you go. Not realizing how much good you do in the world.

He walked confidently and optimistically out of the gate area and past the security line and went down the escalator and was halfway across the terminal's main entrance lobby before he realized how foolish it would be to take a cab now. All during the past week—when he'd first had the idea to pay his father a visit, when he'd been sitting in the special chair in Carol's home/workshop and being turned into someone else, when he'd had a few quiet moments during the flight—he'd pictured himself arriving at his father's front door: the big surprise of it, the warm welcome. In his imagination he stepped out of a white and green cab—Atlantic Taxi, it was—and went up the walkway in the early evening light, and pressed the doorbell. He saw the whole thing clearly, a dream, a triumph.

But in the middle of the airport lobby the dream wrinkled around its edges like a sagging hot air balloon that was losing heat. The cab idea was nuts. Sure, beyond the city limits, Atlantic and the other Revere cabs weren't allowed to cruise for passengers or wait in the airport queue. But there might still be a few Revere guys, old friends of his, who drove a Boston taxi as a living or to make an extra dollar now and then. The second he opened his mouth and stuttered his way through the address they'd know it was him. Two minutes after they dropped him on Proctor Avenue word would be all over Greater Boston: Pete Imbesalacqua was back. Not smart.

So, as much as he loathed public transportation, he forced himself to go and stand at the shuttle bus stop, and ride with the other sheep to the airport subway station, and wait there, at one end of the platform, with his heart going ninety miles an hour, and his face turned away from the other passengers so nobody could see the profile, the famous nose, and make a lucky guess. The skin of his hands was cup-of-coffee-brown— the pill had worked beautifully; still, as he'd worried from the start, there was only so much Carol had been able to do with the nose.

That late at night—it was quarter to eleven—the trains ran only every twenty minutes or so, and he must have just missed one because it seemed to take at least a century before he heard the rumbling on the tracks and saw the headlights coming. He found a seat near the front of the first car and sat there with his briefcase on his knees, the shiny brass clips glinting in the train lights, his mind racing. It seemed to him—and it had been years since he'd felt this way—that he and his father were linked by an electric cable, heart to heart. Look at what they'd been through together! They'd had their fights, sure, like any kid and parent, but his father had never given up on him, never. He'd come down and bailed him out of jail that night when he was drunk and worried sick about his debt. He'd gone in person to see Eddie Crevine, *at his house*, for God's sake, and offered to pay it off. He'd been there every day during the Witness Protection interviews. Old School, sure, but Old School was all about loyalty to family above everything, and so it seemed brave and right and classy that he'd taken a risk like this to come see the old man before it was too late. He didn't know what they'd do. Just sit around the house and talk and watch TV, maybe, or maybe his father would cook him a meal. He had a ticket back to Detroit and Montana the next day at noon so maybe his father would drive him to the airport and kiss him good-bye in the car, or take him down to Darcy's house first so he could drop off the gift from Austin. It wasn't much to look forward to, but it felt right, coming back, and he knew, once his father figured out who it was, and why he'd had to come in disguise, that it would be the greatest gift he could possibly give him. Besides, the risk, from this angle, seemed minuscule, the odds of getting caught or even getting in trouble were about the same as the odds of winning the Massachusetts State Lottery on any given night. Even on the tiny, tiny chance that somebody recognized him, he'd be long gone before the word reached Eddie or one of his goons. No longer so worried about the famous nose, he looked down the car in a satisfied way, proud of himself, feeling like he used to feel, like he had royal blood, like God loved him in a special way. He felt a little surge of pity for the poor people who had to ride this noisy cage to work and back every day of their lives. He'd broken free of that. Paid the price and broken free.

The Blue Line ran behind Suffolk Downs—more great memories there—and through the lowland behind the condos on Ocean Avenue. He felt one small stab of regret when the train brought him close to the building where he used to live. He thought of the first night he'd taken Elsie back there, to the fifteenth-floor condo with the ocean view, after having had a nice day with her at the track. He'd gotten a bottle of champagne all ready in a bucket of ice. They'd had a little to drink, stood out on the balcony and looked at the stars and listened to the waves. A sweet kiss there, then they'd gone into the bedroom and made love. He remembered it like it was yesterday, the warmth of her, the way, when it was over, she'd told him the story of her life as if there needed to be a full confession before they went any farther with things. Her shitty parents, shitty ex-husband; her absolute and total and all-consuming love for her son.

I'm going to rescue you from all that bad history, he thought then, lying beside her and listening. *I'm going to show you and your kid what it's like to have a decent man in your life.*

He left the train at its last stop, Wonderland Station, and stood there in the raw salty air, remembering the route numbers from when he'd been a kid. The 116 bus would be better than the 110 because it would take him up Park Avenue and leave him only a couple blocks to walk before he came to his father's place. He made a little wager with himself. A thousand bucks on the 116. Not two minutes later there it was, swinging its square bulk around the entrance road and puffing to a stop right in front of him. A good sign.

Up Beach Street they went, between the blocks of leaning triple-deckers there, then through Bell Circle, past the road that led to the high school, up Central Ave. Thirty years ago he'd taken accordion lessons there, sitting next to Mr. Rindone and squeezing away to make his father and mother happy. He remembered the one recital he'd ever signed up for, the way he'd frozen solid on stage so that Mr. Rindone himself had to come out and play a duet with him. The truth was, he'd been lousy at music, faking his way through, never practicing much, getting by on charm.

On the heels of that thought came a swarm of others: it occurred to him that he hadn't been very good at sports, either, and no good in school. Not much of a businessman. A fuck-up in a lot of ways if he was really honest about it. He was caught by some old echo of a voice. It followed him as the bus turned left on Broadway and immediately right onto Park Avenue. He felt himself sinking down into an old familiar pool, all negative, exactly the thing that Elsie had rescued him from . . . and he thought he was going to rescue *her!*

There was the softball field where he used to stand and watch the more coordinated guys play in the men's summer league. There was the football stadium where he used to sit in the stands and stare at the cheerleaders and wish his mother had let him go out for the team. Even if all he'd ever done was get knocked around in practice and sit on the bench during games, it would have made a difference in the way he felt about himself. Instead, he'd tried to make up for it with smiles and backslaps in the high school hallways, by being a big talker, and then later, by going to see Tony Mer at his used-car lot near the beach and buying a T-Bird he couldn't afford, and living in a top-floor condo, and conning everybody a little bit. He'd spent his whole adult life living behind a curtain of personality, working the levers of other people's approval. The Prince of Revere Beach Boulevard, the Wizard of Oz. He saw it now. His mother had seen it the whole time. All those things she'd said to him in her moods, they were all true. He was a fuck-up with a flashy smile, a forty-year embarrassment. Maybe his father wouldn't be so happy to see him, after all.

The bus went past the alphabet streets—Allston, Barrett, Cambridge, Dedham—and it was like he'd all of a sudden fallen into some dark, oily swimming pool and was splashing around there trying not to sink. He hadn't even been good at swimming!

He got off at the bottom of Essex, tried to shake it off. Just thoughts, he told himself. Just a little river of thought that came out of the lake of nervousness. Give yourself a little credit, pal. Look what you're doing to make your father happy. Look at the way you've been living lately. Look at the great woman you have, and all the people you've been nice to over the years. How many guys would drop two hundred bills on a necklace for their adopted son's girlfriend?

But near the top of the short hill that was Essex Street it suddenly seemed to him that the risk was larger than he'd imagined, that Eddie might somehow know about this trip after all. Eddie Three Hands, they called him. There was always something going on in the background, something you couldn't expect. A third hand. Eddie would still have plenty of clout in Greater Boston, contacts, guys working for him, reporting to his son, John, no doubt, or, before the big arrest, to Johnny Cut. How hard would it be to pay somebody to watch his father's house, drive by now and again and see if the son had decided to pay a visit, or harass the old man, call him and hang up, throw stuff on the lawn, beep the horn late at night when you drove by? It would be just like Eddie to pull that kind of shit.

He waited for a white van to go by, decent looking blond behind the wheel, then he crossed Mountain Avenue near the old hospital. By then a small tornado of paranoia had wound itself up inside his mind. For the fun of it—for old time's sake, to reduce the odds of being seen, to try to recover the old optimistic city kid inside him, the Pete Imbesalacqua who'd been sucked away into the mountains of Montana—for the fun of it, instead of continuing along the sidewalk to Proctor Avenue, he turned left and walked a hundred yards, then ducked into Mrs.

Antonelli's driveway. If things hadn't changed over the winter, a chest-high picket fence would separate the back of her yard from the back of his father's. It would be nothing to hop that fence. He'd done it five hundred times as a kid, playing kick-the-can or just running from some bigger guy he'd pissed off. It would make him feel young again. And on the slim, slim chance there was somebody watching the house in front, he'd make a fool of the guy and sneak in unmolested.

There was a light on in Mrs. Antonelli's living room but no one at the window. His father had said in one of his letters that she'd lost her husband. Peter went down the driveway—no one had even bothered to shovel it—past her old car, across twenty steps of yard. The fence was more or less as he remembered it, maybe a bit smaller, needing paint. In the old days he'd get a running start, put two hands on the picket points and just swing his body up and over like a gymnast on the pummel horse or whatever they called it. Standing there, though, he wasn't sure if he could still do it. If Austin was beside him he'd say, "Lay you a double sawbuck I can jump it." The kid would be impressed. There was nothing breakable in his briefcase. He tossed it over into the thin layer of snow on the other side— two seconds of getting wet wouldn't matter—then stepped back and gave himself a running start. The footing was only so-so and his right shoe slipped just as he was pushing off, and though he managed to get airborne, the shoulder he'd hurt on the rectory sidewalk felt like it was being ripped open, and he didn't get his feet high enough, and one picket just caught the cloth near his left knee so he lost control and made a very ugly landing on the other side. Small rip in the priest's pants. Little wet spot on his ass. Shoulder on fire. Still, he'd made it. Austin owed him twenty bills.

On his own turf now, at last, the Prince of Revere Beach Boulevard grabbed his briefcase and stood up. He brushed the snow off the borrowed pants, checked to see how bad they'd been torn, then went forward into the last part of his big surprise.

Fifty Eight

Eight o'clock it was when they left Manhattan. Eddie guessed he'd make it to Boston somewhere around eleven. The driver tried to make small talk as the cab headed out of the city, but Eddie just said, "Wake me up when we get close and I'll tell you the address," and closed his eyes.

What greeted him there, in his dark inner world, was a vision of Alicia. She was alive again, looking like she'd looked when he'd first seen her—that tremendous body, that heavy load of red hair falling on either side of her face, the nice green eyes looking straight at him like he was the best thing she'd ever seen. She'd never been afraid of him, that's what he'd always liked about her. Or one of the things he'd liked. And she didn't seem afraid now, not at all. He kept waiting for her to say something but she wouldn't. She just looked, didn't open her mouth, didn't blink, and then she reached out like she used to do and put the palm of her hand against the side of his face. It froze him solid, that touch. He couldn't respond. She reached down and took his hand and was moving it toward her chest in a sexy way. . . but before he could touch her there she just disappeared. Gone.

At that moment Eddie realized he'd made a mistake. A sin, his father's mother would have called it. A real sin. All the other people he'd killed—including the mother of his sons, AnnaMaria—they'd all done something to deserve it, every one of them. But what had Alicia done? She liked to get manicures, and shop for food, and cook, and fuck, and stupid asshole that he was he'd put a bullet in the back of her head. For really the first time ever in his life it felt like he'd committed a sin, and it made him think about what was going to happen when he got on the other side of the dark place, the other side of his last breath. Nothing, he'd always told himself. Dust. The blank TV screen. But now he let his thoughts go to the idea that maybe there would be something, after all. A bad surprise, maybe. Maybe you paid for things. He thought he heard Alicia's voice saying, "Eddie, you're right, there is something. You're not going to like it very much, but something's there, waiting for you." He opened his eyes and for the smallest second thought he saw her sitting in the front seat with the cabbie. But it was only the light reflecting off the plastic barrier. A shitty dream.

Still, after that he couldn't sleep. Somewhere when he was riding in the car with Jimmy he'd felt the pain starting to come back. And here it was again. Worse now. Fucking pills were in the suitcase and fucking suitcase was in the trunk. Now somebody had a spike, a long metal stick with a sharp end, and this person was jamming it up underneath him and through him. He remembered AnnaMaria describing to him what having a baby felt like—not that he'd really wanted to know. A pain that was bigger than pain should be, she said, right up through the middle of you, bang, bang, bang. He had it now, same thing, even worse.

And then, a minute down the road, it went away.

He waited for it to come back, but it didn't. He wondered whether he should pay the cabbie the other grand he'd mentioned or stiff the fucking guy. His hair looked like rags that had been tied up into rope and dragged through the dirt. What was he going to do if he didn't get the other thousand, call the cops? What would the cops say, too bad, you only got a thousand bucks for a few hours driving, take it to court. Probably better to pay him what he'd promised, though, stay clear of any trouble. And what did the money mean now, anyway? What was he going to do with it? Leave it to his kids?

He dozed off finally, had a little snatch of another bad dream: the red edge of a pool of blood pushing up against the bottom of the kitchen cabinets, then Jimmy's face, then what seemed to be the flash of police lights against the right-side car window. He woke up feeling lousy and wondering if it was real. They were in Massachusetts now. He saw a sign for Cedar Junction—the new name for the jail where Xavier was. The people in Walpole didn't want the jail to have the same name as their nice little town. Fuck them. Fuck him. He saw a sign that said QUINCY—and by then he was hungry and stiff and exhausted and his mood had gone completely sour. For a minute he told himself: you could be sleeping in your own bed right now, you moron, getting a meal cooked for you, getting laid; you could wake up and go sit by the pool. But that was no good and he knew it. Sitting by the pool wasn't life. This was life, getting back to his territory, straightening people out, arranging payback. He was a people person, he told himself. Right there was the whole problem with Florida.

The cabbie looked at him in the mirror. "Where to, mahn?"

"Revere," Eddie said. "Over the bridge. You'll see a sign."

Revere, where? He thought. His old place on Reservoir Ave? Vito Imbesalacqua's house for a little visit? He'd left Florida with no exact idea what he was going to do and, three days later, he still had no exact idea. He needed to sleep, sit still someplace, think it through, because every time he tried to decide what he was going to do, all that happened was the dark thing showed up. It had been a pool at the beginning, a stinking black swamp, but now it was a wall, a black wall made of bad air. He had to go through it, he knew that, and the thought of it was like torture, like hell. A sinner's payment, his grandmother would have said. Screw that idea.

"There's a hotel on the other side of the airport. Forget the bridge. Go through the airport tunnel and on the other side after a little ways there'll be a hotel on the right. Holiday Inn or something."

"Ya meetin her there, mahn?"

"Who?"

"Ya woman."

"Yeah," Eddie said. "You'll see it."

It was hard to miss. On the hill behind it stood a giant cross, lit up. Nursing home or nuns' home or something. The cabbie pulled up to the front door of the hotel and before he got out Eddie squeezed another grand through the plastic window and told him to remember not to write it down in his log.

"Nevah, mahn," the cabbie said.

Amazing, Eddie thought, what money could do.

It made him nervous, though, when the cabbie left and he had to carry the suitcase and suiter in through the front door and go up to the desk by himself. It was late enough—eleven-fifteen now—that there weren't any other people around. He even had to ring the bell to get the girl to come out of the back room and check him in. She'd been on the phone in there, gabbing away. It made him nervous. They wanted a credit card now, an I.D., not like the old days when you could just walk in and pay and go to the room. The girl took her time. Eddie kept his shoulders hunched a little and kept pretending to bend down and get something out of his bag, zip and unzip it. Somebody came through the door behind him. A woman's voice, then her husband, then kids. Another second and he was going to scream at the girl to hurry up!

But she was finished, finally. The room was down the first floor, near the exit door at the end. He would have liked an upper floor better, but it didn't really matter. He carried his bags

312

down there and locked the door behind him right away and got out the Sauer and put it on the night table and pissed and took off his clothes and lay down on the bed . . . and couldn't sleep. He rolled this way and that way. He was hungry but didn't know if he should order out for pizza or not. He listened to a plane coming in to Logan. *A sin*, he was thinking. So this is what a sin feels like. He sat up against the headboard and flicked on the TV and went through the channels—sports, news, movies, shit. He decided to order a pizza. When the kid came, he just wouldn't show his face. He made the call and went through the channels a second time, then a third time, and came to a woman who was talking about God. Fairly fat woman, nothing to look at, walking back and forth on the stage and talking about God this, God fucking that.

"The miraculous thing about being a Christian," she was saying, "is that God's forgiveness is constantly open to us. Constantly. Always. Every minute. "I shall not turn my face from Thee," it says in the scripture. No matter what. We sin. We all sin. That's who we are, that's how we're made. No one is without it. But the miracle of Jesus Christ is that all we have to do is admit our failings and turn to Him and say, "Lord Jesus Christ, have mercy on me, a sinner." This is his great, eternal gift to us."

Eddie flicked off the set, but the woman's face stayed in his mind. The room was mostly dark, little bit of light shining in on one side of the curtain. He felt Alicia starting to come to him again and he was tired of that. So it had been a mistake. Fine, so what? What was she going to do, haunt him for the rest of whatever time he had left? The pizza came—a broad—and he handed her the money out from behind the door and said, "I'm naked in here," because, he thought, he was a fucking genius.

He had three slices and half a Coke. All you had to do was ask, the woman on the TV said. Fine. He hadn't said a prayer in a hundred years. Since First Communion. Since getting lost down south. Now he asked. Too tired to sit up straighter in the chair, too old now to get on his knees, he looked up at the ceiling and he said, "Okay, God. I'm sorry. It was a mistake. Give me a little sign now that we're okay with each other. I'm sorry, Alicia, okay? I am. If you're out there someplace, I'm sorry. If I had it to do over again, I wouldn't, alright?"

Satisfied, feeling himself mostly absolved, telling himself he'd decide in the morning what shape, exactly, his revenge would take, Chelsea Eddie Crevine slid down under the covers and soon fell into a peaceful sleep.

Fifty Nine

Ever since Vito lost his wife, Roberta Antonelli had made a point of looking out for her neighbor and old friend. Bringing over a hot dish now and then. Finding reasons to stop by for conversation. Having become widowed herself only a few months earlier, she knew with a painful clarity what old-age loneliness felt like, and she knew, also, how people took advantage of senior citizens who lived alone. Not that anything like that had happened to her, but she'd seen it enough on the TV—her main friend now that Patsy was gone—and read about it every week in the *Revere Journal*'s Police Report. Home invasions. Muggings. Various scam-artists plying their evil trade. The city wasn't the place it used to be, everybody said so. There were a lot of colored now in Revere, and although you were supposed to love everybody, and see everybody the same under God's eyes, and although she tried to do that in her mind, still, it was hard to argue against the idea that when the city had been all white, things were better. Yes, there were bad people even then, Mafia and so on. Her husband had told her about them, and how this or that man had been found dead somewhere. Vito's own son had gotten in trouble with them.

But that had always seemed to her to be happening in some other dimension of life, far away from their own existence. Most of the men who were killed weren't hardworking family men like her husband, an usher at Immaculate Conception. Vito's son was a good boy, true, but it said in the paper that he had a terrible addiction to gambling, and that was what had gotten him involved. And so she was able to tell herself that the Mafia really only hurt people who deserved it in some way. If you led a clean life they left you alone.

Now, though, now that the city was filled with all kinds of people, now that the Mafia had mostly disappeared and been replaced by the types you sometimes saw on Broadway or Shirley Avenue, with floppy pants and hooded sweatshirts and phones pressed up against their ears . . . now the evil in the world seemed closer. Anybody could be hurt now, good people and bad. On the TV news you heard something every night about a killing connected to drugs, carjacking, assault, domestic violence. It wasn't just Revere: the whole country seemed to have been taken over by a devil. She liked to watch the TV shows where the cops caught these people and put handcuffs on them because the shows made her feel a little bit safer. At least *some* of the bad ones were going to jail.

The shows kept her up late but there was nothing to get up early for now anyway, so she didn't mind. She'd just finished watching one of them and had stood up out of her chair and turned off the TV and was moving toward the window to pull the shade down and get herself ready for bed, when she thought she saw a shadow moving along her driveway. For just a moment she wondered if the new medication she was taking had made her confuse TV and the real world again because it was a scene right out of her worst nightmare, right out of the shows. Next second the police would come running up out of breath, and they'd catch the man and throw him down and sit on him and make him put his hands behind his back. You'd see them holding the top of his head so he wouldn't bump it on the roof of the police car. You'd see an interview with the arresting officer, lights flashing in the background.

But the longer she looked the more certain she became that

the shadow was an actual man, a Negro it looked like, and right in her yard. She pressed her face to the glass and watched him leaving footprints at the end of her driveway, where the streetlight shone on the little bit of snow they had left. She thought the man was about to break into her car, but he walked right past it. He made it as far as the fence and stopped and it occurred to her only then that the intruder might be heading for Vito's house. Vito would be asleep. The man would break in and strangle him and steal everything he had. Another second and she was on the phone with the 911. "A Negro in the yard, Vito's yard," she said excitedly. "Imbesalacqua! He's going to break in! He's going to kill Vito!"

The operator asked patiently—too patiently, she thought— for the address. Mrs. Antonelli gave him not her own, but Vito's, because that's where the intruder was headed: 299 Proctor Avenue.

Sixty

Like everybody else in the city, Patrolman Mitchell Robson knew the story: Alfonse's brother or stepbrother or something had gotten in over his head with Eddie Crevine and worn some kind of wire to their last meeting and ended up in Witness Protection. Crevine was gone, in hiding; the whole world looking for him. They had probably eight or ten sightings a week, tipsters calling the station, hoping for the reward. To him it was more or less irrelevant. He thought the chances of Crevine ever being caught were nil. Guys like that made one mistake and didn't usually follow it up with a second one. They had money set aside in various places around the country and probably overseas, too. You didn't get to that level in that business without having some brains in your head and so, as the months went by and they wasted time on one false lead after another, the whole thing started to seem to him like a joke. He knew Captain Romano had a kind of obsession about Crevine. Who wouldn't, if the guy had tried to kill your brother? And he knew the sister was a big-shot anchorwoman on Channel 8, and that she was obsessed with Crevine, too. Also normal. For his money, though, the whole thing was a made-for-TV movie. He, himself, preferred to concentrate on other matters. A pregnant wife, for example. The idea that maybe he'd earn a promotion one of these days and bring home a little more cash so they could end up moving out of the crappy Malden Street apartment and into a house of their own. A condo on Revere Beach, maybe. Or a house on Reservoir Ave with a rental unit upstairs. He was only a rookie; the higher-ups didn't realize what he could do yet. He was made for this job. He'd been dreaming of being a cop since he was old enough to push a plastic cruiser around on the living room floor. So far it had been one piddley-shit assignment after another but he was biding his time, doing everything he was asked, not complaining, not bending a single rule, not giving the captains any lip. There had been one or two screwups but otherwise a pretty clean record.

When he got asked to drive up and park opposite 299 Proctor and keep an eye on the house, he knew what it was about and who was doing the asking. People said Captain Romano was in line to be chief someday. This was his father's house. It meant they'd had yet another fake tip on the Crevine case, and he was supposed to sit there and stay awake and call in if he saw anything suspicious. Easy enough.

It ended up working the other way, though. Not long before midnight, half an hour or less before his shift was supposed to end and he could go home to Susie and a warm bed, the radio squawked and Silovksy said they'd had a call about a possible intruder. 299 Proctor. Robson knew one thing: as soon as Captain Romano overheard the call he'd come flying up here. So he was out of the car in the time it took to say, "Got it, captain." He crossed the street, unsnapping his holster as he went. He ran his eyes over the property—ranch house with shrubs out front, a carport to the left side, all dark—and then, walking slowly into the mouth of the driveway, he took out his service pistol just in case. A tip was one thing. You didn't usually get an intruder call with an address for no reason.

In the distance he thought he heard a siren, but rather than wait for backup he went slowly, step by quiet step, the rest of the way down the driveway, past the car in the carport, into the back yard. Almost completely dark there. He could feel just the thinnest film of sweat on his gun hand. He could see a fence around what appeared to be a garden. A little bit of old, crusty snow. Light glinted off the fence wire, just a bit of light from Mountain Avenue, partially blocked by the house behind. He thought he heard something. He stopped, crouched, held the pistol out in front of him, peered into blackness. Something again. The sound of faint footsteps, it had to be, crunching in the snow, going slowly up the other side of the house. He walked around back—no lights on inside here either—then up the narrow snow-covered lane between the side of the house and the next door neighbor's fence. He saw a figure in front of him, all in black, barely visible, just making the corner. Robson went up the lane as quietly as he could, trying to get his breathing under control. When he reached the corner he realized that a large round shrub blocked his view of the front door. He leaned his head out carefully around it and saw the guy, going up the steps, at midnight, dressed all dark. He leapt out from behind the shrub and yelled, but what came out instead of "Halt" or "police!" was just a syllable of sound. "Ay!" it sounded like, but loud. The home invader heard it and whirled around and then the world seemed to go into super-fast motion: something glinted off what the intruder was holding in his hand, a gun it had to be, he was going to shoot. Susie was going to end up a single mother. There was a sound, a kick against his right hand and at the same time the intruder made a comical backflip, like something from a funny movie, flying backwards over the porch railing and into the snow on the other side of the steps. There had been a shot. He wasn't hit. Something was echoing in the yard and the sirens were getting closer. A light went on in the house next door. He kept the pistol out in front of him and went forward. The sirens were on the next block now, and underneath them, a few feet away, a low choking sound. The intruder was lying on his face with his legs twisted up all crooked against the side of the front porch, a dark brief-case beside him in the snow. Robson could hear him breathing, fast small wet breaths that didn't sound good. He approached and knelt beside the man, a black man it was, African American, and saw the bloody exit hole in the back of his jacket. He looked for a gun and didn't see it because it had to be under the body. The face was turned sideways, blood bubbling around the guy's mouth and onto the snow. He was trying to speak. "El . . . El . . . Eh-el," he was saying. Asking for help. Patrolman Robson tried to say something but couldn't. He put his left hand flat on the exit wound, felt the sticky warmth there, listened to the blood gurgling in the man's throat, and heard what sounded like every siren in the city crawling up his own backbone, then cruisers screeching to the curb, one, another one, a third, and he thought that, at last, after a year and a half of small mistakes and little-boy assignments, he'd finally done something big.

Sixty-One

"I never slept in a hotel once," his father said to him as Alfonse used the card-key in the door and opened it onto a clean first-floor room with two beds. After thinking about it for a minute, he'd decided on the Holiday Inn. Far enough away from Vito's house. Close enough to the station if he needed to get back in a hurry.

"You're not missing much, *Babbo*," he said, but two-thirds of his mind was somewhere else. A few minutes earlier Joanie had called him back. "I decided I was being foolish," she said. "My source was China Louis. It seemed like he was telling the truth."

Alfonse had tried again to get her to leave her condo, but she wouldn't, so he thanked her and hung up, and relayed the information to his boss, and his thoughts were running hard now, trying to get a step ahead of Chelsea Eddie. Here's what he knew: China Louis had given Joanie the plate number of a car that was supposedly carrying Eddie north up Route 95. Which meant Louis somehow knew that Eddie had abandoned his hiding place. Which meant he'd known all along where Eddie had been and had left him there, unmolested, unreported, the half-million-dollar reward hanging in the air around his ears along with the possibility of an abetting-fugitive rap. So maybe China Louis had set Eddie up from the get-go in a move to grab his territory; or maybe they'd been working together the whole time and he'd pissed Eddie off somehow, and now Louis was worried Eddie might be on his way back to Boston to get revenge.

But Eddie could easily have had someone else—his son Johnny, for example—try for the revenge, so that made no sense.

Or maybe Louis was playing some kind of a trick, trying to get Joanie upset, make a fool of the Revere police and the FBI and everyone else, all at the same time.

Or maybe his own theory was right, and Eddie's exile had finally driven him nuts and—this was the worst possibility—there was no logic at all behind what he was doing, no plan to unravel, just a crazy man, a killer, coming this way.

"The bed, she's nice," Vito was saying, but Alfonse could tell that his mind was somewhere else, also. Half of him wanted to be at the station and half of him wanted to be here. His father was exhausted, he could see the weight on his eyes—he'd been shaken out of a deep sleep. Vito was looking at him. "You thinking about him, too," he said.

Alfonse nodded.

"Thinking what things?"

"Where's he's going right now."

"Joanie's house," Vito said confidently.

"The BPD has somebody there. She has a gun, she's locked in."

"My house, then."

"We have somebody there, too, but I think Eddie's too smart for that. I thought—until a little while ago—that he was too smart to leave the place he was hiding, but maybe he's smarter than we think and has some other idea."

"Like what other idea?"

"I can't put my mind in his mind," Alfonse said. "You know him. What would he do? What kind of thoughts would make him leave a safe hiding place where he's been for seven months and get in a car and drive in this direction?"

"You hurt Eddie like Peter hurt him," Vito said, as if he'd been pondering the question every hour since the previous September, "it's like steppin on a snake. The snake she don't want to run, she wants to bite."

"But he ran."

"At the first, sure. Later on he wishes maybe he didn't."

"His father went to jail, is what puzzles me. Eddie was away, too. Four years in Danbury, with Xavier Manzo and Pitchie Luglio. Why would he risk going back?"

Vito sat on the bed and took off his shoes and socks and placed them neatly next to his feet. He looked up, "Because like a fire the hate's burnin inside him."

"But why not just send somebody else—his son, one of his goons?"

"Same reason why he didn't send somebody else to the meeting with Peter that night. He could. That's what he did most of the time. But this time, with Peter, with me, with Joanie, there's something in it past business. There's a big shame. Because we're the Italian family that didn't kill nobody, didn't hurt, didn't steal."

"And Eddie spent his life doing those things."

"Sure. The people in your girl's country, in Cambodia. Look at them. They killed the smart ones, the good ones, because inside themselves it was like a burnin that they weren't good or smart. The good people, their goodness was like a hot light on the other ones. And me and Lucy we were like a light on Eddie. Me, Lucy, Joanie . . . you."

"Eddie didn't know . . . about me . . . that you're my father."

Vito shrugged. "He knew you were helpin'." He took off his pants and shirt and lay them neatly on the half of his bed he didn't plan to use, then he got under the covers and adjusted the pillow beneath his head. "Like the club he had, the girls. He wants to take and make them naked in front of everybody, so they feel like he feels, ashamed all the time, instead of the way they could."

"Alright. So now what? He's driving or being driven north. Maybe he won't come here, but maybe he will. And if he does, then what?"

"Then," Vito said, as if he'd come to the end of a page he'd been reciting from memory, "he plays games with people first, then he kills them. Joanie, if he can. Me, if he can. You."

Alfonse felt the beeper buzz at his hip. He looked at the number. "Sleep, *Babbo*," he said. "I'm going out to make a call. I have the key. No matter what, don't open the door. Sleep."

"I am already," Vito said, and it seemed that he was.

Alfonse went out into the hallway, dialed the station on his cell phone and heard: "Captain Silovsky."

"Mike," he said, into the phone. "It's Alfonse. You beeped me."

The voice said. "Shots fired at 299 Proctor."

"Inside or outside?"

"Outside. An intruder. Youngish black guy. Robson shot him at the front door, but the guy turned out to have no weapon. He's on his way to Mass General but he's going to be D.O.A. And Robson is going to be up shit creek."

"Black guy? You sure?"

"Seems so. Nobody's in the house."

"It's my father's house. He's with me."

"Want to bring him here?"

"I might. I didn't want him spending the night in a cell, but now I might. If you can send somebody else over here, I'd appreciate it. What else?"

"Staties and the FBI picked up Jimmy Crellin, a.k.a James

Crevine."

"And?"

"The kid drove his father north as far as New York. They got that out of him then let him go."

"Let him go?"

"They have somebody on him. They're hoping he'll lead them to Daddy. Maybe Daddy told him what he was planning to do."

"All right, I'm—" Alfonse started to say, but Captain Silovsky interrupted him.

"Hang on." There was a pause, voices. Silovsky was talking into another phone. "Alfonse," he said, when he came back on the line, and the voice had gone bad all of a sudden. Alfonse could feel him struggling to get a word out. "The guy," he said at last, and then he stopped himself and there was more background noise. "Listen, where are you again?"

"Holiday Inn."

"Okay, listen . . . stay right there, I'm coming up. Wait outside. I'll be there in four minutes." And he closed the line before Alfonse could ask what had happened.

Sixty Two

Very dark now, Peter thought. No kind of darkness he'd ever seen before. No pain, but very very hard to breathe and a huge weight pressing down on him. His eyes flickered, bright lights. All sticky wet in his mouth, and the weight was unbelievably heavy. Cold against his face. He understood, that was the surprise of it. Understood it like you understood what to do the first time you ever make love—like you'd done it before in some other dimension and were just now remembering. He didn't know what had happened but he knew what this was now. It felt like you'd been flung out far from what you thought was your own life and now you were at the edge of the known world, trying to hold on like that world was real and permanent but something was forcing you to see it wasn't. There was a face. His mother. No, Elsie. He tried to say her name and then he couldn't breathe at all and there was pain that felt like pure weight on his chest and then he had the sense of something so big, so gigantically big, it made you feel like the tiniest little speck of awareness at the bottom of the ocean, far far far from the surface light, not at all who you thought you were all this time. Not at all. "Hi," he started to say to this new self, but he couldn't get the word to come out.

Sixty Three

Joanna hung up the phone and went to the sliding door, then opened it and stepped out onto the balcony in only her flannel pajamas. It was just past midnight in Boston and the harbor in front of her was quiet and dark, spots of light on the islands, and straight lines of blue lamps marking the airport runways. Setting the receiver in place, she'd felt as though her mind had ceased to work, the place words emerged from had been shut down and locked by what Alfonse had just told her. He had followed the news with a string of apologies for not delivering it in person—just like her father, she thought—but when she tried to absorb what had happened her mind seemed to freeze. It was too much, too sad. Too impossible and at the same time somehow exactly right. They had all circled around Peter's desperate need, all these years. Her father, Alfonse, she and Leslie . . . even Eddie Crevine had been caught up in it. And now the energy at the center of the tornado had ceased to be and they were all lying flat in the wreckage. She had a brother so absolutely crazy that he'd dressed himself up as a black man and sneaked back to see his father when the most vicious killer in America wanted nothing more than to find him and end his life. Absolute illogic, she thought, with tears coursing down her face. Pure craziness! He didn't even die a hero, in some big, dramatic fashion that would make the headlines the next day. He died because of a nervous cop. A mistake. On his father's doorstep. It was too sad to hold in your mind.

It was freezing cold out there. The skin on her hands and face seemed to shrink back from the bite of the wind, but she didn't move. Alfonse had told her it would be on the news—there was nothing they could do about that. The Boston radio stations were broadcasting it even as he spoke to her, he said, and she knew 'SBT would have to announce it, morning, noon, and night. They'd do an investigation. The story would drag on and on for days, Marty Lincoln stumbling over it and smiling his idiot's smile. Peter Imbesalacqua, the Revere man who'd tricked the famous Eddie Crevine, had dressed up as an African American, a black priest—wouldn't the public love that detail!—and sneaked home to see his father and been shot to death in a tragic accident. It was too much.

This time, she thought, it would probably kill her father. He'd never survive this. And then, in a strange, bitter way, she would have gotten what she wanted—to be free of all of them. She could retire and live on her savings, or get a job in Arizona or Oregon and just soak in the misery of it, the guilt, the waste, the puzzle of how the same two parents could produce children so different. She thought of Elsie and Austin and closed her wet eyes against the pain of that. This is what people like Peter did: they went cruising carelessly through the world in a convertible Thunderbird, laughing over their shoulder while left and right friends and family members were knocked into a ditch, all broken bones and blood. A wave of bitterness caught her, cutting through the sadness like a blade.

She could hop over the railing, endure ten seconds of terror, and forget it that way, too.

The phone rang, calling her inside. What could happen now that could possibly be worse? That Peter was not dead but paralyzed, and she'd have to take care of him for the rest of his days? That her father had been killed, too? That Eddie Crevine had blown up their house, set the studio on fire, was torturing

Elsie on live TV somewhere in the Cayman Islands?

It was Leslie's voice on the machine, and it stopped her dead in the middle of the room. "Joanna . . . it's me. I just heard. I'm sorry I'm sorry I'm sorry a thousand times. I'm coming over and I want you to let me in. Will you? I know you're there. I'm sorry. Will you let me in?"

Sixty Four

Austin liked the fact that his mother went to bed at nine and he was free to stay up as late as he wanted. She was good that way. And Peter was good that way, too, and would sometimes stay up with him and watch a hockey game or a cop show. His friends at school were always complaining about being treated like little kids, drowned in advice and pressure about college, forced to go to bed or put on their coats or told to drive safe . . . spoken to as though they were eight-year-olds. He had the coolest parents, he was thinking, right at the moment when the phone rang.

He thought—for just one second—that it might be Darcy. Maybe Peter had sneaked down to her house already and slipped her the phone number on a piece of paper and she was calling just to hear his voice and say how beautiful the necklace was. His mother had gone to bed an hour ago. He picked up the phone and heard a voice he partly recognized. It wasn't Darcy or Peter. After a few seconds of confusion he understood it was the policeman they'd gotten to know a little bit right before all the shit hit the fan and they'd had to leave Revere in a hurry. Alfonse. Peter's half-brother or something. Alfonse asked him if his mother was there, and Austin said no, she was asleep, and then there was a too-long pause on the line, and then the words, "Some bad news, Austin. Bad as can be." And in another minute, like in a dream, he'd hung up the phone without noticing and he was standing outside his mother's bedroom, wondering whether or not he should knock. He stood there. The hall was dark. At that moment he wanted only to die, to stop being, to stop feeling anything. That was how his mother was going to feel, too, he knew that. Going in there now and telling her what Alfonse had told him would be the same as going in there and lighting her hair on fire and watching her burn and scream. He put his fingers on the door handle and turned. It was mostly dark inside, his mother lying on her stomach with her face turned toward the door and her mouth open a little ways. The hair was down over the right half of her face and for a second then he saw that she was pretty. She looked happy there, peaceful, unworried, really pretty. He waited. He felt, almost, like he could hear Peter's voice in the room. "Feel like ta-taking the wheel?" Peter was saying. Austin had tears going down the front of his face. His lips were shaking so bad he didn't know if he could talk. He made himself step over to the bed and he touched his mother on the shoulder and her eyes were open right away and she was looking up at him like she knew.

Sixty Five

Eddie woke up starving. He got up and pissed and turned on the TV and ate one cold slice of pizza and opened his suitcase to find something clean to wear. More shit on the screen. They were selling diamonds, or what they said were diamonds. They were talking about Easter. They were showing a baseball highlight from the night before. Eddie could give a shit. He flipped the channels and was about to turn it off when he passed too quickly across the local news and then went back and saw a face on the screen. Rat's face. He listened. He heard his own name. He slapped himself to be sure he was awake, and then he laughed, loud, and looked up at the ceiling. "God," he said. "God my God," and all of a sudden it was absolutely clear to him what he had to do. The whole thing was clear. All planned out now in his mind, perfect.

He got dressed and went out the side door of the hotel and around to where three cabs were waiting to take pilots and stewardesses to the airport, and he got in and handed a fifty over the seat and told the blond girl driver to take him to Oak Island, in Revere eight minutes away. He told himself it didn't matter now if somebody recognized him, not really. He had a gun, he had his plan, he had God watching out for him.

Oak Island wasn't exactly an island but a strip of flat lowland pinched between the beach and a tidal river with fishing boats in it and a marsh on the other side. Eddie made the cabbie drop him off a block away from where he was actually going. He walked to 55 Elbrus Street and was happy to see that a car he recognized was in the driveway. He slipped around the house and found the back door unlocked, as he knew it would be, and he went very quietly up the stairs and inside. The clock on the table said 6:20. Nobody up yet. Eddie was tempted to make himself coffee and breakfast but he decided that Pitchie was going to do that for him . . . that and some other things.

He pulled a kitchen chair over to the corner of the room and he sat there and waited. There was a time, years ago, when he used to come here and play cards until late, so there were some good memories. After a few minutes, when he couldn't take the waiting or the hunger anymore, he put two pieces of Italian bread in the toaster and smothered them with butter and wolfed them down. The smell, the noise of the toast popping up, he thought it would be enough to get Pitchie out of bed, but it wasn't, so at 7:05 Eddie took off his shoes and padded quietly down the hallway in just his stocking feet. A bathroom, a little storage room or something. A closed door. He took the Sauer out of his pocket and opened the door without making any sound at all and he padded into the bedroom and got down beside the extra-long bed and put the barrel of the pistol an inch from the big man's nose. "Pitch," he whispered. "Pitchie Luglio. This here's God. It's your time. God's here to collect a favor. Pitch. Pitchie, baby! Your wife's hungry, time to make her breakfast."

The eyelids flickered and the man's mouth twitched once. When the eyes opened and focused on the gun, a quick splash of fear showed itself, but no panic. Pitchie Luglio, Eddie thought, was exactly the right guy for this job.

"Eddie," Pitch said calmly, half his face still in the pillow. "I like the hair."

Eddie's smile widened. He scratched the barrel of the gun against Pitchie's big old nose and he said, "Came for that little favor you owe me."

Sixty Six

Two days after seeing the news report about Peter Imbesalacqua, James woke up to the clear understanding of where his father would be. It seemed, almost, as if they had the same mind, or as if God had sent him the information in a dream. Of course he'd be there. Where else would he go to finish his business with the Imbesalacqua family? It would be a suicide mission, but everything would be a suicide mission for his father now. That was why he'd killed Alicia—because he knew there was nothing left, no more time, and he'd wanted to control her life, too, and not leave her behind to marry somebody else.

He left Sean still asleep in their bed—one last, loving look—and got dressed and drove in to Melrose to his brother's house. He didn't check to see if someone was following him. He was possessed by an idea. The idea was that there was no escape for him either. He'd been suckled on the milk of mistrust. For the police especially. And with his new and absolutely clear mind he understood now that, if the FBI wanted to, they could arrest him at any time and he'd end up in Concord Prison or someplace like that and then it would be better for him if he were dead. If his father found out that he'd talked, which he surely would if he lived, then either his father would have someone kill him, too, the way he'd killed his mother and Alicia, or he'd invent a way to torment him for the rest of his life, make him do things he didn't want to do, make him live in constant fear that he'd be sent to prison. On some level he'd always known it, but seeing the photograph had convinced him of it: there was nothing his father wouldn't do, nothing. He'd have Sean kidnapped and tortured. He'd kill his own son. He had certainly killed his children's mother. If there was a line that marked the extreme edge of the human moral spectrum, then his father lived on the far side of it.

So there was no way out for him now, none at all. The police wouldn't protect him, that had been made clear enough. Once his father was caught, if he was caught—there had been no news about him on the TV—he'd figure out what had happened and put the word out: Jimmy's a rat, Jimmy's finished. Maybe his brother John would be assigned to kill him. Yes, probably he would. And that would be perfect, the perfect revenge.

He parked the car in the driveway of his brother's house, and walked up the front steps with his mind clear and clean but at the center of a tornado. Johnny didn't know their father was coming north. If he'd known, there would have been some contact, he would have called. It would have been on the news. When Johnny's wife, Ann, a woman he liked and pitied, answered the door, he said he had to talk with Johnny, it was urgent. Johnny was asleep, she said, but he told her it didn't matter, it couldn't wait. He went up to the bedroom, two steps at a time, and his brother was just pulling himself out of bed.

"What the fuck?" was his greeting. He had half a hard-on. He didn't know anything.

"I need a gun," James said. "I need to borrow a pistol. Somebody's after me. Today. Now."

"Huh? For what, you gonna shoot yourself or something?"

"This second," James said. "Just give me something and I'll explain later on."

"Sure. In the drawer. Two of them. Take either one. Boyfriend cheat on you or what? What's going on?"

"I'll tell you later," James said, and he was gone, down the steps and out the door. Fake moustache and dark glasses on the seat of the car, a little joke on his fucking father.

Sixty Seven

Father Dominic Bucci had learned long ago that the priest's life was a mixture of the most ordinary events and the most extraordinary. In this way, it seemed to him, his work was not unlike that of a policeman. Directing traffic at a worksite one day, and then responding to a shooting or fatal accident the next. Going to the homes of parishioners for Sunday lunch, and then sitting in the dark confessional and listening to a man confess to cheating on his wife with a sixteen-year-old, or hearing a woman he knew say she was contemplating suicide. Sick with the flu and tired of his own voice, he'd say weekday mass on a winter morning to a congregation of three, and then have to go to the hospital and find a way to console parents who'd just lost a nine-year-old daughter to brain cancer. If nothing else, decades of work like that imbued you with an understanding of the terrible majesty of the human condition, a spectrum of emotion that stretched from ecstasy to despair with a million stopping places in between. The absolute authority of God.

There were times, of course, many times, when it also turned up the volume on the choir of doubt. What kind of God would do this to people He supposedly loved? What if the story of Jesus Christ was nothing more than a soothing fantasy that had been embellished over two thousand years, a myth, a narcotic, a lie to ease the raw pain of being? What if your individual consciousness, that collection of cells and impulses that went, in his case, by the name Dominic Bucci, simply ceased to exist

when you took your last breath, just went into the soil and rot-
ted there, food for some other creature?

Sitting now in his plainly furnished upstairs room in the
rectory on Revere Street, Wednesday of Holy Week, watching
yet another April snow fall beyond the window, and listening
through the wall to Father Ghirardelli's Chopin, such a tumult
of despair came over him that it was all he could do to summon
the energy to pray. He offered up one quiet Hail Mary for the
soul of Peter Imbesalacqua. Another for Peter's father and sister and half-brother and wife and adopted son. "Lord," he
whispered, barely loud enough for the sound to reach his own
ears, "why would you torment a man like my friend? An emi-
nently pure and selfless man, with one stain upon his soul?
Why should a man like that have to suffer the things he's suf-
fered? Why now, in his lonely old age, would you visit him with
the greatest pain a human being can know?"

He stopped there. Holy Week. The words made him think
of Mary, and the tone of his complaint caused him to be vaguely ashamed. To have been asked, first, to bear a child in disgrace; to have borne a son as special as Jesus; to have seen him
tormented and tortured in front of her eyes—the mystery of it
stood at the very heart of the Christian tradition. It might even
be possible to say—he wasn't sure, he wasn't a student of other
religions—that what differentiated Christianity from all other
systems of belief was this emphasis on clinging to one's faith in
the face of the absolute inexplicability of human misery. That
was the true meaning of the symbol of the cross. That was the
whole point and purpose of the holiday they were about to celebrate and honor.

Comforted by that, comforted to a small degree at least, he
went downstairs and put on his coat and hat and stepped outside into the storm. It was another in a series of "weather
events" as the meteorologists called them now, a freakish, cold

April of snow, sleet, and rain, the perfect background, it seemed to him, for the sorrow of the past forty-eight hours.

He went across the empty parking lot, thinking he should have worn his snow boots. How many times had he made this trip—from the front door of St. Anthony's Rectory to the front door of Bruno's Funeral Parlor? A hundred? Five hundred? This time—it was understandable but still bizarre—there were three State Police cruisers parked on the curve of Revere Street, their roofs and fenders coated in white, and several troopers in their black raincoats and snow-dusted Stetsons standing on the sidewalk. Their shoulders were thrown back, their faces stern, eyes watching for trouble. Alfonse Romano was there, out of uniform, talking to one of them. After some debate, the family had decided on a closed casket, but a wake that was open to the public. Alfonse and the police and Joanie had all been against it, but Vito had insisted, his tortured face going red with the effort of arguing with them. "Peter's friends, they're gonna come!" he practically yelled out, sitting like a shattered man on the sofa in his living room. "My friends, they're all gonna come! No devil, no Eddie is gonna stop em!" It seemed to Dommy that his friend's grief had driven him right up to the border of insanity and perhaps a little distance beyond.

Father Dom went up to Alfonse and hugged him tight, held their bodies together for a moment, and then went inside to stand with his oldest friend, and to face, for the thousandth time, the inadequacy of the spoken word.

Alfonse embraced Father Dom, thinking he looked atypically broken-up on that afternoon, thinking they all probably looked that way. He held the front door for the old priest, but instead of going inside he decided to make a tour of the back of the building in the snow. He wouldn't put it past Eddie to find a way to shoot a mortar onto the roof of Bruno's, or set off a bomb in a car parked in the rear lot. Or, maybe, Eddie wouldn't do anything. Maybe he wasn't interested in coming here at all, didn't care anymore about the Imbesalacquas. Maybe he'd gone as far as New York then chartered a plane and flown to Bimini, Panama, or a hilltop village in Sicily, and the fact of Peter's death was nothing more than a blip of happy news as he made his big escape.

As he rounded the corner on the Revere Street side of the building, Alfonse saw Joanie and her friend getting out of a black company car, fifteen minutes late. No one was guarding them, none of the Staties were paying attention, so he called out "Joanie" and saw her turn her head and he went there to escort her inside. Just as she was holding him in an embrace and introducing him to her friend, Alfonse saw, out of the corner of one eye, a giant of an old man slipping around the far side of the building and stepping through the front door. Pitchie Luglio it was, holding an umbrella down close to his face. It wasn't easy to see through the snow at that distance, but it looked like Luglio was accompanied by a woman—his wife, Alfonse guessed. He thought she'd passed away but he must have gotten that wrong. Half his size, heavy-looking, shuffling along in the protection of the umbrella, dressed all in black, a long black coat, black gloves, the black veil, she was like a glimpse of the Old World rising up through these streets. Years ago you'd see plenty of women like her, gone heavy from decades of cooking and housework, wearing black from the day their husband or brother or sister died until the hour they themselves passed away, shuffling around the city from bakery to meat market to cemetery and spotting the pews at St. Anthony's like so many quiet old crows on a wire.

Joanie was clinging to his hands, and saying something about her father, and the burial, and what they were going to do now, and Alfonse was listening and trying to find something to say, and at the same time thinking how strange it was that Pitchie Luglio would make the effort to come to Peter's wake in a snowstorm. Luglio had worked for Eddie for years, then been arrested and spent a short while in jail with him, and then—this was decades ago—he'd seemed to decide he wanted out of the business. It was an unusual case, an atypical chapter in the underworld lore they'd all grown up on. Pitchie had apparently undergone some type of mid-life conversion, had started going to church, had taken a job at the dog track and gotten married—no doubt to this same woman—and seemed, according to everyone involved, to have put his criminal days behind him for good. Even more strange, Chelsea Eddie had allowed him to do that, granting Luglio special dispensation, turning the ex-bodyguard and disguise expert into an un-made man, rarest of creatures in that world.

"Please come to the house tonight," Joanie was saying, in a voice that didn't resemble her TV voice at all. "I don't want my father to be alone there. I don't think he could stand it."

As if, Alfonse thought, he needed to be asked. As if he had someplace better to go. As if he wasn't truly part of the family. He nodded, his mind whirling off to a dozen different points of worry. Why hadn't somebody been watching Joanie? The Revere Police and the Staties and the FBI, they'd supposedly coordinated everything. They had men in and around the house now, in unmarked cars here and there along Proctor Avenue. Vito believed that if he had stayed home that night, stayed home instead of going with Alfonse to the hotel, nothing would have happened to Peter, and now he couldn't be convinced to sleep anywhere else but in his own bed. Officer Robson had been placed on leave and was probably, justifiably, finished. Vito was half-crazy. Elsie had arrived that same morning, looking like she'd be unable even to walk unless her son was standing there, holding her up. Lily and Estelle were strong—they'd been through worse—but he could see the strain on them, too, and he was worried about the baby. Joanie had a certain physical presence, an on-air dignity that had belonged to her, somehow, even in her gangliest teenage years. But underneath that he could see that her insides—like his own—were being torn apart. He thought it a good sign, something mildly positive, that she'd decided to bring her girlfriend to the wake. He accompanied them as far as the front door, started to go in, and then thought better of it again and decided to remain out on the sidewalk for another few minutes and make sure Eddie didn't try to play one of his famous tricks.

The snow squall and a fender-bender on the Mystic Bridge had delayed them a bit and Joanna was surprised at how many people were already inside the funeral home. The lines of folding chairs in the room where Peter's casket stood were already full, and the wide doorway there was so crowded that she had to say "excuse me" five times simply to reach her father, who was standing next to the casket and already being hugged and kissed and spoken to by the first group of mourners in a line. There was a whole choreography to this ritual. She remembered it so well from her mother's wake: the casket there in front of a background of flower arrangements and a standing crucifix; the family members in a crooked row beside it—Elsie and Austin and her father. Joanie hugged them and took her place there, dreading the next few hours with their hundreds of expressions of condolence. She preferred to mourn in private, but that wasn't the way it was done in this culture, and it was her father she worried most about now, his health, his sanity, his ability to bear a load like this. His priest friend, Father Bucci, had taken him off to one side and was talking to him in low tones with his hands on both shoulders. Leslie, as they'd agreed, had stayed out of the receiving line; she'd found a place to sit, in the back right corner of the room, and looked terribly alone there. Joanna scanned the room and saw familiar faces here and there—Peter's high school friends and old gambling buddies, second cousins, neighbors from long ago. Marty Lincoln coming through the door with his hands clasped in front of him. Mike McGowan. The rest of the 'SBT crew. Alfonse's fiancé and her daughter—a smart, alert Cambodian girl whom she'd met only that morning. Walking into the building had been like running a loose gauntlet of State Troopers and Revere cops, and there was the feeling, floating like sour incense in the air of the room, that Eddie or someone linked to Eddie might use the sad gathering to cause further havoc in their lives. But only the most wretched of souls, she thought, would do something like that.

Darcy had been crying most of the day, crying for what had happened and crying because it seemed like now there was a chance Austin would come back home for good. In the middle of the day today they'd sneaked off to her friend Lizzy's house and made love in the bedroom there, and he'd been crying the whole time, worried about his mother, sad beyond anything she'd ever seen. He was holding his mother's hand now. She looked like she was on something. Her eyes were glazed and she had a funny smile frozen on her face and was talking to people in a weird way, like she was in a room by herself someplace and trying to keep awake by pretending there were other people nearby.

Darcy felt awkward and alone and she was glad when Alfonse's girlfriend's daughter came over and stood next to her and held her hand. She was a nice kid, a little older, Cambodian or something, but friendly and cool and it didn't feel weird to have her there holding her hand. "Sucks, doesn't it," she said to the girl, quietly, and the girl nodded a bunch of times and kept her eyes out on the people in the room.

Eddie Crevine stood off against the side wall in the back part of the room, sweating profusely in his layers of women's clothing, half-hidden behind the massive bulk of Pitchie Luglio. His legs had started to shake from the nervousness, and the pain was punching up under him again, up behind his balls, and his mind was going in crazy circles like there were a million clowns in there, jumping and yelling and clapping, and this one shadowy figure in the background, the ringmaster, watching it all, waiting. Pitchie was standing half a step in front of him, little bit to the right. There was a head-high flower arrangement on a stand against his left shoulder. Everybody near them was facing forward, looking at the casket. Shame to have the casket closed, Eddie thought; he would have liked to see the little prick's shot-up body one last time and be sure he was dead. He lost focus for a few seconds, wondering how they'd laid out Alicia. Where? Who showed? Then his thoughts jumped crazily this way and that—he'd forgotten about visiting his son Johnny to say good-bye, he'd forgotten to even check out of the hotel, he'd spent the night at Pitchie's and made the old giant cook for him, and get out a trunk of his wife's clothes, and go out and buy a pair of boots that fit and looked like they weren't necessarily a man's. A last favor called in, bringing him here. But what choice did Pitchie have, really?

His thoughts seemed to circle and circle—like pigeons on the trellis at the Beachmont subway station when he was a kid—then settle back to now. He knew he had only a few minutes now, before somebody figured out who he was, or before he did what he had to do and went through the black wall and found out what was on the other side, and his heart was banging around hard in his chest and throat. The pistol was in his hand in the right-side pocket of the old musty dress, and he could feel the sweat between his skin and the metal. He saw her come in, with her girlfriend at first, and then the girlfriend was coming over and practically sitting right there in front of them. He didn't care a shit about the girlfriend. He was going to leave the old man with nothing now, nobody. It would be better than killing him. But something was holding him back a little, just for a second. And then, inside his mind, the shadowy guy behind the clowns was stepping forward. There, right in front of him, was the black wall. No time left. He'd shoot her and then shoot himself and he had to make himself do it or they'd have him in jail within the hour and he'd go like his old man had gone, in a prison hospital, in agony, and that was never going to happen. He had to make himself. He thought he saw her looking in his direction and then he realized he couldn't wait another second. He nudged Pitchie and they went sideways along the back of the room and cut into the line that was moving by the casket. Maybe eight people in front of them now. Seven people. One of them—funny—was Xavier's little brother, another Manzo monster, almost Pitchie's size, good camouflage between him and the TV star. Another little gift from God. He caught a glimpse of her famous face and he tilted his head down and let the veil hang and his heart slam around and he moved the Sauer an inch to make sure it wouldn't get caught in the pocket of the dress when he started to lift it out.

Joanna thought, for a moment, that they were being visited by a cadre of retired professional football players. The young man in front of her was a giant, six-four or six-five, probably two hundred and fifty pounds. "I'm a carpenter with your father," he said. Twice. Her hand was enveloped in both of his and it was as if she'd reached into the sleeve of a leather coat. He wouldn't let go, wouldn't stop saying how sorry he was, how bad it was what had happened. The line stretched behind him. Another giant there, much older, and then she had a quick glimpse of an old Italian woman all in black who was more or less hiding behind him, veil and all. Someone was coming through the door, pushing people in a way that seemed rude. "I know how sorry you are," she said to the younger giant. "Thank you for coming." The young man finally released her and moved on to wrap his massive arms around her father and she looked up into the next face and saw something, a strange movement just behind him and then there was an explosion and a spray of blood all over the front of her dress, in her face, in her mouth and eyes, then a tremendous screaming, stampeding panic. She was being shoved sideways, aware only of desperate snatches of noise and color—glimpse of a moustache, a pistol, the young giant turning to stand in front of her, the taste of blood, the screams, the coffin wobbling hideously on its stand as if it would topple over, and then she was on the floor, her legs tangled up in the coffin stand and there was something in front of her, part of a human brain, it seemed to be, a bloody veil, a body. Then, like a producer's voice in her earpiece in mid-sentence, Alfonse, miles above her, saying the strangest thing: "Jimmy, let it go now. Let the gun go. Let me take it." And then another loud shot, and then all hell.

Epilogue

It was the last day of August and the outside of her mother's new house was nearly finished. Not much time to spare, either, because the baby was due in two weeks. Windows in, siding nailed on and primed with a first coat of paint, roof done, steps done, front and back doors that locked so that she and Vito and the other men no longer had to keep their tools in the little shed overnight. Estelle loved the sight of it, a two-story L-shaped mansion, it seemed to her, with an old-fashioned look that fit right in with the houses to either side. She and Vito were nailing the upstairs baseboards now, a difficult job that killed Vito's knees—she could tell—but was giving her the strongest grip of any girl she'd ever met. You had to hit the finish nails in just so in order to keep from denting the wood. After this, the painters would come in and paint the walls, and then, according to what Vito said, her mother and Alfonse could move in.

She watched him every chance she got, partly because she'd long ago fallen in love with the old guy and partly because she worried that one day he was going to just fall to pieces, literally, an arm going this way and an ear going the other. Since Peter had been killed, since the bloodbath that was the wake and the almost military event that was the funeral, the cargo of sadness Vito carried around with him had swollen to an impossible size. That cargo was familiar to her: the same look and feel as what her mother had always carried, until she found herself with Alfonse. It was the same color, in her mind at least, as the mark she saw on the faces of her older Cambodian friends: the understanding that life was so much bigger and harder and nastier than you'd ever thought it could possibly be.

She watched him. They went out to eat every Thursday night, sometimes Cambodian, which he really seemed to like, sometimes Italian, sometimes to Kelly's at the beach for fried clams and coffee. Cooking, eating, banging nails, talking about her mother's pregnancy and the baby to come—they were the only things that seemed to take Vito's mind off the bad stuff. On Sundays her mother and Alfonse and Elsie and Austin and Austin's girl, Darcy, and, once, Joanie and Leslie—they'd all go over to Proctor Avenue for a huge Sunday meal. Julian had come a couple of times, sitting there in his semi-stupor, eating three times what anyone else ate, carrying the dirty plates into the kitchen in a big wobbling stack, then sitting next to Vito on the couch, with a baseball game on the TV.

It had become almost like a hobby of hers now, caring for Vito. She felt about him almost the way you were supposed to feel about a grandfather. She kept waiting for the right moment to ask him again if he would sit for her, but it was still too early, she thought. She didn't want to have that much sadness on his face when she painted it and she didn't think she'd get any second chances. Maybe that winter, when the house was totally done and his grandchild born, when a little more healing time had passed, when his pain wasn't quite so sharp, maybe then she'd paint the Italian American Buddha at his best and keep the painting in her house when he was gone, as a memory.

On this night they'd worked until late and finished the last of the upstairs trim. Julian had gone off in his truck, and she and Vito had driven to the beach and had roast beef sandwiches and onion rings on a bench there, with seagulls diving around them making noise, and the last families packing up and

349

leaving the sand. When the food was finished, she'd said she wanted to go home with him for a little while, and she was surprised he hadn't objected, and now the two of them were sitting out in his quiet yard with glasses of iced coffee, waiting for the moon to come up. Full, it was going to be on that night, Vito said. They couldn't see it yet—the moon hadn't broken the horizon—but the sky above the neighboring rooftops was lit with the most amazing colors: shades of muted pink and scarlet, a display to make you believe in something larger than this life. They said nothing to each other, watching it, waiting. There weren't many people, she thought, with whom she could sit for so long and not say anything, and thinking that, she let herself sink into an ancient Buddhist meditation her grandmother had taught her. She breathed in Vito's pain, breathed out love, peace, hope, her breaths quiet and steady, her mind settling down and down into a stillness she loved. It was like shaking one of those American snow-globes Vito had in his house and then letting the thoughts and worries settle and the blue space go clear and still. That still place, she thought, was where you understood the way it all worked. Everything in life pointed you there if you let it.

Here was the tip of the moon now, orangey-pink as the inside of a peach. Here was the world, never still, and here they were in the beating heart of it, alive, alive, alive.

"You prayin now?" Vito asked her, breaking the long silence. He wasn't looking at her, but staring up into the sky above the nearby houses.

She turned to look at him. "How'd you know?"

"Because I'm prayin, too," he said. "Because it's the only thing left."

"I'm left," she said. "Alfonse and my mother and Joanie and the baby."

Vito didn't answer. The moon looked huge and there was

something majestic in the way it moved, the way the earth moved—slow, unstoppable, revealing it. She realized, really for the first time she could remember, that she wasn't afraid anymore. She believed she could deal with anything that came down the road now. Pain, illness, anger, violence, disappointment, death—she'd seen so much of it already, and somehow reached that place where she knew she could deal with any of it and all of it and still have something inside her to give to another person. A husband one day. Maybe even a child. She reached out and put her hand on Vito's forearm and she took a risk and said, *"Tutto a posto."*

Everything's in its place. She thought he might be angry, but he only turned his face to her and lifted his eyebrows once and let them fall back. It was a gesture she'd seen often during these months of work, a sad, resigned gesture that seemed to mean both "do you think so?" and "maybe". She kept her hand on his old arm and watched him turn his face toward the moon. He fixed his eyes on the light there and stared, as if there might, after all, be some reason to keep breathing.

The End

Some Other Books By PFP / AJAR Contemporaries

a four-sided bed - Elizabeth Searle

A Russian Requiem - Roland Merullo

Ambassador of the Dead - Askold Melnyczuk

Blind Tongues - Sterling Watson

Celebrities in Disgrace - (eBook only) - Elizabeth Searle

Demons of the Blank Page - Roland Merullo

Fighting Gravity - Peggy Rambach

Girl to Girl: The Real Deal on Being A Girl Today - Anne Driscoll

"Last Call" - *(eBook "single")* - Roland Merullo

Leaving Losapas - Roland Merullo

Lunch with Buddha - Roland Merullo

Make A Wish But Not For Money - Suzanne Strempek Shea

Music In and On the Air - Lloyd Schwartz

My Ground Trilogy - Joseph Torra

Passion for Golf: In Pursuit of the Innermost Game - Roland Merullo

Revere Beach Boulevard - Roland Merullo

Revere Beach Elegy - Roland Merullo

Taking the Kids to Italy - Roland Merullo

Talk Show - Jaime Clarke

Temporary Sojourner - Tony Eprile

the Book of Dreams - Craig Nova

The Calling - Sterling Watson

The Family Business - John DiNatale

The Indestructibles - Matthew Phillion

The Indestructibles: Breakout - Matthew Phillion

*The Winding Stream: The Carters, the Cashes and the Course
of Country Music* - Beth Harrington

"The Young and the Rest of Us" *(eBook "single")* - Elizabeth Searle

*This is Paradise: An Irish Mother's Grief, an African Village's Plight and the
Medical Clinic That Brought Fresh Hope to Both* - Suzanne Strempek Shea

Tornado Alley - Craig Nova

"What A Father Leaves" *(eBook "single" & audio book)* - Roland Merullo

What Is Told - Askold Melnyczuk

21455706R00218

Made in the USA
San Bernardino, CA
21 May 2015